**HELEN WALTON**

**EVERNIGHT PUBLISHING ®**

**www.evernightpublishing.com**

# HELEN WALTON

# DEDICATION

For Dannielle and her inspiration choices of Keanu Reeves and Ben Barnes.

# HELEN WALTON

# THEIR LOVE DEAL

## *Billionaires' Reluctant Brides, 1*

### Helen Walton

### Copyright © 2021

### Chapter One

Loving Dieter was as easy as breathing. Loving just Dieter was as hard as breathing under water. It seemed I enjoyed living under water. Either that or I didn't enjoy breathing.

Dieter drove Mom and me through the busy streets of Los Angeles after the college graduation ceremony. He was ever so attractive in his suit and tie, but then he always was. There was an allure to his tanned complexion and dark looks from the moment I'd set eyes on him in the college library.

"Thanks for driving my mom home, Dieter," I said.

"Anytime, Tiff. You know that." Dieter shot me a smile. The sexy grin melted my insides with the lure of his passionate lips.

"Yes, thank you, young man." Mom squeezed her hand to his shoulder from the back seat of his new shiny

Jaguar, a graduation present from his parents.

I wished my parents could afford to buy me a Jag.

Instead, Dad was a chauffeur for a billionaire. Not that there was anything wrong with his job, except for today when he should have driven *us* home from my graduation ceremony, he'd driven Mr. Burberry and Prue home instead.

"You'd think Mr. Burberry would have given Dad the day off for my graduation," I huffed.

"He did," Mom said. "Your pappa chose to drive them today. You know he thinks of William as a son."

"Yeah, but still…"

"Tiffany Louise Herringer, stop acting like a little girl." Mom flicked my ear with her finger. "Prue is your friend too."

"Yes, Mom." I hung my head, but not before catching the twitch of Dieter's lips. Chastised by my mom in front of one of my boyfriends was not how I expected my graduation day to go. I don't know why he thought this was so funny.

"Here we are." Dieter parked his car in my parents' driveway outside their modest three-bedroom house. "Nice to see you again, Mrs. Herringer."

He was always so polite. Dieter could do no wrong in my mom's eyes—the perfect student at college, and caring boyfriend. He was soon to be a successful financial advisor in his father's firm to the rich and famous of Los Angeles. With a rich and famous actress mother too, the great Octavia Brant.

Mom sighed with an exaggerated exhale. "When will I get to see my baby's wedding? I'm not getting any younger."

"Mom," I scalded. "I'm too young for marriage."

Dieter chuckled, his dark eyes alight with humor at my expense again.

"Pish, posh. Your friend Prue married years ago and she's the same age as you."

I groaned. I was 23, for goodness sake.

Dieter slid his hand into mine across the console of the car. "We have plenty of time to decide on marriage."

She flicked his ear.

"Ow." He ducked his head.

Mom opened the car door and paused halfway out of the car. "I'll see you two tomorrow at the Burberry's graduation pool party."

*Oh, no, she didn't.* She knew damn well I hadn't invited either of the men I was dating. Her bloody single-minded determination to see me married. I scowled at my mother over my shoulder. She smiled with a cunningness only she managed when it came to my future wedding. Seemed she had Dieter as the groom in her sights.

If I didn't love two men, then I wouldn't be so against Dieter as my husband. What started out as a little fun—dating two men at once just to prove to Mom I wasn't ready for marriage—backfired when I fell in love with them both. And marrying two men was out of the question. The law didn't condone those sorts of relationships.

Dieter rubbed his ear, ruffling his dark hair. "Graduation party?"

"Yeah." I chewed my top lip. "You can come if you like."

He shoved the car into reverse. "That's okay, you would have invited me if you wanted me to come."

"I want you to come." I tugged his tie until he faced me. "Please, Dieter. It's your graduation too."

"Do you already have a date?"

"No."

"All right, I'll come then." He kissed the tip of

my nose.

I released his tie and smoothed my hands over his chest. "It'll be good to see you without a suit and tie."

His dark brown eyes sparkled. "How about when I drop you home, I show you my birthday suit instead?"

I flicked my wrist and shoved the sleeve of the graduation gown back to peer at my watch. "Sorry, I won't have time."

He lifted his foot off the brake, and we moved out of the driveway onto the road. He drove back into town to my tiny studio apartment near campus. I guess now that I'd graduated I could look for a bigger place with my new job, an entry level position at Ozwald Delante, a top fashion designer I'd admired since I could say the word "fashion." A position I planned to work my butt off to get to the top. One day I'd be a famous fashion designer with my name on a label and legendary. One day I'd have enough money so Dad could retire. Mom's words made me wonder if Dad would retire if he had the chance.

Dieter's sullenness filled the car.

"Do you want to come up for coffee?" I asked.

His dark eyebrows rose. "I thought you didn't have time."

"I have half an hour to get ready."

He parked his car in the lot behind my apartment building.

"You need like three minutes to get ready. You're gorgeous as you are."

I laughed and opened the door. He climbed out and stared at me over the roof of his low-slung car.

"I'm serious, Tiff."

"Come on, Dieter." I nodded my head at my apartment building. "You can see my birthday suit while I'm changing out of this graduation gown."

"That's an invitation I can't refuse."

We walked over to the main entrance, and I punched in the code to unlock the door. Dieter made sure it locked behind us. You could never be too careful in this part of Los Angeles. We climbed the stairs to my third-floor apartment. At my apartment door, I slid my hand under my gown and fetched my key.

Dieter laughed. "What else do you have under the gown?"

"Wouldn't you like to know?" I smirked and stepped inside my small one-bedroom apartment.

He locked the door behind him and grabbed my waist from behind. "I'd love to know." His husky breath skated over my ear.

"It's unfair you took your gown off before leaving."

He nibbled on my ear. "I couldn't drive in it."

I took another step inside my apartment.

"Where do you think you're going?" His body followed mine while his lips sucked on my earlobe.

"My bedroom." I shivered as his lips continued their trail over the shell of my ear.

"Nope. We don't have time for that." He turned my head and kissed my lips.

I sunk into his fervent adoration of my mouth. His tongue stroked mine with a sensuality and familiarity that made my body ache with need. Dieter's hands tugged at the length of my gown until it gathered around my waist.

"Let's get you off."

I giggled. "I need to get the gown off."

"After." His eyes darkened with passion. "What do you have on underneath?"

"Just a summer dress."

"Nothing is just a dress with you." His hand slid

under the short hem of my dress and up the inside of my thigh.

My skin exploded into rippling goose bumps.

His thumb brushed over my aching flesh.

"I bet you made a dress special for today. Something as gorgeous as you."

He slid his fingers inside my panties and found me wet with desire already. It took little effort from Dieter to get me going.

I grabbed his forearms in a tight grip.

He nibbled on my ear again. My clever boyfriend knew all the spots that sent me crazy with lust. His thumb circled my clit with a slowness that made me rock my hips, trying to get more friction.

"That's it, ride my hand." He slid a long, thick digit into my aching channel. "I'd rather you ride my cock."

My inner muscles clenched with need.

"Pity we don't have the time." He ran his nose along my ear.

I turned my head. He captured my lips with his again. He tugged on my bottom lip with his teeth until my mouth ached for a soothing caress. I rocked against his hand, his finger so hard and insistent on my flesh. He picked up the pace of his fingers, stroking my insides into an aching build of ecstasy.

I ripped my mouth away from his. "Oh God."

My orgasm burst free, clenching around his finger in a tight ball of muscles Dieter commanded at his will with such ease.

"God?" He chuckled, withdrew his hand, and wrenched my gown over my head. "Did I have you seeing heaven?"

"Not quite." I tugged his tie, so he'd follow me into my bedroom.

"I'll have to try harder next time." He stretched out on my bed and crossed his arms behind his head.

"You don't need to do anything different. I love you the way you are."

"Tiff." He sighed. "I wish you were coming to my parents' graduation party with me tonight."

I unzipped my short summer dress in a bold floral print that hugged my waist and flared at my hips. One of my many creations.

"We both know it's better I don't go."

"Screw my mom," he said.

I dropped my dress to my ankles and stepped out of it. "She's never going to believe I'm not after you for your money."

"It doesn't matter what she believes."

His gaze raked my body in a matching delicate mauve lace bra and panty set.

"Do you have a date for tonight?" I asked, not wanting the answer and wanting it at the same time. When we'd first started dating three years ago, we'd agreed to keep it casual and not discuss who else we were seeing. It'd kept things light between us, but the last three months after I'd ended my relationships with both Dieter and Dex to date just one man, which didn't work out, and I'd gone running back to both my loves, well, things had changed. I couldn't quite put my finger on the exact change, but it was there.

"I do." He sat up.

It shouldn't hurt, but it kind of did.

I yanked on a pair of designer jeans—ones I'd designed myself—and a shiny black top with an open back and a silver chain as a halter neck. Another of my designs.

"From sweet and adorable to sexy and smoldering." Dieter stood and wrapped his arms around my waist. "You'd pull off any look."

"Thanks." I wriggled out of his embrace. Damn stupid jealousy. I sat at my dressing table and coated my face in a thick layer of makeup, hoping it'd hide the green beast inside me.

"You don't need that shit," he said, his brows dipping into a deep scowl in the mirror behind me.

"I'm going clubbing," I said as an excuse. I had too much of a sweet girl-next-door look when I didn't wear makeup, with a button nose and full cheeks that Mom pinched like crazy when I was little. She still did sometimes.

I unpinned my updo and let my dark curls fall to my shoulders, then fluffed my fingers through the strands.

"I wish neither of us had other plans tonight." Dieter's gaze shot to the bed.

I slid on a pair of high heels and stood. I'd never be close to Dieter's six-foot-three height, even in heels. But a girl could try. I placed a kiss on his cheek, leaving behind a bright red kiss mark of lipstick.

"Wouldn't want your date to see that." I scrubbed the smudge from his face with my thumb.

"I'm taking Selena tonight," he blurted.

"Selena has a girlfriend." My juvenile jealousy jumped for joy at his admission.

"Yes." He checked his shiny silver Versace watch, a graduation gift from his grandmother. His mother's side of the family came from a long line of rich and famous actors. I couldn't fault his family's taste in fashion.

I grabbed my clutch and keys and walked to the apartment door. Dieter followed, a knowing smile on his face. We left the building in silence. Ridiculous happiness bubbled inside my chest that I had nothing to be jealous about with Dieter and his date when I was about to meet my other boyfriend, Dex.

"Do you need a ride anywhere?" he asked on the sidewalk.

"No, I arranged an Uber."

"Okay." He drew me into his embrace and ran his fingers up my bare back, making my skin explode in goose bumps. He whispered in my ear, "Your date is a lucky man."

I squeezed his ass. "So is Selena."

He chuckled and released me. "Perhaps I can convince her and her girlfriend to have a threesome with me?"

And my jealousy was back.

*Stupid.*

I bit the inside of my cheek to stop myself from saying anything. The Uber stopped at the curb. I scampered into the car and slammed the door. It wasn't the first time Dieter made comments about threesomes. Ever since we got back together, he dropped a hint at least once a week that he'd be into it. I sagged back in the car seat. Was I that type of girl? I dated two men at once, but together?

My cell phone pinged with a message.

Dex: Ready and waiting.

Me: I'm coming.

Dex: Without me?

I laughed and sent him back a laughing face. The other man I loved put a smile on my face. The Uber driver weaved through the heavy traffic and stopped outside a trendy nightclub. I stepped out into the muscular arms of Dex, and I forgot about Dieter, my jealousy, and his threesome comment. Dex twirled me around in the air with ease. I was small, but his muscles from an intense workout routine and his job as a mechanic helped. I giggled and slapped his shoulders.

Dex lowered me to my feet, a sexy lift to both his dark eyebrows. "Hot damn, Fluff, you're smoking tonight." He brushed the tip of my nose with his.

The brush of his trimmed beard tickled. I rubbed my nose to get rid of the sensation. His deep brown eyes sparkled with passion. The top buttons on his black shirt gaped open, affording me with an uninhibited view of his tattooed upper chest. My heart flip-flopped inside my rib cage. The two men I loved were so different, yet they treated me the same.

"Ready to party all night?" he asked.

"You betcha." I grinned. "It's not every day I graduate from college."

"Come on, smarty-pants." He tugged my hand and drew me inside the nightclub bypassing the already long line of people waiting to get inside.

I don't know how he did it, but he always got us into the hippest places.

Dex had secrets. Ones he didn't share with me.

*But didn't we all?*

## Chapter Two

The music inside Heaven on a Stick thumped so loud it reverberated through my body. Dex tugged me through the crowd to the bar and ordered us drinks. The bartender slapped two shots of tequila on the bar and two bottles of beer. Dex and I clinked the shot glasses and slammed them back. The fiery liquid burned the back of my throat. I gulped a mouthful of beer to soothe the burn.

"Lightweight." Dex's eyes twinkled with amusement.

"Sorry, I still can't handle shots like you."

He slid his arm around my waist and drew me into his side. "I love that you can't handle your shots. It makes for a fun night."

"Are you trying to get me drunk so you can get in my pants?"

"Yep." He slid his fingers into the waistband of my jeans.

"Good." I smiled and spun out of his arms. "Let's dance."

Dex groaned but followed me onto the dance floor. I sashayed up against his body while he stood still.

"I'm not drunk enough for dancing," he yelled over the music.

I pouted and turned around to rub my ass against his groin in a dance move that never failed to get him moving with me.

Dex's spare hand landed on my hip and he ground against me. I grinned and kept swaying to the music and sipped my beer. On my next sip, Dex tapped his finger to the bottom of the bottle until I drained the contents. He snagged the bottle from my hand and placed it on a table by the dance floor.

He stalked back to me with heated passion

burning in his eyes. My body quivered in excitement. Dex yanked me into his arms and ravaged my mouth on the dance floor amongst the crowd of partiers. He stroked his fingers into the length of my hair and tugged. I moaned against his thrusting tongue. If he kept this up, I'd be ready to leave in a few minutes and end the night in his bed now. I ripped my mouth away from his with reluctance. My friends from college were meeting me here tonight. I couldn't run off yet as much as Dex made me want to.

"Keep that thought until later." I rubbed the lipstick from around his lips.

He quirked an eyebrow and cupped his dick. "You're such a tease."

"You love it." I spun around and walked back to the bar.

He crowded me from behind. "I love you."

I tipped my head back onto his shoulder. "Love you too."

We found my friends at the bar waiting to be served amongst the crowd. Dex snagged the bartender's attention with ease and ordered another round of shots for everyone. I groaned but slammed the shot back. You only live once, right? We danced, we drank, and we danced more. I laughed with my friends. Danced with my friends. Danced with Dex again. He caressed his fingers over the expanse of my bare back. My body tingled from so much overstimulation, and Dex called *me* the tease.

Much later, our group staggered outside into the muggy summer night. I hugged and kissed my friends in the way a drunk person does. To think I'd do this all again tomorrow night with Prue's friends from college.

My stomach churned. I wrapped my arms around my middle.

Dex peered into my face with concern etched on

his brows. "Let's get some greasy food into you."

Hand in hand, we walked along the sidewalk amongst the crowd of partiers. This Friday night was extra busy on the strip. The mouthwatering aroma of herbs, garlic, and melted cheese wafted from a nearby all-night pizzeria.

"Pizza." I drooled.

Dex laughed. "Pizza it is for my drunk little Fluff."

I giggled. "Drunk Fluff."

Dex guided me into the pizzeria. "You're wasted."

I held up my thumb and forefinger. "Just a wee bit."

"Wait here." He parked me on a seat. "I'll be back in a sec."

I ogled his tight behind in the dark denim jeans while he bought us a piece of pizza each. The man was tastier looking than the pizza. Although my mouth watered for the food when he returned with a large slice of pepperoni pizza.

"Here, eat this."

"I love you," I said.

"I know you do." He tugged me to my feet.

"I was talking to the pizza." I took a bite and chewed.

Dex rolled his eyes at my lame joke. I giggled again. We wandered back outside into the muggy summer night. Dex handed me a bottle of water and I gulped the contents and ate the pizza. By the time we'd walked to his apartment a few streets away, I'd sobered up enough to think about Dieter again. Was he having a threesome right now with two other women?

I sat on Dex's bed and hiccupped.

"Want to tell me what's wrong?" He tugged off

my heels.

"I'm sorry I ruined our night." I cupped Dex's face.

"You couldn't ruin any night I'm with you."

He eased my top over my head and threw it onto a chair by his bed. With a deftness which always astounded me, he stripped me of my bra in milliseconds and that too followed the top. He urged me back on the bed and eased my jeans and panties down at the same time.

"But—"

Dex placed a finger to my lips.

"No buts. This is us. We take what we can get when we can get it. That was our deal."

I pursed my lips and kissed his finger. I wanted Dex so much right now, but how could I do this to him? And Dieter? They were both perfect in their own way and deserved one woman to love them. They didn't deserve this half-life I led with them.

Dex paused. "What's wrong?"

"I love you both so much. How do I choose?"

"I've never asked you to choose."

"Don't you want more, though? Don't you want to get married and have kids?"

"Tiff…" He sighed and unbuttoned his shirt.

"Well?"

"Has your mom been nagging you about marriage again?" He threw his shirt on the chair on top of my clothes.

I nodded and whispered, "Do you?"

"I guess one day." His hands dropped to his jeans.

"So, what am I doing with you?"

"You're loving me." He tugged the zip down and stripped his jeans. "I'm loving you." He threw the jeans on top of his shirt. "Right now, I'm going to be loving you a lot."

My gaze raked his naked body from his bare chest, decorated with tattoos over his six-pack stomach, to the erection straining from his dark curls. He crooked his finger.

I crawled across the mattress to Dex. He tilted my chin up with his finger.

"Stop worrying. I'm happy. Aren't you?"

"You make me happy." I ran my hands up his thighs to cup his balls in one hand and his enormous erection in the other. I stroked my hand up and down his shaft.

"You keep that up and I'll be happy all over your face."

I laughed. "It wouldn't be the first time."

"Or the last." He wrapped his arms around my shoulders and drew my head onto his stomach in a gentle embrace.

Dex was happy with this arrangement. To have me whenever he could and spend time with me in any way. To share me with another man. I guess Mom's words about marriage were getting to me. Or perhaps it was the time I'd broken up with them both that had gotten to me. I'd been so lost without my two loves. I couldn't lose them again.

"Feel better now?" he asked.

"Yeah." I sighed.

"Good." He scooped me up into his arms. "Because you're about to see the moon and the stars."

"Dex." I kicked my legs, but he carried me to the balcony of his apartment. Naked. "Let's go back inside."

There were so many Peeping Toms with telescopes, there were sure to be some looking our way.

"Nope." He placed my bottom on the thick metal balcony railing.

I gripped the rail in a hurry.

He rolled on a condom. "Look up."

I tipped my head back. The abundance of city lights made it almost impossible to see the stars, but tonight a layer sparkled across the dark sky.

Dex's mouth latched onto my nipple. I kept my grip on the railing instead of grabbing his head. He sucked and flicked the hard tip with his tongue until I couldn't stand it any longer.

"Dex…" I moaned.

He rubbed his thick erection on my swollen lips.

He released my nipple. "You ready for me?"

"I've been ready all night."

He impaled me with his hardness in a thrust that almost sent me toppling from the first-floor balcony over his workshop. He laughed and anchored me against his body with his powerful arms.

"Sorry, Fluff."

I glanced at the ground below. "Don't let me fall."

"I won't." He tightened his hold and thrust again.

This time I stayed in place on the balcony railing. I hooked my legs over his hips. I glanced down again.

"Stop worrying about the fall and look up."

Dex tugged my hair until my chin raised to the sky. He thrust into me with a hard precision of his cock inside my damp flesh a constant stroke on nerve endings that shot pleasure through my body. The fear of falling off the railing produced my impending orgasm quicker than I would have imagined. With each thrust, Dex's fingers tugged the tips of my hair. My scalp tingled. Deep inside, the tension built.

My fingers turned numb on the bar. Dex's hot breath brushed against my neck. His rough beard scraped against my cheek. He shifted one hand to stroke my clit. I clenched the railing tighter instead of gripping him. If I fell back, I wouldn't take him with me. He meant too much to me.

The stars above blurred as my vision wavered with the pleasure of his cock, and fingers strummed from me. It all centered on the one place he stroked me. My breaths turned ragged. So much pleasure. Each slide inside. Each stroke outside. It all became too much. Too sensitive. Too good. My body fragmented in a release so exquisite I didn't want it to end.

Dex tugged my hair harder, thrust his hips faster, and exploded with his own release. He sucked the skin on my collarbone.

I blinked until my vision returned to the stars shining in the sky. I kissed his cheek. His lips sought mine in a tender, loving kiss. He carried me back to his bed and tossed me on the mattress like I was a rag doll. I bounced and giggled. He discarded the condom, crawled onto the bed, and scooped me in his arms.

"What are your plans for tomorrow?" he asked.

Guilt surged into my stomach. "I'm spending the day here with you in bed then I have another graduation party."

"I gotta go into the workshop tomorrow."

"Shit. On a Saturday?" I pouted.

"Yeah, I got a Mercedes coming in for a service that was supposed to come in today, but they needed to rearrange. I couldn't say no when they offered triple the money." He stroked my back. "I'll cook you a nice greasy breakfast of bacon and eggs first."

"Ugh," I groaned. "I can't think about eating now."

"You'll need it if you're partying tomorrow night too." He squinted at the clock. "Or should I say tonight?"

"Don't remind me." I placed my head on his

chest. "No more shots for me."

"That's what everyone says." He chuckled.

"Mmm. This is nice." I closed my eyes.

"Nice. Is that all I get?" He stopped stroking my back.

"Perfect."

"Better." He resumed his caress on my skin.

Perfect. Being with Dex was perfect. It bummed me I wouldn't get to spend the day with him like I'd planned, but when you run your own successful high-performance mechanics shop at the young age of 26, I guess sacrifices had to be made. It helped his father left him the legacy, but Dex turned the garage into more in the last two years since his dad's death. He'd be proud of his son. I was proud of Dex and all he'd accomplished.

Maybe one day, Dex would be proud of my accomplishments too.

## Chapter Three

Dieter texted and said he was running late so Mom and I caught an Uber to Prue's mansion since Dad was delayed at work. I didn't understand how when Dad was Mr. Burberry's driver, and since he was married to Prue, they should both be at the mansion for the party. I guess I'd find out in a minute.

Prue waved to us from the other side of the pool underneath the rows of golden fairy lights and glowing pink lanterns hanging from the outdoor entertaining area. The water shone a royal blue with the underwater lights. People milled about the poolside sitting in chairs and tables Prue ordered for the special occasion.

"Hey, bestie." Prue drew me in for a quick hug dressed in a gauzy see-through dress and bright pink bikini underneath. More of my fashion creations.

"Great party," I said.

"Thanks for coming, Mrs. Herringer." Prue hugged my mom too.

"I wouldn't miss it." Mom's eyes sparkled with the chance to mingle with wealthy people. "I'm checking out the buffet table. Do you girls want anything?"

"No, thank you," I said.

The conniving woman inviting Dieter along. If she thought she would get in his ear about marriage again, then I'd just have to keep her away from him all night. It shouldn't be too hard with the amount of people at the party.

"Where's Mr. Burberry?" I asked.

Prue laughed. "When will you call him William?"

"Sorry, no can do. He'll always be Mr. Burberry to me. So where is he?"

"He had to run Gabe to the mechanics to pick up the Mercedes. There was a problem, and they took longer fixing it than we thought. He should be back soon. Why? Do you still have the hots for my husband?"

"No," I spluttered when in truth Mr. Burberry would always be my first man crush. But I had to play it cooler these days, what with my best friend married to Mr. Burberry. Not that I ever had a chance with him. He always thought of me as Gabe's kid.

"Let's get you a cocktail since I can't drink." She towed me over to the bar and handed me a pre-made bright red cocktail with fruit swimming on top of the liquid and a tiny umbrella poking out from the side. "I can't believe I let Will knock me up before graduation."

I laughed and sipped the drink. "Fruity."

"Der," Prue drawled.

"Mom invited Dieter to the party tonight."

"So." Prue shrugged. "Either of your boyfriends are welcome here. Wait, did you invite Dex?"

"No." We parked ourselves at a table. "I'd planned on coming alone."

"Then what's the problem?"

"You know how she is with her marriage talk." I sipped the cocktail and scanned the crowd. "I'll need to keep her away from him."

"Does Dieter want to marry you?" Prue slid closer.

I shrugged. "We avoid the topic, but I believe he does."

"And Dex?"

"I asked him last night, and he said he did one day. Whenever one day is."

"They could have a duel for your hand in marriage?" Prue sipped her iced tea.

"So funny." I rolled my eyes. "How did I end up in this mess?"

"I can tell you how, but you already know." She

beamed.

I groaned and banged my head on the table. "I'm an idiot."

She patted my back in consolation but stopped with abruptness. "Oh. Oh, no. Don't look."

"What?" I tried to sit up, but she rammed my face into the table.

"Prue," I mumbled into the tabletop with my squished lips.

"Tiff, you're in an even bigger mess now."

"Why?" I asked with trepidation.

"You can sneak out now before anyone sees you."

"Prue." I wriggled on the chair and slid out from under her hand and landed with a thump on the timber decking. "What the?"

She waved her hand at me. "Shush, and you can still hide."

"Hide from what?" I peered over the top of the table. "Fuck me two ways from Sunday. What is Dad doing here with Dex?"

Dad, Dex, and Mr. Burberry caught sight of Prue and strode over to the table. There was nowhere for me to hide except under the table and I doubt I'd fit. I peeked to the nearest pot plant. Even that wasn't big enough to hide me.

"I'm so screwed."

Prue shot me a pitying look seconds before the three men came into view.

"Are you drunk already, Fluff?" Dex asked.

"No." I scrambled to my feet. "That's my first cocktail of the night."

And it wouldn't be the last. Damn, he looked so hot in a loose white tank top draped over his tattooed chest with large armholes leaving a view of his smooth ribs.

"Hi, Gabe, Dex. Is the car all fixed now?" Prue asked.

Mr. Burberry rubbed Prue's shoulders.

I could smack my head on the table again. Dex was Mr. Burberry's mechanic. Why hadn't I put two and two together before today?

"Sure is," Dex said. "You're lucky I squeezed it in today, if you'd left the Mercedes any longer, you'd have had a big problem."

"Thanks, Dex," Prue said.

"No problem. I hope you don't mind Gabe asking me to the party tonight. William said it was okay for me to come."

"No, not at all." Prue stood. "You're always welcome." She lifted her gaze to Mr. Burberry. "We might go check on Kennedy and the twins. We'll be back soon."

I grabbed her hand. "Hurry back, this is all for you."

"I will. I'm not missing this night for anything." She squeezed my hand and walked off with her shoulders shaking.

"I see your mom has found the buffet," Dad said. "I'll go join her."

I eyeballed Dad, but he turned his back and left me alone with Dex. Dex sat in the chair Prue vacated, picked up my cocktail, and chugged half the fancy glass.

"Damn, that's sweet," Dex said.

"Mmm-hmm." I flicked my gaze around the pool.

"Do you think Prue and William are getting it on with their nanny?"

"What?" I gasped. "No."

"Kennedy is hot," he said with a teasing smile.

I punched his arm. "No, Prue would have said

something." *What was it with everyone thinking of threesomes these days?* I scanned the crowded pool area looking for my other boyfriend. Guilt churned my stomach.

"Are you okay?" Dex touched my arm.

I jumped. "I'm fine."

"Ah, you've got a date?" His smile fell from his face.

I picked up the glass and gulped the rest of the contents. I couldn't say it to his face this time.

"It's okay, Tiff." He stood.

"Dex." I grabbed his arm.

He stroked my hand. His deep brown eyes met my searching gaze. I swallowed the guilt filling my mouth. This was bound to happen at some time. Karma always caught up with you, and mine was coming in full tonight.

"Hey, aren't you Dex Munroe?" a young man asked.

"Yeah, that's me." Dex detached my hand from his arm like he didn't want my touch on him anymore.

"Cool. I can't believe I'm meeting you here. I bought the last tricked-out Dodge you worked on with that rad engine." He flicked his long locks back from his forehead.

"Yeah? Nice." Dex shook his hand. "How's the Dodge running?"

"It's running like a beast," he said and launched into a mechanical description. I had no idea what he talked about.

I tilted my empty glass and pointed at the bar. Dex nodded, and I slipped away from his side. I threaded my way through the crowd to the bar. A row of people waited for the bartender to mix cocktails. Everyone drank them faster than he made them now.

A pair of familiar arms slid around my bare waist between my bikini top and sarong skirt from behind.

"Hey, Tiff, sorry I'm late," Dieter said.

I stiffened in his arms.

"Not a problem." I wriggled out of his arms and held his hand.

"Dad was going through paperwork with me at the firm. I told him it could wait, but the great Richard Brant always knows better."

"Are you sure you want to work with your dad?" I stepped up to the bar and ordered us two cocktails.

"It's what they expect of me." Dieter picked up the cocktails.

I led him in the opposite direction to where I'd left Dex.

"Doesn't mean you have to do it."

I found a table tucked away in a dark corner of the patio down the side of the house. Dieter peered at me through the sudden dimness.

"Why are we hiding back here?" he asked.

A strangled laugh bubbled out. "We're not hiding."

He drank his cocktail and licked his lips. Damn, he looked good in a pair of cargo shorts and a casual white t-shirt with his deep tan skin. I leaned toward him and slid my hand onto his thigh.

"What are you doing back here?" Mom asked settling herself on a chair and placing a plate of fruit on the table. "The party is by the pool."

"We just wanted a quieter place to talk." I shifted back from almost kissing Dieter.

"What are you talking about?" Mom plucked a piece of fruit from her plate and popped a strawberry in her mouth.

"Mom." I sighed.

"Don't you go breaking his sweet heart again, Tiffany." She wagged her finger at me.

"I wasn't." I folded my arms and glared her way.

"Good girl." She leaned across the table and pinched my cheeks.

I swatted her hands away. Where was Dad when I needed him?

"We were talking about Dieter's job if you must know," I said.

"Such an honorable thing to do, joining your father in his firm. I bet he's very proud," Mom said.

"Yes, he's thrilled I followed in his footsteps," Dieter said.

"Do you think we'll meet your family soon?"

"Mom," I hissed.

"What? You two have been dating for three years now. If that's not serious, I don't know what is."

I slurped my cocktail until the straw sucked air. So much for keeping Dieter away from my mom tonight.

"I, ah, I'll get you another drink." Dieter fled.

I didn't blame him.

"Stop chasing him off with your wedding talk," I seethed.

"I didn't even mention a wedding."

I shoved back my chair and stood. "Can we just have fun tonight at this party with no serious talk?"

"Tiffany." She stood and circled the table. "Life is serious."

"Yeah, yeah," I muttered and stomped off.

## Chapter Four

Prue slid her arm around my waist while I waited in line at the bar again. Dieter never returned with my drink, and he'd somehow disappeared in the crowd. Not that I searched that hard, with Dex here and Mom on her wedding rampage. Would the woman never stop talking about marriage?

"Your two dicks are playing with each other," Prue said.

"What?" I blinked fast. Surely, I heard her wrong.

"I said your two dicks—"

I waved my hands in front of Prue's face. She grabbed my shoulders and spun me around to face the pool. Dieter and Dex were drool-worthy topless in the pool playing volleyball together … on the same team.

"No," I moaned.

Prue collected a cocktail for me and shoved the fancy glass in my numb hands. My entire body froze. This night couldn't be happening. I must be asleep.

"Pinch me," I said.

Prue pinched my arm.

"Ow." I rubbed my arm.

"You said pinch you." She tugged me over to the side of the pool for a closer view of my "two dicks," as she called them.

"How did this happen?" I sucked on the straw watching them slam the ball back and forth over the net. Beads of water dripped from their hair and down their muscled bodies. Dex and Dieter high-fived each other when they won the point.

Prue rubbed her hands together. "You're so lucky."

"Lucky?" I hissed.

"Look at them." She nodded her head in their

direction. "They look happy together."

I narrowed my eyes and studied Dieter and Dex. There was something about the way they were playing volleyball together with well-timed ease that sung out like this wasn't their first time. It was in the way they read each other's movements. But I'd never introduced them. They'd never said they knew each other. Did they both know I dated each of them? So many questions and emotions bubbled inside my stomach.

Prue heaved a deep breath. "You're about to live every woman's fantasy."

I swung my gaze away from my two boyfriends playing with each other.

"What fantasy?" Mr. Burberry asked wrapping his arms around Prue's shoulders and pulling her back into his embrace.

"Tiff is about to have a threesome." Prue smirked.

Mr. Burberry stroked his hands down Prue's arms. "I thought you'd told me all your fantasies."

My cheeks heated, and I gazed back at my two men in the water.

Prue giggled. "All but that one."

"Hmm." Mr. Burberry lowered his mouth to Prue's ear, his voice quiet so I couldn't hear.

"No," Prue said. "I love you."

"Think about it," Mr. Burberry said. "I can arrange it."

"Anyway." Prue tapped me on the shoulder. "What about you and your threesome?"

"I'm not having a threesome." I folded my arms.

"Whoa…" She dropped her hand. "Why the angry face?"

I pointed at Dieter and Dex. "They know each other, and they didn't tell me."

"How do you know?" she asked.

"I've known them both long enough to recognize the way they act with people they know and with people they've just met. And let me tell you, those two know each other."

"Isn't that a good thing?" Prue asked.

"Good?" I screeched so loud Dieter and Dex's heads swung our way. No, this wasn't good. I'd kept them separate. I'd kept my love for them both separate. I couldn't have them be friends. How the hell had this happened?

Dieter and Dex exchanged a look. Yeah, those two knew each other all right, and if they'd kept that a secret from me, what other secrets had they kept?

"I'm leaving," I said.

"No," Prue cried. "You can't leave yet, we haven't even danced. You're my best friend, you can't leave!"

"You're pulling the best friend card now?"

"I'll use anything I have to."

Mr. Burberry grinned. "You might as well stay, Tiff. Prue always gets what she wants."

"I do not." She pouted.

He cocked his eyebrow. "You just got me to—"

Prue slapped her hand over his mouth. "And you enjoyed it too, so you can keep Dex and Dieter from interrupting us while we dance."

Mr. Burberry laughed. "I'm not promising anything, but go and dance."

She batted her eyelashes at her husband and tugged my hand to the makeshift dance floor underneath flashing lights and music blaring from glowing speakers. I glared at Dieter and Dex still playing in the pool then turned my back on them. Those two had a lot of explaining to do and dancing might take my mind off it.

A bunch of Prue's friends from her art classes joined us and the dance floor soon became packed with bumping-and-grinding bodies. Sweat and alcohol streamed from my pores. A hippy blond man stayed close to me and attempted to get my attention, but as fun as dancing was, my mind was on my two boyfriends and how they knew each other.

*How didn't I know?*

Prue and I got separated in the crowd. I swung in a circle to find her but ended up facing the blond man. He circled my waist and tugged me into his body. I shoved at his chest. He let go and held up his hands. Lucky for him, otherwise in the mood I was in, I might have kneed him in the balls. I spun around and came face to face with Dieter and Dex.

Neither of them looked at me. They both glowered at the man behind me. I shoved between them and left the dance floor.

"Tiff," Dieter called.

I kept walking.

"Fluff," Dex said catching up to my side.

"No." I stomped into the house away from the party. Prue wouldn't mind me escaping inside wherever she'd disappeared to. Maybe off having sex with Mr. Burberry again.

"Where are you going?" Dieter asked.

"I don't know." I paused and glanced around the house, then headed to the front door. "Home."

"Stop," Dex said.

I stopped with my hand on the doorknob.

"Turn around and tell me what's going on in that head of yours," Dex said.

I spun around. "You two know each other," I hissed. "I'm a fool."

"Tiff, no, you're not." Dieter stepped closer.

I held my hand up, but he walked right into my palm. My fingers clenched on their own accord into his warm muscles.

"Why are you so angry we know each other?" Dieter asked.

"Am not." I hiccupped.

"You're drunk again, Fluff." Dex stepped closer.

I shifted my other hand and held my palm against Dex's stomach to stop him scooping me up like I knew he would. Their warm bodies seeped into my palms. Both the men I loved together in front of me. Prue was right. A small part of me fantasized about having them together. I loved them both. Why couldn't I have them both? I dropped my hands and head.

"How do you know each other?" I whispered.

"Did you drive your Jag tonight?" Dex asked.

"Yes," Dieter said.

"Let's go back to my place and talk this over," Dex said.

"What about my place?" Dieter asked.

"Any will do. We need to get out of here before Tiff has a meltdown."

"I'm not about to have a meltdown." I hiccupped and raised my head. "Who says I want to talk to either of you?"

Dieter nodded at Dex. Dex swooped me up into his arms. Dieter opened the front door and Dex carried me outside.

"Put me down, you Neanderthal." I kicked my legs. "I don't want to leave Prue's party."

"You were just trying to leave." Dex stopped.

"On my own," I huffed.

"As if we'd let you leave on your own when you're like this," he said.

We? We? What was with all the *we*?

Dieter stepped into my view. "Do you want to go back to the party? We can talk to your mom again."

I narrowed my eyes. "Screw you. Screw the both of you."

The Neanderthals both laughed. Men. Why did I love the two?

Dex carried me to Dieter's car without another word from me. I narrowed my gaze to slits, because I was drunk, but I wouldn't give them the satisfaction of admitting that. Stupid cocktails. Stupid party. Stupid men.

Dieter opened the car door and Dex slid me onto the seat then climbed in after me as though I'd clamber out if he weren't by my side. It was a possibility. Would Prue help me? She thought this was a fantasy come to life. She'd throw condoms at me and tell me to have fun.

Friends. Ugh. Almost as bad as boyfriends.

My head lolled against the window. Dieter started the car and drove down the driveway of the Burberry mansion. At the end of the driveway the car jolted through a dip smacking my head into the glass with a loud clunk.

"Ow." I rubbed my head. As if it didn't hurt enough as it was.

"Come here," Dex said lifting his arm.

As annoyed as I was, I dropped my head on Dex's chest. My favorite place. Dex ran his fingers through my hair. I bit my lip to stop a sigh of happiness escaping. Dieter peeked in the rearview mirror at us in the back seat. To my surprise he appeared happy to see me snuggled against Dex. I shut my eyes. This was way too confusing for my inebriated mind.

"I'm never drinking again."

"That's what everyone says." Dex's chest rumbled under my ear.

"This everyone means it." I hiccupped.

"Lightweight, Fluff," he teased. "You're a real lightweight."

I giggled.

He stroked his hand down my arm and across my hip. "If you weren't so drunk..."

I opened my eyes to catch Dieter's ardent gaze blazing at us in the rearview mirror. He flicked the indicator, turned into a park in front of his apartment building, and turned off the engine. Dieter climbed out of the car and opened the back door. He helped me out and stared at me with such lust I thought I'd self-combust into an orgasm.

Dex exited the car. "Can you walk, or should I carry you?"

I raised my chin. "I'll walk." Shit. Dieter's apartment complex meant an elevator ride up to the penthouse. My stomach churned. I bent into the gutter and dry-heaved.

Dex swooped me up into his arms again. I closed my eyes. Best to pretend I'd fallen asleep. I was in no fit state to talk to either of them tonight. I doubt I would be in the morning either. But I guess at least I'd only have Dieter to talk to in the morning since this was his apartment. One minor consolation in my messed-up life.

The two men I loved together when I'd kept them apart for years.

What would happen now?

## Chapter Five

I'd slept at Dieter's apartment enough times to know I wasn't in his bed when I woke. The summer sun streamed through the sides of the blinds in a gold laser beam. I rolled over with a groan. Time to face the disaster of my love life. I crawled out of the soft Egyptian cotton sheets his mom was fond of buying. The woman had impeccable taste and spared no expense. I suppose when you made millions of dollars per movie you could afford anything you wanted. At least Dieter's father liked me. Maybe one day, his mother would too. Perhaps if I proved I could earn lots of money and became a famous designer, she'd see I wasn't with Dieter for money.

I stepped into the adjoining bathroom and shucked my clothes. This was so different from being in Dieter's bedroom and bathroom. I almost felt like a guest instead of his girlfriend. If I was still his girlfriend after last night. I wasn't sure what either man was to me now. I brushed my teeth with the toothbrush I found in a drawer, loving the fresh mint burst of the toothpaste in my mouth. Feeling somewhat refreshed after a shower, I made my way back into the bedroom.

A black t-shirt sat folded on the bed—the one I loved to wear when I stayed over. I shook out the t-shirt and slipped it on over my head. The familiarity eased the churning nerves in my stomach at talking to Dieter. I could do this. It was just Dieter I would talk to.

I opened the bedroom door and padded down the tiled hallway in my bare feet until I got to the kitchen. I dove at the coffeepot like a crazed person and almost drank from the jug. With restraint, I opened the cupboard and fetched a mug to drink the coffee from. I drained one cupful of coffee, filled the cup again, and ventured to the window gazing over the communal pool of the three massive apartments in the building.

"I thought I heard you in here," Dieter said.

I turned from the refreshing view of the water and drank in the sight of Dieter dressed in casual clothes. He looked good in anything, but he was fond of dressing in suits and ties so when he dressed in sweats it was like seeing a different version of him.

"Coffee," I mumbled and drank.

He flexed his fingers then walked toward me. I jolted and almost spilled the remaining coffee down my favorite t-shirt. Dieter extracted the mug from my hands with gentleness and placed it on the counter then hauled me in for a hug.

I sighed, wrapped my arms around his waist, and buried my face in his chest. The sweet, musky scent of his expensive aftershave filled my senses. I clutched his t-shirt with my fingers.

"How are you?" he asked.

"Not too bad," I said with surprise. "I'm still never drinking again."

Dieter's chest boomed with laughter.

"You're such a liar, Fluff," Dex's voice rumbled with humor.

I released Dieter's t-shirt and scooted out of his embrace. Guilt churned my stomach, but Dex smiled at me.

"Do I get a hug too?" Dex asked.

"I ... ah..." I glanced at Dieter who smiled. "I guess."

Dex opened his arms. I walked over to Dex and hugged him. His muscular arms wrapped around my back and hauled me close until every inch of our bodies were together. I squeezed him back and wriggled out of his arms. I glanced between both men while they watched me with smiles on their faces. If anything, I'd say they looked happy. But how could they be? Wasn't this every man's worst nightmare, meeting your girlfriend's other lover?

I scooped up the mug and drank the rest of the coffee then heaved in a deep breath.

"Okay." I put the mug down. "How do you know each other? How long have you known each other? Why didn't you tell me you knew each other? How…"

"Slow down, Tiff." Dieter took my hand in his. "Let's sit down on the sofa and we'll answer your questions."

I nodded and let him lead me into the lounge room. I sat on the white leather modular sofa and stared out the floor-to-ceiling windows. Dieter sat next to me on my right and Dex on my left. I watched a bird fly across the sky unable to look at either of them.

"We met about a year ago," Dieter said.

I settled my gaze on his face and waited for Dieter to continue.

His dark eyes searched mine. "Remember the day you left your watch here? I tried to drop it off at your apartment, but you weren't there so I rang your cell. Your mom answered and said you were at her house. I drove over there to return the watch but when I got to the house, there was a party. Your mom opened the door, waved me in, and took me around and introduced me to everyone, including Dex. We started talking about cars and other stuff, we hit it off as they say."

I swung my gaze to Dex.

He grinned. "Your mom sent you to the grocery store that day on an errand to find a jar of those special sundried tomatoes. You left for ages."

"I couldn't find those tomatoes anywhere and she'd been so obsessed with getting them for her parents.

I drove to ten stores to find them before finding out they no longer ship them here." I rubbed my hands on my bare thighs.

Both their gazes dropped to my hands. I stopped rubbing my thighs and tugged the hem of the t-shirt lower.

Damn, my mother was a conniving woman. I bet she'd come up with the pointless errand on purpose. "So what, you've been friends for a year?"

"I guess you could say we were," Dieter said. "We met up a few times, but we realized we were both dating you. Things were a little awkward between us after that."

That made me feel a hell of a lot better. I wasn't the only one finding this situation uncomfortable.

"Yeah, we met less often and decided we wouldn't talk about you," Dex said.

"Um, gee, thanks." Way to make a woman feel unimportant.

"Not that we didn't want to." Dex shifted on the sofa. "We didn't want to sway you into choosing one of us."

I blew air out through my mouth. "So, friends for a year and you didn't tell me. Why?"

"Why would we? You made it clear you didn't want an exclusive relationship and didn't want to know who we were seeing," Dieter said.

"Wait." I stood. "Are you saying you two are dating?"

Dex laughed and tugged the hem of my t-shirt. "Sit back down, you're flashing us."

I sat with a thud on the leather sofa.

"No, we're not dating," Dieter said. "Although…"

"Although what?" I chewed my top lip.

"What Dieter is trying to say is, when you dumped both of us, we did a few things together."

"What things? Wait, back it up, did something happen when I broke up with you both?" I waved my hands in the air.

"You broke our hearts," Dex said with a gruffness to his voice.

"Dex," I whispered and grasped his hand.

"What about me?" Dieter asked.

I twined my fingers with Dieter's. "I didn't want to break up with you both, but I thought it was the right thing to do."

"We know. It still hurt," Dieter said. "When you dumped Dex first, he showed up here and found you'd dumped me too. We got blind drunk together that night, and every night for the next week."

"I crashed here for almost a month." Dex squeezed my fingers. "After we'd drowned our sorrows, we started reminiscing about you together."

I tugged my hands free and rubbed my temples. "What sort of reminiscing?"

"We talked about all the things you liked us to do to you," Dex said without a hint of apology or embarrassment. "After a few weeks of talking and not actually doing those things to you, we were both a bit … what's the word I'm looking for?"

"Horny?" I supplied.

Dex and Dieter chuckled and glanced at each other.

I slid to the edge of the sofa. I was a little hot and bothered myself with them sitting beside me and telling me they shared intimate details and enjoyed it. Holy hotness, what did they talk about? What did they do together? My mind raced a million miles per hour imagining the two of them together. I tugged the collar of the t-shirt.

"What happened?" I said with a huskiness that didn't hide the desire racing through me.

"It was sort of like watching porn together except we were telling the porn," Dieter said. "Guys take matters into their own hands in those situations when there's no woman around."

I waved the top of the t-shirt back and forth to cool my overheated body. I pictured it so easily. Dieter and Dex stroking themselves to release while talking about me. I wanted to see it. Would they do it now if I asked? I stood and stepped to the window. Horniness aside, it still hurt me they were friends and didn't tell me. Hell, they were more than friends. They'd lived together. Done sexual things together.

I spun around with a sudden thought. "Are you two gay?"

"No." They both laughed.

"It was just a release," Dex said, "while we were in the same room together."

"Do you want to do more?"

"We want to do more to you," Dex said.

I dropped the collar of the t-shirt and stepped back until my butt hit the window. *We*, he'd said we. They'd talked together and now they were a *we*?

"I should go home." I peered down at the street below.

"Spend the day with us," Dieter said.

"And do what?"

"Whatever you want." Dieter patted the sofa. "We can watch a movie or do other stuff."

"And by other stuff you mean..." I waved my hand between the two of them.

Dieter chuckled. "Whatever you want."

I squeezed my head between my palms. "I can't."

*Wasn't it bad enough I dated them both?*

Dex stood and walked toward me. He eased my hands from my head. "Stop flashing me, you know how much it turns me on."

I couldn't stop the smile tugging my lips.

"Dieter and I have talked about this. It seems like an excellent solution. We both love you. You love us both. Why don't you love us together and we love you together?"

I tugged my hands from his and frowned. "So, you've both decided this is the solution? Thank you very much for deciding for me."

"That wasn't what we were saying." Dieter stood and moved next to Dex.

"Right? So, you both think I'll jump into bed with you together and we'll be one big happy threesome? And we'll live happily ever after?"

"Why not?" Dieter asked.

"*Why not*?" I screeched. "For one, it's illegal. Two, all of our parents would go apeshit. Three, we couldn't get married. Four, I've already told you both I'm not trying anal. Five, five, five," I spluttered stopping on the image of having sex with them both together.

Dex smirked like he knew where my thoughts went.

"Argh." I shoved past them both. "I'm getting dressed then going home."

"We'll drive you," Dieter said.

"I can catch an Uber."

"We'll drive you," Dex said in his commanding voice.

"Fine," I snapped. "You can buy me hotcakes on the way too."

## Chapter Six

After I'd relented to them driving me home, I'd demanded to sit in the back seat by myself and stew. Or marinate. Whatever. One second, I was all for going back to Dieter's apartment and seeing how the three of us would be together. The next I was a prude. What was wrong with me? The two men I loved wanted to be together with me. It should make me happy, but I was more confused than anything.

I devoured the hotcakes in the café like they were the answer to my life's dilemma. Which they weren't. No big surprise there. But they were tasty. Dex and Dieter chatted about cars while eating brunch with me. They seemed to know I needed the space to think. And stew some more. I drank another two cups of coffee. Geez, the extra caffeine would wire me today. I'd put the energy into creating a new design. At least then the day wouldn't be all about my two boyfriends.

"Would you like anything else?" Dieter asked.

"Nope." I twirled the coffee mug.

Dex placed his hand on top of it before the mug spun off the table. "You can talk to us."

"I don't want to." I shoved out of the café chair and stomped back to the car. Way to act like a grown-up. Mom would be so furious with my behavior.

Dex and Dieter joined me at the car.

"I'm sorry," I said. "It's a lot to take in."

"It's okay, Tiff." Dieter opened the car door for me. "We're not going anywhere and whatever you decide we'll be happy so long as you're in our lives, however you want us to be."

My heart almost fluttered out of my chest. How could I act like such a brat when I had two wonderful men who loved me?

I slid into the back seat and buckled my seat belt. I could have walked from here, but I wanted more time with them.

Dieter drove us to my apartment building and stopped at the curb by the front door.

"Thanks for the ride." I opened the car door and hurried to the front steps of my apartment building.

The door swung open and one of my neighbors, Maz, bounded through the gap, arms laden with suitcases, and almost knocked me on my ass.

"Are you going on a holiday?" I asked.

Maz frowned with her dark eyebrows so at odds to her spiky purple hair.

"No, dummy. Did you forget about the fumigation?"

"What fumigation?"

More of my neighbors exited the building with suitcases in hand. Dread settled in my limbs.

"The one they're doing tomorrow. We got an email about it."

"I didn't get an email." I snatched my cell phone out of my purse and opened my emails. "See." I waved my phone in front of her face.

Maz shrugged her shoulders. "Did you check your spam folder?"

"Why would it be in my spam?" I tapped on the folder anyway and there sat the notification email of the fumigation. "No."

"Is everything all right, Tiff?" Dex asked.

"No. I mean yes. No problem."

"I'll see you next week when we can move back in," Maz said and trundled off down the street with her suitcase.

Dex frowned and folded his arms.

"Crap." I kicked the step then wished I hadn't

when I hit my big toe too hard. "They're fumigating. I'll have to stay with my parents."

Dex grinned. "We'll help you pack." He waved Dieter over.

Dieter climbed out of his Jag and sauntered over to us.

"They're fumigating Tiff's apartment building," Dex said to Dieter.

Dieter grinned. "Come stay with me."

"No, I can't." I glanced between the two men. I couldn't live with one of them and not the other, besides, how would Dex feel about me living with Dieter and not him? Why hadn't Dex offered for me to stay with him?

"Good idea," Dex said. "We can all stay at Dieter's apartment."

"All of us?" I squeaked. That explained why he didn't offer.

"Sure," Dex said. "I've stayed there before. You've stayed there before. We can all hang out and see what it's like to live together."

"I don't think so." I opened the front door and climbed the stairs to my apartment.

"Why not?" Dieter asked. "My place is big enough for all of us."

"I already said I can't do a threesome." I unlocked my door and entered my apartment.

"You don't have to if you don't want to. My place has three bedrooms. We can all have our own bedroom," Dieter said.

I walked into my bedroom and tugged my suitcase from the wardrobe. Dex took the case from me and tossed it on the bed. I opened my drawers and stuffed clothes inside. Dieter had three bedrooms, would it work?

"And what? We'll all be roomies? No sex?" I

opened my underwear drawer and dumped an armload of thongs and bras into the suitcase.

Dex groaned. "Who said anything about no sex?"

"Um, me." I paused and placed my hands on the lid of the suitcase. "I can't go hopping from one bedroom to the other when they're right next door to each other."

Dex laughed. "You can be such a prude sometimes. You're dating two men."

"But … but…" I flapped my mouth open and closed. I didn't have any excuse.

"No sex," Dieter jumped to my rescue. "Okay? Or would you rather live with your mom for a week?"

I squinted at Dieter. He knew I'd never hear the end of marriage talk if I lived at home for the week.

"Pack my sewing gear." I pointed to the lounge room where I kept my sketch books, fabric, cottons, needles, scissors, and other supplies.

Dieter left my bedroom to do my bidding. Dex frowned.

"What?" I asked.

"Do you think any of us will go a week without sex?"

"Those are my terms." I zipped up the suitcase.

"Your terms?" He cocked his eyebrow then crossed the small space and ran his hands down both my arms. "You shouldn't have said that, because you only said no sex." He leaned his head close and brushed the tip of my nose with his. "You didn't say no kissing." His lips landed on mine. He stroked his tongue over the seam of my mouth until my lips parted for his searching tongue. Dex's tongue wrapped around mine in a consuming kiss that made me clutch his back to keep my legs from giving way. He kissed his way down my neck and cupped his hand to my breast and brushed his thumb over my nipple until it hardened under his expert strokes.

"You didn't say no touching either."

"I … it … Dex…" I moaned as he pinched my nipple. "I implied it."

"You should have been more specific, Fluff." Dex stopped kissing and touching me and grabbed the handle of the suitcase and left my bedroom.

I scurried after him. "Dex, that's not fair."

Was I talking about the way he'd stopped and left me turned on or that I'd implied we shouldn't do anything sexual while we all lived together? My mind was a mess of conflict.

"What's not fair?" Dieter hoisted the packed sewing bags.

"I reminded her she only said no sex." Dex opened my apartment door.

"Ah, yes, she did only say no sex, didn't she?" Dieter stepped out of the apartment, his arms laden with my sewing machine and bags of gear.

Dex followed him with my suitcase.

"Guys, wait, that wasn't what I meant." I hurried after them and locked the door behind me.

Dieter whistled while walking down the stairs. Dex ignored me. Annoying boyfriends. They both knew I had little willpower when it came to being pleasured by them. My heart raced and my stomach churned. This was all so wrong yet exciting.

They threw my bags into the trunk of the Jag and I climbed into the car with a loud huff of frustration. Dieter met my gaze in the rearview mirror.

"I guess we're spending today together anyway," he said.

"Shut up." I stuck out my tongue.

Dieter chuckled. "I'll take you up on that when we get back home."

"I am not, I repeat, I am *not* having sex with

either or both of you." I crossed my arms. "You're both too annoying."

"Annoying?" Dex asked. "I thought we were handsome, hot, and amazing in bed. I recall you saying those things to me a few times."

"Yeah, you've said that to me too," Dieter agreed.

"Oh. My. God. Would you two shut up? This is like a nightmare. Why would I want two boyfriends when one is infuriating? Two of you together ganging up on me is ridiculous."

"So, I'll drive you to your parents then, shall I?" Dieter asked.

I flipped him the finger.

Dex and Dieter fist-bumped.

"Ugh," I groaned. "At least we'll all be at work during the week. We won't see much of each other."

"We'll see plenty of each other," Dieter assured me.

I opened my cell phone and contemplated calling Dad to tell him I needed a place to stay for the week. But then I'd have to listen to Mom, and as much as I wanted to eat her cooking, it wasn't worth it at the moment with her incessant marriage talk the last few months. She'd been nonstop since I got back together with Dieter and Dex. I tapped the screen. Was she capable of orchestrating the fumigation just so I'd end up with one of them? No, impossible—or was it? I wouldn't put anything past her.

I dialed my home number. "Hi, Mom."

"Hi, Tiffany. You left early last night. I trust Dieter took you home."

"Yes, Mom. Dieter drove me to his house."

"He's such a wonderful boyfriend," she gushed.

"I know. Listen, they're fumigating my apartment."

Dieter flicked his gaze to the rearview mirror. Dex turned around in his seat and eyeballed me. I smiled with evilness. Let them stew this time and think I was about to go stay with my parents. It served them both right for teasing me.

"Do you want your father to pick you up and take you home?"

"I can stay with you…"

Dex leaned over the seat and grabbed my phone.

"Hi, Mrs. Herringer, Dieter has already offered Tiff a room at his apartment and we're taking her stuff there now."

I scrambled forward and slapped Dex's shoulder trying to get my cell phone back, but he ducked forward and kept talking to my mom.

"Yes, we'll take good care of her. I give you my word."

Dieter parked his Jag in front of his apartment building and took the cell from Dex.

"Hello," he said.

I slapped at his shoulder too, but he climbed out of the car. I scrambled out after him.

"Yes, we'd all love to come to dinner Friday night," Dieter said.

My mouth dropped open. Dieter tapped my chin shut and handed my cell back.

"Dinner?" I squeaked.

"Yes, dinner," Mom said. "You bring both those young men here for dinner."

"Together?" I gulped.

Mom sighed. "Yes." She hung up.

I stared at my blank screen. What the hell was she up to now?

Dieter and Dex fetched my bags from the trunk and carried them inside. I followed behind them more worried about dinner Friday night than spending the week with the two men I loved in the same apartment and not having sex.

## Chapter Seven

Dex dumped my suitcase in the room I'd slept in last night while Dieter set up my sewing gear in his sitting room.

"I'll head back to my place and grab a bag of gear. I'll be back soon." Dex hauled me in for a knee-wobbling kiss.

I unpacked my clothes and dithered around in the bedroom before venturing into the sitting room where Dieter was still setting up my sewing machine.

"Thanks for letting me stay." I stood fidgeting my feet by his side while he kneeled on the floor plugging in the power cord.

"You can stay as long as you like." He gazed up at me.

"Won't this be awkward for you?"

"No. I love it when you stay here."

"What about Dex?"

"I like Dex." He slid his hands under my sarong skirt and along the insides of my legs. "I liked it when he stayed here too."

"You're not jealous when I'm with him?"

"No. We've never had that sort of relationship." He brushed his thumbs against my inner thighs.

"So, if I dated someone else you wouldn't be jealous?"

"I never said that." He moved his thumbs higher until they teased the fabric of my thong. "I was jealous when you dumped both of us and dated that jerk."

"Yeah?" I bit my top lip. "I was jealous of your date the other night thinking you were having a threesome with them."

Dieter laughed. "I wanted you to be jealous."

"Are you dating other people?"

"Not anymore."

His thumbs inched closer to my aching clit right where I wanted his talented hands. Dex's kisses made me long for more with either of them. With Dex out of the apartment I didn't suffer the guilt of loving them both. I didn't experience the awkwardness of doing sexual things with one while the other was nearby.

Dieter's thumb slid under my panties.

The front door slammed shut.

I jumped back out of Dieter's reach and almost ran from the room. I barreled into Dex.

"Whoa." Dex grabbed by shoulders. "What are you running from?"

"Nothing." I flicked a glance over my shoulder.

Dieter wandered out of the sitting room. "You're all set to go in there."

"Thanks," I said. "I think I'll shut myself in and work." I squeezed through the tiny gap he'd left between him and the door. My body tingled from the brush against his. Damn it, I hadn't even been living with them for a day and I was almost ready to jump in bed with them.

I shoved Dieter's back and shut the door in their faces.

Their voices mumbled through the closed door. I pressed my ear against the wood, but I couldn't make out what they were saying. Ugh. I stomped over to my gear and let my creative side take over.

****

A gentle knock rapped on the door.

"Come in," I called without even thinking while swapping one piece of pale pink fabric for a delicate ivory onto the sketch. Yes, that was the right material for this design. I gazed up with a satisfied smile.

Dex and Dieter stood inside the doorway. I'd

forgotten about them while designing. Good thing too, because they both looked good enough for me to drag into bed.

"Would you like to go out for dinner or order in?" Dieter asked.

"Is it that time already?" I scooped the design off the floor where I'd sprawled and stood.

"Yep, you've been hiding for hours, come out and play with us." Dex winked.

My lips tugged into a smile. "I'm not playing with you."

"Aww, but…" Dex said.

"Nope, no car racing games, I'm not having both of you beat me. We can order in and watch a movie instead."

"Fine, but no horror movie," Dex said.

"Or car racing," I said.

"No thrillers," Dieter added.

"Comedy then?" I asked.

Dex rubbed the back of his neck. "I can't believe I'm saying this, but what about that chick flick you wanted to watch?"

"No, that's okay." I cringed. The chick flick was well known for its raunchy sex scenes.

"Yeah," Dieter said. "You keep saying you want to watch it."

"Um, we don't have to watch it." I dropped the design on the coffee table.

My cell phone rang. I swiped to answer it.

"Some best friend you are. Why haven't you rung me yet and told me how your threesome went? I've been waiting all day," Prue's voice rang out through the speaker on the cell.

Shit. I always had my cell set to answer on speaker when I was designing.

"Hi, Prue, I didn't have a threesome." I fumbled with the cell, and it slid from the table onto the floor.

"Why not? You keep saying how great your dicks are. Why wouldn't you want them both at the same time?"

"Prue!" I cried, "you're on speaker."

"So, you always answer on speaker when you're working."

I stared at Dex and Dieter who were both wearing shit-eating grins. I'd never live this down.

"I'm at Dieter's apartment," I said.

Silence.

"Oh," Prue said. "Hi, Dieter."

"Hi, Prue," Dieter called out.

I picked up the cell phone.

"Hi, Prue," Dex said.

"Shit, did I interrupt you three together?" Prue asked.

"No, it's not like that," I said.

Dex stepped closer. "It could be."

"Girl, get off the cell phone and get you a threesome. I'll come by your place tomorrow after work for all the details."

"Prue," I snapped.

"Yeah?" She stopped her gushing to ask.

"I'm not at my place. I'm staying at Dieter's while they fumigate the building."

Prue clapped her hands. "Meet me at my art gallery for lunch then."

"Okay."

I sure needed to talk to someone about this situation I'd gotten myself in.

"Will," Prue called out. "I need to cancel our lunch sex tomorrow. I think you should spank me for being so naughty."

"You didn't hang up," I yelled at Prue.

Mr. Burberry's deep voice laughed in the background before Prue hung up the cell phone. Dex and Dieter chuckled. I made sure I ended the call before looking at either of them.

Dieter leaned against the doorjamb and crossed his legs. "Are you taking your best friend's advice?"

I drank in the sight of him looking so relaxed and amused. "Huh?"

"Get you a threesome?"

"Pfft," I scoffed. "The answer is still no."

Dex stepped up behind me and placed his large hands on my shoulders. "You're tense. Would you like a massage?"

His thumbs worked on the tight ball of muscles where my shoulders met my neck. I dropped my chin forward letting his thumbs ease lower under the material of the t-shirt and massage the stiff muscles lower down my back.

A quiet moan slipped out.

"I love the sounds you make," Dieter said still lounging against the doorjamb.

I raised my head and met his intense gaze.

"Me too," Dex said.

Dex's voice ruffled my hair and sent a shiver down my spine. His fingers drifted higher to the sides of my neck and eased the muscles with a soothing rub. Dieter watched Dex's fingers on my neck. Did he enjoy watching Dex touch me? Or was he jealous?

I stepped forward. "Thanks, Dex. I'm hungry, let's order Chinese."

"Chinese it is." Dieter thrust off the doorjamb and whipped out his cell phone. He tapped away on the screen. "It'll be here in twenty minutes. What do you want to do while we wait?" His gaze raked my body from head to foot.

The pressure of Dex's fingers still echoed on my skin. Dieter stared at me like he wanted to shove his hand in my panties and find out if I was wet. I wouldn't disappoint him.

"I'll pack up a few things in here, then I'll be out." I walked over to the sewing machine and fiddled with the bobbins and threads avoiding eye contact.

Dex and Dieter got the message and left me alone. At least they took my no for a no. They might push for us all to be together, but they respected me enough to know when to back off. I loved them even more.

Would it be so bad for all three of us to be together?

Dieter said he wasn't jealous of Dex, and he didn't look jealous a few minutes ago when Dex massaged my shoulders. But what about Dex? Would he be jealous when Dieter touched me?

It was a conversation I needed to have with him before … wait, was I considering a threesome when I'd been so against it? Shit. It wasn't even a day, and they were swaying me to their way of thinking.

A week.

I could last a week without making this decision. We'd all live together and see if we'd be happy with this arrangement before bringing sex into it. Because once we involved sex things would either get more complicated or a lot easier.

The doorbell pealed through the apartment. I left the safety of the sitting room/sewing room and found Dex and Dieter unpacking the takeout boxes on the coffee table in the lounge room.

"We thought we'd eat in here and watch the movie," Dex said.

"Okay. Did you get honey chicken?" I asked.

"Here." Dieter handed me a takeout box and chopsticks.

I settled on the sofa then plucked a piece of chicken and put it in my mouth.

Dieter flicked on the television, picked up a takeout box, and sat next to me. Dex sat on the other side of me. I didn't think this through. I should have sat in the armchair. It was too late now to reposition without it being obvious I'd moved away from them.

"Drink?" Dex scooped up a soda can from the coffee table.

I shook my head and focused on my food instead of the way each of their thighs brushed against mine.

The movie introduction flashed on the screen. I shifted my attention to the television. The movie started with a bang. Literally. A couple banging up against a door in a bathroom. Dex and I had done that the first night we'd dated. Heat flooded my face. I swallowed the chicken and choked. Dieter slapped my back.

"Cough it up," he said with a firmer thud on my back.

The lump of chicken ejected from my windpipe. Dex handed me a napkin and I spat the offending piece of food into it.

"Thanks," I croaked.

"Are you okay?" Dex peered into my eyes.

"Yep," I rasped.

He laughed. "You're thinking about our first time, aren't you?"

My face boiled to an inferno.

Dieter paused the movie. "We've never talked about our first times with Tiff."

I shoved my half-eaten food onto the table and picked up the soda can. I popped the ring with a fizz and gulped the liquid. *Please don't. Please don't,* I chanted inside my head. Both my first times with them had been epic.

Dex waved at the screen of the frozen couple mid-bang. "Imagine that, but better. Tiff and I met at a pub. There was a band playing, I can't even remember their name, all I remember is seeing Tiff grinding her hot bod on the dance floor and thinking I had to have her."

"Mechanic Mouth," I said. "That was the band."

"Right." Dex placed his takeout box on the coffee table. "You were smoking that night, you had on this tiny white dress with knee-high black boots. Your hair was in a crazy crinkle mess like you'd just been fucked. It made me want to have you so bad."

Dex slid his hand onto my thigh. Tingles raced up my body.

"Then what happened?" Dieter leaned forward with his elbows on his knees watching us.

"Dex came up to me on the dance floor and told me I was about to have the best sex of my life. I told him he was crazy and went back to dancing with my date." I laughed.

"That guy didn't stand a chance with you," Dex said. "I let her dance and watched her from the bar."

"You did nothing?" Dieter asked.

"I did plenty when she followed me down the hallway."

Dieter peered at me with raised eyebrows.

"I was going to the restroom," I said.

"Sure you were," Dex drawled. "We ended up in a bathroom, and she dry-humped me so hard I didn't wait to take her home. I rolled on a condom, lifted her dress, slid her thong to the side, and fucked her hard against the bathroom door."

"I had a bruise on my back for days from the

doorknob," I said.

Dex chuckled and slid his other hand into my hair. He drew my head closer until our lips met and our tongues tangled in a kiss reminiscent of our first kiss in the bathroom full of passion and heat. Blinding lust. Our lust had turned into love somewhere along our many best-sex-ever sessions. Dex nibbled his way from my lips to my ear. I let out a moan.

"Fuck, that's hot," Dieter said.

I snapped open my eyes to Dieter's blazing gaze beside me. The usual guilt surged in my stomach. I shifted out of Dex's hold and smoothed my hands through my hair.

"It was," I said and turned back to the screen.

Dex didn't remove his hand from my thigh though.

"It is." Dieter placed his arm behind my shoulders and ran his fingers through my hair. "I'm so freaking hard I doubt I'll remember any of this movie." He pressed the "resume" button.

The couple on the screen sprang back to banging life. The woman's moans and the man's grunts filled the apartment and sent my raging desires even higher. I'd hoped to watch the movie with one of them so I could bonk their brains out afterward, but now with them both here I didn't have that option.

Unless…

No. It was too soon to jump into bed with them both. I still needed to talk to Dex. And what would everyone else say?

I'd disappoint Mom because I wouldn't be able to have a wedding with two men. At least it'd stop her talking about marriage if I were in a threesome. I should say the hell with it and take them up on their offer. Heaven knows they turned me on enough to do it right now. But in the morning, how would I feel?

The movie ended, and I stood in a rush. "Good night."

"Tiff?" Dieter asked.

"I'm up early tomorrow for work. I'll see you both in the morning." Excitement thrummed at seeing them both in the morning. I'd never stayed over at either of their houses on what used to be school days and were now workdays. Another new experience of spending time with them.

"Yes, you'll see us before work," Dieter said.

"Not me," Dex said. "I'll be at the gym."

My excitement plummeted a fraction. At least I'd see Dieter in the morning, but I'd miss seeing Dex too. Loving two men wasn't easy.

## Chapter Eight

"Good morning." Dieter handed me a large mug of coffee.

"Good morning." I accepted the mug and placed a kiss on his cheek.

"Is that all I get for providing you with lifesaving nectar?"

I laughed and kissed his lips. He deepened the kiss with a tug of his teeth on my bottom lip and a swipe of his tongue inside my mouth. I fumbled with the mug trying to put it on the counter. Dieter stopped kissing me long enough to take the mug from my hands then returned to kissing me.

He hoisted me onto the counter. I spread my legs and wrapped them around his waist. His tongue and lips stroked mine until my breathing turned ragged and I rocked my hips against the hard erection jutting between my legs. Dieter ground his hips.

"I've been hard like this since last night." He let out a long breath and stepped back. "But you said no sex."

I pouted. "But Dex isn't here."

Dieter fiddled with his suit jacket. "Are you worried about us hearing you?"

I nodded my head and bit my top lip.

"We love hearing the noises you make." Dieter handed me the mug again.

I sipped the caffeine fuel for my day.

"So, how about it?" I asked.

Dieter shook his head. "No, it'd feel wrong for me."

"How?"

"It's just, you said no sex this week, yet the second one of us isn't here you're keen for sex. It'd feel like I'm cheating."

"Cheating on Dex?" I frowned. Now he said that it sounded true. If Dieter and I had sex without Dex knowing, then it would be like we were hiding it from him, and I'd never done that with either man. They'd always known I was with someone else, but Dieter was right. "Yeah, I get it."

"You do?" he asked with surprise.

"I love you, Dieter. You've got an amazing heart to put up with me. You could have any woman you wanted and not have to worry about her loving someone else."

"Tiff." He brushed his knuckles over my cheek. "I love you too. I wouldn't have you any other way."

"Including Dex?"

"Including Dex. We can make this work. All three of us, if you give us a chance."

I cupped his handsome face. "Give me time. It's a lot, you know, finding out you two knew each other threw me off. And then hearing you two..." I slid one hand down his suit to cup his erection.

"Tiff," he groaned.

"I've got to say, it was hot hearing you both touch yourselves while talking about me."

"Don't make a mess of my suit before work."

I giggled and withdrew my hand. "Don't say I didn't offer you more." I finished the coffee.

Dieter walked over to the fridge, opened the door, and stared inside.

"What are you looking for?"

"Something cold to tip down my pants." He threw me an anguished smile over his shoulder.

I jumped off the counter. "Good luck with that. I'll see you tonight after work."

"Wait." He slammed the fridge. "I have a key for

you."

He fetched a key hanging from a shiny gold key chain with a jagged cut down each side.

Dieter held up his key chain. "I have one third, Dex has the other. You have the middle piece because you bring us all together."

I swallowed the lump in my throat. "I'm only here for the week."

"We're hoping you love living with us enough you'll want to stay."

"Um." I stared at the shiny piece of the key chain that was an accurate representation of my heart split into pieces. Yet together with the two men I loved my heart would be whole.

"Don't say anything now. Think about it," Dieter said.

"Okay." I curled my fingers around the key. "I should get going."

"Yeah, me too. Dad wouldn't be too happy if his prodigal son were late to work."

I laughed. "Your dad loves you, he wouldn't care if you turned up at three in the afternoon."

"True." Dieter pecked the tip of my nose. "Have a good day at work."

"You too." I smiled.

This was nice having someone to wish you a good morning, a good day at work, and to look forward to seeing them at the end of the day. I could get used to this.

**** 

During my hour lunch break I walked the three blocks to Prue's art studio from the Ozwald Delante studio. It was handy having my best friend close by when I needed advice on how to handle a situation. Except Prue would tell me to enjoy the sex and not worry about the consequences—if I didn't have my parents to worry about.

Prue waved and excused herself from talking to a couple. "Hey." She grabbed my arm and marched me into her office.

"Do we have to eat in here?" I groaned. Prue and Will didn't keep their lunch sex a secret, and I didn't want to eat in a room where they'd probably screwed on every surface.

"I'm grabbing my lunch." Prue rolled her eyes at my prudishness. She picked up a Tupperware container and waved me out of her office. "Let's eat in the park, it's not too hot today. Martha is making me these extra healthy lunches since I'm pregnant again. I can't wait to get my hands on a greasy cheeseburger once this baby is out."

I laughed. "Don't think I'm joining you. I'm buying a hot dog today."

"Man, you're the worst best friend ever."

We stopped at the hot dog cart, and I purchased my lunch. We crossed the street to the small park nestled in the abundance of the busy streets of Los Angeles and settled on the grass under the shade of a tree.

Prue opened her Tupperware container, peered at the contents with a sad expression then dug into it with her fork.

"So, um, I'm staying at Dieter's and so is Dex. They want to have a threesome, but I said no, and I said no sex while we're all living together."

Prue stopped crunching her salad and waved her fork.

"I don't know if I can do that. Two men at once. What sort of woman would that make me? And then what about marriage? And kids? How would you decide who would be the father? Or would you just take a potluck in whoever's sperm made it to the egg in time? What would my parents say? What would anyone say?" I huffed and puffed.

Prue resumed eating, her silence more telling than words.

"Would you do it?" I asked.

"If I loved two men and they loved me and wanted us all to be together, I'd at least try."

I took a bite of my hot dog wishing I had Prue's healthy lunch, but I wouldn't tell her that.

"I didn't think you wanted marriage and kids," Prue said.

"That's the thing, I do. I'm scared of screwing it up though. Mom and Dad are always so happy and perfect together, what if my marriage wasn't?"

"So, you dated two men to stop from failing?" she asked.

I finished the hot dog. My stomach churned, I'd let out my fears. Maybe from the hot dog too.

"When you say it like that it sounds stupid." I frowned.

"It's not stupid. What's stupid is you."

"Me?"

"Yeah, you. Do you really think your parents are perfect and happy all the time?"

"Yes, so are you and Mr. Burberry," I said with conviction.

"Lies. No one is. Least of all your parents."

"But you and Mr. Burberry…"

"We have our problems. But we always work it out in the bedroom." She grinned.

"So, you're saying I'm stupid for saying no sex."

"Bingo." She closed the lid of the container and rubbed her small stomach. "How about an ice cream?"

"Are you allowed to eat them while pregnant?"

"Don't you start." She glared. "Of course, I can eat ice cream."

"Yeah, okay. You're buying though, since you pointed out how stupid I am."

"It'll be my treat for the stupid woman with two men wanting to give her orgasmic bliss and she says no." Prue smacked my ass.

"Hey, I'm not the one who likes spankings."

"You never know what you'll like until you try it." Her eyes twinkled with mischief.

I sliced my hand through the air. "Zip it, I don't want to hear how talented Mr. Burberry is in bed."

"Bed, who said anything about bed?" Prue tossed her long black hair back and laughed.

She'd always been gorgeous, but she had the pregnancy glow to her complexion of pale skin and dark hair. She also boasted the "in love with my husband" glow. The same glow I saw on Mom every day of her life. It was no wonder Mom was pressuring me to get married when she was so happy, but what if Prue was right, what if she wasn't always happy? Had I been running from marriage for all the wrong reasons?

And if I had, would that change the way I felt about Dieter and Dex? Would I be able to love one more than the other and choose who to marry?

My heart twisted in pain at the notion. I'd tried giving them both up. I'd tried moving on from loving them, yet I'd gone back. What if this solution of theirs was the solution to us being happy forever?

If it was, then there'd be no wedding and marriage to two men. I would have to give up the idea of being happily married like my parents. Was that something I could do for the two men I loved?

"Prue?"

"Yeah?" She paused outside the ice cream parlor.

"Do you think it's wrong to love two people?"

"No," she scoffed. "Love comes in all shapes and sizes, the same as relationships. There is no one type we all have to stick to. The world is changing, Tiff, gay marriages used to be illegal. One day polyamory won't be illegal either. One day I'll be your matron of honor at your wedding to your two dicks."

"Stop calling them that."

"You picked two men whose names start with 'D', what else am I supposed to call them?"

"They have names." I opened the parlor door. "Dieter and Dex."

"Put them together and you get … Dix." She giggled.

I giggled with her. How could I not when my best friend gave a ray of hope to my situation? She painted a pretty picture, one I saw, me marrying Dieter and Dex. Together. At the same time. Would they want marriage though? Or did they just want threesome sex?

## Chapter Nine

I caught an Uber to Dieter's apartment after work. The summer heat was too much to walk home in. *Home.* How easy it was to imagine I was going home to the two men I loved. I slid the key into the front door and stepped inside the cool apartment. A sigh left my lungs at the central air-conditioning system blowing cool air over my sticky skin. The Uber car's air conditioning had been appalling.

Noises clanged from the kitchen. I kicked off my heels and made my way to the kitchen. Dex stood at the stovetop stirring a pot with a wooden spoon. Dieter sat on the bench sipping on a beer bottle. Dieter's suit jacket was off, his tie missing, and his top buttons undone affording me a view of his bronzed chest. He was handsome. Dex put the spoon down and picked up a beer bottle. His thick bicep tugged at the tight band on his black t-shirt. He was gorgeous too. How did I get so lucky to have two good-looking men love me?

"Hi," I said.

Dieter slid off the bench. "Hi, how was your day?"

"Good," I said. "Apart from this heat."

"Hi, Fluff. Would you like a beer?" Dex said.

"No, thanks. I'm never drinking again, remember?" I sat at the kitchen table. "Something smells good."

"That'd be my one-pot wonder." Dex grinned.

"What's in it?" I asked.

"That's the wonder." He laughed.

Dieter shrugged his shoulders. "Don't ask me, he was already cooking when I got home."

"I started work early, so I finished early." Dex removed the pan and slopped the contents into three bowls. "Bon appetit."

I took the bowl he held out to me. Dex and Dieter joined me at the table. Dieter scooped a spoon into his bowl and stared at the beige contents with hesitation. I dug in. Dex's cooking might not look the greatest, but his meals always tasted great.

"Tomorrow we're ordering in," Dieter said.

"Just try it, you pussy." Dex slapped him on the shoulder.

The contents of the spoon sloshed back into the bowl.

I placed my hand over my mouth to smother my laughter and watched Dieter eat his first spoonful, his expression full of reservations. A slow smile spread from his lips.

"Not bad," Dieter said.

They clinked beer bottles. I wished I'd said yes to a beer bottle now just to join them. I stopped scooping up the liquid and gazed at them. They got along well together. They were friends without me around. I saw it in the way they were at ease with each other. But if we had sex together, would I ruin that for them?

I cleared my throat. They both stopped eating to look at me. I blinked. No, I couldn't.

"How was work?" I asked instead.

"Good," Dex said. "The latest shipment arrived with no hassles and all the parts were there for the project car."

"What are you doing up this time?" Dieter asked.

"We're doing a Plymouth Barracuda," Dex said.

"Nice." Dieter nodded his head.

"Yeah, she'll be a real beauty when we're finished." Dex grinned.

"Isn't that a fish?" I asked.

They both laughed.

Dieter leaned over the table and smooched his lips against mine. "You're adorable."

"But it is." I pushed my bowl away.

Dex shook his head and cleared our bowls. Dieter followed him and placed them in the dishwasher. This was nice. Dinner cooked for me. Dishes cleaned for me. A woman could get used to two men waiting on her like this when she got home from work.

"Do you want ice cream?" Dieter asked.

"No, thanks, I ate some with Prue today at lunch."

Dex nodded and Dieter filled two bowls for them. It was like they had the kitchen routine down pat. How long did they say they lived together? A month. It seemed like they'd been together for years with the way they read each other so well.

"How did that go?" he asked.

"Good." I stretched my arms over my head. "She pointed out I was stupid for saying no sex."

"I like Prue even more now." Dieter grinned.

"Hey, you said no this morning." I folded my arms on the table and pouted.

"You did?" Dex asked.

"Yeah." Dieter swallowed his ice cream.

Dex swung his spoon and clinked it with Dieter's spoon. "You're better than me, I would have said yes."

"Dex," I said. "Let's have sex."

Dex chuckled. "I'm going to have to say no too."

"What? Why?" I shoved back my chair and stood.

Dex nodded his head at Dieter. "I think you'll like it more with both of us."

"Ugh." I threw up my hands. "I'm going to work on my designing."

"But you've been working all day," Dex said. "Don't you want to watch a movie and chill with us?"

I did, but I wouldn't admit to it. Because them saying all of us together or nothing was just blackmail. I only had myself to blame for putting the no-sex ban on for the week. Perhaps after the week was over, we'd go back to the way things were.

But did I want to go back to my little apartment? Did I want to go back to keeping the two men I loved separate?

"Fine," I relented. "We can watch *Runway Stars*."

"Anything but that," Dieter groaned.

"Yeah, Fluff, the only woman we want to see prancing around is you," Dex said.

"How about after the show I prance around in my latest swimwear design?"

They both opened their mouths but no sounds came out. Score one for me.

\*\*\*\*

I sang to the music playing on the radio in the shower. Last night had been fun. We'd laughed, ate popcorn, Dex and Dieter had thrown popcorn at the designs that were over the top and outrageous, then they'd tickled me into agreeing never to make anything that hideous. By the time we'd gone to our separate beds I'd abandoned the idea of prancing around in my swimwear. I hadn't wanted to lose the easy and relaxed atmosphere we enjoyed together.

The bathroom door opened and Dex stepped into the bathroom naked. In all his hard morning glory. I dropped the bar of soap. He slid open the shower door.

"What are you doing?" I squealed.

"Showering. Move over." He placed his hands on my hips and wriggled me out of the way so he could fit into the cubicle with me.

"Together?"

"It's not the first time," he said.

The water gushed down his naked body over his hard muscles and to the even harder one sticking out from his groin.

"Yeah, but…" I wet my lips.

"You put so many buts into everything." He glanced around the shower. "Where's the soap?" He spotted the bar on the floor. "I see what's going on." He pointed at the soap. "We're playing 'who dropped the soap' game."

I shook my head, but it was too late. Dex squatted on the floor and picked up the soap. He slid the bar up the inside of my thighs running his other hand over the soap trail. My body combusted into a longing need to experience his hard length deep inside me. I gazed down at his dark hair slick with water and his face level with the place I wanted him to bury it.

He slid the soap higher over my throbbing mound.

"I love this bit of fluff you keep just for me."

"Who said it's for you?" I panted.

His other hand followed the soap and brushed through my curls.

"You did." He stood stroking his hands up my stomach, around my ribs, and under my breasts.

I dropped my head to his hard chest. "Dex."

"Yeah?" He soaped my back.

"This isn't fair."

"You know I don't play fair." He molded my body against his.

His hardness pressed into my stomach too far from where I wanted it.

"Why do you want us all together?"

"I told you, I think you'll love it."

"What about you?" I slid my hands to his back and ran them over his firm buttocks. "Will you love it?"

"I love anything about you." He massaged my buttocks in return.

Damn him, if he kept this up, I wouldn't be able to function for the rest of the day. I released my hold on him and ducked under the warm spray rinsing all the suds off my body. I stepped from the shower with a last longing look at his erection.

Dex chuckled and ran his hand along his length. "When you say yes, I'm going to come all over you."

"What makes you think I'll say yes?" I rubbed myself dry with a towel.

"You've already said yes. You just have to admit it."

He was right. I wanted them both and I couldn't admit it.

I left him to finish washing, wondering if he'd relieve himself in the shower and wishing I'd stayed to watch. The man was too sexy. I dressed in a hurry before I returned to the bathroom.

Dieter was crunching a bowl of cereal in the kitchen.

"Good morning," he said.

My cheeks heated thinking about Dex in the shower and what it would be like if all three of us were in there together. It wouldn't be a tight fit in Dieter's bathroom. His shower was big enough for a good sex romp, which we'd enjoyed many times.

"Morning," I mumbled and made myself a bowl of cereal.

"What's up?" He cocked his hip against the counter.

My gaze dropped to his pants.

"Nothing." I crunched the cereal.

"Did you have the shower too hot? Your face is flushed."

"Maybe." I waved the hem of my lemon-yellow shirt to fan my overheated body.

"That'd be my fault," Dex said walking into the kitchen. "Tiff and I shared a shower. She's such a hog with the soap."

My face and body heated even more.

Dieter chuckled. "Remember the first shower we took together?"

"Yes." I placed my finished cereal bowl in the sink and fetched a cup of coffee.

Dex waggled his fingers my way, so I poured him a cup too.

"I want to hear this," Dex said.

"We ended up on the floor in the sixty-nine position and almost drowned each other." Dieter laughed. "The orgasms were worth it though."

It had been worth the lack of oxygen. I sculled the rest of my coffee and rinsed my cup and bowl then placed them in the dishwasher trying to ignore the way my body hummed in arousal at the memory and Dex's hands in the shower.

I grabbed my bag. "I'm off to work."

"How about a kiss good-bye?" Dieter stepped closer.

I rose on my tiptoes and kissed his cheek.

"You call that a kiss?" Dex asked.

"No." Dieter placed both hands on the side of my face and claimed my lips.

His tongue swirled with mine. His lips molded against mine. He stroked his thumbs along my jaw and coaxed me to open my mouth wider, so the kiss grew hotter until it centered all my thoughts on his taste inside my mouth.

I sunk my fingers into the lapels of his jacket and hung on while he plundered my mouth in a kiss that would stay with me for the rest of the day. And night. The rest of the week too.

He released my mouth from his and pecked the tip of my nose. "Have a great day at work."

Dex slapped him on the back, and they walked to the front door.

"Are you coming?" Dieter called out when I hadn't moved.

"Yeah." I flapped my shirt again. I almost came from the kiss alone. I walked from the kitchen to the front door.

Dex held it open and waved me through. "See you tonight, Fluff."

"I'm ordering dinner tonight," Dieter said.

"What's wrong with my cooking?" Dex asked.

"Not a thing."

I shook my head at their easy banter. Life was taking an unexpected turn. Who would have thought I'd end up here with the two of them together? Yet we hadn't been together in all the ways we could be. And they were taking my week of no sex serious so we'd have to wait to find out if it'd work between us in bed.

"Have a good day," I said to them both.

"I will," Dex said. "I'll be thinking of you all wet and soapy all day."

"Yeah, the kiss will stick in my mind all day," Dieter said.

*Mine too.* But I didn't say that to them.

## Chapter Ten

The day passed in a blur of fabric and thoughts of my two men. I often found my mind drifting to what they were doing and if they were thinking about me. If they were as sexually frustrated as me. And it was only Tuesday. Four more days and then I would either jump into bed with them together or go home to my tiny apartment alone.

My apartment was less and less appealing. It wasn't like I held any emotional attachment to the place either. The four years I'd lived there were only a necessity as it was close to the college campus. Those days were behind me now and a new future loomed bright with a job I loved and two men I loved wanting to love me together instead of separately. If I let them.

When I returned to the apartment, I found Dieter sprawled on the sofa with his eyes closed and soft classical music playing from the surround-sound speakers. His foot bounced in time to the tune and his fingers drummed on his thigh. He was way too talented with those fingers. He should have been a musician. I pictured him playing the guitar with the gentle strokes of his sure fingers. I imagined him stroking me with his fingers.

"Hey." I kicked off my shoes and slid onto the sofa next to Dieter.

His tapping fingers transferred to my thigh instead of his.

"Bad day?" I asked.

"Long day," he said.

"Do you want to talk about it?" I asked.

"No, it'll upset you."

"Your mom?"

"Yeah." He sighed.

I shifted to sit up. Dieter's arm trapped me against his side.

"Don't go," he said.

I slid my arm around his stomach. "I don't want to." There was truth in my words. I didn't want to leave Dieter and his apartment.

"She'll get over it one day."

"Yep, as soon as I make my first million." I laughed with bitterness.

"Don't take it personally, no girlfriend has ever been good enough for me in her eyes." He stroked my back in a gentle caress. "Besides, you will make millions."

"I'm glad you're so confident." I fiddled with the buttons on his shirt.

"I have insider knowledge."

"Yeah?" I frowned. "What?"

"I've seen your designs in person, and I want to see your latest one right now." He sat up dragging me with him. "Dex does too. He's waiting for us in the pool."

"What about dinner?"

"We can eat by the pool."

I smiled. "Like a pool picnic at night. I love it."

"We thought you would."

I wriggled out of his arms. How well did they both know me? How much did they talk to each other about me? I didn't know whether to be annoyed or pleased.

"I'll get changed," I said.

"Me too. Meet me back here in five."

I nodded and walked to my bedroom. It was strange staying in this room instead of with Dieter where we'd change into our swimsuits together and race each other to the pool. If I gave up my inhibition about being with them together, we'd do that again. I undressed and shimmied into the orange and white polka dot bikini I'd designed and made with tiny flares of fabric at my hips. Wrapping a matching sheer sarong around my waist and sliding on a pair of flip-flops, I left my bedroom.

Dieter waited by the door in a pair of navy board shorts, his arms laden with takeout bags.

"Wow," he gasped. "You look stunning."

"Thanks." I twirled and curtsied. "I'm working on the swimwear line at work."

His gaze heated with an appreciative glance up and down my body. "I can see why."

Tingles of desire raced through my body. I opened the door since Dieter's hands were full.

"I prefer making gowns though."

"Have you told them?" he asked.

We made our way down the stairs to the pool.

"No, I haven't worked there long."

"It shouldn't matter with how talented you are."

"You're full of compliments tonight." I opened the glass door to the outside pool.

"You deserve them." He stepped through the door.

I ogled the draw of his muscles across his shoulders as he carried the bags to the lounge chairs and set to work unpacking our picnic.

Dex's head popped up from the crystal blue water. "Hey, Fluff, you look so hot you need cooling down." He rose from the side of the pool with a quick hoist up from his powerful arms and stomped toward me. Water flicked from his feet with each step, but I couldn't move because the sight of Dex all wet and delicious-looking made my mouth water.

He scooped me up into his arms.

"Dex," I squealed.

His wet body dripped onto mine and he marched us back to the side of the pool.

"No, don't," I cried when I realized he was about to launch us into the water together.

He paused.

I sighed with relief.

"Live a little." He chuckled then launched us into the water together.

I sucked in a breath a second before my head sunk under the water. Dex held me tight in his arms and kicked us back to the surface as my sarong floated free.

"I washed my hair this morning," I spluttered.

"I'll wash it for you tonight." He stroked a hand over my damp hair.

"You're such a dick sometimes."

He urged my legs around my waist. "You like my dick."

I anchored my ankles behind his back and bobbed in the water with him.

"Yeah, but you won't let me like it this week."

Dex's eyes lit with laughter. "You made the terms."

"I'm regretting those terms." I bit my top lip and peered at Dieter sitting on the lounge chair watching us.

"What's going on in that pretty head of yours besides liking my dick?" He tugged the ends of my damp hair floating in the water.

A tingle raced down my spine and I pressed my body tighter to his. His dick swelled between us. I wanted him so bad, but Dieter watched us.

"Dieter says he's not jealous when we're together."

Dex flicked his gaze to Dieter.

"What about you? Are you jealous when I'm with Dieter?" It wasn't something I considered when I'd kept them separate because I'd always believed they didn't know each other. It was harder to be jealous of someone you didn't know, but when it was a person you knew and a person you saw with the woman you loved, how weren't they jealous? And this morning he'd watched me kiss Dieter, but he hadn't kissed me too.

"I used to be." His hands dropped to my lower back. "After we realized we were both dating you and I found out you saw him every day at college, I was jealous it wasn't me seeing you every day."

"Dex," I whispered. "I didn't know you wanted to see me every day."

"No, you didn't want to know."

"That's not fair." I stiffened in his arms.

He kneaded my ass with his firm fingers. "Life isn't fair. We take what we can get. That's always been the way with us. And what we can have now, I'd be happy, you'd be happy, and Dieter would be happy."

"How can you be so sure it'll work out?"

"I'm not." His fingers slid lower.

I shifted in his hold trying to get him to dip lower still where I ached for Dex most, where I ached for Dieter too.

"Then why?" My breath puffed out in shallow pants as his fingers massaged my flesh.

"Why not?" His fingers skimmed the material of my bikini.

I whimpered with desire. Dex kissed my lips with a chaste kiss and released me from his hold. I sank under the water with a gasp. Floating back to the surface I splashed him in the face. He laughed and wiped the water from his eyes.

"Come on, Fluff, let's eat this dinner Dieter put together for us." He dove under the water and swam to the end of the pool.

Dieter threw Dex a towel. I swam with slow strokes to the steps in the pool trying to calm the raging desire pounding through my body. Seeing them both in board shorts wasn't helping either. Dieter stood and made his way over to me with a towel in his hands. I climbed out of the pool. Dieter wrapped the towel around my shoulders and kissed the end of my nose.

"Have fun?" he asked.

"You know Dex." I sighed. "He always likes to have fun."

Dieter frowned. "Not always."

"No, you're right." Dex might give the impression of being a fun-loving man, but losing his dad affected him. I'd been with Dex when his dad died and hugged him when he needed. I'd been there to let him lose himself in my body to forget the pain for a few blissful hours. The over-the-top fun was his way of living life knowing any day might be the last like his dad's. Dex's attitude to life was right. Why not? Why not try to see where this thing between us went?

I settled on the lounge chair next to Dex and placed my hand on his thigh. "Why not?" I nodded.

"Yeah?" His eyes glittered.

Dieter settled on the lounge chair across from us. "Why not what?"

"This. Us," I said.

"You're considering it?" Dieter asked.

"Yes."

Dieter smiled like it was Christmas morning. "Which flavor bowl would you like?"

"Did you get Little Tokyo?" I bounced on the lounger.

"I did." He offered two bowls. "Remix combo or Doner salad?"

"Remix, please. Is it chicken?"

"Yes, it's chicken." He handed me a bowl.

I removed the lid and inhaled the lemon dressing with hunger.

"What's this?" Dex asked opening his bowl.

"It's a combination of chicken, lemon-herb tahini dressing, cabbage slaw, feta, tomato, cucumber, roasted corn, harissa, Kalamata olives, and crispy marinated garbanzos." I licked my lips. "Try it, you'll like it."

"Yeah, I don't know." Dex poked at the contents of his bowl with a fork.

"Why not?" I raised my brows.

Dex chuckled and scooped a forkful into his mouth. He chewed and swallowed.

"Well?" I asked.

"It's great," he said.

"You're a terrible liar." I laughed.

He shrugged. "I've eaten worse. Next time get me a wrap or something."

Next time. He was already thinking ahead to us doing this again.

"Sure thing," Dieter said and ate his food.

A warm glow filled my body at the thought of us doing this again. And again, for the rest of our lives.

Dex passed me a bottle of apple juice like he knew I needed a drink. Dieter passed me a napkin. It was nice they both doted on me. I finished my bowl and stood with a stretch of my arms.

"I'm going to float on the blow-up lounger and if either of you tips me off then…" I trailed off.

"Then what?" Dex cocked his eyebrow.

"Then…" I scrambled for something that'd put them off disturbing me. "Then I'll key both your cars."

They both gasped.

"You wouldn't," Dex scowled.

I turned my back on them and made my way to

the pool.

"She wouldn't," Dieter said.

They followed me into the water, but they both eyed me with caution as I climbed onto the blow-up lounger. Yeah, they wouldn't take the chance of me hurting their cars. Dieter was right, I wouldn't, but the threat was enough to give me a peaceful time in the pool. Except I kept watching them. Kept staring at their glistening bodies. And kept imagining what it'd be like to have them both pressed up against me.

The week couldn't be over fast enough.

## Chapter Eleven

Dex didn't make good on his promise to wash my hair. I was both glad and disappointed. After a few days of their constant presence I was ready to jump them. It was like Dex knew I'd reached my limit and kept away.

In the morning, he pecked me on the lips and fled the apartment. Dieter followed suit and muttered something about a meeting.

If this didn't suck, I didn't know what did.

I wanted to try with them both and they were running the other way.

Work dragged for the first time in my life and my creative side didn't want to play. I left work and returned to a silent apartment. I walked into the kitchen, opened the fridge, and contemplated cooking them dinner. Thumbing my cell, I sent a group text to them and both replied they wouldn't be home for dinner. I frowned. No further explanation. It was Wednesday, where were they?

What if they were out with another woman? One who didn't have a hang-up about sleeping with two men at once? What if they were with her right now enjoying what should be mine?

I slammed the fridge door.

How stupid was I? They were both sexual men and if I weren't giving it to them then they'd get sex from someone else. Wouldn't they?

But they said they loved me and wanted to be with me.

My phone rang, and I picked it up hoping it was one of them.

"Hello," Dad said.

"Hey, Dad." I sighed with disappointment.

"What's wrong, sweetheart?"

"Nothing." I opened the pantry door and peered

inside. "Just trying to decide what to eat for dinner."

"Is that all?" he asked in his way-too-perceptive way.

"It's Dieter and Dex," I said.

"What about them?"

I puffed out a breath. If I could talk to anyone, it was my dad. He'd always been there for me and never judged me. I spilled my guts about what happened between us the last few days.

Dad's silence traveled down the phone line.

"Dad, are you still there?"

"Yes," he said.

"Well?"

"What do you want me to say?" he asked.

"Give me some fatherly advice, please." I found a tin of soup and left the pantry.

"Hmm. Do what makes you happy, Tiff, that's it."

I put the call on speaker and opened the tin. "But what will other people think?"

"Who cares? Your mother and I won't think any less of you."

"You won't?"

"How could we? We love you and want you to be happy. It's all any parent wants for their child. Dex and Dieter love you, we've seen that ourselves over the years."

"They do, don't they?" I tipped the soup into a saucepan.

"As if you have to ask."

I pictured Dad rolling his eyes.

"Any reason you called?" I asked.

"I thought you'd want to hear the latest gossip," Dad said.

"Yes." I tapped the spoon on the saucepan. "What

have Prue and Mr. Burberry been up to?"

Dad laughed and launched into the latest escapades from my best friend. She hadn't always been my best friend, not until she'd married Mr. Burberry. Dad worked for Mr. Burberry for years and always gossiped about the billionaire and his family, so when Mr. Burberry fell for a waitress at his restaurant it'd been the biggest gossip of Dad's life. Mom and I heard all about it and continued to hear all about how the sassy ex-waitress mouthed off to Mr. Burberry whenever they were in private. Except Dad got to witness it firsthand as their driver. When Prue married Mr. Burberry, she'd needed a fashion consultant and Dad suggested I take her shopping. We'd hit it off straightaway, hard not to when I felt like I already knew her, but Prue was awesome too.

I sipped on the soup straight from the saucepan and listened to Dad's latest Prue and Mr. Burberry rendition. I giggled and Dad ended the call. Trust my dad to cheer me up.

"Does Prue know your dad gossips about her to you?" Dieter asked.

I screamed and dropped the spoon. I didn't even hear Dex and Dieter return to the apartment.

"Shit, when did you two get home?" I clutched my hands over my racing heart.

Dex squinted at the clock. "About five minutes ago."

"Rude much? Eavesdropping."

"Hey, you put your cell on speaker." Dex shrugged.

I guess it was unavoidable for them to not overhear when I had the phone on speaker. It was a habit I was used to living alone. I'd have to change that staying here.

"Yes, Prue knows. I'm not sure if Mr. Burberry

does." My cheeks heated. What would Mr. Burberry say if he knew what my dad said to me?

"Mr. Burberry?" Dieter raised his eyebrows. "Why don't you call him William?"

I touched my cheeks to see if they were as hot as they felt.

"Because she has the hots for him," Dex said.

"I do not," I spluttered.

Dex pointed at my face. "You do too."

"You have the hots for their nanny Kennedy," I snapped.

"I said she was hot, not that I had the hots for her." Dex crossed his arms over his muscular chest.

Dieter walked over to me and tilted my chin up, so I'd meet his gaze. "Do you?"

I flicked my gaze away. "He's a good-looking man."

"That's so funny. Are you jealous of Prue?"

"No, I'm not," I snapped. "Just because I think he's hot it doesn't mean anything."

Dieter dropped my chin and burst out in laughter.

"We're teasing you." Dex laughed too and picked up my dropped spoon. "You're so cute when you're all flustered."

I folded my arms over my chest and narrowed my eyes at them both. "Where were you tonight?"

"I was at work," Dex said. "There was a problem with the car due to leave tomorrow for a show."

"And you?" I tipped my chin at Dieter.

"Work too. A Zoom meeting ran overtime." Dieter's gaze scanned my face and his smile dropped. "What's wrong?"

"I thought … never mind."

"What did you think?" Dex stepped behind me.

His body heat soothed my tense muscles. I

wanted nothing more than for them both to touch me.

"That you might be with another woman," I admitted.

Dieter tipped my chin up again and held my gaze captive. "Why would you think that?"

I jerked my shoulders. "Because I'm not giving you sex, I thought you might get it somewhere else."

"Tiff, there's only you." He cupped my cheeks.

Dex's hands landed on my hips from behind. "Yeah, Fluff, I'm not going anywhere else for sex."

I let out a loud exhale.

"Why would you think that?" Dex asked.

I blinked fast. Dieter's gaze flicked to Dex behind me. Whatever passed between them spurred Dieter into kissing me. His fingers slid into my hair and massaged the back of my scalp. I moaned against his demanding lips. Dex's fingers stroked my hips and his chest pressed against my back. He hauled my hips back into his erection. I wriggled against the firmness pressed near my ass. Dex grunted with a deep sexy sound that sent my heart pounding.

"You keep that up and I'll mess my pants," Dex said with huskiness.

Dieter raised his head and watched me wriggle against Dex. Dieter yanked up the hem of my tight skirt. Dex pulled back enough for the skirt to wrap around my waist and leave my smooth ass in a thong for Dex to rub against again.

"You're so sexy," Dieter's voice lowered.

He smoothed his fingers over my satin-covered mound. I inched my legs apart, and he took my invitation and dipped his fingers into my thong.

"She's so wet," Dieter groaned.

I fumbled with Dieter's zipper and wrapped my hand around his hard length.

Dex brushed my hair aside and kissed my neck. "I need to feel you too." He slid a hand under my thong to join Dieter's.

I stared at both their hands inside my panties.

Dex's thick finger slid inside me. "You want us both, don't you?"

Dieter's finger circled my clit.

My legs quivered, and I pushed against Dex's erection harder, grinding my hips in time to both their fingers. Dex inside. Dieter outside. I dropped my head to Dieter's chest and pumped my fist on his erection trying to concentrate on him instead of the way they both were so perfect together.

Dex's hand gripped my hip hard and stopped me from grinding against him and their hands.

I whimpered at the sudden loss of the heady sensation.

"Say it," Dex demanded.

"Yes," I spat out. "Damn it, I want you both."

"Good girl." Dex thrust his finger inside me again.

Dieter's finger joined his.

"Oh God," I moaned.

The fullness from both their fingers made me grip Dieter's erection harder. Dex pumped his finger inside me and yanked my hips against his with each thrust. Dieter's finger worked in opposite time to Dex's, so I had no reprieve from the pleasure. My blood pounded in my ears. This was so good. Too good. I let go thinking this was wrong when it felt so perfect. Two men. My two loves pleasing me in a way I never imagined. I moaned.

"She's close," Dieter said.

"Yep," Dex said. "I'm going to mess my pants when she comes."

"Me too," Dieter said. "But it'll be worth it."

"For sure."

"Stop. Talking." I panted.

"Are we distracting you, Fluff?" Dex's finger slowed.

"Not slower," I whined. "Faster."

Dex chuckled but kept his slow torturous pace and Dieter copied him until both their fingers were thrusting inside me together. In they stretched me. Out they dragged over my throbbing clit together. In again with a slowness that made my legs shake. Out over my clit again. Their fingers circled my entrance until I thought I'd die from not having them inside me. I dropped my hand from Dieter's suit and clawed at Dex's arm. They slid their fingers inside. Every tight muscle exploded into a bouncing ball of pleasure racing from their fingers and through my entire body.

Somewhere through the ringing in my ears, I heard Dex and Dieter's grunts of pleasure. Warmth exploded over my hand. Dex sagged against my back. Ripples of aftershocks squeezed their fingers still buried inside me. I didn't want them to leave. They were where they were meant to be. All of us together.

Dieter kissed the top of my head and eased my hand from around his softening cock. I dropped it to his arm with his finger still inside me. Dex nibbled the back of my neck. Goose bumps tingled down my shoulders.

"Better now?" Dieter asked moving back.

"Wait." I gripped his arm harder.

"Tiff, gorgeous, if I keep my finger in you then I'll get hard again," Dieter said.

"Would that be so bad?" I met his heated gaze.

"We still have the rest of the week before we can have sex," he reminded me.

"I thought…"

"That we'd ignore your request? No. We agreed,"

Dieter said.

"Right." I let go of both their arms, a little miffed they were still agreeing to the week without sex after what just happened.

They withdrew their hands from my panties. Dex turned me around.

"Don't make us go back on our word. We'd feel like shit if we did," Dex said. "Just because you're all happy and sated now doesn't mean you're ready for more."

I kissed his cheek. I was so lucky to have two caring men who put my needs first.

"I love you both so much."

"We love you too." Dieter hugged me from behind.

"You're all wet." I squirmed and giggled.

"You're wetter," Dex said.

I wriggled out of their arms. He was right. Moisture coated my thighs where their fingers commanded me to an intense orgasm. They were right about a lot of things, but I wouldn't tell them since they already thought they knew everything.

"I'm showering then going to bed to read for a bit," I said.

Dieter zipped up his pants. "So long as you're happy and you don't need to talk about what happened here."

I leaned up on my tiptoes and kissed his cheek. "I'm happy and I'm good with what we did."

I was more than good. I floated on ecstasy. For years I'd worried about choosing one of them over the other and now I didn't have to. I could have them both.

Three more days and I'd have them both in all ways.

## Chapter Twelve

I woke with the book flopped against my chest. I hadn't even read a chapter I'd been that relaxed and sated after my mind-blowing orgasm in the kitchen. Heat drifted into my cheeks and I thought I might never be able to walk into the kitchen again without blushing. I glimpsed the clock surprised to find it was four in the morning. My body was still in sleep mode, but my mind raced with ideas for the gown I'd started designing the other night.

I flicked the flashlight on my cell and padded through the quiet apartment to the sitting/sewing room. The sketch paper called to me like a homing beacon. I turned on the lamp and settled on the floor with the design. Excitement for the ideas bounced through my head and sent a zing through my body.

"Tiff, you'll be late for work." Dieter smiled from the doorway.

"What are you doing up so early?" I raised my arms behind my back and stretched out the strain of muscles from being hunched over the design.

"It's almost eight."

"What?" I screeched and scrambled from the floor. How had I lost four hours? "Out of the way."

Dieter stood aside, and I hurried from the room to my bedroom. I threw on an outfit of a leaf green dress with a side split up my thigh. Dieter followed me and watched from the doorway. I sat on the bed and buckled my strappy sandals.

"I can't believe how lucky we are." His gaze ran the length of my exposed thigh.

I twirled my hair up onto my head and stuck bobby pins in it then slapped on a coat of lip gloss and mascara.

"Why didn't you tell me the time sooner?" I rushed to the door.

"I didn't want to disturb you when you're creating." He followed me to the front door of the apartment. "Besides, this way I have a reason to drive you to work."

I picked up my handbag from the hall table. "That'd be great."

"If you tell me how much you love me, I'll even buy you a coffee on the way."

I laughed. "I love you like the best Grande Americano in a tall cup."

Dieter grinned. "One Grande Americano in a tall cup coming up."

"Wait, where's Dex, I haven't said good-bye?" I swung around expecting to see Dex's cheeky smile.

"He got a phone call from his mom and left to pick her up from the airport."

"Why didn't he tell me?" I turned back around, a little hurt Dex told Dieter and not me. I liked his mom. She exuded this cool hippy vibe that always made me smile.

"He didn't want to interrupt you either."

We made our way down the stairs.

"Don't be stupid. You can both talk to me when I'm designing."

Dieter chuckled. "We could but you wouldn't remember what we said. You have a one-track focus once you start."

"Okay, you might be right, but I want you both to be able to talk to me even when I'm working."

"All right. We're still getting used to living together, there's bound to be kinks."

*Kinks*—as if I needed to hear that word from Dieter's sexy lips. We left the building and jumped into his Jag.

"Dex's mom is staying at Dex's apartment for a while so he's going to stay at my place. Our place." He flicked me a quick look. "He said he'll be late tonight because he's going to pack up more of his stuff to bring over."

"Okay." I fiddled with the split in my dress.

"We know you haven't decided to stay, we're hoping you will, but if you want to go back to your apartment after this week, then you can."

"It's a big decision."

He placed his hand on my thigh and squeezed. "We know."

Dieter ordered my caffeine fix at the drive-through.

"Thanks." I sipped the hot liquid and burned my tongue. "Ow."

He shook his head. "You couldn't wait."

"No," I said sounding like I'd come from the dentist.

He parked the car in front of my work building. "Let me kiss it better."

I poked my tongue out, and he sucked it into his mouth. I giggled and clutched the coffee with care, so I didn't spill it as I'd need the triple shot of espresso after waking up so early.

"I'll see you tonight." I opened the car door.

"Have a good day."

"You too." I flung him a smile through the door then closed it.

A bounce of happiness jumped through each step into work. Dieter was special. I was glad I didn't have to choose between them because I loved them both too much.

\*\*\*\*

It was strange knowing Dex wouldn't be at the apartment when I got home. Dieter greeted me with a kiss on the tip of my nose. We settled on the sofa to the gentle sounds of classical music through the surround sound and chatted about our day. I relaxed, and we fell back into a comfortable atmosphere instead of the sexual tension between the three of us while I decided if I could be with them both. Our kitchen tryst relieved more than the sexual tension. It'd shown us all a threesome was possible.

Dieter ordered sushi, and we ate it on the sofa while watching the sunset and the sky darken. The city lights twinkled. Where was Dex?

"Should we call Dex and see if he needs help?" I asked.

"I offered to help him, but he said he wanted to catch up with his mom."

"Yeah, she's been traveling for six months. He's missed her." I'd missed her too.

"I haven't met her. What's she like?" Dieter asked.

"Sienna is great, she's like a hippy car enthusiast if there was such a thing."

Dieter laughed. "Those two things don't go together."

"When you meet her, you'll see what I mean."

"Nothing like my mom then."

"Nope. Worlds apart. But ours are too."

"Three different moms. I wonder how they'll get along?" Dieter frowned.

No doubt he wondered how his famous mother would fit in with Dex's and mine. My mother spent her life working at the local corner store, while Dieter's acted for the world to see, and Dex's mother did whatever she pleased. It was strange to think how similar

Dex and Dieter were in the way they treated me, yet their parents raised them in a different way.

Voices muffled from the other side of the front door. Dex and his mom walked into the apartment. Dex looked a little disheveled and carried a box. His mom looked stunning in a tight pair of denim jeans and a paisley shirt in bright teal and purple matching the streaks in her hair.

"*Eeek*," she cried. "Tiff!"

I scrambled from the sofa and ran into her open arms. We hugged and swayed side to side. Dex grinned at us.

"It's so good to see you." I shifted out of her arms and kissed Dex's cheek. "You too. I missed you this morning."

"Yeah?" He swiped his knuckles over my cheek.

I kissed him on the lips with all my love. His lips moved against mine in a gentle G-rated kiss. Nothing like normal, but his mom was beside us.

"Hi, I'm Dieter."

Dex and I pulled apart to see Sienna hugging Dieter. Dieter bugged his eyes at us like he didn't know what to do. I mimed wrapping my arms. Dieter hugged her back with awkwardness.

"So, you're the other man," Sienna said squeezing Dieter's biceps. "I can see why, Tiff." She winked at me.

Dieter blushed a deep red.

"Come, sit down." I tugged her away from Dieter. "I want to hear about your trip."

We settled on the sofa and Dieter and Dex took the separate armchairs.

"Where did you go? Who did you see?" I asked.

Sienna launched into an hour-long description of her travels across the other side of America to Nashville where she met a handsome younger man and stayed for a month until she broke the man's heart because she hadn't finished traveling and he owned a farm he wouldn't leave. I pictured the poor man now. Sienna was a knockout and full of life. A lot like her son.

"So, I'm staying here for a few months until I decide where I'm heading next."

"To where you want to break the next heart?" Dex asked.

"Smartass." She shook her hands at Dex making the bangles on her wrists jingle.

Dieter chuckled.

Dex punched him in the arm.

"Now, now, boys, there's no need to fight, you've both got the girl. How's that going? All three of you together?"

My face burned like I'd slept the day away under the California sun.

"No need to be embarrassed," Sienna said. "We're all adults here. Your father and I enjoyed a threesome once with this beautiful girl, what was her name, Cara? Claire? It started with a C or was it a K? Who knows?"

"Mom," Dex groaned.

Sienna settled her arms along the back of the sofa. "Sorry, honey, but I have to say it was a spiritual experience between the three of us. We would have been more than willing to repeat it, but she had a boyfriend so that was the end of that."

"Someone rip my ears off now," Dex said.

"I'll do it," Dieter stretched out his hand and tugged Dex's ear.

"Piss off." He slapped Dieter's hand.

"You asked."

I giggled at their ridiculous antics. Sienna waved

her hands sending the sound of clinging metal through the apartment.

"Aren't you two sweet," Sienna said. "I don't need to read your tea leaves to see you'll be happy."

Dieter's eyebrows rose. "Tea leaves?"

"There's quite an art to it, young stud."

Dieter coughed and blushed again.

"I should get going and leave you three to your night." Sienna stood.

"You don't have to go, Mom," Dex said.

"Please stay, Mrs. Munroe," Dieter said.

"Call me Sienna." She patted Dieter's head then Dex's. "I must be off. I'm meeting up with an old friend at a bar in..." She glanced at her watch and laughed. "Half an hour ago."

"I'll walk you out," Dex said.

"I'll see you all later no doubt." She turned to me. "And you, my dear girl, if my son wasn't in the mix, I'd be envious."

Dex cursed under his breath and strode over to the front door.

"That's my cue." Sienna grinned and strutted to the front door. She patted Dex's cheek. "Have fun, honey."

Dex shut the front door behind her and flopped on the sofa beside me. "Remind me why I missed her?"

"Because she's wonderful and you love her," I said.

"Yeah, she's amazing," Dieter said. "My mom would never be so open with me about sex and what we have here. You're lucky, Dex, to have her support."

I stroked my hands on Dex's neck and massaged his muscles in the way he liked. He always got a little tense around her when she was so open about everything. I was open with my parents, but Sienna took it to another level.

Dex hauled me onto his lap and buried his face in my neck. "Why is your hair up?"

"I didn't have time to do it this morning."

Dieter shifted to sit on the coffee table, slid the bobby pins free, and ran his fingers through my hair until the strands fell in Dex's face.

"Better?" Dieter asked.

"Much." Dex sighed. "I think my mom has the hots for Dieter."

"Nah," I said, "she was teasing like you do."

"Thank fuck," Dieter said. "I was worried she'd try to turn this into an orgy."

Dex raised his head. "Dude, shut your mouth."

My stomach quivered with repressed laughter.

"Are you laughing?" Dex slid his hands to my ribs.

"I think she is." Dieter grabbed my feet.

"I'm not," I squealed in horror they were about to tickle me.

"How about we give you something to laugh about?" Dex quirked his eyebrow.

Dieter's fingers ran against the soles of my feet. I squirmed in their hold but Dex's fingers found my most vulnerable spot under my ribs. Laughter peeled from my aching lungs and I slithered around on Dex's lap until I slid to the floor to escape their fingers toying with my sensitive spots. I crawled across the floor, scrambled to my feet and ran to my bedroom, and slammed the door.

"That's cheating, Tiff," Dieter said through the door.

"I call it winning."

A quiet rap of knuckles knocked on the door.

"I'm not falling for that, Dex."

"Okay, Fluff," Dex's deep voice came loud and

clear through the door. "We wanted to kiss you good night, but never mind."

I creaked the door open a fraction and poked my head out while keeping my body out of reach of their tickling fingers.

"Good night." Dieter pecked my lips.

"Good night, Dieter."

Dex stepped closer and caught my chin in his hand. "Fuck, I love you." He kissed me in the same way Dieter did, a gentle peck of lips on lips. Nothing sexual about it, but I wanted it to be more.

He let go and stepped back.

"Hey," I said. "I love you too, Dex."

He winked at me and walked to his bedroom. I let out a sigh and closed the door. I wanted more than anything to be in the same bedroom as him snuggled against his side with my head on his chest in my favorite spot.

Two more days and I'd be back there again.

Two more days and I'd be in bed with them both for the first time.

I don't know who suffered more from my no-sex terms—me or them.

## Chapter Thirteen

"I'm going to be sick." I hung my head between my knees in the back seat of Dex's canary-yellow convertible 1965 Pontiac GTO. The rumble of the V-8 engine did nothing to ease the queasiness churning my stomach about the dinner at my parents' house. How the hell would I eat anything when I knew Mom would talk about marriage to the two men I loved? Why had she insisted on the dinner anyway?

Parents were crazy.

"Hang on, we're almost there." Dieter stretched behind him and rubbed the top of my head. As if that would help. All it did was send tingles of desire down my spine.

"Stop touching me," I snapped and raised my head.

Dex frowned at me in the rearview mirror. Under normal circumstances, I loved riding in this car with the top down and the wind blowing my hair. But not tonight. Tonight, I wanted to vomit.

"Tiff, relax," Dex said.

His voice always held a hint of command to it. One that always made me eager to do what he said. As if on demand the tension in my body eased a fraction.

"How did you and Dieter get together?" Dex asked.

"You're asking me now?" I gripped the armrest in a white-knuckle grip.

"We met at the college library," Dieter said. "I was studying for an exam and Tiff wafted into the place smelling like a bouquet and looking like a fashion model from a magazine. I didn't read a single word after I set eyes on her. I returned to the library every day for the next week just to see her. I almost failed my exam."

"I didn't know," I said looking at our meeting in a different light.

"You saw her and had to have her," Dex said. "It was that way for me too."

"Yeah," Dieter said.

"Did you kiss her in the library?" Dex asked.

"She kissed me," Dieter said.

"I did not," I spluttered. "You kissed me."

"Nope, I remember every little detail. We met in aisle twenty-three, section two hundred and one. The business books. You were wearing ripped jeans and a white halter-neck top that showed a little of your side boob when you stretched for the same book as me."

"Did it?" I chewed my top lip recalling the moment our fingers touched and the fly of sparks. I'd noticed Dieter that week, who wouldn't? He was way too handsome to be hiding in a library, he should've been strutting in front of a camera for the world to see his hotness.

Dieter chuckled. "As if you don't know how clothes sit on your body, Miss Fashion Designer."

"Then what happened?" Dex asked.

"We played tug-of-war with the book and fought over who needed it most," I said. It'd been so much fun tugging each other closer with every yank until our toes touched and our breaths mingled.

"Then she landed one on my lips. I let go of the book and she skipped down the aisle laughing."

I giggled. "It was too easy to win the book from you."

"That's it?" Dex asked.

"I let her win," Dieter said. "The next day in the library I followed her to the back stacks, otherwise known as the make-out area. She expected to kiss me again."

"Is that right, Fluff?" Dex flicked me a heated look in the rearview mirror while stopped at a red light. "Did you lure poor Dieter to the back of the library to make out with him?"

"I was looking for a book." I shoved my hands between my thighs because what happened next had me all hot and bothered remembering Dieter on his knees with his head buried under my dress.

"So, you didn't kiss her?" Dex turned around at the green light and drove off.

"I kissed her all right, just not on the lips on her face." Dieter threw me a blazing look over his shoulder like he wanted to do it again now.

I shifted on the seat now glad for the cool breeze blowing in through the convertible top.

Dex swung the car into my parents' driveway, unbuckled his belt, and faced me. "Did you come all over Dieter's face in the library?"

I wet my lips. How I'd come with my hands pressed over my mouth to stop making a sound. "Yes."

Dex smirked. "Whose face do you want to come on first tonight?"

"What?" I squeaked.

The outside light on the house flicked on. I scurried out of the car.

Dex caught hold of my hand. "So?"

"I'm not answering."

Dieter took hold of my other hand. "We'll take turns and see who makes you come first."

I tugged my hands, but they held on. "Stop."

"Stop what?" Dex kissed my cheek. "Making you wet? Not happening."

"We're about to go into my parents' house," I whined. I was way too turned on to even want to be on the same street as my parents let alone in the same room.

"So we are…" Dieter tugged my hand, and we walked to the front door. "But we're never going to stop pleasing you. It makes us happy."

"Stop trying to please me sexually and help me with Mom. That'd make me happy."

"Done." Dieter kissed the tip of my nose and knocked on the door. "Your mom loves me. What about you, Dex?"

"Yeah, she's always happy to see me," Dex said.

Which was true on both counts. Mom and Dad were always happy to see me with either of them.

The front door swung open, and Mom stood in the interior's glow, her face an expressionless mask of politeness. The churning in my stomach started again instead of the aching need for Dieter and Dex which they'd created with ease talking about me coming on their faces. Heat traveled up my neck to my cheeks.

"Tiffany, are you all right, you look like you might be coming down with something?" Mom pressed her palm to my forehead.

"I'm fine, Mom." I stepped inside and kissed her cheek.

Mom shuffled me along to greet my two men. "Dieter, Dex, so lovely of you to come tonight."

"Thank you for inviting us," Dieter said.

"Wouldn't miss it," Dex said and winked at me over Mom's head.

"Come in, come in, this way, your father is in the sitting room pouring everyone a drink." Mom led us down the short hallway to the room on the right.

"Hi, Dad." I crossed the room and hugged him.

"Gabe," Dieter shook Dad's hand.

"How's the car running?" Dex shook Dad's hand after Dieter.

"Perfect since you tuned it." He handed them

both glasses with a smidgeon of amber liquid.

I picked up another glass and poured the bourbon halfway. Dad raised his brows but said nothing.

"Dinner shouldn't be long," Mom fussed. "I'll go check on the progress. Tiffany, perhaps you'd like to help?"

"Me, nah, I'm good here." I indicated my glass. There was no way in hell I'd let her get me alone tonight to question me.

Dex stepped forward and slid his arm into my mom's. "I'd love to help."

"Such a good young man." She patted Dex's arm and tutted my way. "I thought we raised you with better manners, Tiffany."

I rolled my eyes and sat on the lounge suite.

Dad parked himself in his favorite armchair. "Why do you have to rile her so much?"

"Come on, Dad, what's this dinner about?" I didn't trust Mom's motives. I heard her voice in my head. Marriage. Blah, blah, blah. Marriage. I so didn't need it or want it now that I contemplated being in a polyamory relationship. We couldn't get married.

"Your mom is trying to be nice," Dad said.

Dieter sat next to me and held my hand.

"How's your job with your father?" Dad asked Dieter.

"Good." Dieter sipped his bourbon. "I like the work, and Dad has built a great company."

I swigged my bourbon. So much for never drinking again. Trust Mom to be the reason I broke my promise. The alcohol warmed my mouth and throat. Dad's gaze dropped to our joined hands.

"I hope you've thought things through," he said.

"Yes, Mom wanted me to be an actor like her, but that sort of life didn't appeal to me, I preferred what Dad did. The stable job, steady hours, living in one place. I'm afraid flying all over the world isn't for me."

"What about when Tiff becomes famous and goes to all the international fashion shows?" Dad asked.

"Dad, that's a long way off." I twirled the glass. I'd never realized Dieter was so against flying around the world and one day it'd be something I did a lot of.

"You never know." Dad sipped his bourbon.

"I suppose it would depend on whether Tiff wanted me to go with her." Dieter squeezed my fingers. "I can take vacations from work if she did. If she didn't, I'd be here for her when she got back from flying around the world."

Dad shook his head. "Young people these days, so willing to let the ones they love go."

"I'm not letting her go." Dieter took the empty glass out of my hand and placed his and mine on the coffee table. "I did that once and I never want to do it again."

"You didn't have a choice." I gave him a grim smile. I'd been the one to break up with him.

Dex and Mom burst into the room laughing. Our heads snapped their way. At least someone was having a good time.

"Dinner is served," Dex said with a flourish of his arm in my direction and yanked me to my feet away from Dieter's side.

We walked from the sitting room to the dining room.

Dex whispered in my ear, "You look way too serious."

"You look way too happy," I whispered back.

"Of course, I'm thinking about you sitting on my face tonight," Dex whispered.

My breath caught in my lungs. Dex tugged the

chair out for me and pushed me in then sat opposite me. Dieter sat beside me while Mom and Dad sat at the ends of the oval table.

"Smells delicious," Dieter said sliding a hand onto my thigh under the table.

"Thank you, Dieter." Mom's smile stretched her face until wrinkles formed in the creases of her cheeks. She loved it when people complimented her cooking.

"I carved the roast lamb," Dex said lifting the plate of meat.

"Good job." I smiled at Dex across the table.

"Dig in, everyone," Mom said.

We passed the serving plates around the table until our dinner plates were full of roast meat and vegetables. The mouthwatering aroma of a home-cooked meal made me want to drool. Mom's cooking was the best.

"How's work?" she asked.

"Great," I said around a mouthful of juicy meat. "I'm helping on the swimwear line."

"Swimwear? A waste of your talent." Mom frowned in disapproval.

"It's a starting place." I dug my fork into a roast potato.

"Don't these people realize you've been designing all your life?" she asked.

"I'm young in their eyes, fresh out of college, of course they won't have me designing haute couture gowns in my first year."

"Have you shown them your work?" she asked.

"Yes, Mom, they've seen my work. How do you think I got the job in the first place?" I rolled my eyes.

"Show them more. They didn't look hard enough," she insisted.

"I like my job. I won't risk losing it."

The three men watched us without a word, too busy enjoying their dinner while mine cooled every minute this conversation lasted.

Mom huffed. "You're going to be famous. You don't need them."

"Mom." I placed my knife and fork on the table.

"And what's this about you three living together as a relationship? I don't approve." Mom frowned.

"Dad." I scowled his way.

Dad kept his gaze on his meal. Wise move.

"Don't blame your father for telling me. I have your best interests at heart, Tiffany. What happens when you're rich and they both want your money? You can't just live with a man, let alone two who will both take you to the cleaners when things don't work out."

"Now, wait just a minute, Dieter and Dex have their own money. In fact, they have more than me."

"But for how long?" She raised her right eyebrow. "Did you ever think of that, Tiffany?"

I picked up the water glass and swallowed half the contents. She was right. If my designing career progressed the way I envisioned, then I'd earn more than both of them combined. And what if it didn't work out with them? Would they take everything I'd worked my entire life for? Would I see my dreams crumble into nothing?

"It's why I keep nagging you about marriage, at least then you can sign a prenuptial agreement like Prue and Mr. Burberry. Smart. Very smart."

I met Dex's gaze across the table. It wasn't something he'd considered. He appeared distraught about what Mom said. I didn't dare look at Dieter.

"Neither of us would take Tiff's money when she has more than us," Dieter said.

Mom sighed. "I like you, Dieter, you too Dex, but

I have to put my daughter first and I don't think her living with you both is the right thing for her."

"Louise, that's enough," Dad said. "Tiff is a grown woman. She can make her own decisions about life."

"But…"

"No, we've all heard enough." Dad pushed back his chair and stood. "She loves them and they love her, shouldn't that be what matters?"

"Gabe, of course it is, but you know how much we struggled to send her to college, I don't want her to lose it all because of sex."

I sucked in a shocked breath unaware they'd struggled to send me to college. I thought it'd been a stretch for them, but not a struggle.

"I'll pay you back," I said.

Dad shook his head. "You won't pay us a dime, you're our daughter and we wanted to send you to college."

Dieter rubbed his hand across my shoulders. I risked a peek at his handsome face to see what he was thinking. He appeared as appalled as Dex.

"I think we should go." I stood dislodging Dieter's arm.

"But dessert…" Mom stood too.

"Thanks, but I've lost my appetite." I kissed Dad on the cheek. "I'll call you."

"Sure." Dad kissed my cheek and ruffled my hair.

Dieter stood. "Thanks for dinner, Mrs. Herringer."

"Yes, it was delicious." Dex followed suit.

"I'll walk you out," Dad said.

Dieter and Dex followed Dad.

I turned back to Mom. "Just so you know, it's not about sex. I've loved each of them for years because they are sweet and caring. This week living with them both they've made me happy, Mom. Why don't you want me to be happy like you and Dad?"

"I do." Mom flopped into her chair and sniffed. "I want all the happiness in the world for you, but I'm thinking about your future."

"I am too, Mom." I spun and walked away. "I am too."

## Chapter Fourteen

I sulked in bed all Saturday morning after the disastrous dinner with my parents. Dieter and Dex said little on the ride home, and neither of them offered to make me come on their faces. It disappointed and relieved me. My heart and body were already with the two of them, but Mom messed with my mind.

What would I do if they both left me?

If one left, I'd have the other, but if we were all together and it didn't work out, then I'd have no one.

I'd been counting down the days to us all being together and this last day was the crunch. It was make-or-break time. I wasn't sure if either of them would go back to the way things were after we'd all lived together this week. We'd fit like puzzle pieces coming together. And it wasn't about the sex, it was about the companionship and love.

My cell rang, and I ignored it. I didn't want to talk to anyone. I wanted to wallow in what might have been, in what I was about to lose.

The stupid cell rang again. I scanned it expecting it to be Dad, but Prue's name flashed across the screen. I hit the speaker button.

"Hey." I sighed.

"What's wrong?" Prue asked.

"Nothing," I lied.

"I'm coming over." She hung up.

Trust my best friend to read my need for a good sob in two words.

True to her word, she was at Dieter's apartment in about thirty minutes and knocking on my bedroom door.

"Tiff, I'm coming in," Prue said.

I said nothing. My sobs were about to crack open.

She swept into the room in a swirl of gorgeous turquoise fabric.

"What's going on? Dieter and Dex look like someone kicked their dog," she said.

I opened my mouth, but a strangled sound rang out.

"What did those two dicks do?" She lunged for the door and swung it open. "Hey, idiots, what did you do?" she yelled.

"No." I scrambled from the bed and fought with her to shut the door. I didn't win, she was stronger than she looked.

"We did nothing." Dex stepped into my bedroom and crossed his massive arms.

Dieter leaned against the doorjamb with a frown marring his handsome face.

"Are you sure?" Prue said in absolute disbelief. "Because if either of you hurt my bestie, I'll make sure your dicks never work again."

"Prue," I spluttered. "Leave their dicks alone, I like them."

Dex smirked and sat on the bed. Damn, he looked good there. So did Dieter with the way he watched me, all concern etched across his brow but a hint of amusement in his eyes at my comment.

"It was Mom," I said finger-combing my hair. I bet I looked hideous and here were the two men I loved looking like they were models.

"For fuck's sake you don't need to get married." Prue sat on my bed next to Dex and rubbed the small bulge in her stomach.

"She made some good points about legal stuff last night, like what if we break up and one of us tries to take the other's money? At least with marriage, there are prenuptial agreements to stop that," I said.

Prue tapped her chin. "There has to be something. I'll ask Will tonight. He has good brains for contracts and his friend Marco is a lawyer."

"I doubt there's anything, but whatever." It seemed like the universe was in on my relationship with two men. My gaze skittered across Dex's tight muscles on his chest and then to Dieter's long legs crossed at the doorway.

Prue scanned all our sullen faces and threw up her hands. "What is wrong with you three? Why haven't you fucked this out by now?"

I tugged on the old t-shirt I'd gone to sleep in. As if they'd find me attractive right at this moment. A threesome would be the last thing on their minds with me looking like a she-devil. My cheeks burned.

"Ugh." Prue flopped back on my bed. "The sexual tension in this room is as bad as when I was serving Will at the restaurant. Thank God I don't have that these days."

Dex stood in a hurry and walked to where Dieter stood. Yeah, I didn't blame him with Prue sprawled out on my bed.

"We'll go for a drive and leave you two to talk," Dex said.

"Okay," I mumbled.

If they told me everything was going to be all right, if they so much as touched me, I'd follow them into Dieter's bedroom and do what Prue said. I wanted them both so bad. A burning need deep inside me to be one with them. They'd asked all week, and now they were running away. Maybe it was time for me to let them both go.

I watched them leave my bedroom wondering if I should have asked them to stay, if I'd just given up on the best two men ever.

"So," Prue said sitting up. "You're going to jump their bones when they get back."

"Ah, no."

"Yes." Prue stood. "First, I need you to design me a dress for this big charity event Will bought a table at."

"A dress I can do." I tugged on a pair of shorts. "Follow me."

I led the way to the sitting room—now my sewing room—and picked up a sketch pad and pencil.

"What do you want?" I asked.

Prue picked up my latest sketch of the one I'd started when I'd been thinking about being with Dex and Dieter together.

"This is stunning, Tiff. You need to make this to wear there too."

"Wear it where?" I tapped my pencil to the page.

"The charity event for underprivileged children of course," she said like it was a given I'd be going. "Will bought an entire table and told me to fill it. Bring your two dicks too. This will be so much fun."

"When is it?"

"Two months, on the twenty-second of July." She sat on a chair and crossed her legs.

"I doubt we'll even be together then."

"Bullshit." She coughed. "We're going to talk about what sort of dress you're going to design me then you're going to wax and buff every inch of your skin, shower off this stink of depression, dress in your skimpiest lingerie, light candles and put on sexy-time music, and jump your two hot dicks when they get home."

She painted a passionate scene with her words.

I opened my mouth.

"Nope, no excuses, let me go home to Will tonight thinking about hot threesome sex. Come on, Tiff,

I'm a married woman with kids and another on the way. Give me something here."

I laughed. "As if you need to think about hot threesome sex when you have Mr. Burberry."

"You have me there." She bounced her foot. "Still, you got to admit thinking about being with them together makes you all hot and bothered. One in your pussy, one in your ass." She drooled.

I sat up straighter. "I, um, don't do that."

"What? Anal?" she asked.

"Yeah." I tapped the pencil so hard it was a wonder the wood didn't break.

"I didn't like it until Will. It has a lot to do with who you're with and whether they see to your pleasure. And Will is all about my pleasure."

Could this conversation get any spicier? I'd thought Mr. Burberry was the hottest older man alive when I was a teenager and hearing this, yeah, hot. I tugged on the collar of my t-shirt.

"So, um, what sort of dress are you after?" I changed the subject.

Prue laughed. "I bet Dieter and Dex would make sure you enjoyed it."

She was right. I squirmed on my seat thinking about all the ways they'd make sure I'd enjoy it.

"You want to try it, don't you?" Her eyes twinkled with mischief.

"Maybe," I admitted. Having them both at once, yeah, okay, I sat in a puddle of wetness. I was so jumping Dieter and Dex when they got home. What did I have to lose besides self-respect if they said no and dumped me?

"So, this charity event dinner thing is fancy. I need something special, but not as special as the one you designed for you. A little less oomph and not white. Will always has a thing for me in a white dress. You should see him when I put on my wedding dress."

"No white." I scribbled in bold writing across the top of the paper.

"I think I'll go home and put my wedding dress on tonight."

I laughed and thought about all the dresses in my wardrobe. I hadn't packed many clothes and the few I did weren't sexy but my matching bra and panty sets were my go-to underwear and sexy. The little racy red set would work for seduction but I had nothing to put over it.

Could I wait for them in just lingerie?

I did a quick sketch on the pad and showed Prue. She smiled in approval.

"You have such a brilliant eye." She stood. "Let me know when I need to come for fittings."

"Will do." I stretched out the kinks in my shoulders.

"Also, let me know how tonight goes."

"What if they say no and I make a fool of myself?" Excitement and worry churned my stomach.

"They won't and you won't."

"They haven't been clamoring all over me today. I can go back to my apartment tomorrow. They don't want me to stay."

"Have they said they want you to go?"

"No."

"Then they want you to stay. Men can be simple sometimes. They're not like women with hidden meanings in everything they do. What you see is what you get. If they said they want this, then they do."

I tucked the pencil into the mess of my hair. "All right. I guess I should shower. I don't even know when they'll be back."

"If they're not back when you're ready just call them," Prue said. "Better yet, send them a photo of you in your lingerie. They'd love that."

A sexy photo? I might do that. Nothing too risque. Perhaps a selfie with a bit of cleavage.

## Chapter Fifteen

I'd set the scene. Candles flickered on the hallway table and in the lounge room, and even in Dieter's bedroom. I'd taken the liberty of going into his bedroom and imagining us ending up there together. All three of us. Screw whatever Mom said. This was my life and these two men made me happy. Even with my angst about all of us being together, it'd been the best week of my life.

Hopefully, it was about to get better.

I paced the room in a pair of stilettos and my red lace lingerie. One minute I felt sexy as hell, the next I felt like a fool. I'd been in this cycle for the last hour and still too nervous to call them or text them. It was any wonder I had heels left on my shoes with the pacing I'd done back and forth.

Their voices muffled on the other side of the door. Guess I didn't need any courage to text them a sexy selfie now. Thank goodness. My limbs shook. The door opened. Dex and Dieter walked inside chatting like old friends. Dieter's gaze landed on the flickering candle with a frown. Dex must have sensed me watching them because he stopped walking and stared at me. Dieter's gaze scanned the room, hit me, and he dropped the paper bag.

"Hot damn, Fluff..." Dex recovered first and strode toward me.

He stopped in front of me and spun me around by the shoulders. Dieter sucked in a deep breath still standing by the front door.

"Dieter, is this okay?" I asked.

"More than okay." Dieter strutted over to me. "Are you saying what I hope you're saying?"

"Yes." I grasped both their hands. "Let's do this

together, all of us."

Dieter puffed out a breath through pursed lips. "I can't tell you how much I've wanted this."

I stood up on tiptoes and kissed him with softness on the lips. His lips molded to mine, and he sighed into my mouth with a deep sexy sound that made my insides clench in need. Dex's work-rough fingers brushed my hair aside and then his mouth was on the back of my neck kissing and suckling on my sensitive skin sending ripples of pleasure down my spine. I ran one hand over Dieter's shoulders while the other caressed Dex's head.

Dieter's lips traveled down my neck, and he turned my head so I could kiss Dex. Dex's lips devoured mine with tongue and teeth. I sunk my fingers into his hair urging him to go harder. He didn't disappoint. Our teeth clanged with the force of our kiss. His hands landed on my hips, and he tugged me back into his hard erection. I rubbed against him. He released my mouth.

"You're not making me come in my pants this time, Fluff," Dex husked out stepping back and stripping his top over his head.

My mouth watered at the sight of all his glorious tight muscles.

"No," I said licking my lips. "Take it all off."

Dex chuckled and continued stripping.

Dieter spun me around, so I didn't have to twist my neck to watch Dex's strip show.

Dex laid on the sofa. "Come here and sit on my face. I've been thinking about it since last night."

"Here?" I gazed toward the bedroom.

Dieter pressed into my back and shuffled us closer to the sofa. Dex moved over and pressed his mouth to my aching mound. He nudged with his chin against my clit. Dieter pressed into me from behind, his thick erection spreading my ass cheeks and making me widen my legs for Dex's seeking tongue. Dex's tongue stroked the length of my thong. Dieter's fingers slipped under my panties and tugged them to the side. Dex's tongue swiped over my clit. My hips bucked and my knees wobbled. Dieter lifted my left leg and dragged it over Dex's shoulder. He held my leg keeping me wide open to Dex's seeking tongue.

Dex's tongue slid deep inside me and swirled against the front wall making my one leg give way. Dieter held me up with his arm tight around my waist.

"Are you going to come on his face?" Dieter asked, his breath hot in my ear. "Like you did on mine in the library the first time?"

"Yes," I panted. *God, yes.*

Dex's tongue swiped over my clit and dragged back inside. Long slow licks. My hips bucked in time to his ministrations. Hanging in midair with Dieter holding me for Dex was way more intense than I could have imagined. I dropped my head back against Dieter's chest. He smiled down at me with carnal need but also love. The love tipped me over the long edge. My inner muscles spasmed and released in wave after wave. Dex kept licking the pleasure from me with his tongue until I sagged so much in Dieter's arms, he dragged my leg back and eased me onto the couch.

"How you doing there, Fluff?" Dex asked.

I pressed the back of my hand to my forehead trying to calm the pounding of blood racing through it with the intensity of the release.

"I'll be back in a sec." Dieter strode from the room.

"Dieter, wait," I called out, "don't go."

"I'm getting condoms." He grinned. "I'm not going anywhere except inside you."

"Okay." I closed my eyes again.

Dex nuzzled the side of my neck. I swear the man was obsessed with it. Pleasure sparked from his bristles on my hot skin. The lazy post-orgasm sensation didn't stay long. Dex stroked his palm down my side and cupped my breast. His thumb toyed with the nub until it was hard with arousal. He latched his mouth onto the hard tip and swiped it with his tongue. Pleasure shot an arrow straight to my core. I ached to have him inside me.

Dieter returned naked and wearing a condom. Dex swapped places with him on the sofa. Dieter spun me over onto my stomach and kissed my lower back, dragged his teeth over my buttocks making me clench them then I unclenched them remembering what Prue said.

"Can we all be together at once?" I asked, my voice muffled against the cushion. Good thing I wasn't facing them either as my face was hot.

"Do you mean here?" Dieter slid his finger into my wetness with ease then dragged it over my puckered hole. "And here?"

Dex chuckled. "From the woman who didn't want to try anal."

Dieter's finger kept sliding inside me and making me squirm. "One day we can. Not today. You'll need a bit of preparation."

"What do you mean?"

His finger skated up near my puckered hole again and I clenched my ass cheeks.

"Like that. You can't be tense for you to enjoy it," Dieter said.

Dex massaged my shoulders from the end of the sofa. "We'll work up to it if it's what you want."

"Okay."

Dieter tugged my hips off the sofa. "All this talk about fucking your ass has me ready to blow."

I pushed up on my hands and knees. "You like it that much?"

"I like you that much," he said.

He rubbed his flared head against my entrance, found me soaking wet and drove inside. I moaned at the sudden sensation of fullness. This was what I'd missed all week being surrounded by them. Filled by them. Loved by them.

Dieter thrust his hips, sliding long and hard along my slick channel.

"Open your mouth," Dex said. "You can have us both at once another way."

Dex's enormous cock strained in my face. Dex wrapped his fingers in my hair and guided my mouth to his cock. I swallowed him down my throat. His thick cock hit the back of my throat and I gagged a little. Dieter's cock swelled inside me. I moaned around Dex's cock in my mouth. He tugged my hair harder and thrust into my mouth. Every nerve ending in my body lit on fire. The two men I loved both loving me at once. My muscles clenched deep inside.

Dieter's dick dragged against the front of my clit. His hands shifted from my waist to my ass cheeks and kneaded the muscles until they were lax. His thumb brushed against my puckered hole. A thousand pleasure nerves sparked and sent me convulsing into another orgasm. Dex pulled out of my mouth—good thing too because my mouth was useless with the silent screams the orgasm ripped from my throat. He rubbed his cock along my shoulder, and he came with a warm spurt over my back. Dieter stroked his hands from my ass and rubbed Dex's release into my back. His pace picked up and then he grunted and came with a force I experienced deep inside me.

"Wow," I got out through the pants in my breaths.

Dieter pulled out, and I landed face-first on the sofa in a pile of oxygen-starved limbs. I listened to the pad of his feet as he left the room again.

"Where did Dieter go?" I mumbled.

"He's getting rid of the condom."

"Oh."

Dex tugged the soaked thong from my hips and down my legs. He unhooked my bra and eased the straps off my arms.

"A bit late now." I giggled.

His fingers slid the stilettos from my feet.

"Not at all. You're going to ride me now."

"I can't move," I whined.

He dragged me into a sitting position and sat me on his lap with my back to his front.

"How are you hard again already?"

"Fluff, you're kidding, right? It's me you're talking to. Lift your butt and slide onto my cock."

"Condom?"

"Already on."

"Okay, but my muscles are like jelly." I sunk onto his thick cock. It was different from Dieter's. Thicker whereas Dieter's was longer. Both were amazing. "I doubt I'll come again either."

"Ye of little faith." Dex arranged my legs until he spread them wide and wrapped his feet around my ankles holding me in place. "Let's wait for Dieter."

"All right." I sat resting on his lap, but the constant fullness of him inside me made me want more. To move and stroke my insides with his thick cock. Time ticked, and I grew more restless. "What's taking him so long?"

Dex stroked his fingers through my fluff but didn't go lower where I ached for him to go. "He hasn't been long."

Dieter strode back into the lounge room and sat on the coffee table facing us. His gaze glued to where my pussy held Dex's dick.

"Look at you spread open." He circled my entrance around Dex's cock.

Pleasure raced its way from his simple touch to every inch of my body. Dex's hands controlled my hips and slid me up and down on his cock in one long slow slide. Dieter's gaze glazed with heat, his cock grew stiff before my eyes, and he wrapped his hand around it.

Dex moved my hips again with infinite slowness. Dieter brushed his finger around my entrance again.

I sucked in a breath and held it.

Dieter circled the hard nub of my clit.

I puffed out my breath.

Dex controlled my movements again. Soon they were working in a rhythm of thrusting and touching that had me hovering in the bliss of pleasure. Slide. Swipe. Slide. Swipe.

"Squeeze your nipples," Dex said.

My fingers squeezed them with eagerness. I needed something to push me over the edge. I couldn't take this hovering anymore.

The slide of Dex's cock didn't change pace. Neither did the swipe of Dieter's finger.

"Please," I begged, my heart and breath stuttering.

Dieter slid his finger inside the same time as Dex slid his cock in and I exploded with the force of a supernova. A scream ripped out of my throat. I needed to close my legs, but Dex's feet kept mine wide as my body rocked on his. The orgasm took on a life of its own and rippled on and on until it fluttered to the occasional spasm. Dex picked my hips up and slammed me down exploding inside me sending ripples of pleasure along with my aftershocks.

I opened my eyes in time to see Dieter's hand bring him to release all over my chest. His long cock twitched in the palm of his hand making my inner muscles clench at the way he felt when he did that inside me. I wet my dry lips.

Dex unhooked my ankles and Dieter helped me from his lap and hugged me. My wet front squished against his.

"Now you're all messy too," I said.

He kissed my nose. "You're worth it."

Dex rubbed his hands down my back. "We all need a shower."

"Okay, but don't get any more ideas about sex for at least…"

"Tomorrow?" Dex said.

"Yeah, tomorrow," Dieter said releasing me.

"I don't know, I think you broke me with the last orgasm," I said.

Dex scooped me into his arms and carried me to Dieter's bedroom and bathroom.

"You lit candles in here too, Fluff."

"Yeah, I thought it would be nice."

Dex chuckled. "You didn't need any of this, we just want you."

"And you both had me. Was it okay?"

"It was more than okay by me. You blew my mind," Dex said, discarding the condom.

Dieter turned on the shower.

"Dieter?"

"Tiff, honey, I've wanted this since Dex, and I figured out we were both dating you. Sharing you with Dex was a huge turn-on, bigger than I imagined, and seeing your pretty pussy take his dick I could watch you all day long."

"Yeah, that ain't happening." I squeezed my well-used lady bits together.

"I knew you were a perv." Dex stepped into the shower and dragged me with him. "So, you like my junk, huh?"

I giggled. The sound reverberated around the tiled bathroom with happiness.

"Shut up." Dieter joined us in the shower and washed his front with the soap.

"I like both your junk if that counts?"

"It does." Dex winked.

## Chapter Sixteen

After our shower (thank goodness it was big enough for the three of us), Dieter tugged his favorite t-shirt over my head. He'd never let me wear it before. The perks of having sex with them both. Dieter ushered me into his bed and flicked on the television hanging from the wall. Dex disappeared and returned in a pair of steel-grey boxer shorts and the takeout bag Dieter dropped earlier.

"Good thing we bought salad wraps." Dex climbed into bed with us and extracted the wraps.

"Dieter doesn't like eating in bed," I said wriggling out from under the sheets.

"Too bad." Dex shrugged and opened his wrap.

Dieter sighed and opened his wrap. "Tonight is fine, but that's it."

Dex chewed his wrap and smirked.

"Don't get any crumbs in the bed."

"You're a bit anal," Dex said.

I giggled. They both shot me an amused look. I bit into the salad wrap and picked up the remote control, flicked through the channels until I found *Runway Stars*. They groaned in unison, but it didn't stop me. I settled back against the pillows and finished the wrap to my favorite show. The night couldn't get any better. Three intense orgasms, a full stomach, my favorite television show, and the two men I loved lounging beside me in bed. A yawn stretched my jaw wide. My eyelids grew heavy. I tugged the sheet up to my chin and fell asleep.

When I woke, the television was still on, but Dieter and Dex were both asleep beside me. I stretched over Dieter's slumbering body and switched off the television plunging the room into darkness. I laid back down, but all I thought about was the dress. The one I'd wear to a charity event with Dieter and Dex as my dates. I should have mentioned the event before we fell asleep. There'd be time when they woke. There'd be time for everything now.

I eased over Dex's body. He didn't move either. What was the time? I got little sleep last night, but the way these two were sleeping it was like they didn't get any sleep at all the night before. I padded out of Dieter's bedroom and into the sewing room and turned on the floor lamp. A mellow golden glow lit up the armchairs. I picked up my sketch pad and drew more of the design for Prue's dress.

I loved creating so much. The peace and calmness descended on me while my fingers drew the image in my mind. A sigh of contentment left my body. I didn't think I'd ever been this happy. All the obstacles I'd thrown in our way had been for nothing. Sex with the three of us hadn't been weird or awkward. It'd been intense and fulfilling in a way I'd never expected. I couldn't wait to tell Prue how amazing tonight went. I scanned the time on my cell. Five o'clock in the morning.

My stomach rumbled. I was so hungry after the sex marathon last night. My taste buds craved a breakfast burrito. I stretched out my neck and shoulders and stood. There was a great food van down at the boardwalk that would be open for breakfast. I'd pop down there, fetch breakfast, and feed my men.

I almost skipped to my bedroom to dress. Breakfast in bed. Dieter wouldn't like it, but he'd relented last night with the wraps and burritos weren't so different to wraps. Mmm, coffee too. I yanked on underwear and a pair of shorts. Took the t-shirt off with reluctance and put on a bra and tank top. I put on a pair of sneakers, grabbed my purse, and left the apartment.

The streetlights were still on, the roads quiet for

Los Angeles, but it was early on a Sunday morning. Birds chirped. I raised my face to the sky. The predawn light filtered through the darkness. I trotted to the end of the street to watch the sunrise through the palm trees. The sun rose in a giant fluorescent ball of orange lighting the sky to match. So beautiful. This day would be amazing—the start of our future. I sensed it in the depth of my heart.

Once the orange glow faded and the sky turned blue, I continued to Carry's Coach, ordered three breakfast burritos, and grande coffees. Balancing the coffee cup tray in one hand and carrying the heavy paper bag with the food in the other, I made my way along the boardwalk. The gentle lap of waves on the beach was a constant sound of happiness, like the way I was feeling.

The street was alive with people, now many couples walking hand in hand, on their way to a romantic breakfast. Or so I imagined. I was on my way to a romantic breakfast in bed with my men. I'd relight the candles and even though my well-used lady parts didn't want another round with them together, my heart did. The things those men made me want.

Everything and then some.

I arrived back at Dieter's apartment with a dizzy glow but the apartment was quiet. Those lazy bums were still asleep. I bounded into Dieter's bedroom and froze. The sheets were hanging half off the bed and the bed was empty. Where were they? I didn't pass them in the lounge room or the kitchen. I checked the bathroom and found that empty too.

"Dieter? Dex?" I called out.

No answer.

Did they leave? My heart sank like the Titanic to the bottom of my stomach. I dropped the bag on the kitchen counter and placed the coffee tray next to it.

They'd both been so happy last night. Where were they? I yanked open my handbag. Where was my cell? I needed to talk to them. I ran to my bedroom and threw books aside looking for my cell in a frantic search.

The tinkling ring of my cell sounded from somewhere in the apartment. I paused, cocked my head, and scurried after it. It stopped ringing. *Damn it*. It rang again. I hurried into the sewing room. Of course, I left my cell in here when I'd been sketching. I swiped the speaker.

"Hello."

"Tiff, honey," Sienna said in a quiet voice, then a sob burst from her.

"Wh-what is it?"

Why is Dex's mom calling me? Was Dex with her? Did he tell her he didn't want to be with me anymore?

"It's Dex and Dieter … they're in the hospital."

I sunk into the armchair.

"Are … are they?" I couldn't ask. "Why?"

How were they in the hospital? I'd left them not long ago, not even two hours. *How?* reverberated through my head.

"They're both in surgery." She sniffed.

"What happened?"

"Dex said a carjacker attacked them. Honey, can you come to the hospital? Dex was asking for you before they wheeled him off to the operating room."

"I'll be there soon."

Sienna hung up. She didn't even say how Dieter was. Was he all right? Were they both all right? Fuck, of course they weren't, they were in the hospital having surgery.

I dialed Dad's number with a shaking hand. Good thing I liked the speakerphone.

"Good morning, Tiff," Dad answered.

"Dad, can you take me to the hospital?"

"Are you okay?" Dad's voice changed to concerned.

"I'm fine. Sienna called me and said a carjacker attacked Dieter and Dex, they're both in surgery." I burst into tears.

"I'll be there soon." Dad hung up.

Good thing too, because the cell's screen was blurry and my fingers didn't work. The tears streamed down my cheeks. I couldn't lose them. This was way worse than believing they'd left me because they didn't want me. I could live without them if they lived. If they lived, I'd give them anything they wanted.

They couldn't die.

I rocked on the armchair. The sketch of the dress taunted me. I'd dreamed of happily-ever-after. Of us living together. Loving each other.

A knock pounded on the door. I dashed at my cheeks with my fingers, scooped up my cell, and ran to the front door.

Dad held his arms open.

I fell into them and blew out a long breath in his comforting hug. He patted my back until I got myself under control.

"Go wash your face, baby girl. Then we'll go."

I hurried to the bathroom and washed my face with cold water until the bright red ring around my eyes dulled and the bleariness from my eyes lightened with the blast of icy water. Satisfied I was at least presentable and wouldn't crumble again, I made my way back to Dad, made sure I held my cell, and left the apartment.

We drove to the hospital in silence and hurried up to the reception desk.

"Can you please tell me where I can find Dex

Munroe and Dieter Brant?" I blurted.

The receptionist tapped away on the computer. She looked up with a compassionate expression. My heart sunk again, and my knees knocked against each other. They couldn't be dead.

"They're both still in surgery. The waiting room is on the third floor. Follow the signs once you get off the elevator."

"Thank you," Dad said since my voice was nonexistent.

I wrung my hands together, and we waited for the elevator which had to be the slowest in the whole city of Los Angeles. We climbed on and my stomach dropped even further making my slow assumption the complete opposite. Dad and I followed the bright blue signs to the waiting room.

Sienna rushed over and hugged me. I squeezed her back and let go before I cried again.

"How's Dex?" I asked through the roughness in my throat.

"He has a broken arm from what they tell me. They're putting screws in it."

I sagged with relief. A broken arm. That wasn't too bad. Sure, he required surgery, but he'd be fine once the bone healed even if he needed rehab. They couldn't have broken his arm so bad he'd never use it again. He needed his arm for work. How would he work on cars with one arm?

"Will it heal okay?" I gulped.

"The doctors are confident he'll heal just fine."

"Thank goodness." I couldn't imagine Dex not having use of both his arms. With his penchant for picking me up and carrying me around, he wouldn't like it. Neither would I.

I skimmed the waiting room, a half-dozen

worried-looking people sat in the hard chairs but not Dieter's parents. Did they know? "What about Dieter?"

"I don't know, honey." She touched my arm. "His parents were in here but they left."

"I need to find out." I stepped to the door. But Dieter's mom didn't like me. Would she even tell me?

"I'll come with you," Dad said.

We stopped at the nurse's station.

"Can you please tell me how Dieter Brant is?" I asked the nurse.

"And you are?" She peered at me over the rim of her glasses.

"I'm his girlfriend."

"Please," Mrs. Brant scoffed from behind.

I spun around.

"Did you ask about your other boyfriend too?" Mrs. Brant sneered.

I cringed.

The nurse stood. "Mr. Brant is still in surgery. If you'd like to wait peacefully in the waiting room for an update as soon as I have one, then you may. If not, then please step outside so you won't disturb anyone else."

Mrs. Brant stomped off down the hallway away from the waiting room. No surprise there. The woman had a huge stick up her ass about me dating Dieter. Let alone dating Dieter and Dex together. She'd be even more horrified if she knew what we'd done last night.

"I'm sorry," I said to the nurse. "Why is Dieter having surgery?"

Her hard expression fell from her face. "He suffered a gunshot wound to the shoulder."

"But ... but ... he'll be okay? Won't he?"

"I'm sorry, I can't tell you more until I hear from the surgeons." She squeezed my lifeless hand laying on the counter. "I'll come to find you as soon as I hear anything."

I nodded my head in muteness. Shot. They shot Dieter. I couldn't wrap my head around it. Bloody images circled my mind. Dad maneuvered me back to the waiting room and sat next to me. Sienna sat on the other side. I stared at the clock; the second arm ticked with slowness. The minute arm was even slower.

This wasn't happening. It must be a nightmare. I was still in bed with them both with their warm bodies. They'd be cold if they died. Perhaps they were cold now?

The nurse walked into the waiting room. "Mr. Munroe is out of surgery and we've moved him to recovery. You'll be able to see him soon. The surgeons will be along in a minute to talk to you."

"Thank you," Sienna said.

"What about Mr. Brant?" I asked.

"No news yet." The nurse walked away.

I shut my eyes. It didn't mean he wouldn't be okay. A bullet wound would take longer. I should have asked. At least Dex was out of surgery.

A doctor strode into the room in his green scrubs and said, "Munroe family?"

"Yes." Sienna stood.

Dad and I stood with her. The doctor walked over to us.

"Mr. Munroe's surgery was satisfactory. The fracture to his humerus required repositioning and stabilizing with internal fixation. He'll be in a fair bit of pain I'm afraid, but we'll give him medicine to reduce the pain. He'll need to keep the arm immobilized with a sling for at least six weeks. Physio will visit with him in the morning and give him further instructions and set up physical therapy appointments, but he should be able to go home tomorrow," the doctor said. "It'll take a few months until he has full use again, but he's a fit young man, so we expect he'll make a full recovery."

Sienna shook the doctor's hand. "Thank you, Doctor."

I watched the doctor leave wishing he'd told me Dieter would be okay too. It was an enormous relief Dex would be fine. But I needed both my men to be okay. I needed them both in my life. How selfish to be thinking of what I needed when they were both in the hospital. Time to put their needs before mine.

And if that meant giving them both up, then that's what I'd do.

## Chapter Seventeen

"We're moving Mr. Munroe to Room 218," the nurse said another hour later. "You can visit with him there."

Sienna stood in a hurry. I pushed to the edge of the hard plastic chair then stopped. What if I left and there was news on Dieter?

The nurse gave me a pitying look. "Mr. Brant is still in surgery. I shouldn't expect it'll be too much longer until we have news."

Sienna peered into my eyes. "Wait here for the news then come see Dex."

I blinked. I should go see Dex and tell him I loved him. I wanted to see he was alive and breathing.

Dieter's parents walked into the waiting room. Mrs. Brant threw me a disgusted look and stomped to the other side of the waiting room. Mr. Brant walked my way. I stood in a rush and clasped his outstretched hands.

"I'm so sorry," I said.

"It wasn't your fault." Dieter's dad held my hands a little tighter.

Sienna dipped her head. "Jonathon."

"You two know each other?" I asked. Did everyone know each other and keep it a secret from me?

"Yes, I take my cars to Munroe's garage. Dex's dad worked on my cars before he passed away. How is Dex?" Mr. Brant asked.

"He's out of surgery. I was about to go see him," she said.

"Don't let me stop you." He dropped my hands and waved her off. "Give him my best for a good recovery."

"I will," she said.

As if the day couldn't get any more difficult. My

poor brain was about to implode. The worrying was getting to me. My temples pounded. My heart still sat in the bottom of my stomach. It would never float again if Dieter... I swallowed. I didn't want to think it.

Dex's mom disappeared from the waiting room leaving me and Dad, Dieter's parents, and one older lady. Everyone else's loved ones had left. Everyone else was out of surgery. How bad did they shoot Dieter?

"How are you holding up, Tiff?" Mr. Brant asked.

I swayed my hand side to side and swallowed the lump in my throat. "Why is it taking so long?"

His bushy brows dropped into a deep frown. He was as worried as me. As worried as his wife pacing by the window.

A doctor rushed into the room. My breathing faltered. All sound stopped reaching my ears. A haze descended over my eyes. This was it. He was here to tell us Dieter had died. The hard line of his mouth said this wasn't good news.

"Brant family?" the doctor asked.

"Yes." Dieter's mom rushed over to her husband's side not even bothering to give me a dirty look.

"Mr. Brant is out of surgery."

Did I sit in the chair or did Dad lower me to it? One second, I was on eye-level with everyone, the next I was looking at their knees.

"The bullet fragmented, and we had a hard time finding all the pieces. We believe we've removed them all. He lost a fair amount of blood and required a unit. The bullet missed the subclavian and brachial arteries and the brachial plexus. He's a very lucky young man," he said.

"I can't thank you enough, our son means everything to us." Mr. Brant shook the doctor's hand.

"You'll be able to see him when they transfer him from recovery to a ward." His lips didn't budge from the hard line. "Depending on whether he gets an infection, which is a chance with a bullet wound, but we'll give him antibiotics to prevent it, he should be able to go home in a couple of days."

"We'll take good care of him," Mrs. Brant said and walked back to the window as far away from me as possible.

I stood in a rush. I could see Dex now. He'd want to know about Dieter too. And who knew if Dieter's mom would let me in Dieter's room. I wouldn't be surprised if she asked the nurses to ban me. I loved Dieter more than she understood.

"I'll get us coffees," Dad said.

I nodded and strode from the room with purpose. My heart rose from the bottom of my stomach like a miracle occurred. It bobbed near its original place, but my heart wouldn't be back until I saw the men I loved and talked to them.

My sneakers squeaked on the linoleum floors as I made my way through the sterile hallways. I found Room 218 and Dex laying in a stark white hospital bed, his face pale instead of his usual bronze. Even his eyes appeared pale like someone put a filter over him and washed him out.

"Dex," I squeaked.

His gaze snapped my way.

"Fluff?" He held out his good arm.

It was all I needed, and I ran to the bed, placed my head in the crook of his neck, and sobbed.

"Shh." He rubbed my back up and down getting way too close to my ass considering his mom was in the room, but I didn't move. If he wanted to feel me up with the entire world watching, I'd let him after almost losing him.

"I'll leave you two alone," Sienna said.

I crawled onto the side of the bed and hugged him with great care. Dex let out a long sigh.

"Am I hurting you?" I sat up, grabbed a handful of tissues, and wiped my face.

Pain lanced across his face.

"Why did you leave?" he asked.

"Leave?" I frowned in confusion.

"This morning, you left … you left us, after everything we shared, why?"

"I left to get breakfast burritos."

He snorted. "You'd disappeared for over an hour before we searched for you, and you never answered your phone."

"You were looking for me when this happened? This is my fault."

Dex brushed his fingers over my trembling lips. "Shh. Were you really getting breakfast?"

I nodded since my throat felt like a home for a thousand rocks.

"Fuck." He dropped his head back on the pristine white pillow. "I'm the biggest idiot. We thought we'd persuaded you into something you didn't want and ran home in the morning."

"No, Dex. I wanted it, both of you. I wasn't running away from either of you."

"Dieter is going to be so pissed we jumped to the wrong idea. How is he? Have you seen him? Mom knew nothing, and he was bleeding pretty bad when I drove us here."

The concern in his voice overwhelmed me. He cared about Dieter as his friend.

"They shot him, but he's going to be okay." I shifted on the bed. "They said you will be too."

"Yeah, I'll be fine, Fluff, it's a broken arm, it'll heal. You were staying with us?"

"Yes." I laid my head on the pillow beside him. "It's us now. Can you live with that?"

"I love it. I'm looking forward to living with you both for as long as I live," he said.

"Don't say that." I sniffed. "I almost lost you both today."

"Sorry." He turned his head and brushed the tip of my nose with his.

"I can't live without you and Dieter. I love you both too much."

"You won't. We'll be home before you know it."

*Home.* Yes. Home was where they both were. Where we all were. But if Dex thought I'd left, then Dieter did too. I'd have to talk to Dieter and make him understand I'd never leave them again. I'd broken all our hearts once and once was more than enough to know this was real between us.

Sienna knocked on the door then entered the room. She smiled when she saw us lying on the bed together. I moved off the side of the hospital bed before Dex stopped me, his motions were slower than usual, and he fumbled at the last second catching my hair in his fingers.

"Ow." I tugged the strands free.

"I'm the one with a broken arm, I should say *ow*."

The first smile I'd experienced since the catastrophe of this morning creased my lips.

"My poor Dex. I'll take good care of you." I smoothed a hand over his forehead.

"You're not coming back to your place?" Sienna asked.

"I wasn't planning to." Dex frowned. "Why?"

"I thought you might like your mom to look after

you," she said.

Dex chuckled then winced. "If it's a choice between my mom and my girlfriend playing nurse, who do you think I'm picking?"

A puff of repressed laughter escaped. "Do not think about buying me a nurse costume."

"Too late, already have. I'm sure Dieter will love it too."

"You're incorrigible." I shook my head.

"I'm looking forward to my sponge baths, Nurse Herringer." He grinned.

"I'm not bathing you."

"But I can't get my plaster wet."

"Fine." I pursed my lips. As if he'd be up for any sort of sexy times when laughing made him wince in pain. Men were so stupid when it came to sex.

Dad knocked on the door and entered carrying three cups of coffee.

"Thanks, Dad." I took a cup.

Dad passed Sienna a cup and drank his coffee. They settled on the chairs, and I dithered by the door.

"Go check on him," Dex said.

"But?"

"And tell him, fuck, I don't know." Dex rubbed his forehead and shut his eyes. "Tell him I'm glad he's okay."

"I will," I whispered.

Dex's concern for Dieter filled my heart with warmth. I was the luckiest woman alive. Two men loved me, neither was jealous, and they showed genuine affection for each other too.

I left Dex's room and made my way to the nurse's desk.

"Excuse me, what room in Dieter Brant in?" I asked.

She held up her finger and scribbled on a clipboard filling the page with writing before looking up.

"Who did you say?" the nurse asked.

"Dieter Brant."

She flicked her gaze to a whiteboard on the wall. "Room 3."

If I'd realized it was that easy, I would have peeked at the whiteboard myself. I hurried to Dieter's room. Lightness filled each step. His surgery went as well as Dex's operation. I still didn't know what happened apart from a carjacker. Whose car were they in? Where were they? Why didn't I ask Dex?

I knocked on the doorjamb and walked inside. Dieter looked worse than Dex. A grey tinge dulled his skin, around his eyes seemed bruised, and his lips were pale.

"Oh, Dieter," I whispered.

He blinked but didn't look at me.

"He doesn't want you here," Mrs. Brant said. She stepped between me and Dieter.

"Ridiculous." I stepped around her. "Dieter, tell her."

"I don't want to talk to you, Tiff," he said with a rasp to his voice.

"You don't understand." I rushed to the bed. "I didn't leave you like you thought, I left to get breakfast for us."

"I'm tired, Tiff, I might be up to talking to you tomorrow," Dieter rasped.

A strangled noise escaped my throat. I turned and fled the room but not before catching the gloating look on Mrs. Brant's face. Screw her. This was a misunderstanding. That's all. I'd clear it up tomorrow with him. It still hurt like he'd stabbed me in the heart. His words smarted. I shoved my hands in my pockets and walked back to Dex's room.

"How is he?" Dex asked.

"He, ah, was asleep." I couldn't even tell Dex what Dieter said.

"He'll be awake later. You can talk to him then." Dex yawned.

"We should go so you can rest." I nodded my head at the door signaling to Dad it was time to go. If I stayed any longer, I'd tell Dex what Dieter said. He didn't need to be upset right now. He needed to rest and heal.

"Aw, no." He yawned again.

I crossed to Dex's side and kissed his forehead. "I'll see you tomorrow."

"Tomorrow is so far away." His eyelids drooped closed.

I left the hospital with Dad's silent support. It wouldn't last though. Dad was too much of a gossip.

"What happened with Dieter?" Dad asked driving out of the hospital parking lot.

"He didn't want to talk to me." I hung my head against the window and watched the road zoom by.

"Did he say why?" Dad frowned.

"It's a big misunderstanding." I sighed.

"You'll work it out."

"Maybe." My stomach revolted at the notion of never taking to Dieter again.

"You will, he's full of pain meds, drowsy from surgery, he might not even know what he was saying to you."

"Can you drop me at my apartment please?" I asked.

"Why don't you come home for the night?"

"I have work tomorrow," I said.

"I'll drive you to work in the morning. You

shouldn't be alone right now. You look too sad. Your mom is cooking her famous lasagna for dinner."

"And homemade garlic bread?" My stomach rumbled reminding me I hadn't eaten all day.

"Yes, she had the dough rising this morning before I left."

"Sold." Even if it meant seeing Mom after her stupid marriage talk the other night.

Dad drove us home. Mom opened the front door the second Dad pulled the car into the driveway and rushed outside.

"How are they?" she asked as I opened the car door.

"Dex has a broken arm, and they shot Dieter," I said. The reality of the situation wouldn't sink in. "Unlucky for you, they're both still alive."

Mom's fingers curled and her lips twitched down. "I'll pretend you didn't say that."

"It'd solve your problem, wouldn't it?" I slammed the car door.

"You're upset, Tiffany, don't take it out on me," she said with softness.

"I…" I flung my arms wide.

"Hush, now." Mom swooped me into her embrace. "I know you didn't mean it."

"I'm sorry, Mom," I mumbled into her shoulder.

Mom's hug was the one I'd needed the most today. It didn't matter what she'd said about marriage, my future, Dex and Dieter. What mattered was she was here giving me the support I needed. We may not see eye to eye on the marriage deal, but she'd always be there for me. Today of all days I needed my mom.

## Chapter Eighteen

I'd stayed in my childhood bedroom staring at the walls half the night. What if Dieter didn't want to talk to me today? Mom cooked breakfast and Dad drove me to my apartment to dress for work then drove me to work. I couldn't focus on the designs in front of me. After my less than stellar workday, I caught an Uber to the hospital.

Neither Dex nor Dieter contacted me all day even though I'd texted them both on my morning break. Their silence spoke more than any words they said. I knew it was over with them. There was no other explanation.

I walked straight to Dieter's room. I wouldn't be able to talk to Dex and lie to him about Dieter.

Dieter was thankfully alone in his room.

"Hi, you look better today." And he did. He had his color back but the enormous bags under his eyes still confirmed he wasn't one hundred percent.

He wriggled up on the pillows, so he was half-sitting. His face twisted with each movement, but he didn't look at me.

"About yesterday … Dex said you thought I'd left. I didn't. I left to get breakfast."

Dieter sighed. "I want to believe you."

"Why don't you?" I shifted closer to his bed.

"Dex and I pushed you into it. I don't blame you for leaving."

"You didn't push me. You gave me a little nudge. I didn't leave. Think logically. All my stuff is at your place still. I wouldn't leave without my sewing gear."

"You were in too much of a hurry to pack."

"Dieter." I touched his hand.

He flinched then cursed under his breath and placed his hand near his shoulder.

"I don't understand where this is coming from," I said.

"We made a mistake." He hung his head.

"We didn't," I whispered.

Silence. I waited. And waited. A different fear from yesterday's poured through my body.

"What are you saying?" I asked.

"It'd be best if you and Dex weren't at my apartment when they release me tomorrow."

I stepped back like he'd slapped me. "You don't want us?"

"Getting shot has made me see things differently. We should have a special someone who'll be there for us." He dug his fingers into the sheets.

"I love you, Dieter. I'll always be there for you."

"And Dex." His lips firmed.

"Yes, and Dex will always be there for you too. He's worried about you."

"How is he?" His face tugged with concern. "His arm was hanging at a weird angle when he drove us here."

"He had to have surgery, but he'll be okay. He wanted me to tell you he's glad you're okay."

"I'm glad he's okay too, but…"

"But you still don't want us. You realize how hard it was for me to do what you wanted." I swallowed, my throat hurting like I swallowed knives. "And one minor bump and you're baling."

I shuffled back from his bed.

"I almost died."

"And I almost lost you." I snorted. "I guess I have, haven't I? The fear I had for losing the man I loved has eventuated."

"You have another one," he said.

"What?"

"You have another man you love. Go be with him." He waved his hand.

"Are you kidding?" I glared. "After you were the one who said it'd feel like cheating?"

"It's not cheating if I'm no longer a part of this," he said.

"You'll always be a part of it." I backed up to the door. "You've got your payback, Dieter, you've broken my heart too."

"Tiff…" He sighed.

I staggered from the room before we said anything else to hurt each other. My heart lay back in the hospital room with Dieter. He'd smashed everything to pieces with one killing blow.

Somehow, I found my way to Dex's room through the tears in my eyes.

"Tiff?" Dex rose from the chair dressed in clothes and with his arm in a sling. "What's wrong?"

"Dieter." I spluttered.

"He's not…"

"No, God, no." I shook my head. That'd break my heart worse than it was now.

"Then what?" Dex tipped my chin up.

"He broke up with me. With us. He wants us to move out of his apartment."

"He what?" Dex ground his teeth. "What room is he in?"

"Dex, don't." I chased after him.

Dex walked the hallway looking in each room until he found Dieter.

"What the fuck?" Dex ground out through his clenched teeth.

"She told you," Dieter said with resignation.

"Of course she did, she's our girl," Dex said.

"Not anymore, she's all yours." Dieter curled his

good hand into a fist.

"Bullshit. This is utter crap you are saying this shit," Dex spurted, his voice raising.

"Dex, keep your voice down, we're in a hospital," I said.

Dex spared me an apologetic look.

"Forget it, Dex." Dieter sighed. "Just leave."

"No way. You wanted this and you flip the switch now because of what? Has your mom been in your ear?"

Dieter straightened in the bed. "My mom has said nothing."

"More bullshit," Dex spat.

Dieter rubbed his forehead. "I'm tired."

"This isn't over," Dex said and stomped out of the room.

"It is," Dieter whispered.

I followed Dex back to his hospital room. He kicked the leg of the chair sending it scuttling across the linoleum with a screech.

"Calm down. You'll get kicked out," I said.

"I'm leaving anyway." He curled his good hand into a fist. "I'm going to punch him in the dick when he gets out of here."

I puffed out a breath.

"Let's get out of here and go back to my place."

"Dex," I said with guilt.

His gaze scanned my face. "No."

"We can't do this without Dieter."

"But. Fuck. Forget punching him in the dick, I'm going to rip it off and jam it up his ass."

"I wondered if you two were into each other."

Dex chuckled and slumped onto the bed. "He'll come around. It was his idea in the first place for all of us to be together."

I stepped in front of him, cupped his rough

cheeks, and kissed him with the bittersweetness of the last kiss.

Dex tugged my hair. "Don't do this, Fluff."

"I didn't. Dieter did." I untangled my hair from his fingers and walked out of his hospital room.

Today might be the last time I saw either of them. My heart longed for it to not be true, but where would we go from here?

I couldn't go to Dieter's apartment. I didn't want to go to my apartment, and I didn't want to go to my parents' house. It left me with one option. I caught an Uber to Prue's mansion. I should have called her first, but what would I say? She'd be expecting juicy details from my threesome. How was it a day ago?

I knocked on the Burberry mansion door. Kennedy Prue's nanny opened the door.

"Hi, is Prue home?"

"Um." Kennedy glanced behind her with a blush staining her cheeks. "They're in the pool."

My emotions fell even more and my face too.

"You can come in and wait if you'd like." She opened the door wider. "The twins and I are watching a kids movie in the theatre room. Prue will come to take them up to bed soon."

"If you don't mind me joining you, a kids movie sounds good." I walked into the grand foyer of the mansion and followed Kennedy to the theatre room.

"Hey, kiddos," I said to the twins. "What are you watching?"

"Swek," they chorused.

"*Shrek*, cool. Kennedy is showing you a great movie." I smiled at Kennedy and settled in a recliner.

The green characters on the screen took me away from my problems for a little while and the boy's obvious enjoyment over the talking donkey. The donkey was pretty cool. Prue strolled into the room with damp hair, flushed cheeks, and a healthy glow. Yeah, she'd been doing more than swimming. I didn't blame her with her gorgeous husband. What wife wouldn't be all over Mr. Burberry?

"Tiff." Prue startled. "What are you doing here?"

"I, ah, I didn't, I couldn't…" I stammered.

She frowned. "I'll put the boys to bed and be back soon. Kennedy, can you get Tiff a drink please?"

"Sure thing." Kennedy jumped up and left the room.

Prue ushered the twins from the room to many protests.

"Good night, boys," I called out to their grumbling backs.

"Night." They waved their chubby little fingers at me.

So adorable and the spitting image of their dad. Those boys would break hearts everywhere when they got older. A lot like Dieter broke mine now.

Kennedy returned with a fancy cocktail for both of us.

"Thanks, Kennedy."

"It looked like you needed a drink." She sipped the bright red liquid.

"I do." I guzzled my drink. "I can't believe how big the boys are getting now."

"They're growing so quick. I can't wait for Prue's next baby to have the baby stage again." Her eyes glimmered with happiness. "What about you? Any plans for babies soon?"

"No," I scoffed. Everything had gone to shit, there'd be no babies from me and Dieter and Dex. I couldn't believe I'd ever hoped we would be together as a happy family.

"Um, sorry."

"That's okay. Things are not good right now." I slurped the rest of the drink. "What about you? Are you dating anyone? Babies in your future?"

A shadow passed over her face before she forced a smile. "No, I'm single."

"You and me both." I raised my glass.

"What?" Prue hurried into the room. "You're single? How? When? Why?"

Kennedy stood. "I'll go so you two can talk."

"Thanks, Kennedy," I said.

She took my glass and left the theatre room shutting the door behind her with a quiet snick.

"What's going on, Tiff?"

I scrubbed my eyes and told Prue everything. From the intense sex with Dex and Dieter, to the carjacking, their injuries, and Dieter breaking up with me. By the time I finished it felt like I'd lived the ordeal again.

"Shit, I can't believe that all happened in a day. I need a drink."

I choked out a laugh. "You're pregnant."

"Shit." She stood and paced the room. "I don't know what to say."

"You don't have to say anything." I rubbed my eyes, so tired I could sleep forever.

"I believed in you three."

"I know you did." I yawned.

"How long do you want to stay here for?"

I shrugged.

Prue's lips pursed. "Wait until I see Dieter. And Dex just let you go too. Those idiots."

"Kind of ruined your threesome fantasy, didn't I?"

Prue laughed and opened the door. "Come on,

Tiff, those descriptions ruined nothing."

A small smile twitched at my lips. Yeah, at least I'd have the memory of one amazing night with the two men I loved. One night where we'd all believed the future was ours.

## Chapter Nineteen

Dex rang my cell first thing in the morning. I ignored it. It wasn't his fault, but if I talked to Dex, I'd want to see him. A clean break was better for all of us. Dad drove me from the Burberry mansion to my apartment and for the first time, I didn't tell him what was going on in my life. If I told the one person who mattered, then it would be real. His concern filled the car with a waiting silence. My cell phone rang another three times, and I ignored Dex each time.

Dad waited for me to change clothes and drove me to work too. How I'd concentrate on designing swimwear was anyone's guess.

"Have a good day," Dad said.

I gave him a grim smile. "You too, Dad."

He squinted his eyes, but I climbed out of the car before he said what was on his mind and disappeared into the building. I strode across the tiled foyer to the elevators and joined my waiting colleagues. The bell dinged and we entered the elevator. A hush descended the interior. Ozwald Delante stood in the middle of the throng.

"Good morning, Mr. Delante," I said. If I was to make a name for myself as a top fashion designer then I needed to make connections now, not just work for the famous man.

"Good morning." His gaze scanned my outfit.

"Tiffany," I said, "Tiffany Herringer."

"Elegant dress," he said.

"Thank you, it's one of my designs." I smoothed a hand down the A-line flare of the dress.

"Did you do the hand beading too?" He peered closer at the bodice of the dress.

"Yes." A thrill buzzed through me that he

admired my design.

"Exquisite work. What are you currently working on?" he asked.

"Swimwear."

His eyebrows rose. "How long have you worked here?"

"This is my fourth month now. I'm loving every minute and learning so much."

His gaze scanned my dress again. "I'll be keeping an eye on you, Tiffany Herringer. You have talent."

"Thank you, sir."

The elevator stopped with a loud ding and the crowd exited. My feet moved of their own accord, cloud nine was under them. Ozwald Delante thought I exhibited talent. A stupid proud grin split my lips. I bet I looked like a crazed shark smiling. My day now had a purpose.

I sat at my desk and got to work. Ozwald Delante would look at these designs and know my name. That was my goal.

My cell rang, and I ignored it without even looking at it. If I saw Dex's name on the screen, it would drag me down. I needed these eight hours to be mine free to design and lose myself in the process. I ate lunch at my desk and placed the finishing touches on the sketch. Satisfied with the effect I chose the fabric, cut out the pieces, and pinned them to the dressmaker mannequin. Pins stuck out of here there and everywhere, including my lips. My phone buzzed. I swiped the screen, too caught up in the moment of putting the design together.

"Yello," I mumbled.

"Tiff, I'm so sorry," Dieter said.

The pins fell from my lips numb with shock. No words would move through their lack of feeling.

"Tiff, are you there?" he asked.

I cleared my throat. "I'm here."

"I'm a fucktard, what can I say?"

"Why are you calling?"

"To apologize and beg your forgiveness."

"Why?" I asked again.

"I just got home from the hospital and found the breakfast you purchased on the kitchen counter."

My heart squeezed tight. "So now that you know I told you the truth you want to apologize?"

"Yeah."

"Good-bye, Dieter."

"Tiff, wait. I'm sorry."

"So you keep saying." I gathered the fallen pins. "I'm at work, Dieter, I can't do this right now."

"Shit, sorry, can you come home tonight, please? I need to see you and apologize in person."

"I'll think about it," I said and hung up. I blew out a breath. What an about-face. The last two days had been the worst in my life. Dieter's moods hurt me. Would I be able to accept his apology? I huffed. I should at least see him once more, shouldn't I?

I got little work accomplished, instead I dithered over whether to see Dieter. In the end, I walked to his apartment. Three years of loving him were too many to ignore. He opened the door with a smile, took one look at me, and his smile fell.

"Hey," I said and walked by him to the lounge room.

"Thanks for coming." He followed me and sat on the sofa, a pained weariness slumped his body.

"I needed to collect a few things anyway."

He swallowed hard. "Sit, please."

I sat in the armchair opposite him. "I'm not sure an apology will fix anything."

"I have to try. You're the love of my life."

I snorted. "That's not what you said yesterday."

He punched the sofa cushion with his good arm. "I felt weird since I woke up from surgery. Everything was hazy and these bizarre thoughts kept running through my head. Last night after you left, I had an episode, my skin broke out in a rash and my breathing became erratic. I thought it was an anxiety attack. Turns out I was allergic to the antibiotics."

I placed my hands between my knees to stop myself from reaching for him. "Are you okay?"

"Yeah, I'm good. They swapped the antibiotics and I'm better now."

"And your shoulder?" I pointed at his body.

"It's sore, but they expect it'll heal in a few weeks."

"That's good."

Poor Dex wasn't so lucky. His arm would be in a cast for six weeks. Why hadn't I answered his calls this morning? Guilt churned my stomach.

"When the thug waved the gun in my face all I thought about was you and never seeing you again." His voice caught on the end.

I gulped.

"I'm so sorry about what I said. I didn't mean it." He swiped invisible lint from his pants. "I guess I was scared."

"Scared of what?" I whispered.

"Scared of losing you. Mom said you saw Dex first. She told me to take it as a sign you love him more, and I could never trust either of you."

"I asked you if you were jealous of Dex. It was the one thing I needed to make sure of before we were all together." I clenched my hands together.

"I wasn't, I'm not. I wasn't in my right mind. Waking up from surgery was hazy." He touched his fingers to his forehead.

"I saw Dex first because he was awake first and I didn't go see him until I knew you were all right."

"Ah." He cradled his injured arm with his good arm.

"Are you in pain?" Concern barreled past the hurt.

"A little."

"Where's your pain medication?" I stood.

"In the kitchen. I can get it." He inched forward and winced.

"Stay there." I walked through to the kitchen, found a package on the bench, poured a glass of water, and carried them back to Dieter.

I handed Dieter the glass and opened the paper bag. Inside were two boxes, one labeled as pain medication, the other antibiotics, and papers with instructions.

"Do you need the antibiotics too?" I popped out a pain pill.

"Yeah, I guess."

"You guess? Aren't you following the instructions?" I waved the paper.

"Um, sure." He dropped his chin and peered up at me.

"I already told Dex I'm not dressing up as a nurse."

Dieter chuckled and placed his hand on his shoulder. "Have you spoken to Dex? He wouldn't talk to me."

"No. He rang me this morning, but I didn't answer."

"Why not?"

"Because we said we'd do this together."

"He loves you, Tiff. Don't punish him because I

was a fucktard."

"I'm not." But I was. I should have talked to Dex. "I'll talk to him."

"Good." He nodded. "So, us?"

"I don't know, Dieter," I said with regret.

His lips firmed into a tight line. "I suppose I deserve that. I am sorry, and I'll keep apologizing until you forgive me."

"I should go." I took a step to the door.

"I don't want you living at your apartment. Not with those thugs targeting the parking lot. What if they go in the building too?"

"They attacked you outside my building?" I stopped.

"Yeah, didn't you know?" His brows dropped.

"No." My stomach churned with guilt and fear.

"Stay here." He stood with another grimace.

"I can't." I walked to the front door.

"Tiff, at least think of your safety. I won't even talk to you if that's what you want."

I sighed and opened the door. "That's not what I want. Besides, I'm staying with Prue."

He gripped the doorjamb. "Can I see you tomorrow?"

"I'll think about it." I left his apartment without a backward glance because if I saw his hangdog expression one second longer, I'd hug him and tell him everything was all right when everything wasn't all right.

I ambled along the busy streets until I stood outside the Munroe Garage. The windows of Dex's apartment on the floor above were lit with a golden glow as the day dimmed into the night. I climbed the outside staircase and knocked on the door.

Sienna opened the door and smiled. "Tiff, about time you got here."

Huh? Didn't Dex tell her what happened?

"Um, I saw Dieter."

"What the fuck for?" Dex yelled from inside.

"I'll leave you two to talk." She stepped out onto the stairs and hurried down to the road.

I shut the door and walked over to Dex sitting on his sofa. "Hey. I'm sorry I didn't answer your calls."

Dex ground his jaw. "What did the fucker have to say?"

"He apologized." I sat next to Dex, so our thighs brushed.

"So he should." He met my gaze. "I'm still punching him."

I puffed out a laugh. "Can I watch?"

Dex laughed. "Yeah."

I rested my head against his uninjured shoulder. "How are you feeling?"

"Like crap."

"Are you in a lot of pain?"

He slid his hand onto my thigh. "Not as much now you're here."

"I'm sorry things got so messy between us all."

"Me too." He squeezed my thigh.

"Where do we go from here?" I sighed.

"Beats me, Fluff. I guess it depends on whether you accept his apology."

"*We*," I said. "He should apologize to you too."

"Guys don't do that shit." He placed his arm around my shoulders.

I snuggled into his side and wrapped my arm around his waist with care not to jostle his arm in the sling.

"I guess this is why three-way relationships aren't a big thing," I said.

"Relationships are messy even with two people."

He stroked my upper arm with his fingers. "I once had a girlfriend who was a complete psycho and ripped my clothes to shreds."

"That's different." I shuddered thinking of him with a psychotic woman. Any woman.

"I even had a normal girlfriend and things weren't easy."

Jealousy churned through my bones. I didn't want Dex with anyone but me. "Is that why you liked our original arrangement?"

"Yeah, it was easy being with you and not having the drama of a clingy girlfriend."

"It was easy, and we were happy," I agreed. "Do you think we can go back to it?"

"I want to say yes, but we had a taste of what it would be like together as a unit and I liked it. I liked it a lot."

"You want to try again?" I asked.

"Yeah, after I punch Dieter in the nuts, then he can watch me fuck you and be in too much pain to join in. Serve the bastard right for hurting you."

I giggled. "You won't be punching or having sex with your arm in a sling."

"My arm is in a sling, not my dick. In fact, my dick is all kinds of good with you snuggled next to me." He slid his finger to the swell of my breast.

I shook my head and slithered out from under his arm.

"Aw, Fluff, don't go. I'll behave." He crossed his heart with his hand.

"Promise to keep it in your pants and I'll stay and watch television with you for a bit before I go to Prue's house," I said eyeing his pants with more longing than I should in his condition.

"You're staying with Prue?"

"Yeah, I needed a friend."

"Come here." He patted the sofa cushion. "I'll be your friend."

I laughed. "A friend who wants in my pants."

"Yep." He winked.

"At least you're honest, Dex. It's one of the things I love about you." I settled back against his side.

"What else do you love about me?"

"Your big…"

Dex shifted on the sofa.

"Ego." I laughed.

"You wait." He tugged me closer. "I might have to get inventive with one arm, but…" He smirked.

Heat flooded my body and swarmed to my lower parts.

"So, how did they break your arm?" I changed the subject before I was the one taking Dex's pants off.

He scowled. "The fuckers tried clobbering me with a crowbar across my head. I ducked and lifted my arm to protect my head, slammed my foot on the accelerator, and got us out of there. He caught me on the upper arm. It wasn't until I tried lifting my hand to the steering wheel that I realized they broke my arm. I sped around a few streets and pulled over to ask Dieter to drive and that's when I saw the blood running down his chest and arm. It scared the shit out of me. I planted my foot and drove us straight to the hospital."

I gasped. "Were you in your dad's Pontiac?"

"Yep, you can understand why I didn't let them take it."

"Of course, it's the last car you and your dad worked on together," I said.

"I knew you'd understand." His chest swelled with a deep breath.

"How's your mom taking this?" I asked.

"Overbearing and a pain in my ass. I hope we can all go back to Dieter's apartment soon."

"We'll see," I said.

"Yeah, make him sweat first." Dex settled back on the sofa and changed the television channel to my favorite show.

"That's not what I'm doing." I frowned.

"Beg then?" He dropped his gaze to my face. "I bet you'd love Dieter on his knees begging."

My face flushed with heat.

Dex brushed his nose against mine.

Trust Dex to fetch me out of my funk. He was always the light and happiness in my life. I couldn't imagine life without him, and to have Dex in it I'd have to forgive Dieter.

Why did I have to make my life so complicated by loving two men?

## Chapter Twenty

"What do you call this, young lady?" Prue held a massive bunch of purple hyacinths.

"Um, flowers?" I walked to the bedroom I was occupying while at the Burberry mansion.

Prue followed me and sprawled out on my bed with the flowers clutched to her chest. "Why did Dieter send you a bunch of 'I'm sorry' flowers?"

"Dieter sent them?" I snatched them from her hands and searched for the card.

Prue held it up between her finger and thumb.

"Give it here." I scrambled to yank the card from her outstretched arm.

"Why are you home so late from work? Were you having a threesome already?" She waggled her eyebrows.

"You and your threesomes." I opened the card.

*I'm sorry. Please let me fix this.*

*Love Dieter*

I hugged the bouquet like I wanted to hug Dieter.

"What does it say?"

"It says he's sorry. Dieter called me to apologize and asked to see me after work. I saw Dex too."

"So, you're all back together?" She sat up.

"I'm not sure what to do."

Prue patted the bed. I sunk on the mattress beside her and dropped the flowers on the bedcovers.

"Take your time. I enjoy having you here. Besides, I want to see what flowers he sends you tomorrow."

I chuckled. "What makes you think he'll send more flowers?"

"Men are idiots. They think flowers are the answer to everything."

I stroked a bloom. "They are pretty."

"Yeah." Prue sighed. "No one ever gave me flowers before Will. Sometimes I act annoyed with him just so he'll buy me flowers."

"You're insane." I shook my head. "He'd buy you flowers every day if you told him you wanted them."

"He likes to give me anything I want."

"You're lucky, Prue."

"I know." She stroked her small stomach. "Who would have thought I'd end up here after growing up with a junkie mother?"

"Some things are meant to be."

"So are you and your two dicks." She stood with an exaggerated back roll. "I'm off to bed to complain about the baby making my back sore so I can get a massage from Will. The vases are in the kitchen cupboard by the pantry."

Prue left with a determined step to her stride. She was after more than a massage from her husband. I sighed. It'd be a long time before I got either of those from the men I loved. They were a lot like Mr. Burberry—if I asked, they'd give it to me, but my poor heart was still smarting from the blow Dieter inflicted.

I hoped Dieter could piece my heart back together.

****

Dex called me first thing in the morning. I answered. It was nice to hear his voice. It wasn't a long call, just enough for Dex to say good morning and wish me a good day, but he filled my heart with love.

Dieter texted me the same sentiments. I scowled at the text. Did he think I wouldn't answer? I wanted to hear his voice too. Stupid since he'd hurt me so much. I texted back a simple thank you.

Dad drove me to my apartment and work again.

"Will you tell me what's going on?" Dad asked.

"No, you're a big gossip, Dad."

"Now, Tiff," he spluttered.

"Nope, I'm figuring this out myself." I jumped out of the car.

A little thrill coursed through my veins as I waited for the elevator. Would Ozwald Delante ride the elevator with me again? I scanned the crowd, but his distinctive face wasn't in the throng of waiting people. I couldn't hope for miracles two days in a row.

My stomach grumbled. Lunchtime. What should I get? An Uber Eats delivery driver appeared in my office.

"Um, I ordered nothing," I said.

"Sushi delivery for Tiffany Herringer, the receipt says it's from Dieter Brant," he said.

"That's for me then, thank you."

He dumped the tray on my desk and fled. I removed the lid and inhaled the mouthwatering aroma. A small smile formed on my lips with every bite I ate.

I rang Dieter.

"Hi, Tiff," he answered.

"Thanks for lunch, and the flowers last night," I said.

"My pleasure."

An awkward silence descended.

"I should get back to work," I said.

"Okay." His voice came out low and dejected.

"Make sure you're taking your pills," I said.

"Yes, Nurse Herringer," he said with a sexy lilt.

I laughed, hung up, and texted Dex.

Me: Dieter sent me flowers and lunch.

Dex: It's a start. Dieter came to see me today and apologized.

Me: Okay. How are you?

Dex: Sore. I want to go to work and the gym.

Me: You need to rest and heal.

Dex: Yes, Nurse Herringer.

I giggled. Those two were so much alike. My heart a little lighter, I returned to work on the swimwear design. Swimwear wasn't my favorite thing to work on, but I'd work on Prue's dress tonight, and that filled my mind with eager anticipation. There was nothing I loved more than creating gorgeous gowns, except for Dieter and Dex.

I went straight to the Burberry mansion after work. Prue greeted me with a grin and a massive bunch of white orchids.

The card read:

*I'm so sorry and mean it.*

*Love Dieter*

"Don't even," I said. "I'm going for a swim."

"Will's swimming laps," Prue said.

"I'll wait then." I hesitated. I'd looked forward to a swim in their pool, it was one of the best things about the mansion.

"Don't be stupid, the pool is big enough for you both to swim."

"Are you coming in?"

"No, I promised the boys we'd play with Play-Doh. We're going to build our sculptures and have an art show. Will is going to come and buy the lot," she said with a smile.

"Sounds like fun." I smiled too. The love Prue had for her family shone from her face. If only I had an uncomplicated relationship like theirs.

"I guess if you don't mind me swimming too."

Prue smirked. "You can ogle Will all you like but touch him and I'll cut your hands off, best friend or not."

I rolled my eyes. "As if."

"Yeah, that's right, you've got two dicks of your

own."

I shoved her out of my bedroom and changed into a swimsuit. I padded through the mansion and outside to the spectacular deck and pool. The cool blue pool looked like an oasis with a fast-moving Mr. Burberry streaming through the water. I took a moment to ogle him, what woman wouldn't? I slipped into the refreshing water and set a slower pace of swimming laps in the pool.

At one stage I sensed Mr. Burberry's gaze. My skin prickled with embarrassment. I stopped swimming and climbed out of the pool.

"Nice form," Mr. Burberry said seated in a lounger wrapped in a toweling robe.

"Thanks. You too." I wrapped the towel around my breasts and tucked the end in to keep it in place.

"How long are you staying?" he asked.

"I'm not sure."

"Prue enjoys having you here, but if I hear about flowers one more time, I'll have to buy a florist shop."

I giggled.

"What did Dieter do?" he asked.

I shuffled my feet. "He broke up with me, then he changed his mind."

"Ah." He tugged the collar of his robe.

"I don't get it since he was the one who…" I trailed off before I told Mr. Burberry about our threesome with Dex. My face burned.

Mr. Burberry crossed his legs. "It's difficult growing up with money and expectations. I was a lot older than Dieter before I put my needs before my family's beliefs."

I gazed at the water. "So I should forgive him?"

"Forgiveness is never for the other person." He stood and walked into the house.

I chewed my top lip. Had I been too hard on

Dieter? He'd grown up different from me and Dex. Dex's money didn't come until later in life, it was why we had fun together, we connected on a lower level. Privileges were never an issue with us. But Dieter, he'd grown up with money and the pressure to do well, in particular from his mom.

I walked inside, collected another vase from the kitchen, and placed the bouquet beside the hyacinths in my bedroom. I didn't call Dieter to thank him. I couldn't make it too easy for Dieter. The damn man was worming his way back with ease as it was.

****

The next two days were repeats. A good-morning call from Dex. A good-morning text and lunch delivery from Dieter, and a flower delivery at the Burberry mansion. I now possessed a bouquet of pink roses with a card reading: *I'm sorry I took you for granted, Love Dieter*; and a bouquet of Lily of the Valley with a card reading: *Please let us start fresh, Love Dieter.*

I rocked up at my parents' house for another Friday night dinner after Mom rang and insisted I be there. Of course, I should have guessed the reason, but it never occurred to me she'd invite Dex and Dieter too.

After a very awkward greeting in the lounge room with nonalcoholic drinks due to their medication, Dex and Dieter sat across the dinner table from me.

"I wanted to apologize about our last dinner," Mom said, "and to make sure you two were all right after that nasty scare."

"We're fine," Dieter said.

"I will be once I get this cast off." Dex tapped the cast on his arm. "At least it's not as sore now."

"I'm glad." Mom passed the plates around the table and eyed us. "How's work, Tiffany?"

"Good. I bumped into Ozwald Delante in the

elevator the other morning and he talked to me." I placed a helping of vegetables on my plate. "He complimented me on my dress."

Mom beamed. "The man has good taste."

"You think?" I rolled my eyes.

Dad laughed. Mom shot him a look. Dad concentrated on his dinner plate.

"Are you working on any dresses?" Mom asked.

"I am. Prue invited me to a charity event so I'm making both our dresses."

"That's exciting." Mom's eyes gleamed.

"And what about you two? Are you back at work yet?" Mom asked.

"Dad gave me two weeks off," Dieter said. "It's rather boring being stuck at home all day. I can't wait to get back to work."

Mom nodded.

"I went into work the last two days," Dex said.

"What? You should rest," I said.

Dex grinned at me over the table. "Relax, I was there for a couple of hours each day and sat in the office."

His foot rubbed against my leg under the table. The contact soothed me. I'd missed being touched by them these past few days. It wasn't the sexual touching I missed the most, it was the affection and caring touches that let me know they loved me. Although gazing at them across the table sitting together, my mind wandered to the last time they'd touched me sexually. Okay, so I missed that too.

Dad asked Dex about a Dodge and the three men launched into a discussion about cars. I tuned out. Engines and pistons weren't my thing. It'd be like me talking to them about fashion designs. Their eyes would glaze over too.

Mom smiled the entire night. She was putting on a good show of trying to accept our arrangement. I was glad I hadn't told her or Dad what happened between us this week. It'd make her question our relationship more. Our relationship? Since when did I think of us together again?

Shit.

"Thanks for dinner, Mom." I stood once everyone finished eating. It was time to get the hell out of here.

"My pleasure. I still want you to consider what I said last time."

She just couldn't let it go.

Dad frowned. "I'll drive you all home since neither of you can drive right now."

Ugh. Dad knew I wasn't living with them, but he picked up his car keys and led us to the car. I climbed into the front seat next to Dad leaving Dieter and Dex in the back seat. At least I wouldn't have to be close to one of them. As it was, my body thrummed with the need for Dex to touch me again.

Dad drove us to Dieter's apartment.

"Thank you for the ride," Dieter said and climbed out.

"Yeah, thanks." Dex followed him.

I sat in the car and watched them.

"Off you go then," Dad said.

"But…"

"You might have fooled your mom tonight, but I know you haven't been living here all week. Whatever it is, don't you think you should talk it over?" he asked.

"Fine." I yanked the door handle and jumped out of the car.

Dex and Dieter watched me with eagerness. I slammed the car door and stalked into the apartment building with them close behind me. Dieter unlocked the door, and we all stood in the entryway.

"We should talk," I said and walked over to the sofa.

Dieter and Dex followed me into the lounge room, but they stood at the floor-to-ceiling window. Neither of them seemed to want to come near me. I stared at them, and they stared back.

"This is ridiculous." I stood. "I'm going. I'll call an Uber and be out of here in a jiff."

"Ah, Tiff, your dad is still waiting at the curb," Dieter said.

"Fuck." I sat back down.

Dieter clenched his hands in front of him. "I know I hurt you, but please, Tiff? I've missed you. I love you."

I flicked my gaze to Dex.

"Make him beg, Fluff," Dex said.

I nodded.

## Chapter Twenty-One

"I'll beg and grovel at your feet for the rest of my life if you'll say yes to us being together again." Dieter dropped to his knees at my feet. "I'll kiss your feet too."

I jerked my feet back. "Don't you dare, they're ticklish."

"I know." A tiny smile twitched at Dieter's lips.

"I can think of better places you can kiss me."

Dieter's eyes lit with heat. "Me too. I'll worship every place you want me to."

Dex shoved his hand in his jeans pocket.

"What about Dex? You hurt him too," I said.

"If that's what he wants, then I'll kiss him too," Dieter said.

"I always knew you liked my junk," Dex said with a smirk.

Dieter rolled his eyes. "I'd do anything Tiff wanted including kissing your hairy ass if that's what she wanted."

I giggled.

"So, what's it going to be?" Dieter asked. "Am I kissing your cute butt or his hairy ass?"

"Stop." I laughed clutching my stomach. "Dex's ass isn't hairy."

Dieter kissed my ankle. "What about here?"

Tingles danced up my legs.

Dieter kissed my knee. "Or here."

Flutters of desire spread through my lower limbs.

"Dex wanted to punch you in the nuts and make you watch us have sex," I said.

Dieter's face twisted into a grimace. "If that's what you both want." He stood with a push off the floor with his uninjured arm and stood in front of Dex. "Go on, I deserve it."

Dex peered over Dieter's shoulder at me. "I would, but we're both injured."

Dieter let out a loud breath.

"We can still do the second part though," Dex said.

"Okay. Here again or the bedroom?" Dieter asked.

"The bed will be more comfortable for my arm," Dex said.

"Hang on a minute." I waved my hands to get their attention. "Who said I'm staying?"

Their smiles fell. Dieter's face paled. Was he about to vomit?

"Just messing with you." A grin tugged at my lips. "I'll text Dad so he can go home." I thumbed my cell, texted Dad and Prue. Prue sent back two eggplants. I laughed, stood, and made my way to Dieter's bedroom. "Are you two coming?" I called over my shoulder.

"I'll wait until you're riding me," Dex said.

They followed me into Dieter's bedroom. I took in Dex's cast and sling. Stepped closer to Dex and eased the hem of his t-shirt up his body and over his limbs. I traced the expanse of his tight muscles and tattoos with my fingers.

"Kiss me," Dex whispered.

I brushed my lips against his in a smooth caress. Dex's lips met mine in a gentleness that spoke volumes of his feelings for me. A quiet moan of rightness left my mouth and entered his. He swallowed my moan, took my love into his body, and wrapped his uninjured arm around my waist. With gentleness he lured me closer. I resisted the urge to plaster myself to his front and jostle his arm in the process. I broke the kiss and unbuttoned his jeans, slid them down his thighs, and kneeled at his feet to undo his shoes.

"On the bed," I said.

"Yes, Nurse." He shuffled to the end of the bed.

I tugged his shoes, socks, and jeans from his feet. "Stop with the nurse fantasy." I flicked a glance at Dieter behind me. "Undress, Dieter, and get in bed with us."

"But?" Dieter asked.

"We're an 'us', so in bed with us."

He tugged his tie free and unbuttoned his bright blue shirt.

Dex shifted up the bed, laid down, and watched me watch Dieter undress. God, they were both so gorgeous. Fit and tanned. Muscled, and the main one large and erect jutting from their bodies with an eagerness I experienced.

Dieter laid on the other side of the bed. I took in the sight of them both like this, ready and waiting for me. They'd always be like this for me. I had to believe it. Had to believe in our love and that it would endure even in the hardest of times like them both almost dying. I unzipped the back of my dress and let it drop to my feet.

Their breathing faltered and their dicks jerked with need for me.

I wet my lips and unbuckled my lace bra. It too fell to the floor. I teased my fingers into the waistband of my panties.

"Take them off and come here," Dex said. "I might not have the use of both arms, but I can still love you."

I slid my panties to the floor, crawled onto the bed, and placed a chaste kiss on Dieter's lips taking him by surprise. He reached for me and winced in pain.

"Damn it," he ground out.

"Karma," I said. "You're meant to watch."

I settled over Dex's hips, leaned down, and brushed my nipples along his chest.

"Let me suck them," Dex said.

I shifted higher and shoved my breasts into Dex's face. He ravished them with eager kisses. Dieter shifted and a warm breeze blew against my dampness. I gasped.

"I'm watching," Dieter said.

Dex's fingers stroked my wet folds and spread them open. Dieter blew me again.

"You're so pretty, Tiff," Dieter said, his words drifting into my aching mound. "Sit on Dex's dick, let me watch you."

I eased down until Dex's erection nudged at my entrance.

"Wait, condom," I said.

"Here." Dieter fetched a wrapper from the bedside table, ripped open the packet with his teeth, and handed it to Dex.

Dex rolled on the condom and slid his hand to my hip and guided me back down. I eased onto Dex's erection with slowness letting the sensation of him filling me take every nerve ending in my body on a quiver of pleasure. I swayed my hips again. Dex's hand urged my hip faster. I let him set the pace, he always knew what I needed better than me. My body coiled tight. Dieter's warm breath gusted between my spread legs and the place I joined with Dex.

"I could watch you two all night," Dieter said.

I puffed out a breath and eased into a sitting position. "It's not a punishment if you're enjoying it."

"You're trying to punish me?" Dieter shifted to look in my face.

I bit my top lip. "I guess not." And I wasn't. I understood he liked to watch. I swayed my hips and fumbled with my hands looking for the perfect place to put them without hurting Dex's arm.

"Here." Dieter held his arm in front of my chest.

I wrapped my fingers around his forearm like it was a pole and gripped his flesh while I rode Dex. Up and down. Dex's cock worked my insides into putty, but no matter how hard I rode him I couldn't reach the orgasm hanging inside my body.

"Rub her clit," Dex said.

*Yes. Why didn't he do it?*

"May I?" Dieter asked me.

I nodded my head. Someone touch it now.

"Words, Tiff, let me know it's okay for me to touch you."

"Yes, Dieter, yes." I rode Dex even faster. Moisture poured from me at the mere thought of Dieter touching me.

Two of Dieter's fingers found my hard nub. I gripped his arm tighter. He spread my wetness over and around it, then got serious with a firm pressure that made me see glistening stars in my vision. I tightened around Dex. My hips lost their rhythm, but Dex's hand kept me going never letting me stop the torturous pace. My thighs quivered and clenched. Every pleasure point focused on Dieter's fingers and Dex's cock.

My release detonated with an explosion deep inside sending quivers of pleasure racing through my body. Dex rocked inside me. Dieter's fingers strummed my throbbing clit. Dex yanked my hip down onto him and exploded in orgasm with a sexy grunt. I dropped my hips on him with all my weight. Dieter's fingers stopped moving and just sat there experiencing both our orgasms.

"You two are so hot together." Dieter's voice came out husky with arousal.

I stared at his raging erection. "Make yourself come, Dieter. I want to watch."

He swiped his fingers through my wetness and wrapped his hand around his shaft without further encouragement. I watched, mesmerized as his palm slid over the hardness of his cock, the veins bulged and throbbed with each stroke. Pre-cum leaked from his tip making his palm slide easier. He jerked harder. His balls drew up tight, and he jetted out so hard his release landed on his chest. He laid back on the bed with a relaxed sigh.

I eased off Dex, tugged the condom off, and walked to the bathroom. I returned with a damp washcloth for them both. I wiped between Dex's legs first then turned my attention to Dieter's chest and cleaned up his mess. Both smiled at me.

"Don't call me Nurse," I said. I tossed the washcloths in the bathroom and slid on one of Dieter's t-shirts. Where was my favorite? In the other bedroom. Should I sleep there tonight or here? "Do you need your medication before I go to bed?"

"Yes, please, Nurse Herringer," Dex said with a cheeky grin.

"What do you mean, go to bed?" Dieter sat up with care. "You're sleeping here. We all are every night."

"I wasn't sure," I said.

"We're all sure. From here on out," Dieter said.

"Okay." I smiled. "I'll get your meds and be right back."

Happiness filled every step, every breath I inhaled, and every bone in my body. Forgiveness was about the one doing the forgiving, because I'd never felt better about my love for Dieter and Dex and what the future would hold for us.

**\*\*\*\***

"What's all this?" I sat up in the bed.

"Breakfast in bed," Dieter said.

"But you don't like food in your bed."

"I'll make an exception for you." Dieter placed a

plate of buttered toast on the bed next to the cup of coffee. "There's more." He left the bedroom and returned with a bunch of deep red roses interspersed with delicate white baby's breath. "I love you forever."

Emotion clouded my vision. Dieter slid back into bed. I slid my arm around his waist.

"I love you too."

Dieter tipped my chin up with his finger and placed his lips on mine. He kissed me with passionate love, morning breath and all. The man loved me. Our lips heated under the others, our tongues tangled. The kiss grew fervent. I ran my hands up his body and connected with the bandage on his shoulder. I broke the kiss and traced the white bandage.

"I almost lost you," I whispered.

"I almost lost you too." He kissed my nose. "I saw a therapist last week. They said my reaction was due to post-traumatic stress at being shot."

"That's good you talked to someone." I traced a finger from his forehead to his chin.

"I'll be fine. I won't let anything come between us again."

"Even my mom and your mom?" I frowned.

"Even the entire world," he declared.

And I believed him.

"Where's Dex?" I asked.

"He went to the gym."

"Already? Should he be doing that yet?" I bit my top lip. "Do you think we can...?"

"Without Dex?"

I nodded. As much as I loved having them both together, I didn't want it to always be the three of us. I'd loved them each separately for years, I couldn't turn it off.

"I'll call him and ask." Dieter stood from the bed

and picked up his cell. "Dex…"

Dieter was quiet. I couldn't hear Dex.

"Give me the phone." I held out my hand.

Dieter handed me his cell.

"Hi, Dex, what are you doing at the gym?" I asked. "Should you be going yet?"

"Hey, Fluff, I have one broken arm, not all of me. I'd go insane if I had to sit at home until it healed."

I sighed. "Okay. How long until you're home?"

"I'm on my way now. What's up?"

"Dieter made me breakfast in bed," I said.

"And?" he asked.

"And now I want sex." I smiled at Dieter.

"Start without me," Dex said.

"Yeah?"

"Yeah, go for it, I'm not cockblocking anyone," he said.

"Thanks, Dex. Love you."

"Love you too, Fluff."

I hung up the phone. "He said it's okay. What about you? Are you okay if Dex and I have sex without you?"

"Tiff." He crawled back into bed. "I'm okay with anything you want."

"Yeah?" I slid a leg over his and rubbed it against his calf. "I want you right now."

"How do you want me?" He rose an eyebrow.

"Any way you can manage with your shoulder."

"Roll over on your side."

We faced each other. He opened a condom and the crinkle sound of a wrapper filled the bedroom.

"Here, let me." I took the condom from his hand and rolled it on his erection. I swung my leg over his waist and guided his hard cock inside me.

Dieter groaned and touched his forehead to mine.

I cupped his face with my hands. We rocked in a lazy give-and-take. A slow build of pleasure, each rock so gentle it was like we were saying how much we loved each other. Our lips melded in a slow kiss. We could have stayed like this for hours loving each other.

A cool breeze hit our warm bodies as Dex tugged the covers from our bodies and slid onto the bed behind me. His lips landed on the back of my neck. I arched into his touch but kept my lips with Dieter's.

Dex slid something slippery between my ass cheeks. I clenched on instinct, but he rubbed it up and down until pleasure tingles ran from where he touched me. Dieter kept loving me with soft kisses and the slow slide of his cock.

Dex pressed against my rear hole. I paused the kiss. Dex retreated and I resumed kissing Dieter again. Dex pressed again. I didn't pause this time. Dex retreated and thrust. Each time was easier, more slippery, more exciting. Whatever he was doing felt good until he drove it in all the way.

I reared back with a yelp. "What is that?"

Whatever he'd thrust inside had my ass burning and an intense sensation of fullness filled my body.

"I picked up a butt plug." He kissed my lower back. "It's a little one to get you started."

I jerked with sparks of pleasure and pain.

Dieter thrust again. Every nerve ending sparked to life.

"Oh my God," I cried.

Dex kissed his way up my back to my ear. "I can't wait until you're taking both of us at once."

God, yes, I wanted that. I imagined the butt plug was Dex. Dieter's cock rubbed against my insides, the bundle of nerves buried deep throbbed, and one more slide of his engorged head across them had me coming around him and the hardness in my ass. I cried out. My body shook with the intensity of the orgasm. Dieter thrust into my orgasm and came with me. Dex rubbed his erection against my spread ass and spurted his warm release between my cheeks.

I dropped my forehead to Dieter's chest and breathed with raggedness trying to calm my racing body.

Dex withdrew the butt plug and disappeared to the bathroom. The shower turned on.

"We should join him," Dieter said.

"I can't move," I mumbled.

Dieter chuckled. "Our turn to clean you up."

He disappeared into the bathroom and returned with a damp washcloth. He wiped between my legs making me jerk with the sensitivity still running through my engorged flesh and the pull on my ass. If that was small, it'd take a bit of practice before I'd take either of their dicks.

But we had all the time in the world.

I rose from the bed with reluctance, stuck my head in the bathroom, and called out, "I'm going to work in the sewing room. I'm inspired."

Dex stepped out of the shower and swapped places with Dieter.

"Are you working on the dresses for the charity event?" Dieter asked through the open shower door.

"I am. I'm way behind schedule if I'm doing these gowns justice."

"They'll be beautiful like everything else you make," Dieter said. "Do you have a date?"

"Well," I said, "there are these two gorgeous men who are amazing in bed I'm thinking of taking as my dates."

Dieter grinned and shut the shower door.

Dex held up the butt plug. "That's good because

this guy here would make a terrible date."

I laughed. "I don't know, he was pretty good in bed too. Maybe he can come along?"

## Chapter Twenty-Two

The ivory silk gown with hand-stitched beading fitted me like a glove. It should since I'd made it. The two months whizzed by, and I'd never been happier than when we were all together. Dieter and Dex. My two loves. Dieter worshipped me, as he said he would. Dex was Dex, and I was glad he hadn't changed. As I stared at my reflection in the mirror, there was one thing holding me back from enjoying having my two men: I'd never get married.

I ran my hands over the beading. What would it be like to walk down an aisle? To declare my love forever. We said those words a lot, but a wedding was special, the words had meaning along with the signed papers. Perhaps Mom was right, and I should've given more consideration to choosing one of them instead of both, but I'd never go back now.

A soft knock rapped on the bedroom door. My old bedroom in Dieter's apartment was my dressing room now, since his bedroom didn't have enough hanging space for all of our clothes. Dex kept his things in the other bedroom, but we all slept together every night.

"Tiff, we need to go," Dieter called through the door.

"Almost ready," I called back.

I fastened the beads on the lace sleeves at my wrists and hurried to the door. Dieter stepped back in a flourish of black and white, stunning in a tuxedo, but then he always was handsome in his suit and ties.

His mouth fell open.

I tapped his chin shut. "You like?"

"I love," he blabbered, and his eyes glistened.

*Were tears in his eyes?*

I strutted out into the living room; pride filled every step I took. This gown was the best garment I'd ever made. I suppose I'd put a lot of dreaming into it. The night would be fabulous with my two loves by my side.

Dex jangled the keys by the front door, his thick shoulders jiggled making the tuxedo jacket draw tight. I don't know who was more relieved for him to have the cast removed, him or me. He turned in slow motion. I held my breath. It wasn't every day I saw Dex in a tuxedo and he was more thigh-clenching sexy than I ever thought possible.

"Look at you," I said. "You're so sexy."

"Yeah?" He raised an eyebrow. "You are one beautiful woman, Fluff, talented too. Your dress is to die for."

An old pain flared in my chest. They both might have died the night of the carjacking. I blinked back the image before I ruined my makeup.

"I can't have that." I placed my hands on my hips. "Perhaps I should take the dress off?"

Dex slid his arms around my waist. Warmth and comfort swarmed my body with his embrace. It was so good to have both his arms around me again.

"Dieter and I will take it off." He fiddled with the buttons on the back of my dress.

Dieter slapped his hand. "Later, we have to wine and dine our girl first."

"And sixty-nine." I giggled.

"Anything you want." Dieter's breath gusted over my ear.

I shivered. Anything. Tonight, I wanted them both at the same time. They'd prepared me enough and yet they'd still held out on anal sex.

"I want you both tonight," I said with a lusty

exhale.

Dex's fingers tightened on my waist. Dieter's breath came faster on my skin.

"Let's go." Dieter marched out of the apartment like it was on fire.

Dex chuckled, gathered my hand in his, and led me from the apartment to Dieter's Jag. They'd fought over who'd drive tonight in a rather immature way that made me laugh and put their names in a bowl and draw one out. Dex wasn't happy, but he was still having therapy on his arm to rebuild his muscles after having it in a cast for six weeks. The man was determined to recover.

Dieter held the door open for me like a chauffeur. I eased into the car and settled the length of the gown around my legs. Dex climbed in next to me.

"What are you doing?" Dieter asked.

"Riding in the back and keeping Tiff company." Dex smirked.

"Keep your hands to yourself until after the dinner," Dieter said.

"What about my hands?" I wiggled my fingers in the air.

Dieter rolled his eyes. "You two are as bad as each other sometimes."

"We love you." I grinned.

Dex chuckled and took my hand in his. That was all, but the warmth of his palm made me imagine it in other places. I fidgeted on the seat.

"Stop wriggling," Dex said. "You're giving me a boner."

"What? Why?" I stopped moving.

"I'm thinking about you doing that on my dick with this dress on."

I giggled. "There's too much material, it'd get in

the way."

"Dieter can hold it for us." He winked.

"Would you two stop!" Dieter said. "I don't want to walk into the charity dinner with an erection. My mother and father are coming tonight."

"They are?" I asked.

"Yes, they've had tickets for ages. It's one of those high socialite events my mother likes."

"Oh God." I hung my head between my knees and sucked in oxygen. The woman hated me. Dieter's relationship with her had been even more strained since he'd told her about our relationship and our living arrangements. It was the reason I'd kept a few things at my apartment and not let the lease go. A backup plan if things went to shit again when I shouldn't want or need one, but there was a small part of me waiting for this all to end.

"Relax." Dex rubbed my back. "She might not even talk to us."

I raised my head and met his gaze. His gaze filled with a sharing compassion. He understood my anxiety. Our relationship wasn't conventional nor was it looked upon favorably.

Dieter drew the car up to the valet parking at the Beverly Intercontinental Hotel, a grand building with curved arches and flags fluttering in the evening breeze. Dex made sure my dress was out of the car and took my arm. Dieter handed the keys to the valet and secured my other arm around his. Completion filled every piece of me with them both by my side. I didn't care what anyone thought, this was my life, and I loved them both equally.

We made our way to the ballroom through the opulent interior of the hotel. Inside, I gazed around in awe at the chandeliers, the tables laid with exquisite bunches of flowers in soft pinks and mauves. A similar glow of lights lit the room giving it an ethereal quality, but it didn't hide the faces of the famous people seated around the ballroom, from actors and actresses to well-known business tycoons, and my boss Ozwald Delante. I smiled when his gaze met mine.

Dieter and Dex escorted me to our table, one on either side of me, but neither held my arm anymore like they knew people wouldn't approve of our relationship. It was something we'd all have to get used to, but maybe one day people wouldn't frown upon relationships with more than one person. I shoved the thought aside and sat with an unladylike eagerness to take it all in. Every petal, light, the silverware, even the tablecloths. I ran my fingers over the damask linens. Dex and Dieter sat on either side of me.

"And you rushed me out of the door," I said.

Dieter shrugged and surveyed the packed room. Immaculately dressed people filled the other tables already. Where were Prue and Mr. Burberry? Speaking of the couple. Prue sashayed into the ballroom in the amethyst gown I'd created for her. The material clung to her ample breasts and fluttered over her growing baby bump. She gave the impression of being the epitome of glowing motherhood. Mr. Burberry, dressed in a tux, had his arm wrapped around Prue's waist in a possessive hold like he knew she was the most beautiful woman in the room tonight. She might well be.

"About time," I said as Prue settled in the chair next to Dex.

"Sorry," Prue said. "All my friends pulled out. The idiots ate dodgy leftovers and are all puking their guts up."

I wrinkled my nose.

"I needed to find more people to fill our table. Otherwise, it would've looked bad for Will." A sparkle lit her eyes.

"Um, who?" A trickle of apprehension ran down my spine.

Dad and Mom walked into the ballroom dressed in a tuxedo and a sparkling emerald dress I'd made her for my cousin's wedding last year.

"My parents?" I squeaked. So much for a fun night of wining and dining. With Dieter's parents and mine in the same room, and our moms not seeing eye to eye on our relationship, it would be a disaster.

"Hello," Dad said and tugged out Mom's chair.

"Thanks for coming on such short notice, Gabe." Mr. Burberry shook hands with Dad.

"Our pleasure." Dad sat next to Mom leaving five empty seats. Who else did Prue invite?

I kept my gaze glued to the doorway. Kennedy walked inside wearing a turquoise gown I'd made Prue— I guess they were almost the same size. A silver fox in a tuxedo followed. Sienna swept into the room in a fuchsia pink gown, another one of my designs I'd made for Sienna to take on her trip in case she ended up somewhere fancy. Dex stood, greeted his mom with a kiss on her cheek, and pulled out the chair next to Dieter. Dieter shot Dex a glare. Dex shrugged and resumed his seat.

"Tiffany, I'm so glad I have a reason to wear this dress you made me," Sienna said.

"You look gorgeous," I said.

"I wrangled my lawyer in too," Mr. Burberry said. "Marco, this is Gabe and Louise, you know Dex, Tiffany, and Dieter."

The men greeted Marco with handshakes. But who would fill the last two empty chairs?

Dieter rubbed his hand on my thigh under the table. "I'm sorry I didn't warn you, but my parents are sitting with us."

I glanced to Dex for help, but he was chatting with Prue. Traitors, all of them. Could I go home now?

"Why?" I hissed under my breath.

Dieter leaned closer and whispered in my ear, "I wanted them to see how happy we are. I wanted to prove to you I don't care what my mother says, and I choose you and Dex."

A lump formed in my throat, and I placed my hand over his.

The waiters served the entrée and Dieter's parents arrived and took their seats. Fashionably late and looking gorgeous as always in a stunning Ozwald Delante gown, Mrs. Brant smiled with her plastic smile and greeted the table as a whole. Mr. Brant exhibited better manners and spoke to each of us. Dieter's mother kept her head facing the other way and talked to my mom and dad. Seemed our parents were hitting it off.

The meal might have been dog food for all I cared. I couldn't taste a thing with the churning in my stomach. The music started after the main course and Dieter took my hand and led me onto the dance floor.

"I'm sorry," he whispered.

I molded into his arms and let him lead me. Out here I pretended it was the two of us, away from the hostility of his mother and the disapproval of my mom.

"Me too," I said. "My mom isn't any better."

He pecked the tip of my nose. "We make a great pair with our mothers."

"We do," I said. "I sometimes wish they were like Dex's mom but as great as she is…"

"She has no filter." Dieter chuckled. "If I hear her tell me how handsome I look tonight one more time, I think I'll have nightmares."

I smoothed a hand over his tie. "You are

handsome and sexy, and mine."

"Always."

The waiters delivered the dessert. We made our way back to the table. Poor Kennedy seemed uncomfortable next to Mr. Burberry's lawyer Marco. Prue appeared happy though. So did Sienna. And my parents. What was going on?

"What did we miss?" I asked.

Prue bounced in her seat. "Marco has come up with a deal for you three."

"A deal?" I frowned.

"Remember I said I'd ask Will," Prue said.

"Yes, but that was months ago," I said.

"Sorry," Marco said. "I did a fair amount of research and hit dead ends, but then I came up with this." He unbuttoned his jacket and removed an envelope.

"What is it?" Dieter asked taking the envelope and opening it.

"It's a contract between you three. A business deal, if you will. It states neither of you are entitled to either of the others' money, even living together that there will be no access to any de facto entitlements should you part ways," Marco said. "I planned to give the papers to William yesterday, but I got caught up at work. I have the other contract for you to look at too." He tugged on his tie.

"Come by my house one night after work and we'll discuss that one then," Mr. Burberry said.

Marco gave a small nod and turned his attention to Dieter. "It's a basic business deal. You can either read the contract now and we'll get the formalities over with considering we have witnesses, or you can take the papers home and go over the terms then make an appointment at my office to sign the deal."

Dieter swung his gaze from the papers. "Up to

you two."

I scanned the faces at the table and settled on Mom's face. Would a contract like this get her to accept our relationship? It was worth trying.

"Read it now, Dieter," I said.

Dieter shuffled plates out of the way and laid the contract on the table in front of me. Dex leaned over one shoulder while Dieter peeped over the other. Together we read the deal. Not that I understood most of it. I doubted Dex did with all the legal jargon. Dieter would though. So would his father.

"This is good," Dieter said. "What do you think, Tiff? Dex?"

"I'm in if you are," Dex said and squeezed my shoulder. "Tiff?"

"I … um." This wasn't how I'd imagined what would in essence be our commitment to each other with disapproving mothers looking on. But what if by signing a contract both of our mothers would have peace of mind our relationship meant more to us than what they thought, and our finances were protected? "Let's do it. Who has a pen?"

Marco swiped a pen from the inside of his jacket. "Sign at all the tabs."

"Wait," Mrs. Brant said. "Can your father at least read the contract first?"

"Sure." Dieter slid the papers to his dad.

Dex shoved back his chair and held his hand out to me. "Come on, it's my turn for a dance with the most beautiful woman here."

I stood with a decadent smile. Thank goodness for Dex taking me away from the table and further judgment from Dieter's mother. Mine too. Would Mom also read the contract? I wouldn't put it past her.

Dex eased me into his hold. I placed my hand on

his arm with care, still used to being careful with the plaster.

"How's it going over there?" I asked.

Dex glanced over my shoulder. "Looks like some words are being said."

"Thanks for getting me out of there."

"Anytime. Sorry, the night hasn't been much fun. I have plans to change that later." He winked.

A snicker escaped. "I bet you do."

"It involves, me, you, Dieter, and a room upstairs."

"You booked a room?" I asked.

"For the weekend." He beamed.

The night held a glimmer of happiness.

## Chapter Twenty-Three

"May I cut in?" a familiar voice said.

Dex scowled.

"Mr. Delante," I said.

"Okay." Dex kissed my cheek and handed me to my boss.

Mr. Delante spun me in his arms. I laughed and fell into step.

"I needed to ask about this dress you're wearing," Mr. Delante said. "It could be a showstopper in one of my fashion shows."

"Thank you." My cheeks warmed with his praise. "It's one of mine."

"All of it?" His eyebrows rose.

"Yes, design to completion. I made all the dresses at our table too, except for Mrs. Brant's of course, she's wearing one of your designs."

"Did you use the Delante premises?"

"No, at home. I've turned poor Dieter's sitting room into a sewing room." I smiled at the image of all my gear taking over Dieter's apartment and he hadn't complained once.

"The man I intruded your dance with?"

"That was Dex." Panic bubbled in the bottom of my stomach he'd ask more questions about my living arrangements. What would I say? I shouldn't have to hide our relationship.

"I have to say, you are talented. This gown is special."

He didn't even ask. The panic fluttered free from my stomach and left me glowing at his praise again. He twirled me around the dance floor like Fred Astaire and walked me back to the table.

"Tiffany, thank you for the lovely dance. Come

see me Monday morning in my office and I'll have you transferred to the couture gowns for the fall fashion show. Who knows, we may even showcase an original Tiffany Herringer gown," Mr. Delante said.

"Thank you," I gushed. My legs wobbled with the surge of adrenaline.

Dex wrenched my chair out before I fell over. I sunk into it gratefully. As soon as Mr. Delante was far enough away Mom squealed.

"Did that just happen?" I asked.

"I knew it," Mom said, the grin on her face so large her cheeks would hurt tomorrow. "You're going to be famous, Tiffany."

"I still have a lot to learn, Mom." I picked up the pen. "Now, where are the papers?"

Mr. Brant passed them across the table. Mrs. Brant put her hand on his arm.

"Sweetheart, he's a grown man, let him live his life," Mr. Brant said.

Her arm fell to the table with a thud. "What will people say?"

Mr. Brant brushed her cheek. "They'll say whatever they want, and they always will no matter what, you should know that more than anyone. Remember when they said you were having an affair with your costar Radan Pette?"

"That wasn't true," she said, her gorgeous face marred with a scowl.

"Yes," he said.

"But this is." She waved her hand at us.

"Let people talk. Besides, all publicity is good publicity, isn't that the saying?" Mr. Brant said.

She let out a strangled sound. "Fine. Be discreet, please."

"I can't guarantee it," Dieter said and took the

pen from my hand and signed his name to the deal.

"Neither can I." Dex signed his name.

"We'll try," I said and placed my signature on the papers.

"If two of you would like to be witnesses," Marco said.

"I'll do it," Prue said and snatched the papers from my hand. "It was my idea."

Mr. Burberry chuckled and signed his name after Prue. He handed the papers to Marco. Marco signed the deal completing the transaction. This night had gone from bad to amazing, and with Dex booking us a room I couldn't wait for the dinner to be over.

"To you three." Prue raised her glass.

Everyone raised their glasses and toasted us. As good as this was there was still the nagging feeling I needed more. I drained my glass then excused myself to go to the ladies' room. Prue raced to go with me.

"What's up? I thought this would help," Prue asked as we slipped inside the opulent restroom.

I slid onto the sofa in the waiting area. "I don't know. The deal was good, and the contract might have helped with Dieter's and my moms, but…"

"Spit it out."

"I guess I'd imagined something romantic when signing the rest of my life to the men I love."

Prue sat next to me. "Most men suck at romance. Besides, multiple orgasms are romantic."

I laughed. "Dex booked a room for the weekend."

"There you go." Prue slapped my arm and raced into the toilet. "Stupid pregnancy bladder," she grumbled from behind the door.

I stared at the garden painting on the wall. Now that was romantic.

"What are you staring at?" Prue stepped in front

of me.

I blinked in a rush. "Nothing." I stood. "I'll be out in a minute. You don't need to wait."

"Okay." She frowned but left.

Alone in the restroom, I stepped closer to the painting and ran a finger over the pink flowers. They reminded me of the pink roses Dieter sent me. Was I overthinking this? Not everyone got married. I freshened up and returned to the table. Dad was the only one sitting there.

"Where is everyone?" I asked.

Dad smiled and stood. "I'll show you. They went this way."

I fell into step with Dad, as we left the ballroom and rode the elevator to the ground floor.

"Did they leave?" It made little sense, since Dex booked us a room.

"You'll see." Dad threaded his arm through mine and walked through a large glass door into an outdoor garden.

Everyone from our table stood in front of a fountain. The fountain squirted colored water to the beats of classical music drifting from the hidden speakers.

"This is pretty. Why didn't they wait for us?"

Dad walked me along the path toward our group. "Prue said you wanted something romantic, and Dieter suggested this."

"Dieter suggested what?"

Dex and Dieter stood in front of me and the fountain with the others gathered on the sides. They held their hands out to me. Dad released my arm, and I took Dex's and Dieter's hands.

"What's going on?" I asked.

Dieter smiled. "You wanted romantic, so we're giving it to you. I promised you once I'd give you anything you wanted, and tonight I'm promising it to you again in front of everyone."

I glanced at the small crowd.

Dex squeezed my hand. "You look like a bride in that dress. We figured we'd make you one."

I gasped. They both kissed my hands.

"I don't know wedding vows," Dex said. "But I promise to always love you."

"I promise to always love you too," I said through the intense emotion clogging my throat.

Dex kissed me on the lips with a soft chaste kiss. So unlike him, but we couldn't go at it like usual at our wedding. Holy shit, this was my wedding, as close as I'd ever get to marrying the two men I loved unless they made polyamory legal one day. Tears glazed my eyes and blurred my vision. I blinked to clear them. I didn't want to miss either of their faces.

"I promise." Dieter gulped. "I promise to love you, to cherish you, and to always put you first."

"I promise to love you, to—" Dieter's lips crushed mine in a deliberate kiss to stop me promising more.

"That's all you need to promise me," he whispered.

"Congratulations," Prue cheered. "You're now a threesome."

I laughed and hugged her.

Mom hugged me next. "This was beautiful." She sniffed. "You look like a radiant bride, Tiffany. I'm happy for you too."

I sniffed too. Mom would stop with the marriage talk and prenuptial agreements. Tonight ticked all her boxes for my future, including a job promotion. I moved on and hugged everyone except Dieter's mom, but she smiled at me. She might never accept our relationship in full, but she'd made a start by coming down to the garden and we had a lifetime to figure things out. So long as I had Dieter and Dex, it'd work out.

This night turned into more than I ever dreamed, and it wasn't over.

\*\*\*\*

"I'd carry you, but my arm might not be strong enough yet," Dex said unlocking the hotel room door.

I smoothed my hands up his back. "I used to think it annoyed me when you picked me up and carried me, but I miss it."

"Me too." He swept us inside and kissed me with so much desire I wrenched at his buttons. They popped free, and I slid my hands inside his shirt to the warmth of his bare skin tracing every bulge of muscle.

Dex forced me against the wall trapping my wandering hands between us. His lips held me hostage. I squirmed but didn't wriggle free. Dieter's hands slid around my ankles and tugged my shoes off my feet. He ran his hands up my legs and teased the sides of my lace panties over my hips with his fingers. Dex ground his erection against me then he stepped back leaving me aching for the pressure of his body against mine.

I didn't ache for too long. Dieter's head disappeared under my dress, and he nuzzled me through my panties. His tongue dipped to the crease and nudged into where I wanted him without the clothes in the way.

"Take them off." I tugged at my dress trying to wrench the expanse of fabric out of my way.

Dex grabbed my hands and pinned them to the wall. "Not yet."

"Dex," I pleaded. "Naked is better."

He grinned. "All we've thought about since you stepped out in that white dress is fucking you in it."

Moisture flooded. Dieter's tongue soaked my

panties, but they were wet from my arousal too. I ached for more from both of them. Dex lowered his head to my chest and kissed along the top of the dress hugging my breasts. My nipples hardened and scraped against the fabric. Dex nuzzled my breasts, finding my hard nipples through the fabric, and he drew one into his mouth.

I gazed down at them both. Dieter on his knees worshipping me in his tuxedo was the sexiest sight. And Dex's mouth working over the fabric leaving damp patches on my dress. At this rate, we'd ruin the dress, but I didn't care.

When I thought I'd almost come from their teasing, Dieter slid my panties down my legs and stood with a triumphant grin.

"I think she's ready," he said.

"Yeah," Dex said taking the panties and scrunching them in his hand. "On the bed, Fluff." He tugged my hands until I walked over to the bed then he placed a hand on my chest and urged me back. The backs of my knees hit the mattress, and I tumbled onto the bed. Dex dropped to his knees and his head disappeared under my dress. One swipe of his tongue over my aching clit, and I jumped.

Dieter undressed, his gaze glued to mine while Dex's tongue fluttered against my clit with such irregularity he aroused me to the point of madness.

Dex bunched my dress to my waist and breathed hard. "Fuck, it's hot under there."

I giggled at his cheeks tinged with pink. "I told you to take the dress off."

"Nope." Dieter rolled on a condom and joined me on the bed.

I ran my hands over his chest and shoulders, stroked the scar of his bullet wound. So close to losing him. The scar would always be a reminder of how quick life could change.

Dieter tugged me on top of him. "Don't think about it."

He slid into my wetness and we both groaned. We ground together in a brutal rhythm both taking what we needed at the moment—a connection, a passion, an aliveness to the feelings of his cock sliding inside me. The pressure built. My inner muscles clenched on his cock. He stopped moving. I tried chasing my orgasm, but I needed him with me. I sat on him a quivering mess of need longing for release.

Dex brushed my hair aside, kissed the back of my neck, and slid two slippery lube-coated fingers into my ass. Pleasure sparked, and I swayed my hips on Dieter again slower this time getting a feel for the peak again with Dex's fingers pumping inside too. Dex removed his fingers, and I whimpered. He pressed against my ass with his slick cock.

I held my breath.

"Breathe," he said.

I let out my breath, and he thrust inside. Dieter gathered my face in his hands.

"Are you okay?"

I took another breath and nodded. "Yes."

Dex eased out and slid back in.

"Oh," I said.

"Oh, good?" Dex asked.

"More than good." It was. Both of them inside me was something I'd fantasied about for a while now and tonight of all nights made it perfect. We'd signed a deal to protect our finances, but it was more. We'd promised each other our love forever.

Dex pumped his cock inside me with slowness. He made my insides burn with pleasure. And then Dieter thrust too. Deep inside sparks of pleasure so intense made me drop my head to Dieter's chest. I couldn't move even if I wanted to. The pleasure was too much. Their cocks rubbed in tandem. One in, one out. How were they so perfectly in sync that I couldn't catch a break in the building intensity? In. Out. In. Out. My body shuddered. My breathing faltered. The orgasm started slow, a tiny flutter inside, and then Dex's cock thrust inside again. The orgasm rippled so hard my ass clenched around his cock while I bucked back into him.

"Fuck," Dex ground out.

I laid all my weight on Dieter, my body no longer felt like my own. Dieter stroked my hair then thrust inside me again. The pleasure I thought had ended burst to life with urgency.

"Faster," I panted.

Dieter pounded into me until I chased another orgasm. Dex bunched my dress higher and joined Dieter in time. I screamed with the intensity of the climax. Dex joined me, but Dieter kept going through my orgasm, and then he exploded on my oversensitive flesh. Flutters of aftershocks quivered against them both.

Neither of us moved for a long time. Dex held half his weight on top of me and brushed the occasional kiss against my neck. Dieter ran his hands up my arms, but I couldn't take my weight off him. Dex stood and disappeared into the bathroom. The shower turned on.

"I need a shower too," I said. "But I don't know if I can move."

Dieter eased me off him and helped me into a sitting position. He unbuttoned my dress and slipped it from my body. We shuffled into the bathroom and shower with Dex. This shower was nowhere near big enough for three, but we washed, dried, and fell back into bed.

I laid my head on Dex's chest and Dieter spooned

me from behind. My insides fluttered at the remembered pleasure. Next time I wanted to experience Dieter from behind while Dex was in front. Hopefully, we'd experience a lot of things in our future together in and out of bed, but in bed was by far the happiest time in my life with the two men I loved, and I never needed to worry about who I loved because they both loved me too.

**** 

The setting sun blazed orange in the sky and over us in the hotel pool. I lounged against Dieter in the shallow end while Dex swam laps. His determination to build strength back up in his arm wouldn't let him lounge around the entire weekend, but if it meant he'd pick me up and carry me again, then I was all for it.

Dieter stroked my damp hair from my shoulders. "Last night after you fell asleep, Dex and I had an idea."

"Hmm," I said with laziness. The night and morning in bed with them both had turned my body and mind to mush.

"Would you like to buy a house together?"

"A house?" I swam out of his arms to look him in his deep brown eyes.

"My bedroom isn't big enough for all our clothes, and when we have kids, we'll need more room," Dieter said.

"Now wait a minute, I'm twenty-three, who said I'm ready for kids?"

Dex scooped me into his arms from behind and laid his rough chin on my shoulder.

"I'm not ready for kids yet either," Dex said. "We need to do a lot more before that."

Dieter threw his hands up in the air flicking us with water. "I didn't mean now, but later."

"Yeah, much later like after Tiff has made her first million." Dex kissed my shoulder. "Let's go back to our room, this is our honeymoon."

I guess in a way it was our honeymoon since we'd sort of married each other last night in the only way three people could—with a business deal and declaring our love for each other in front of close family and friends. I'd never have to wonder what it would be like to have a wedding. I knew nothing would top the perfect moment we shared last night.

"If I didn't know any better, I'd say you two planned last night," I said.

"Who says we didn't?" Dex spun me in his arms and winked.

"So, the house?" Dieter asked.

Dieter stepped behind me and pressed his wet front to my back sending a shiver of arousal through my body.

"Will it have a pool?" I asked.

"If you want." Dieter's warm breath hit my damp neck.

"Yes," I said. I'd say yes to anything they wanted. Even kids, but not yet. Dex was right, we had a lot more to accomplish before kids came along and burst our little pleasure bubble.

Including going back to our hotel room and making love in every way possible with the two men I loved.

**The End**

THEIR LOVE DEAL

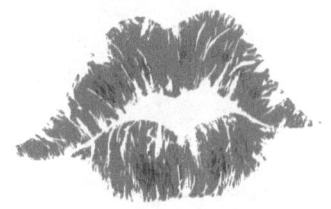

**EVERNIGHT PUBLISHING ®**

To my parents, Kelly and Annetta.
I still remember everything about our trip to
Tennessee. I love you mucho.

# Acknowledgments

Thanks for my cover designer, Kerry Prater, and editor, Lauren Hanson, for knocking out this project when life got hectic.

I never thought having internet at the drop of a hat was such a luxury until I've had to struggle through life without it. It's hard to research, download, upload, write, market, etc. without the wonderful internet. Thank you to the places with free Wifi that I was able to visit or park outside and work from my car: McDonalds, Chick Fil A, Starbucks, a few churches, a few motels, the list goes on.

Thank you to my beta readers: Carolyn Rogers, Kerry Prater, Megan Wyatt, Danielle Pfeil, and Sarah Marshall. I value your input, and thank you for taking the time to help me!

Thank you to my attorney friend, Sara, for answering all kinds of questions for me in regards to property law. Any elaborations or stretches are of my own making.

And thank you to my readers. It's a joy to write for you.

# «PROLOGUE»

*"It's always odd not* having Ramsey Jenkins around the harbor." Matthew Summers clapped the gentle giant of a man on the shoulder as he winked at his new wife, Olivia.

"Do you really have to leave town, Ramsey?" Olivia asked, her stunning blue eyes melting him to the core. Matthew had definitely met his match when Olivia came back to Friday Harbor for the summer to manage her grandparents' boutique. The beautiful and sweet woman had not only transformed his friend, but everyone she encountered. Her enthusiasm for Friday Harbor, and life in general, was contagious and Ramsey had taken an instant liking to her. Now he counted her as a friend, and considering she married his best friend, he was grateful he liked her.

"It's tradition." Ramsey tugged on her blonde ponytail.

"A chance to relax," Matthew explained. "Ramsey's one of the hardest working residents on the harbor."

"Says the guy who runs an orca tour cruise, sailing tours, and helps catch fish for my clients." Ramsey shook his head at Matthew's modesty and then continued packing his fishing gear into his truck.

"But what about the bar?" Olivia asked. "Who watches the bar while you're gone?"

"Jake."

Olivia looked doubtful and the men laughed.

"Believe it or not, he's quite the businessman," Ramsey assured her. "Besides, I have plenty of people keeping an eye on things. My brother being one of them."

"True, but Reagan is busy trying to find out who the harbor burglar is," she sighed, slightly disappointed. "How long will you be gone?" Olivia asked, taking a sip of her water bottle as she shifted her weight from one foot to the other. His friends were dressed for their evening sailing trip and her tennis shoes were laced and ready to go.

Ramsey knew their last-minute stop by his house was to wish him well on his trip.

He'd drive out to his brother's house so Reagan could help him load up on the last ferry towards Seattle. From there, he'd hop a flight to McGhee Tyson Airport in Knoxville, Tennessee. And when his feet hit the ground, he'd find a cab to take him the rest of the way to Gatlinburg, to his grandfather's cabin nestled in the Great Smoky Mountains. It was tradition, as well as a need for him. He'd been traveling each autumn to Gatlinburg since he was eleven years old, his family packing up their life in Friday Harbor after the busy season to take time to rest and replenish before the next. His brother had stopped traveling to Gatlinburg years ago, as did the rest of his family, but Ramsey needed the cabin. The peace and quiet, the secluded serenity that replenished his spirit was just as important to him as it was to those around him. Because if he didn't get the break from his hectic life at the harbor each fall, he was a bear to those around him. Mentally, physically, and spiritually, he had to escape each year for a break. He knew it. Everyone else knew it. And though it was always a bit bittersweet to leave the harbor, there was always excitement about his trip.

"Keep me updated on Reagan's investigation," he told Matthew. "Bro won't be bothering me while I'm gone, so the only news will come from you."

"Or me," Olivia added.

Ramsey grinned. "Now that would be nice. A phone call from a pretty female is always welcome."
"Hey now," Matthew teased, sliding a protective arm around Olivia and tucking her into his side. "This one's taken."

"A shame too." Ramsey rubbed a hand over his scraggily beard. "Because I'm pretty sure Olivia would have fallen in love with me right quick if you hadn't stepped in."

Flashing her dazzling smile, Olivia kissed Ramsey's cheek, her blue eyes turning serious. "Take care of yourself, Ramsey. And touch base with us every now and then."

Touched that she'd grown to care for him as he did her, he nodded. "Will do. You take care of him." He tilted his head towards Matthew. "Keep him out of trouble."

"I can't promise anything, but I will do my best." She saluted toward him and smiled adoringly up at Matthew.

"See you in a few months." Ramsey slid behind the wheel, the door creaking as it closed the final farewell to his friends before he backed out of the alley behind his bar and headed towards Reagan's

and the promise of rest in the Tennessee mountains.

## « CHAPTER ONE »

*The birthday candle's flame* flickered as she contemplated just what exactly she wanted to wish for in her life for the upcoming year. Clearly, she'd been thinking about it for a while, because a drop of wax began dripping down the side of the purple candle, followed by another. She rested her chin in her palm and stared. Annoyed that she couldn't think of a single wish, she blew the candle out in frustration and in simple eagerness for a taste of the buttery cake smothered in chocolate icing. She picked up her fork and dived right in, not even slicing a proportionate slice for one person. No, she was just going to eat from the platter. It was just her, after all. Just her.

Autumn Simpson set her fork aside as she hurried towards her briefcase. It was time. She'd put off her current assignment long enough and knew her boss expected the situation to be handled by this afternoon. It wasn't like she wasn't prepared. She'd handled similar foreclosures before. Representing the law firm in such matters was her job. The frustration came from having to coordinate with the local sheriff's office. She and Sheriff Hendricks were to drive out to the abandoned cabin this afternoon, slap a foreclosure notice on the door, and she'd be back in the office by three. That was her plan anyway. Birthday cake for lunch, however, was not. That happened to be a spur of the moment decision when she ran home to check on her kitten. And the cake she'd prepared the night before had been too tempting. She had to sample it while she was here. She'd have a full piece this evening to fully celebrate her birthday. Alone. Well, besides her new kitten, Puddin'.

Autumn had accepted the position as lead attorney for the foreclosures and acquisitions department one year ago in Gatlinburg. Her law firm, Rochester and McGee, covered Gatlinburg and the surrounding areas. What she hadn't realized at the time was that she would be making trips to random abandoned cabins in Gatlinburg. Thankfully, she had a great working relationship with the sheriff, and he insisted on accompanying her on all postings, which she didn't quite mind,

considering some were deep into the mountains, secluded, and, if she were being honest, sometimes creepy. She also had her fair share of confrontations at certain properties. People were not typically the happy sort when you threatened to foreclose upon their home. And though she understood that feeling, she also respected the law and felt compelled to uphold it.

She pulled into the parking lot in front of the Sevier County Sheriff's Department and Sheriff Hendricks came walking out the door as she shifted into park. He was a short man, she mused. Though what he lacked in stature he made up for in character. He was fierce when it came to justice, kind when it came to empathy, and loyal when it came to his county. It was no wonder the people of Sevier County re-elected him in the last election. She grabbed her briefcase from her seat and hurried towards him. "I hope this means you're ready to escort me." She handed him a copy of the posting and watched as he scanned it over.

"Sounds easy enough. I called the police chief over in Gatlinburg and since this sits a ways into the mountains, he didn't seem to mind me taking the reins on this one with you. Said he hasn't seen anyone up that direction in a while. Not even sure anyone even owns it. So, this shouldn't be too difficult."

"It's part of an estate. Not uncommon to see houses fall through the cracks when relatives don't wish to take on the property taxes. It's probably another abandoned piece the family has long forgotten about." Autumn slipped the paper back into her briefcase.

"I have to follow you this time, instead of riding together." He motioned to his own vehicle. "I have to be over in Pigeon Forge this afternoon."

"That's fine. I don't mind following you." She slipped back into her car and patiently waited as the sheriff gave her a solid nod of mutual encouragement: "Let's do this," he seemed to say. Autumn took a deep breath and prepared herself for the winding trip up into the mountains.

~

Ramsey shut the door to the rusty pickup with a satisfied grunt as he shifted the shopping bags to one arm to fumble for the cabin key in his pant pocket. He'd spent his entire morning tuning the vehicle. It'd sat in the small shop next to the cabin for an entire year collecting dust, the gears were rusty, and he'd needed to swap out the spark plugs before it would budge, but he'd gotten it cranked and successfully made a trip to the small "Grab n Go" a few miles down the mountain. Now, laden with groceries to help him survive the week, he was ready to officially start his vacation. He slid the key into the lock and paused as he heard tires

on gravel. Turning, he spotted the sheriff's car as it pulled into the small alcove beside the house. Another car, a sporty silver one, pulled in beside it.

Ramsey stepped down from the porch, resting his grocery bags on the bottom step as he waited to greet the strangers.

"Hello there," the sheriff called as he walked forward, a petite brunette walking alongside him in a form-fitting pencil skirt and stilettos that caused each of her steps to sink into the moist earth. She maintained her balance, though she stumbled a few times.

"May I help you?" Ramsey asked, extending his hand and accepting the firm shake from the sheriff in response.

"Perhaps so. You live here?"

Ramsey crossed his arms over his robust chest. "For now. Just here for the season."

"You rent it out from someone?" the sheriff asked.

"No sir. Don't have to," Ramsey explained. "It belongs to my family."

"That so?" The sheriff looked to the woman beside him. "What's the name?"

"Ramsey Jenkins. Is there some sort of problem?"

"I believe so," the sheriff said. "Or perhaps it's just a mix up. Ms. Simpson will be able to clarify that for us."

The attractive Ms. Simpson fished around in her briefcase and withdrew a slip of paper. "This is the cabin belonging to the Donald Rover Estate, is it not?"

"Yes. That's my maternal grandfather," Ramsey replied.

"I see." She straightened her shoulders. "Well, I hate to tell you this, Mr. Jenkins, but this property is in foreclosure." She handed him the paper. "Seems the property taxes have not been paid."

"What?" Ramsey looked down at the paper and his eyes widened at the amount. "This can't be right. The estate covers the property taxes, always has."

"That may have been the case in the past, but the property has been delinquent for the past five years. Tennessee law states that the unpaid amount becomes a lien on your home. The house can then be foreclosed through the court system and sold at a public auction to satisfy the tax lien. That is where we are at now." She gripped the handle of her briefcase in both hands as if waiting for an outburst. The sheriff eyed him curiously.

"There has to be some sort of mistake," Ramsey stated.

"Are you the executor of the estate, Mr. Jenkins?" Ms. Simpson asked.

"No ma'am. That's my aunt."

"Perhaps you should give her a call," Ms. Simpson suggested. "The public auction is in two weeks, Mr. Jenkins. If the back taxes and fees are not paid by then, the house will go up on the auction block."

"You can't sell it." Ramsey turned panicked eyes on the small woman. She didn't shrink back from his harsh tone. Instead, she rolled her shoulders and faced him calmly.

"I'm afraid that's the way it is, Mr. Jenkins."

"There's no way I can collect this amount in just two weeks."

"Here's my card. Should you find the resources, that is where you can reach me."

Ramsey eyed the small card and then looked up at the sheriff and the polite, but disinterested eyes of Ms. Simpson, *Attorney at Law*, as her card stated. He shook his head in dismay and walked back towards the house, swooping up his groceries and hurrying inside

before he let his temper take control and he said something he knew he'd later regret. The screen door slammed behind him, and he heard muttered voices outside before the sound of car doors closing, tires on gravel, and blessed silence assured him his unwanted visitors were gone. Perplexed and fuming, Ramsey pulled out his cell phone to call his brother. Reagan answered on the first ring. "Already miss me?"

"Sure," Ramsey replied, his upset tone carrying through the line.

"This doesn't sound good." The sound of a door closing told Ramsey that his brother was at the police station and now tucked away in his office. "What's going on? You make it to the cabin okay?"

"Oh, I made it alright," Ramsey answered. "However, I just encountered a major problem."

"What's going on baby brother?"

"Seems the taxes haven't been paid on the property and it's being foreclosed upon."

He could hear the squeak of Reagan's chair as he undoubtedly dropped his feet off his desk and sat up straight. "That can't be right. Aunt Ceecee handles the estate."

"I know. You have a number for her? Or should I just call Mom?"

"Mom would be the best bet, though she'll be furious and demand to confront Ceecee herself. Let me do some digging and I'll see if I can find a number for dear old Auntie. How long do you have?"

"Two weeks," Ramsey replied. "And there's no way I can come up with this money on my own. If the family wants to keep the property, I'm going to need some help with this."

"How much is it?"

"A little over fifteen grand." Ramsey heard a long whistle on the other end.

"Yeah, that's a chunk. I could probably pitch in a couple grand, but that's about it."

"That's where I'm at as well, though I'll pull what I can together since I'm mainly the one that uses the cabin. I had a good season there at the harbor. My renovations to the bar may have to be put on hold, but I could use that money to help towards this, which will give a few more thousand. But it still won't be enough."

Typing sounded on the line and Reagan grunted. "Found a number for Aunt Ceecee." He

read it out and Ramsey jotted it down on a slip of paper before tucking it into his shirt pocket.

"If you need me to help rally the family, let me know. Though I doubt anyone will be willing to help. No one has ever really used that cabin except for us. And since I haven't been out that way in a long time, I imagine you are its sole inhabitant. Don't expect much help, Ramsey."

"I know. I just want to know why the estate hasn't been paying the taxes. The family trust should cover it. Something is going on."

"Agreed. Well, let me know what Ceecee says."

Sighing, Ramsey eased into one of the old wooden chairs at the small dinette table, the seat creaking under his weight. "Yeah, will do." He hung up and drummed his fingers on the tabletop, working through what to say or ask Aunt Ceecee. Dreading the phone conversation to his eccentric aunt, he dialed her number and held his phone to his ear.

"I don't know this number, so if you're a telemarketer, an identity thief, or the government you might as well hang up now because I'm about to start singing. And I'm not a good singer." He heard her tuning up her voice and tried to speak over the sound.

"Aunt Ceecee, wait. Aunt Ceecee?" he called into the phone, holding it out in front of his mouth. He heard a pause.

"Who is this?" she asked again.

Relieved she'd stopped with the pipe tuning, Ramsey's shoulders relaxed. "It's Ramsey. Your nephew."

"Rammmmseeeey!!!" an elated voice called over the line. "Now, why on Earth are you calling me?" He could hear the pleasure in her voice and hoped his conversation wouldn't turn sour. Ceecee was known for her erratic emotional spells.

"Well, I'm at the family cabin in Gatlinburg," Ramsey began.

"That old dump?" she asked. "I was hoping it'd burned down by now or blown away or something. Why would you want to go there?"

"Been coming here since I was a kid, Aunt Ceecee. I come every fall for a break from the harbor."

"I don't blame you on that front. I enjoy Friday Harbor when I visit, but I sure am glad to leave. Too much water there."

Ramsey inwardly screamed for patience. He knew Ceecee didn't enjoy Friday Harbor, her visits

were rare and few over the years. She preferred her quiet life in Wyoming, if that's where she was still located.

"Well, I've run into a bit of a snag here, and I wanted to run it by you and get your thoughts." He kept his voice light so as not to sound accusing, and hoped that she'd maintain her chattiness.

"Alright, what seems to be happening?"

"Well, the sheriff stopped by with a lawyer and served me foreclosure papers. Apparently, the property taxes haven't been paid for several years. I was thinking," He paused to try and carefully craft his next sentence. "that Grandfather's estate covered the taxes. The trust you and Mom and Uncle Howard set up with it."

"It does," she confirmed with a continuous murmur of agreement.

"Then do we have proof of those payments? Maybe that's all I need to show them."

"Oh," she paused. "Well, the trust should cover the taxes. I should have worded that differently."

"But it doesn't anymore? Is that what you're saying?"

"Exactly." She seemed pleased he was keeping up.

"Why not?" he asked.

"Oh, I needed help a few years back with getting settled in Wisconsin."

"I thought you lived in Wyoming?"

"I did."

"But you moved to Wisconsin?"

"Yes." She seemed completely fine with what she was telling him, and Ramsey struggled for patience.

"So, you're telling me that you took money from the trust to cover the costs of moving?"

"Well that and to help buy a house. I needed a down payment, Ramsey." Her tone took on a hint of condescension, as though he didn't know how real estate worked.

"Do Mom and Uncle Howard know?"

"That I'm in Wisconsin?" She seemed baffled by the thought. "Of course they do."

"No, I meant do they know you used the estate funding towards your move and not towards the property taxes here in Gatlinburg?"

"Oh, no. Which, they don't have to know. I'm the executor of the estate and the trust. It's up to me on how it should be dispersed and used."

"What about the cabin?" Ramsey pressed. "There's nothing in the trust to go towards its taxes?"

"I think there might be a few hundred left in there for now, though your mom and Howard pay into the trust each year to go towards the property. I believe that is in December, though."

"So they've been paying money towards taking care of the property and you've been spending it?" Ramsey leaned back in his chair and rubbed a hand over his beard.

"Only for the last few years. I planned to stop this year since I'm settled. They'd understand." Ceecee's tone remained cheerful, as if her lovely life, despite her stealing from family, was everyone's concern and wish.

"What am I to do about the back taxes then? They are going to put the property up for auction in two weeks if taxes aren't paid by then, Aunt Ceecee."

"Oh, that is such a shame. I didn't realize they did that."

"You didn't realize that you could lose property if you didn't pay for it?" Ramsey rolled his eyes as he pinched the bridge of his nose.

"Oh, Ramsey, of course I know that, I just didn't realize they'd collect so soon."

"It's five years delinquent." His voice rose a smidgen and he inhaled a calming breath.

"Ah. Wow, time flies," Ceecee, still unapologetic, hummed. "You know, you could contact your Uncle Howard and mom and ask for their financial help. If they wanted to put their usual amount for the trust towards the back taxes instead of in the trust, that would be fine this year."

Growing angrier by the minute, Ramsey gritted his teeth. "Yeah, I'll do that."

"Well, just let me know how it goes, Ramsey. You know, if anything happens to that property I need to know for paperwork and such."

"I'm sure you do."

"Alright, I need to jet. I've got a nail appointment at four. Angela works wonders. You know, if you're ever out this way I'll have to introduce the two of you. You're still single, right?"

---

"Goodbye, Aunt Ceecee." Ramsey hung up and beat his head on the table. His aunt had been stealing from other family members and had absolutely no regret or conviction over it. How was he to approach his mother and uncle about their family trust being robbed blind by their sister? Looked like he'd have several more uncomfortable phone calls ahead. Texting an update to Reagan, Ramsey then dialed his mother's number and prayed she wouldn't hunt his aunt down and kill her.

## « CHAPTER TWO »

*There was nothing more* satisfying than slipping high heels off your feet after a long day, and Autumn basked in the moment, burying her relieved toes into the fluffy rug on her living room floor. She sat ungracefully on the couch with a plop, and Puddin' jumped onto the cushion next to her with happy purrs. She rubbed a hand over his sleek tabby coat. "It was a long day, Puddin', but I think we handled it."

She thought of the foreclosure that'd had her venturing into the mountains and confronting the large man that'd occupied the run-down cabin. She'd never seen such a man before, except in movies. She wasn't quite sure they even existed, but now the proof resided just a few miles up the road. He was built like a Greek god, tall, wide, and

fearsome. His face, though not particularly handsome in the traditional sort of way, was arresting to look at. His beard was too long, his hair barely even there as if he typically shaved his head but was letting it grow, and he'd had a chipped tooth. When it came to appearances, he could pass as an intimidating pirate who battled Hercules on the weekends; a man who could easily crush you in the palm of his hand and then have a pint afterwards with his buddies. But there was a softness to his eyes despite his hard exterior. Also, a vulnerability when she'd handed him the paper. She still remembered the look of shock on his face as he read the words for the first time. She'd felt sorry for him, finding out the way he had, but it was her job. And though she hoped he'd be able to come up with the money to save the cabin, which seemed important to him, she could not involve herself any further, other than processing the foreclosure should it happen.

Puddin' hopped down to the floor and weaved his way around her ankles. "Alright, I'll feed you." Autumn rose and walked towards her small kitchen, the efficiency apartment offering just enough room for the essential appliances before becoming too cramped. She had a small table, with one chair, set against the wall, Puddin's bowls nestled underneath it and out of the way. She filled his bowl with food and then stroked him one last time before walking towards the covered cake on her counter. "Happy Birthday," she said to

herself quietly. She'd finish off the leftover salad she'd mixed last night and then she'd indulge in more cake. She'd thought about it all day, and it made leaving work that much sweeter.

She ate the salad without enthusiasm but considered it her debt to herself, as she planned on pouring a cold glass of Moscato to go with the cake she intended to consume. She checked the hand-drawn chart stuck to the front of her refrigerator, running her finger over the weekly grid and landing on Thursday. "Ah. Looks like we get to watch a little romance tonight," she reported to Puddin', who raised his head in acknowledgement. She'd drafted the small chart to record what days and times her favorite television shows came on. She had a terrible memory when it came to scheduled shows, and she found she enjoyed her quiet evenings in front of the TV when she knew exactly what show to expect at a certain time. She was the queen of structure and organization. It just made life easier and smoother. She grabbed a fresh fork and the cake platter and walked towards the couch. Setting them on the round coffee table, she then fetched her glass of wine. She sat on the floor instead of the sofa as she turned on the television. Cozy. Comfortable. And only a smidgen lonely, she basked in the noise. She slipped the first bite of cake into her mouth and closed her eyes to savor it. Yes, this was a delicious way to top off her day. Puddin', thoroughly licking

paws and cleaning his face, settled beside her on the rug.

As she lifted the fork for her second bite, a knock sounded on her door. She eyed Puddin', who scampered beneath the couch. "Coward," she muttered, climbing to her feet. She peeked through the peephole and immediately pulled back. *What was he doing at her house?* She peeked again. Yep, it was that Jenkins man standing at her door, and by the looks of it, he was not happy. She eyed her phone across the room and quickly fetched it as he knocked for a second time.

"Just a minute," she called out, and began pre-dialing 911 just in case she needed it. She wasn't accustomed to strange men knocking on her door, much less men to whom she'd just delivered terrible news. She opened the door as far as the bolted chain lock would allow and peeked through. "May I help you?"

The man offered what she assumed he thought a polite smile, but his lips strained into a tight grimace. "Ms. Simpson, right?"

"Yes."

"I know you don't know me, and I apologize for coming to your personal residence, but I needed to talk with you about... well, about my family's cabin situation."

"The foreclosure," she corrected.

"Yes, that."
*There were those soft eyes again*, she thought. Pleading for a moment of her time.

"Like I said, I hate to bother you. I was at the local bank trying to negotiate with them about the ordeal and they kept saying I had to go through you to even talk to them." He moved his hands in a step by step manner that she could tell clearly irritated him. "The sheriff happened to be there and told me where I could find you. He's in the parking lot still, if that gives you peace of mind." He pointed, and the sheriff offered a brief wave.

Autumn closed the door and unlocked the chain and opened it again, stepping out onto the welcome rug outside her door. She waved towards Sheriff Hendricks and he nodded, stepping out of his vehicle to be of service if needed. He'd never brought someone by her house for a spur of the moment consultation. She eyed the man before her and crossed her arms over her chest. Thankfully, she had yet to change out of her work clothes, though her feet were bare, so she still felt somewhat professional. However, she now fell feet below him, her head coming to right below his chest.

He slipped his hands in his pockets. "Can I have a minute to discuss the... foreclosure?" He forced out the last word as if it tasted bitter in his mouth.

"What do you need to discuss, Mr. Jenkins?"

"It's Ramsey, please," he corrected. "Mr. Jenkins makes me feel old."

That comment had her relaxing a moment and his eyes briefly warmed as he said it.

"Alright, Mr. Ramsey."

He rolled his eyes at her use of "mister," but continued anyway. "I've spoken to multiple family members to try and figure out this mess. Turns out my Aunt Ceecee has been stealing from the family trust, which is a whole issue in and of itself, so my mother and uncle are handling that situation, but as far as the payment on the taxes, that's why they weren't being made."

"I'm sorry, but I really don't see—"

"Just wait," he interrupted. "What I'm saying is, I can't afford that chunk of money on my own. My brother is going to help, but even then, I can't get that amount in the allotted two weeks."

"I hate to hear that, Mr. Jen— Ramsey," she corrected. "But that's when the property will go up for auction."

"The sheriff was telling me that in some circumstances, if the owner showed good faith in regards to paying the amount, then you could offer an extension."

"Did he?" Her brows rose as she surveyed the aloof Sheriff Hendricks as he leaned against his car and watched traffic pass by. *What was it about the man in front of her that had garnered such support from the sheriff?*

"Yes. And look, I will pay back every penny and will even take over the property taxes each year, I just need a little more time to pull together the money. I've got my brother wiring me money, I've got my bank back in Washington transferring money to an account I *just* opened here to make it easier. I'm working on it."

"Washington?" she asked, surprised that he was in Tennessee from such a distance.

"Yes, that's where I live." Not skipping a beat, he continued. "I even have friends there who have offered to help me out by running a fundraiser at my bar."

"Bar?" she asked, her brows once again rising in surprise at what she'd heard.

"Yes, I own a place. Anyways, that will take a bit of time to raise the funds, but I do intend to. Can you help me?"

Autumn leaned against her door and almost fell back into her apartment. Ramsey's hand shot out and caught her before she stumbled over the threshold. His grip was firm, but gentle, as if he wasn't quite sure if he should touch her, but his reflexes had taken over. Recovering quickly, she smoothed a hand over her skirt. "I thought I had closed that," she mumbled, slightly embarrassed. Her door remained ajar now and Puddin', now brave, ventured out. Ramsey's eyes flashed down to the cat, their eyes meeting one another and holding. Then, to her surprise, Puddin' began his weaving around Ramsey's ankles. "So sorry. Puddin', stop that." She bent down to scoop him up. "He never does that to people he doesn't know."

Ramsey waited patiently for her answer.

"I can't make any promises, Mr. Ramsey, but I can talk to my client tomorrow and see about getting you an extension. I'll warn you, it may not be what you're after, but I'll push for as long as I can."

His face split into a wide smile, that chipped tooth giving a brief appearance before he began vigorously shaking her hand like an old well pump. "Thank you. Thank you so much." He blew a relieved breath and lifted his hands to the back of his head as he marveled at what he'd just been offered. His biceps had her eyes widening, the sheer size of them bigger than her head. *Well, not that big,* she amended to herself, but they showed the muscles and strain of a man who was used to hard work. *There was no way this man just owned a bar,* she thought.

"I, uh," he stammered as he fished in his pant pocket. "Here's my cell number. If you can call me when you know something, that'd be great. I appreciate you giving me the opportunity."

"Like I said, I can't promise anything."

"Yes, but you're giving it a shot, and that's all I can ask for at this point. Thank you."

She set her cat down and Puddin' wandered his way slowly back into the small apartment. Ramsey's eyes followed the creature and she saw his eyes narrow. She turned and realized her party of one was still showcased on the table.

"Celebrating?" he asked curiously. "I think I might go celebrate myself." He chuckled, the sound deep and genuine as it rumbled from his broad chest.

Embarrassed he'd seen her cake platter, not a single slice, but the *entire* platter with one pathetic fork digging into it, she fumbled for what to say. "It's my birthday." The words spilled out quickly.

"Oh." His face changed from curiosity to kindness. "Well, that is definitely worth celebrating, then. I'm sorry I interrupted."

"It was no problem, not much of a celebration with just me anyway." *Why did she say that?* She inwardly kicked herself. *Tell him goodbye, Autumn,* she warned herself.

He offered a genuine smile this time, much different than the one she'd first seen when she opened her door. And she liked it; the way it lit up his bright blue eyes. "Well, enjoy it nonetheless. That cake looks awesome." He gave a small nod of his head and headed down the stairs towards Sheriff Hendricks, the two men briefly exchanging hearty pats on the shoulder before heading across the parkway to one of the many restaurants on the strip. Again, she wondered why the sheriff was so invested in this stranger. She made a mental note to ask him.

~

"At this point it is just a waiting game," Ramsey said, shifting the phone on his shoulder so he could cast his line into the water. "I've set the ball in motion and now once the money arrives, I

can see where I'm at and how far I have to go. I should hear from her today on what extension I should be getting."

"That's great news." Matthew's voice came over the line. "Well, Olivia is determined. She's got buckets and signs set up all over the harbor. At Anchors Aweigh, your bar, the pizza place, even on my orca tours." He laughed. "Hopefully we'll have a couple of weeks to rally up some support."

"Man, I appreciate that more than you know. I just can't lose this place."

"I get it," Matthew assured him.

"How are things there? Other than you being completely blinded by your little blonde bombshell."

Laughing, Matthew continued. "Well, things are slowing down as per usual. Bumped into your brother on the boardwalk, said they had another burglary at the resort, so he was looking into that."

"Still no lead on that?"

"Not that he can tell... or tell me about, anyway. Said he doesn't believe it's kids like everyone first thought. Said they seem to be going after certain types of property or money."

"What kind of property?"

"He didn't say. But I'm figuring it's only things that can fetch a pretty penny."

"Hmph." Ramsey set his rod down and gripped the phone as he listened. "Well, keep me updated. How's Jake doing at the bar? Haven't talked to him in a couple of days."

"Seems to be doing fine. I think he enjoys it more than the pizza place."

"Good."

"So tell me more about this lawyer," Matthew prodded. "You went to her house. That's a bit unorthodox."

"I was desperate. *Am* desperate. I needed to plead my case. She was nice enough to answer, even though it was her birthday."

"Wow, interrupting a party, huh? Yikes."

"Not quite. She was alone. Eating cake out of the pan, alone."

"Oh. That's kind of sad."

"Yeah, not what I would have pictured. I mean, she's not bad to look at. I figured she'd have

someone special or at least a big group of friends or something. Heck, maybe she does. It's none of my business."

"But you felt sorry for her?" Matthew asked.

"A little," Ramsey admitted. "Hard not to. But I'm not exactly the guy that can ask her to go celebrate, whether out of pity or friendliness, because of her role in the foreclosure."

"That's a shame. Sounds like she could use good 'ol Ramsey Jenkins in her life. Spice it up a bit," Matthew teased.

"Right. No thanks. Ramsey Jenkins is a single man. Always has been. Always will be."

Guffawing with laughter, Matthew jested. "I highly doubt that. You'd steal Olivia right out from under me if we weren't such good friends."

"That's true," Ramsey teased. "But that's Olivia."

"Awe, thanks Ramsey!" Olivia's voice yelled from somewhere in the room with Matthew.

"Great, now you've outdone me," Matthew chuckled. "Maybe being friends with this attorney would be helpful to you. Maybe she'd be more accommodating."

"Doubt it. She seems pretty strait-laced to me. And that's fine. It's her career. I wouldn't want her to jeopardize it. I can do this. If she can get me an extension, I can get the money."

"The hardworking Ramsey who went to Tennessee for a break." Matthew pitied him. "Sorry this is all going down, man. Keep us posted on everything."

"Thanks. Take care." Ramsey hung up, thankful for good friends who supported him, and even more grateful when he saw the nibble on his fishing line. No sooner had he hung up with Matthew, when his phone rang again.

"This is Ramsey," he greeted, thinking Jake was finally calling him with an update on the bar.

"Mr. Jenkins." The cool, calm voice of Ms. Simpson drifted through the line.

"Yes. Hello." He felt somewhat awkward as he fumbled his fishing pole and phone, the phone falling to the ground. He pulled up his line and reeled in as fast as possible while snatching the phone up. "Sorry about that, dropped the phone."

"Not a problem. I'm calling in regards to your request for an extension."

"Yes?"

"I can grant you a total of 30 days."

"Thirty?!" his voice boomed into the line.

"I'm sorry that's all I could negotiate, but—"

"Are you kidding? That's fantastic!" He turned his face up to the sun and gave a relieved sigh that carried through the phone. "You have no idea how grateful I am." He held a hand to his heart.

"I will need you to sign some paperwork. I would just like to have on record that you've requested the extension."

"Of course."

"If you will be at the residence this afternoon, I can swing by with the paperwork."

"I'll be here," Ramsey assured her.

"Wonderful. See you then." She hung up and he stared out over the pond in complete peace. He was going to save the cabin. Yes, he still needed to come up with the money, but he knew he would. Every last cent. He fisted his hand into the pebbled bank and let the tiny rocks sift through his fingers. His grandfather's legacy, hard work, and life would be saved. Yes, he'd be saving it for the family trust, but he'd work on negotiating with his mom and uncle about buying it outright. He was, as his Aunt

Ceecee pointed out, the only one who even cared to use it, which was a shame. His fondest childhood memories were of the cabin. He and Reagan would come spend summers and school holidays with his grandparents every year. A chance for his parents to have some peace, his mom used to say. With two rambunctious boys, who could blame them? He'd grown up here. From boy to awkward teenager to man. He'd had his first taste of moonshine, courtesy of his grandfather, right on the banks of this pond. The taste was terrible, he remembered, but the experience was priceless. He'd chipped his tooth here too; the one he'd yet to have fixed even though the incident happened more than twenty years prior. He and Reagan had laid into one another, fighting over only God knew what, and pounded on one another. It was their way back then. They sorted it. Ramsey walked away with a black eye and chipped tooth, and Reagan, well, he lost his tooth altogether. Ramsey was still quite proud of that accomplishment. And each year, despite years of weather and erosion, he looked for that tooth amongst the pebbles. His grandparents lived in the cabin year-round, his mother having grown up in Gatlinburg. When she met his dad in college, they married, and shortly after made the move to Washington. His dad, being a Friday Harbor boy, had brought his new wife to the San Juan Islands, and she'd never wanted to leave. Who could blame her? It was beautiful.

And most thought Ramsey crazy for trading the Olympic and Wenatchee Mountains around the islands for the Smoky Mountains of Tennessee each fall, but it was his home too. So much of his life happened here that he couldn't possibly let it fall by the wayside. And one, no matter how beautiful the islands are, needed a break from the familiar now and again to refresh and recoup.

He leaned back on the rocks, arms crossed behind his head, and stared up at the sky, his fishing pole forgotten, and for a moment, his stress and worry along with it.

# « CHAPTER THREE »

*She parked her car* behind the ancient pickup truck that she assumed belonged to the grandfather whose name established the estate. Like the cabin, the truck looked neglected and worn. However, it was clearly still in use by the giant man she saw sleeping by the pond. Hesitant, not sure if she should wake him or leave, her shoes crunched against the rocks as she stepped closer. It wouldn't hurt to make sure he was sleeping and not dead, right? She drew nearer and saw the steady rise and fall of his chest. He was alive, that was good. A bit relieved, she stepped closer. "Mr. Jenkins," she said, her voice gentle so as not to spook a bear. A small scream of surprise flew from her lips and she ran behind two large boulders as he bolted to his feet with the

speed of a leopard. Seeing it was her, his shoulders relaxed.

Her heart pounded in her chest and she held a hand there to steady it. "You scared me." She let out a nervous laugh as she tried to steady her quaking heart and legs.

"Sorry." He cleared the sleep from his voice and blinked his eyes. "I must have drifted off." He eyed his fishing pole and picked it up, winding his line up and setting it against one of the boulders she now stepped around. The hand on her briefcase was white knuckled from nerves and she mentally forced her body to relax.

"I have those papers."

"We can go in the cabin." He motioned, leading the way and ducking through the doorway. And he *had* to duck, which she thought was extraordinary. But once inside, the small space was open and welcoming, and surprisingly not crowded with his presence. It was clean. The bed in the corner was made, the cushions on the worn couch were fluffed for fresh comfort, and the kitchen was free of dirty dishes and debris. It smelled of lemon wood polish and man, the musky soap smell of a freshly showered man that seemed to make women swoon with the first sniff. She was not immune and found herself grateful for the chair at the small table. She fished in her briefcase and withdrew three forms.

"This first form is just a pledge of sorts. Basically, it states that you requested the extension because you want to pay back the taxes. It's more for me than anything. I don't like to waste time, and if someone fails to pay back the amount after the extension this form sort of helps me save face with my clients. And then this one is the actual extension." She motioned to where he needed to sign. "I've also faxed these forms to your mother, Deena Jenkins, as she is now executor of the estate of Donald Rover. She has signed an agreement letting you act on behalf of the estate, and I need your signature of agreement to do so here," she pointed. He signed. "And that's it." She stacked the papers on the table and then stuck them back in her bag.

"Easy enough." Ramsey leaned back in the chair, the creak causing her to glance towards its legs to make sure it held. "It's stronger than it looks." He smirked as she blushed. "Do I pay in full or can I pay in installments?"

"In full."

"Got it. I'm about halfway there."

"That's great. I'm happy for you." She nodded in farewell as she stood to leave.

"Why don't you stay for supper?"

"Oh, I can't. I'm sorry."

"Look, I won't bug you about the foreclosure stuff. It will just be a friendly supper that saves me from eating alone."

She looked at her watch for absolutely no reason other than to buy herself a few seconds to come up with an excuse.

"Call it a belated birthday dinner," he grinned. "I'll go get the fish off the line. You do eat fish, right?" Without waiting for her answer, he walked out the door and towards the pond, reaching into the cool water and withdrawing a line of flopping fish. He looked up as she stood on the small porch. "Won't take but a minute to clean them."

"Mr. Jenkins, I can't."

He walked by her and grabbed a skinning knife that rested on the outdoor wooden table used for such purposes as cleaning fish or wild game. Without replying, he set to work, the knife slicing through the first fish. She gagged a moment as he tossed the head aside. Holding a hand to her mouth, she turned away.

Seeing this, Ramsey chuckled. "Squeamish?"

"I just... I wasn't prepared to watch you do that."

"Sorry. Best to do it right out of the water. No sense in prolonging their fate." He tossed fish pieces into a bowl of water he'd set aside.

"Do you like fried, baked, broiled, or smoked?" He glanced up, those blue eyes dancing as he knew she struggled to contain the contents of her stomach.

"I really can't stay," Autumn repeated.

Setting the knife aside, Ramsey rested his bloody hands on the table, completely at home in his surroundings. "You always this skittish, or do I scare you? Because I know I may look like the scary sort, but I assure you I'm not."

"Oh, it's not that. I just don't want to complicate our business relationship. I have to be impartial. No conflict of interest. You understand." She smiled.

"Then let's call it a consultation." He grinned, that small chip in front adding charm to his tough face. He'd trimmed his beard, she noted, and looked friendlier and less roguish.

"Then you would have to actually be counseled," she added on a sigh.

"I will be. I have some questions." He winked.

Unsure what he would want to consult with her, she eased onto a wooden stump that was typically used for chopping wood.

"You can set your bag down." He continued slicing and expertly cleaning the fish.

She rested the briefcase against the stump.

"You grow up around here?" he asked.

"Yes. Though in Pigeon Forge, not Gatlinburg," she replied.

"Your parents live here too?"

"Yes."

He grunted in acknowledgment and his big hands continued working the knife over the fish. "You ever say more than a couple words?" he asked.

"Sometimes."

He chuckled at her response. "How's the cat?"

She blinked. "What?"

"Your cat," he repeated. "How is he?"

"How'd you know he was a boy?"

"The way he sized me up last night, there was no mistaking it. He was letting me know what was what. You're his girl." He smiled as she flushed. "Not that I had intentions, but it's just what we guys do. We need to set the record straight up front, so another man won't infringe on our lady."

"Your territory," she confirmed.
"I always hated that phrase, but yeah, I guess so."

"He's just a cat," she said. "Not like he can lay claim to anything other than the mice he brings to the door."

"Tell him that and he might just find somewhere else to go." Ramsey went back to cutting fish and she diverted her gaze to the sunset over the pond.

"How long have you been coming here? I've never seen you before," she commented.

He set aside the knife and lifted the bowl of fish cuts.
"Mind opening the door?" He nodded towards the cabin and she darted up the steps and held open the screen door and followed him inside, her briefcase forgotten by the stump. "I've been here every year since I was seven years old. Mostly summers as a kid, but more this time of year as I've gotten older. My work keeps me pretty busy

during the summer with the tourist months and fishing months."

"So you're a fisherman as well?"

"Sometimes. Mostly run a fishing business. I have several boats and have teams that go out and make catches for the day. I have clients that buy the fish from me to use in their restaurants or markets."

"Oh. Where are you from in Washington?"

"Friday Harbor."

She tilted her head and squinted at him. "Is that a real place?" she asked skeptically.

He chuckled. "Yes, it's a real place. It's in the San Juan Islands."

"Interesting. I've never heard of it before. Though I haven't ever left Tennessee."

"Ever?" he asked.

"Ever," she replied. "I know it's crazy, but I've just never had a reason to leave. All my family is here."

"That's nice. That's somewhat how it is for me now at the harbor. Growing up, though, my grandparents lived here." He pointed towards the floor of the cabin.

"I can see why you're trying to save it then."

"Yes. Though we'll see if I actually can. I'm determined to, and I usually tackle whatever obstacle I set my mind to, but you never know." He pointed to the fish. "You never answered me earlier. Fried, baked, broiled, or smoked?"

"Oh, um... however you like it best."

He shrugged and she watched as he turned towards the counter, his back towards her, and began working in the kitchen, rinsing the fish and then his hands. Seasonings were opened, veggies washed and sliced. He seemed to know what he was doing.

"What did you wish to consult with me about?" she asked, trying to maintain the professionalism of her visit.

"Oh, right. Forgot about that." He flashed a smile over his shoulder before turning back to his cooking. He began sautéing veggies, the smell making her stomach rumble. "Can I just share with you an idea I have and you can tell me if it's feasible?"

"You mean legal?"

"Well, yes and no. I'm not sure if what I'm wanting to do is even necessary or makes sense."

"Alright, go ahead." She waved him onward.

"Would you like a beer? Or wine? Or tea? I know you southerners are pretty partial to your sweet tea. I don't have any, but I could make some."

"Since I'm technically on the clock, I should go with water."

"But it's after five," he pointed out.

"And this is a consultation," she countered.

He held up his hands in surrender. "Alright, you win. I can't loosen you up, can I? One ice water, coming up." He quickly made a glass and handed it to her as she sat at the table. "My mother gave me liberty to act on behalf of the estate to clear this whole matter up."

"Right."

"Once I do, I plan to either purchase the property from the estate or see if they just want to deed it over to me since no one comes here but me. Either way, I'll do what I need to do to get the place."

"Well our firm could definitely help with the transfer or sale."

"That's not what I'm needing."

"Oh."

"I'd like to set up my own trust or a limited liability company or something, and have this property in there. Ideally, I'm thinking maybe I could open up a small business that funds the trust or LLC and the trust/LLC pays the taxes, maintenance, or updates and improvements I would like to do here."

"You want to start a business?"

"Maybe."

"Here?"

"I thought that would be easiest," Ramsey continued, trying to understand why she seemed confused.

"But you don't live here," she clarified.

"I don't really have to."

"But to run a business you would need to."

"No. I would have employees."

"But a business takes time. You have to obtain certain licenses in some cases. A location. Accounts. Taxes."

"I know. I own several businesses in Friday Harbor, so I'm familiar with what it takes."

"Well," She took a deep breath as she processed what he was telling her. "An LLC could establish your business and give you an operating structure, but salaries, supplies, fees, costs, earnings... everything would have to be reported under that LLC. And you're wanting to have earnings go towards this property?"

"I'm talking about creating a business, earnings obviously go towards the business first, but that I would draw, let's say it's a salary, that I would not take but instead have it go towards this property/trust."

"A percentage of earnings towards a trust would be easiest, in my opinion. But you would need to set up what type of trust you'd like, and there are several options."

"Think you could get me a list and information on those?"

"I could," she agreed. "Seems like a lot to take on in the next 30 days."

"I have assets in Friday Harbor that I can sell to make this happen. I love the land in the harbor, but I have a friend who's been wanting it since we were kids. I know he'd buy it and I could use that money to start a small business here that could carry the trust for this property."

"Ambitious."

"Family trait," he replied, slipping a piece of fish onto a plate and adding veggies. He brought the plate to her and sat across from her with his own. "Voila."

She eyed her plate in wonder. "Wow. This looks impressive."

"Did I mention my bar also has food?" Ramsey asked.

She smiled, continually impressed with each new detail she discovered about him. "You're full of surprises, Mr. Jenkins."

"It's Ramsey," he reminded her. "Just Ramsey. No mister. Just Ramsey."

"Alright."

"And you?"

"What?"

"Your name?" he asked. "I only know you as Ms. Simpson."

"Oh." She shyly tucked her hair behind her ear as she unfolded her napkin and placed it in her lap. "It's Autumn. Autumn Simpson."

Ramsey held up his glass of water and waited for her to raise her own. "Happy belated birthday, Autumn." And tapped his glass to hers.

~

Ramsey offered a friendly wave from the porch as Autumn climbed into her zippy little car and headed back towards Gatlinburg. He'd enjoyed their visit. He was thankful the ball was rolling in regards to the property, and she'd given him plenty to think about in the direction of his possible new business venture; a business venture that he needed to wrestle with. First things first, he needed to free up some property in Friday Harbor and plant the seeds in Matthew's mind that he needed to buy the Lookout Point he and Olivia loved so much. Once that money was freed up, he could pay the back taxes, get the property in his name, and then invest in a way to provide for the property in the future. It was important that he keep this land. On more than one occasion he and his grandfather had sat on the banks of the pond and talked about life, work, and women. He'd received wisdom and advice, some he wished he'd

taken and some he'd heeded. He was the man he was today because of his grandfather, and he would one day want to pass this property on to his own children, should he have any. If not, well, he'd cross that bridge when he got there. But this place was special, and he intended to keep it.

He turned to head back into the cabin when he spotted her briefcase resting against the stump by the cleaning table. He scooped it up; the leather was soft and supple and most definitely expensive. Now he understood why she did not want to lay it down near his fish guts table. He smirked. She'd be back. He was certain that Autumn Simpson was the kind of woman who'd know when she'd left her lifeline out of sight. He couldn't remember ever meeting such an uptight woman. Though he couldn't quite determine whether she was uptight or just socially awkward. He assumed both based on their interactions. An all-business introvert who spent most evenings alone with her cat. *Sad*, he thought, *that a pretty girl like Autumn hadn't been scooped up by someone.* She was classy, educated, and very easy on the eyes with that rich auburn hair and creamy complexion. Her brown eyes were deep and dark and shy, he remembered, as he noticed her blush several times throughout the evening. She was particular in her movements, in her speech, and a bit too tidy and buttoned up. He wondered if she ever wore her hair in one of those little messy buns women tended to favor when they were relaxed and comfortable, or if she

always made it a point to look the part of the professional young attorney. Probably the latter. He'd run the bag by her office tomorrow if he didn't receive a pounding on his door before then and relieve her of the worry he knew she'd feel when she couldn't find it in the morning.

His phone dinged with a text message. He'd sent Matthew a teaser about Lookout Point and he knew it wouldn't take long for him to reply. To his surprise, it was from Jake.

*Jake: Call when you have a minute.*

Ramsey dialed, Jake answering on the first ring. "Jake," he greeted.

"Ramsey, hey man, that was quick."

"I'm free. What's up?"

"So, things are good. Supplier brought in fresh inventory of booze and food supplies today. We're going into tomorrow and the weekend with a full kitchen and bar, so that should be good."

"Yes. And what else?" Ramsey asked, knowing full well something was wrong if Jake was calling him and starting off with a positive affirmation of how well things are going.

"Well... have you talked to your brother?" Jake asked.

"No, not since yesterday. Why?"

"Well, last night we had a bit of an incident."

"What kind of incident?"

"More rods were snatched," Jake reported. "Reagan came out and took stock of what was stolen. Seems your place is a hot spot for the recent burglaries."

"We just replaced those fishing rods. Can't leave anything out these days." Ramsey sighed. "Well, see what rods need to be replaced immediately. Anything that can wait until next season, we'll do then. And lock them up inside at night."

"Where?" Jake asked. "Health code won't let you lock them up inside the bar or kitchen."

"Then lock them up in a boat or one of the sheds somewhere. All I know is, is I can't keep replacing rods. So, if the men want something to fish with, have them lock them up," he growled, not in annoyance at Jake but the circumstances.

"Gotcha. I'll figure out a place. So, how was the flight down? All set up for a relaxing season?"

"If people would stop stealing my stuff at the harbor I might be," Ramsey muttered. "And trying to get this property issue taken care of."

"Yeah, heard about that from Matt and Olivia. Got several buckets around the bar for you. Olivia even made flyers."

Ramsey cringed at the thought of flyers being passed around on his behalf, but knew Olivia was determined to help. "Please tell me they don't say I have a property foreclosure."

"They don't. I'm pretty sure it said something like you're 'raising funds for a new venture' or something like that. It was discreet."

"A new venture." Ramsey chuckled. "Little does she know," he mumbled.

"What was that?" Jake asked.

"Nothing. Thanks for filling me in on the rods."

"No problem. Any good fishing down there?"

"Didn't do too bad this evening. Was able to whip up a feast for myself and Autumn."

"Who's Autumn?" Jake asked, intrigued. "Ramsey got a lady?"

"No. She's the attorney handling the foreclosure. I had to sign some papers."

"And you just decided to cook for her?" Jake asked.

"She was here," Ramsey added noncommittally.

"Right. Well, *Autumn* sounds like an impressive woman."

"Why?"

"She's an attorney. Is she good looking?"

"What does that matter?" Ramsey challenged.

"So that's a yes," Jake laughed.

"I guess she is," Ramsey conceded. "But a bit too... delicate for my taste."

"Delicate?"

"I mean small," Ramsey said. "Well, not small, just dainty. She's not very tall and she's tiny. Well, not tiny, just small compared to me. I'm a giant."

Jake's laughter continued in his ear. "You didn't check her out at all did you?" he teased.

"I just... no. It was just an observation."

"Right. Well, I have to go, customers just walked in. You have fun with Autumn and good luck down there."

Before he could debate any further, Jake hung up and Ramsey was left staring at the phone in his hand. *What in the world had he just said? Dainty? Tiny? Delicate?* Groaning, he walked to the sink to finish washing dishes and get ready for bed. The last thing he needed to think about was a pretty face. His focus was saving his grandfather's cabin and Autumn was needed to make that happen. That was it. That was all.

# « CHAPTER FOUR »

*She'd left it.* She'd left her briefcase at Ramsey's house. *Great.* Not only would she be late for work, but she wouldn't have the papers he'd signed to grant the extension. Fighting back her frustration and panic, because since she also did not have her cell phone due to it being in the bag, she could not even call him last night to have him grab it from outside. So her beautiful leather bag was now going to marred from the dew. Or something. She huffed as she pulled into her parking space at the law office. She'd run in, check her emails, and then make an excuse for her departure at a client's request. Her entire day was going to be thrown off schedule. And she liked her schedule. She had phone calls to make, clients to meet with, and papers to file at the courthouse. She slammed her car door and stomped her way

towards the office. When she reached the door, it was locked. She was early, as was her usual way of arriving to work, and so she would unlock the doors, disarm the alarm, and start the coffee for everyone. When she reached for her keys, she fisted her hand. She'd locked them in her car. She stomped a foot and let out a frustrated growl.

"Bad morning?"

She jumped, one foot slipping out of her black stiletto and onto bare concrete. She cringed as she quickly tried to stuff it back into her shoe. Wriggling her ankle back and forth to no avail, she dipped down to adjust the fit and get her foot in her shoe.

Cars pulled into the parking lot and several of her coworkers hopped out with morning smiles, thankful that it was Friday. They eyed Ramsey in curiosity as they saw a flustered Autumn.

"You forgot this at my place last night."

Her coworkers took their precious time unlocking the door at the sound of that, intrigued by the giant man holding Autumn's briefcase. She wished she could disappear. Maybe the ground would do her a favor and just swallow her up. Attempting to maintain a smidgen of control over her day, she forced a smile.

"Thanks for bringing it to me." She reached out and his fingers brushed hers as he handed it over, and cursed skies, she felt a bolt of attraction shoot up her arm at the contact. Her coworkers bit back smiles as they walked into the building, but she noticed they lingered in the lobby, trying to appear consumed with straightening up the office so as to watch her scene play out on the sidewalk. Ramsey stuffed his hands in his pockets and nodded to her car. "Need some help with that?"

"It's fine. I mean, I locked my keys in there, but I'll just call the sheriff and have him send someone to help."

"I can do it." Walking towards the small car, Ramsey peered inside and saw her keys sitting in the driver's seat. "Hate when I do that. Give me a second." He started to walk towards his truck, and she placed a hand on his arm.

"Really, it's okay. I don't need my car right now, and the office is already unlocked, so I can just wait for the sheriff."

"I imagine he has more important things to do than I do," Ramsey told her. "I don't mind." He offered a friendly smile as he walked towards his truck in long, powerful strides. Everything about the man screamed power and strength. Even dressed in a simple plaid button up and jeans, he looked the part of mighty warrior undercover, and

when she looked at the office, it was not difficult to see her female coworkers admiring his physique from afar. He walked back carrying a slim jim, a thin metal bar she knew he'd slip through the seam of her window and car door to the inside and pop the lock. "Shouldn't take but a second." He started working on it when a woman with blonde hair and a friendly smile popped her head out the door. "Autumn, you have a phone call."

Autumn, torn between whether she should take the scheduled call or stay and monitor Ramsey's work, deliberated a full second before he spoke. "Go on. I'll bring you your keys when I'm done."

"I just—"

He looked at her. "Autumn, go. I'm not going to steal your car."

"I know that," she barked back.

"Then trust me and go handle your business. I'll be just a minute and then bring you your keys."

She heard the annoyance in his tone at her lack of trust, but she didn't know him. It was only natural for her to be cautious. "Fine. Alright. Just... have them buzz my intercom and I'll come to the lobby when you're done."

"Fine."

She hurried into the building, bypassing the questioning glances and shut the door to her office. Taking a deep breath to calm herself, she then picked up the receiver. "This is Autumn Simpson."

~

"You know, it's a crime to break into someone's car. Though I give you points for bravery, doing it bright and early in the morning." The sheriff's voice carried towards Ramsey as he finally saw the lock pop up.

He grinned at the man. "Autumn locked her keys in the car," he explained, opening the door. He inhaled a deep breath of feminine lotion when he bent to snatch the keys. He held them up for the sheriff to see.

"And she called you?" the sheriff asked curiously.

"No. I was here, returning some paperwork." Ramsey did not expound upon the fact he was returning her briefcase because she'd had dinner with him and left it at his house. He wasn't quite sure how the sheriff would feel about that, even though he'd seemed to like him well enough. He didn't want to trouble the waters for Autumn.

Ramsey tapped the key fob and locked her doors from the outside.

"I've got to pow wow with one of her associates," Sheriff Hendricks explained. "Seems I spend more time at this law office than I do my own some days. Used to be I'd just receive a call every now and then, but now I've got to come all the way down here, give up my mornin' moon pie and talk legalities."

"I don't envy you," Ramsey chuckled as he held the office door open for the sheriff to walk inside.

"How's the money coming along?"

"Slowly, but it's coming. Autumn was able to get me an extension."

"That's great news." Sheriff Hendricks smiled.

"I have friends back in Washington doing some fundraising for me as well, so hopefully we can gather it all together."

The sheriff leaned a hip on the secretary's desk. "Becky, I would sure love a cup of coffee if you can manage it."

"Of course." She smiled warmly. "And you, sir?"

"I'm okay, thank you," Ramsey replied.

"Oh, he'll have one too," the sheriff corrected and pointed to two chairs in the lobby. "Fundraising, you said?"

"Yes. Setting up some buckets at some of my local businesses and others," Ramsey explained.

"What kind of businesses?"

"Fishing mostly, though I have a bar as well."

The sheriff scratched his chin. "Ya know, if you get creative you might could think of something to do for the Smoky Mountain Harvest Festival coming up. Have a vendor booth of some sort."

"A festival?" Ramsey pondered that a moment. "Like food?"

"Food, gifts, trinkets, crafts, you name it, there's a spot for it. The festival brings in thousands of people, locals and tourists alike. Might be a chance to make some money."

"I will look into that. How do I go about signing up for a booth space?"

"Oh," the sheriff paused to accept the coffee from Becky as she handed each man their own. "Becky, is the chamber handling vendor applications for the festival?"

"Yes sir. Donna's overseeing all of that again this year."

"Give her a buzz, will you? Tell her I'm sending a gentleman over to fill one out."

"Yes sir."

Becky obediently picked up the phone and dialed.

"I appreciate this." Ramsey shook the man's hand.

"Not a problem. We want good folks around. I looked into your family. Didn't realize Donald Rover was the Donald my daddy knew so well. Fishing buddies back in the day."

"Really?"

"Oh yeah, stumbled across some old clippings in the newspaper about them. I figured if my daddy liked your grandfather, then he must have been a decent man. So, I'm giving you the benefit of the doubt."

"Thank you." Ramsey took a swig of the coffee and his face blanched.

"Oh, yes, it's terrible if Becky makes it," the sheriff whispered. "But coffee's coffee when you need it bad enough."

Ramsey nodded at the man's logic. "Well, I better give Autumn her keys. She's probably stressing each second they're not in her possession."

The sheriff chuckled. "For having just met her, you seem to know her pretty well already."

"Is she always so..."

"Put together?" the sheriff finished graciously.

Ramsey pointed at him like they'd go with his answer over anything he was about to say.

"Her momma is the same way. The Simpsons are what you would call upper crust in Pigeon Forge. Autumn attended the best private schools growing up, received the best college education in the state, and is held in high regard just due to her last name. However, the young woman is impressive enough on her own. Smart as a whip. A bit shy in the social aspects of life, but that's her parents' fault. They sheltered that girl from the time she was born. I'm surprised she turned out as normal as she is."

Blunt honesty was something Ramsey always appreciated, and Sheriff Hendricks dealt it out in spades. Standing, Ramsey flipped Autumn's key around his finger. He smiled at the secretary as he towered over her. "Can you see if Autumn is available, please?"

Nodding, Becky glanced at the phone system. "She's off the phone. Her office is the last one on the right." She pointed down the small hallway. "Go on back."

He shook the sheriff's hand once more. "I'll head to the Chamber after this. I appreciate the tip about the festival."

"More than welcome." Hendricks smiled as he watched Ramsey navigate his way towards Autumn.

Tapping his knuckles against her door, he heard a muffled, "Come in," and opened the door to find her furiously typing away on her computer. She glanced up, back down, and then did a double take. She slapped a hand to her forehead as she rushed to stand to her feet. "I am so sorry, I completely forgot about my keys."

Ramsey held them out to her. "I was busted by the sheriff trying to break into your car."

Her face flamed. "You're not in trouble, are you?"

Ramsey crossed his arms, liking the alarm and concern pictured on her face. Concern for him. "I may have to do some time."

She gasped. "I'll talk to him. He'll understand once I explain."

Ramsey bit back a smile. "He said I could get by this one time if I could do one thing for him."

"Oh? What's that? Community service of some sort?"

"Take you to dinner." He watched as his words processed in her mind and her eyes finally squinted in doubt. She sized him up in one quick glance and then tightened her jaw and sat back at her desk.

"Not funny, Mr. Jenkins. I thought you were in serious trouble for helping me." She clicked away on her computer, attempting to ignore his presence.

Ramsey laughed. "If I had been, it's good to know you would come to my rescue."

Her dark eyes glanced at him a brief moment. "Of course, I would. You were helping me."

"My offer still stands."

"What offer?" she asked.

"Dinner."

She sighed as if exhausted with the subject. "You know I cannot accept, Mr. Jen—"

"Thought we'd been over this? No more Mr. Jenkins. My name is Ramsey. And yes, you can accept. Because I need another consultation."

"I have fifteen minutes right now before my next appointment. We can meet now."

His lips quirked. "I'm afraid it will take longer than fifteen minutes. Dinner tonight, at six. I'll pick you up."

She fumbled, sputtering. He knew she was trying to think of an excuse. He stood to his feet and she shrunk back in her chair a bit. He knew he intimidated her, and he didn't mean to. It was just

sort of something that happened with a lot of people due to his size. He was used to it. But with Autumn, he didn't want to intimidate. He found himself wanting her to be comfortable around him. At ease. He wasn't sure if she was like that with anyone in her life, but based on what the sheriff had mentioned about her and her childhood, he could understand why she was the way she was. But he liked challenges. They required his full attention and efforts, and Autumn Simpson was definitely a challenge, but one which he knew required a delicate touch. Goodness, he just wanted to be her friend. He wasn't sure she had any. His eyes roamed around her clean and tidy office. Every paper and folder had a designated spot. There were three framed photographs on a bookshelf in the corner. He walked over and peered at them.

"My family," she explained.

And they were. The older version of Autumn standing with her arms around a fresh college graduate Autumn had to be her mother. She also had a picture of her with her dad and one, he assumed, of the entire family, siblings and all. She had three siblings. Two sisters and a brother. "Are you the oldest?" he asked.

"Yes."

He could see that; the weight of that responsibility. It was one he knew Reagan felt from time to time in wanting to set a good example

for his younger brother. "I have an older brother. Reagan."

"Is he... like you?" she asked.

"You mean big?" Ramsey turned to face her. Her cheeks stained red.

"No, I just meant in general."

He knew she hadn't, but it didn't bother him. "Not really. He's older, but I'm bigger. A source of constant debates and fights growing up." He grinned mischievously. "Reagan was bummed he couldn't beat me up when we were younger." He pointed at his tooth.

"Your brother did that?" Appalled, she shook her head in bewilderment.

"Yep. Don't worry, I knocked his out."

Her astonishment had him laughing. "It's what boys do," he explained.

"My brother does not fight." She pointed to the gangly kid in the photograph. "And if he did, my parents would flip."

"Different times." Ramsey shrugged. He smelled the faint scent of the lotion he'd smelled in her car. Honey, vanilla, and something floral, he'd guess. Just lotion. Autumn wasn't the perfume type of woman, he figured. Lotion was necessary and therefore easiest to apply. She probably even

carried a small bottle in her leather bag. She came up to his mid-bicep in height. *Was she even five feet tall?* He took a step back, feeling a bit crowded in her space. "I should head to the Chamber of Commerce."

"What for?" she asked, walking him towards her door.

"Well, I guess I'll just have to tell you about it over dinner." He winked as she rolled her eyes.

"Consultation," she corrected.

"Whatever you want to call it." He headed down the hallway and back towards the lobby. She followed listlessly behind him. He extended a wave. "Nice to meet you, Becky. Happy Friday."

The secretary gushed at the attentive response from the stranger, but Ramsey didn't notice.

"Oh." He turned, and Autumn bounced off of him with a small gasp. He gripped her arms to stabilize her and bit back a laugh. He'd embarrassed her again, though that was not his goal. "Be sure to wear tennis shoes."

"But—"

"Autumn..." his tone warned.

"Fine. Tennis shoes. Got it."

"Do you own any?" he asked.

Crossly, she placed her hands on her hips. "Of course I do."

Ramsey nodded in approval. "Just making sure." Winking, he walked out the door.

## « CHAPTER FIVE »

*Tennis shoes. Of course* she owned tennis shoes. Who didn't? She laced up her left shoe and stood just as a knock sounded on her door. Still irritated that he assumed she'd eat dinner with him, she swung the door open. Ramsey stood, arms gently holding Puddin' and stroking the cat's head. Baffled, she eyed them both.

"This guy was roaming the sidewalk. Wasn't sure if he was supposed to." Puddin's purrs grew louder when Ramsey stopped petting him, and the cat nudged its head against the man's chin for attention. Ramsey chuckled and nudged the cat back into the crook of his elbow and pet him. "Ready?"

"I suppose so." Her stiff tone had Ramsey raising a brow.

"Is there a problem?"

"I just don't see why I need to wear tennis shoes to a consultation."

He eyed her outfit. The same slacks and button up shirt she'd worn to the office, but instead of heels, she wore the requested footwear. "You might want to change into different clothes."

"Why?"

"Because you might get messy."

"Ramsey—" She pinched the bridge of her nose. "Look, I think we need to talk."

"I know, I know. You're the attorney representing the bank that plans to foreclose on my property. But the way I see it, you're also representing me in my new business venture. So technically I'm a client, right?"

"You have yet to pay me a retainer fee," she pointed out.

He reached into his pocket and withdrew a dollar. "We'll settle the rest later." He shoved the crumbled bill into her palm. "Now, will you please relax and come to dinner with me?"

"It has to be business related, Ramsey."

"It is."

"Doesn't sound like it." She pointed at her shoes.

"I'm just trying to be courteous," he replied in mock innocence.

Deliberating, Autumn reached out and took Puddin' from Ramsey's arms. "Give me five minutes."

"I can do that." He grinned and eased onto the top step of stairs outside as she shut her door and hurried to her bedroom.

She pulled a pair of jeans from the closet and a lightweight long sleeve shirt from a hanger. Slipping them on, she eyed herself in the mirror and fluffed her hair. Puddin' rested on the edge of her bed watching. "You, sir, are not to go wandering the neighborhood. You know better."

Unapologetic, Puddin' stretched out on Autumn's comforter and purred.

"Well, here it goes." Autumn opened the door to nag Ramsey further, but he wasn't there. She peered up and down the walkway of her upstairs level and he was nowhere to be seen. She walked to the balcony edge and glanced towards the parking lot and didn't see him. Confused, she turned and rammed into the solid wall she knew was his chest once more. She swatted out and shoved. "Why do you keep doing that?" Flustered,

she tugged on the hem of her shirt and tucked her hair behind her ear as his lips blossomed into his customary smirk.

"I was trying not to scare you."

"By sneaking up on me?"

"I wasn't sneaking. My steps could be heard a mile away."

"Well, I didn't hear them," she mumbled, gripping the handle of her leather briefcase.

"That stays here." He pointed at the bag.

"What? Why? I thought we were going to be discussing your business venture. I have that list of the different types of trusts. Also, the steps to forming an LLC."

"I bet you do."

Mouth agape, she stepped back in offense. "What is that supposed to mean?"

"That you're organized. A little anal." He tilted his head back and forth as if considering. "But it suits you. The bag stays here."

He turned to walk down the stairs. She glanced at her bag and feeling put off by his demand, she started to follow him. He paused on the steps and did not turn around. "I swear, Autumn, I will burn that bag if you bring it."

Self-preservation had her quickly unlocking her front door and tossing the bag inside. Appeased, Ramsey's steps continued down the stairs and to the ancient truck.

"Where are we going?" she asked.

"Maw's."

"The backwoods diner in the mountains?"

"That's the one."

"That place is disgusting."

He opened the passenger door and waited for her to step off the sidewalk. "Have you ever been?"

"Well, no, but it has a reputation."

"For the best food in the Smokies," Ramsey elaborated. "Hop in."

"But—"

"Autumn!" Exasperated, Ramsey pointed to the passenger seat. "Do you have to make everything complicated?"

Offended, she shook her head. "I'm not making anything complicated. I'm simply stating that—" Ramsey pressed a finger gently to her lips, her eyes forming two large saucers at his audacity. He leaned in close and though she was shocked, her pulse danced at his nearness.

"It's dinner at a hole in the wall diner. Fancy? No. Good? Yes. I would appreciate if you would just hop in the truck." He took a step closer, his face nearer to hers since she stood on the curb of the sidewalk and he on ground level. She still had to look up at him. Nodding to him, she was relieved when he dropped his finger and waited for her to climb in the truck. When she did, he shut the door and made his way around the front to the driver's side.

The drive took a half hour, Ramsey making small talk as they wound their way up into the mountains. She'd never eaten at Maw's Diner. As they pulled into the parking lot, she reminded herself why. The old wooden structure looked a thousand years old, the signage askew on its hinges above the roof awning, and the entire building seemed to sag. The parking lot was crowded, as she knew there were many people who frequented the place, especially those who lived up in the mountains and didn't venture to town much. But it was not for her. She would have preferred a quaint or chain restaurant in town or in Pigeon Forge, but she doubted, glancing at Ramsey's excited expression, that she could convince him of those options.

"I try to eat here every year when I come back."

She forced a smile as she dreaded every step towards the building. Ramsey opened the door and placed a polite hand at the small of her

back as he escorted her inside. Music—banjos, *go figure*— played softly in the background. Conversations fluttered about the room. Surprisingly, Autumn noted that not all the clientele were dressed in denim overalls and raggedy clothing. Perhaps Maw's had broadened their customer base.

"Table for two?" a cheerful teen asked, her face scarred by unfortunate acne, but her smile radiant and friendly as she led them towards a booth.

"Autumn?" A familiar voice had her stopping in her tracks, Ramsey behind her, as she looked down into the face of her mother.

"Mom?" In equal surprise, Autumn glanced across from her mother. "Dad? What are you doing here?"

Her father chuckled until his gaze landed on Ramsey behind her. "We could ask you the same thing."

"Oh, I have a... consultation."

Her mother's appraising eye soaked in the casual wardrobe in distaste. "Is that so?"

"Yes. Um... Mr. Jenkins." She stepped aside as Ramsey extended his giant bear claw towards her elegant mother.

"Ramsey," he corrected, as he gently shook hands with her mother and father. "Nice to meet you."

"You two should join us," her father invited, Autumn already waving away the invitation.

"We'd love to." Ramsey grinned at her annoyed expression as the waitress quickly rearranged the tabletop for two additional guests. Ramsey pulled out a chair for Autumn and she sat as if in slow motion. She had to be dreaming. *A nightmare*, she concluded. A terrible nightmare that she'd wake up from any minute now. Under the table, she pinched the top of her hand. *Nope. No dream.* She watched as Ramsey adjusted his legs to fit them somewhat under the table.

"So, you're a client of Autumn's?" her mother asked.

"Sort of." Ramsey beamed.

"A potential client," Autumn clarified, giving him a warning glance. "And what are you guys doing all the way out here?" She looked to her dad.

"Date night." Her parents smiled and held one another's hands on top of the table.

"Date? Here?" Her face held disgust.

"Of course," her dad replied. "We've been coming here for years."

"Wait," Autumn held up her hand. "You always said Maw's was disgusting."

"Maybe we just wanted it for ourselves." Her dad chuckled. "Ever think about that? Maybe your parents wanted some alone time, away from you kiddos."

Ramsey tapped her shoulder, her mouth closing as she turned to him. He pointed upward at the awaiting waitress. "Drink?"

~

"Water," Autumn replied, and Ramsey ordered a beer.

"She'll have a glass of wine as well," Autumn's mother cut in before the waitress ventured away.

"Mom, I cannot drink when I'm here on business."

"Nonsense." Her dad rolled his eyes. "So, Ramsey, are you a local?"

"No sir. I'm not. Just here for the season."

"Interesting. What brings you here?"

"Vacation."

"Ramsey is from the San Juan Islands in Washington," Autumn explained.

Her dad's brows rose. "Beautiful country up there. Tennessee doesn't seem like much of a retreat compared to that."

"It's tradition." Ramsey explained about his grandparents living in Gatlinburg.

"How wonderful to have such a place." Autumn's mom looked pleased.

"Yes ma'am. I'm hoping I can keep it. That's how Autumn and I crossed paths. Apparently the property taxes had been neglected by my Aunt for the last five years and the property is in the midst of foreclosure. I'm determined to save it."

"My goodness." Her mother placed a hand over her heart. "I hate to hear that. And Autumn is helping you?"

"Actually, I represent the bank in this matter."

"So you're just going to sell his family home?" Her mother looked appalled at her daughter for doing such a thing.

"It's not like I have a choice, Mom. And it's not me, it's the bank."

"But surely you could tell them Ramsey plans to pay."

Ramsey counted it as a win that he'd visited with her parents less than ten minutes and they already seemed to like him. It was a nice surprise to meet the people he'd seen in photographs just that morning.

"I have, okay?" Autumn waved her hands as if cutting off the discussion. "I can't really talk about this with you guys. You aren't my client."

"But Ramsey is." Her dad pointed across the table to a grinning Ramsey.

"She hasn't quite adjusted to that idea yet," Ramsey admitted.

"In a completely different manner. I cannot represent him in the foreclosure because I represent the bank. I'm *potentially* representing Ramsey in another matter."

"Ah. I see." Her dad bit back a grin at his flustered daughter and looked to the man across from him. "Do you think you will be able to save the property?"

"I think so." Ramsey took a sip of his beer as Autumn's dad did the same. "I've got a few financial contributions lined up and then Sheriff Hendricks told me about the Smoky Mountains Harvest Festival coming up. I plan to have a vendor's booth there to raise money as well."

"Selling what?" Autumn looked to him in surprise.

"Food." He grinned at her. "I can cook. I'm used to cooking for people." He shrugged.

"Are you a chef?" her mother asked.

"Not quite." He chuckled. "I own a bar that serves a few items on the menu, but I think I could easily come up with a unique festival food to offer that would bring in some dollars."

"You know," her father continued. "we attend the festival every year. Do you have any help?"

Ramsey started to reply when the waitress walked up to take their orders. Autumn turned to him and leaned close. "You cannot accept his help," she whispered.

"Why's that? I could use a helping hand, and he's the only one that's offered."

"Because he is my dad."

"And?"

"That's just... out of the question," she growled, and then forced a polite smile up at the waitress.

"No," Ramsey replied to her dad. "I don't have any help yet."

"Well, count me in. It's been years since I've volunteered at the festival, and it sounds like fun."

"Dad, you don't even know him." Autumn attempted to apply logic to the situation.

"Don't have to." Her dad extended his hand towards Ramsey. "The name's Bobby."

Beaming, Ramsey returned the handshake. "I would appreciate all the help I can get, Bobby. Thank you."

Her mother sighed. "And what am I to do while you help whip up greasy festival food all day?"

"Spread the word," Bobby told her. "You and Autumn can walk around and shop like you usually do and help spread the word."

"Can't." Autumn held up her hand. "Conflict of interest." She pointed at herself.

"Well, then you can entertain your mother. So, Ramsey, how's the fishing up at this cabin of yours? Has the temperature been dropping up there?"

"A bit. The water is pretty chilly, but I've been able to make several good catches. I'll be out there quite a bit over the next couple weeks catching as much as possible. I plan to do fried fish at the festival. If I can catch all the fish needed, I won't have the overhead cost of purchasing it."

"It won't be fresh." Autumn's nose curled.

"It will be frozen and sealed until I need to use it." Ramsey nudged her shoulder. "Wipe that disgusted look off your face. You liked my fish last night."

Her parents exchanged a curious glance.

"It wasn't fried," she pointed out. "But yes, I will admit, it was delicious. You will have to catch a lot of fish to feed the masses."

"I can do it."

"Especially with help." Her dad winked again. "I've got plenty of time on my hands this next week, if you'll have me?"

"Dad, oh my word." Autumn looked to her mother in complete shock. "Again, you don't know him. You can't just invite yourself over to his house. In the mountains. By yourself."

Ramsey, a bit surprised she seemed concerned about her dad's safety around him, felt as if he'd been slapped. He thought after the last couple days, especially the night before, that she saw what kind of guy he was. Apparently, he still scared her or made her nervous. Not his intention.

Bobby ignored her interruption. "I can bring my son tomorrow. He's not the most avid fisherman, but an extra rod in the water may not be bad."

"If you're sure." Ramsey said, unsure now how to move forward.

"Consider it done." Bobby smiled, pleased he had an open invitation to fish in the mountains. "And Autumn, close your mouth. You look like the very fish I plan to snag this week." He pretended to toss a line in her direction and reel her in. Ramsey

started to laugh and felt the sharp pointy elbow land in his ribs and met Autumn's full scowl straight on.

"I'm Wendy," Autumn's mom announced. "Since you and my husband are now fishing buddies it only seems right that you know me as well." Her smile was more focused, her eyes narrowed as she soaked Ramsey in. *Momma Bear*, he thought, surveying whether or not he was to be trusted. He hoped to put her mind at ease.

"Nice to meet you, Wendy. I appreciate you two allowing us to join you tonight. I thought I was going to have to talk boring law and legal jargon throughout dinner."

Bobby guffawed as Autumn sat miserably to the side, swirling her straw in her glass. "Autumn does tend to have a laser focus on her work."

"I'm right here." Autumn motioned to herself as she propped her chin in her hand and continued swirling her water glass, her wine untouched.

~

A warm hand pressed in between her shoulder blades and she blinked away the fog of her mental to do list as she realized she sat alone at the table with Ramsey. Straightening in her chair, she looked around. "Where'd my parents go?"

"They went to walk the back deck to look at the stars and have a glass of wine. You okay? You've been quiet." Ramsey's concerned gaze softened her annoyance.

"Are you done charming them?"

"Charming? I was just talking with them. If anything, they charmed me. They're wonderful people, Autumn."

"I know they are."

"And—"

"We're headed out." Her dad's voice interrupted them, and Ramsey stood to shake his hand and accepted the friendly hug from her mother. Autumn did the same. "I have to say this was a fun evening. Ramsey, I'll aim to be there by nine tomorrow morning."

"I'll hold you to it." Ramsey smiled and accepted the friendly pat on his shoulder as Bobby pointed to Autumn. "And you, young lady, better come by to see your mother and me on Sunday so we can celebrate that birthday of yours."

"I will."

"Good."

Wendy brushed a kiss on Autumn's cheek. "I'm making your cake tomorrow, so you better be there, or we'll all celebrate without you."

"I'll be there, Mom."

"And bring Ramsey." She pointed to the easy-going man laughing at one of her dad's corny jokes as the two men conversed by the door. "He's a delight. And handsome, in a gladiator sort of way."

"Mom!" Autumn blushed at the direction of her mother's thoughts.

"He is. Don't think I've ever seen a man that big before, but he carries it well."

"Carries what well?" Autumn asked. "His size?"

"Confidence." Her mom gently rested a hand on Autumn's back as they walked towards the two men. "And humility. Those are important traits."

"He's just a client."

"I know, but it seems to me he could use a friend around here as well." Wendy accepted the mint her husband picked up for her out of a small bowl on the checkout counter.

"You two be careful heading home," Ramsey told them as her parents walked out hand in hand. "Ready?" Ramsey asked her.

"Yes." She headed out the door and to his old truck in relief.

He took the mountain roads at a snail's pace. Yes, he was being careful, but she was more

than ready to be home. It was Friday, her chance to have a glass of wine and unwind watching a movie she'd snagged from the kiosk outside the market during her lunch break. She and Puddin' would snuggle on the couch with her favorite blanket, she'd fall asleep before the movie ended and wake up around two or three and shuffle towards her bed. It was the same every Friday.

"I'm sorry." Ramsey's voice cut through her mind.

"What?"

"I'm sorry."

"For what?"

"For imposing."

Confused, she turned in her seat to face him. "On what?"

Sighing, he scratched his bearded chin. "Well, for accepting the invite at your parents' table. I could see you did not want me to meet them and I forced it any way. I apologize."

"Oh." Her voice was quiet as she watched him guide the steering wheel around a curve.

"It's just... I guess I'm missing my family and friends more than usual. With everything going on with the foreclosure, I could just really use my family right about now. It was nice to be surrounded by one, even if it wasn't mine."

She saw the slight embarrassment that stained his cheeks at admitting he was somewhat lonely and homesick. She understood those feelings. Not the homesick, but definitely the lonely, and she had yet to even think about how it must feel to face the foreclosure on his home in Tennessee.

"Well, if we're being honest..." She rubbed nervous palms over her thighs. "I actually liked Maw's."

A slow smile spread over his face as he turned to grin at her. "Oh really?"

A giggle escaped as she nodded. "Those French fries were incredible. I'm pretty sure they were hand breaded by God himself."

Ramsey laughed. "Maybe I should copy her recipe for the festival."

"You'd sell out, for sure. And look," she shifted in her seat, tucking her left ankle under her right leg to face him instead of the front. "I'm sorry for acting like a spoiled brat most of the evening. I just try really hard to keep my private and professional lives separate."

"I get that, and again, am sorry for forcing you to merge the two tonight."

"Apology accepted. However, that being said, I know my parents. It would not have mattered who

I walked in with, they would have joined us if we hadn't joined them."

"They're nice."

"Sometimes too nice." Though she smiled when she said it.

"I appreciate your dad being willing to help me out. That doesn't cause complications for you does it? Legally, I mean?"

"No. He's his own person. But I won't be able to help you at the festival, Ramsey."

"I understand that, and I wouldn't expect you to. Heck, I don't expect anyone to help me. I planned to do it myself."

"Then I'm glad my dad will at least be an extra pair of hands for you. And you made his day allowing him to come fish with you tomorrow. He loves to fish."

"Allowing? He's more than welcome. I was going to run some trot lines and nets, but another rod in the water, like he said, is helpful." Before she could respond, his cellphone rang. A warm smile flooded his face. "Well, well, well. Hello, beautiful."

Autumn's brow rose as she turned to face the front once again, wondering who might be on the other side of his phone call. She wasn't aware that he had someone special in his life, though she wasn't surprised. Her mother was right in

assessing Ramsey's charm. Autumn had even found herself thinking of him several times throughout the day, which was completely unprofessional and annoying.

"Man, I appreciate you so much. You have no idea," Ramsey continued. "I'll send you the bank information and you can wire it there whenever you're ready. You're a rockstar, Olivia. And I owe you a hot meal when I get back." He chuckled. "Calm down, Summers, you're invited too." He hung up. "Some friends have raised a couple grand already. They're going to wire it on Monday."

"Friends?" she asked, attempting to sound nonchalant.

"Yeah, my best bud got married recently, and his wife is incredible. They've been soldiers for me, raising funds to help."

Why did she feel relieved knowing this Olivia woman was married? "That's great, Ramsey. I'm happy for you."

"You know, you'd probably like Olivia. She's real business driven and can be quite a pistol when she wants to be."

"She sounds great."

"She is." He pulled the truck into the parking lot of her apartment complex and to a stop. He

unbuckled his seatbelt and she rested a hand on his arm.

"You don't have to walk me up. Thanks for the evening. And thanks for dinner."

"Thank your dad. He wouldn't let me pay."

A tender smile washed over her face. "Typical."

"And I don't mind." He hopped out of the truck before she could respond and opened her door.

She fished in her pocket for her keys and her hands nervously gripped them as they walked up the steps. When she unlocked the door, Puddin' sat two feet inside, waiting. Ramsey chuckled. "I'll have you know she is five minutes early." He pointed to the cat. "He informed me of your curfew before we left."

"Did he?" She quirked a brow and hid a smile as she walked inside and set her keys on a small entry table. She picked up Puddin' and nuzzled him against her cheek, the cat purring, but keeping those watchful eyes on Ramsey. "Would you like to come in?" she asked.

Ramsey filled the doorway, hands in pockets. He looked towards the stairs. "I should probably head back."

"Oh. Right. Well, thanks for this evening. I'd offer you a piece of cake, but I haven't exactly been

slicing from it, so it wouldn't be the most sanitary of offers." She blushed.

"You know, cake sounds good."

Surprised, she set Puddin' down on the floor. "But you just said—"

"I changed my mind." Ramsey shrugged as he stepped inside, shutting the door behind him. "Besides, my plan was to take you to dinner and then on a small hike around Maw's. We ate the dinner, but that lasted longer than planned."

"That's why you asked me to wear tennis shoes." Understanding donned Autumn's face.

"You got it. Now, where's that cake?"

## « CHAPTER SIX »

*"So you graduated top* of your class in high school, college, and law school?" Ramsey leaned back against the cushions as he watched Autumn take a hearty bite from the cake on her plate. "I'm impressed."

A sweet tinge of pink stained her cheeks. "Don't be."

Ramsey gave a low whistle under his breath. "Hard not to be. I never even went to college. I barely graduated high school, though not due to bad grades," he clarified. "I just hated it." He chuckled at her surprised expression. "I wanted to be outdoors and didn't like to be contained."

"Did you play sports in school?" she asked.

He grinned. "Let me guess, I look like the football type?"

A brief look of horror crossed her face and she waved her hand. "I didn't mean—"

He gently grabbed her frantic hand and brushed his thumb over her knuckles to calm her nerves. "You didn't offend me, Autumn. I'm pretty used to the question by now." He released her hand, regrettably, and took a sip of his tea. The best sweet tea he'd ever tasted. Homemade. He held up the glass in front of him. "Please tell me you are the one who made this tea."

"Yes. Why? Is it awful?" She shifted as if to rise and walk to the small kitchen.

He rested a hand on her arm. "No. It's incredible."

"Oh. Thanks." She smiled shyly as she eased back into the corner of the couch and tucked her legs underneath her. "My grandma taught me the 'proper' way to make sweet tea."

He lifted a brow. "Want to share your secret?"

She shook her head. "I don't have many secrets, Ramsey Jenkins, but that is one of them."

He chuckled. "I was going to borrow it for the festival. This would sell better than my fish."

Her face grew thoughtful. "You think so?"

"I know so."

She set her plate on the coffee table and stood. Puddin', annoyed at being disturbed beside her, rolled to his other side to shun her presence. She extended a hand towards Ramsey. "Come on."

Curious, he grabbed her hand and accepted her help off the couch. He continued holding it, though he knew she had meant only to help him. But she led him to her kitchen. "You have to promise never to share the recipe and technique with anyone else," she warned.

"Do I need to sign a legal form?" He took a step closer, Autumn nestled between him and the counter.

She leaned her head back to look up at him. "Possibly."

He grinned as he reached up and lightly looped a finger in the hair that framed her face. He could feel the nervous energy emanating from her in pulses and took a step back to look around the small kitchen. "Show me your ways, Autumn Simpson."

She reached for a saucepan and added water to boil. She then grabbed another one and poured ample amounts of sugar into the bottom and covered it with water, explaining measurements as she went. "The trick is the syrup."

"So you boil tea separately from the 'simple syrup', as you call it."

"Yes. *And*—" She withdrew three tea leaves and placed them in the boiling water. "Leaves, not tea bags."

"Why would that make a difference?"

She shrugged. "Stronger, I guess. All I know is that I've done this with tea bags as well and it just doesn't taste the same."

"Fair enough." Ramsey nodded and watched as she stirred the sugar mixture, the sugar slowly melting and blending. "Why are you sharing your secret with me?"

Those calm, cool liquid pools of chocolate glanced up at him. Sighing, she stopped stirring. "If anyone asks, you did not receive anything from me."

"Okay..."

"Because technically it may be misconstrued as helping you."

"Ah. I see."

"If it can help you, Ramsey, use it. If you choose something else to serve at the festival, then you just have a great recipe under your belt for another day." She tucked her hair behind her ear as she turned back to stir the sugar.

She wanted to help him save the property. Her hands were legally tied, but she genuinely wanted to help him. Pleased that she'd offer such help, and also that she'd share a family recipe with him, Ramsey leaned against the counter and watched her every movement. *She had graceful hands*, he thought. Small, but graceful. He tried to remember the way they felt in his own. He hadn't paid attention, and now he wished he had.

She poured the tea into the syrup mixture and stirred. Turning off the burners, she grabbed a glass pitcher and filled it. She then added a few handfuls of ice. "Tada!"

"Taste test. Let's see if it's as good as the other one." He grabbed his glass and handed it to her. She topped it off with a smug smile. "Don't get cocky," he muttered, making her laugh. He liked the sound. And the way her eyes lit up when she did, and the laugh lines around her lips that smoothed away when she sobered.

"Just taste it," she ordered.

He took a sip and swished the tea around his mouth in expert tasting fashion. "It's—" He paused and cast a look at her hopeful expression. "Delicious." There was that beautiful smile again. "You sure you don't mind me using it at the festival?"

"Go for it. You'll want to make as much beforehand as possible. I doubt you'll have the stovetop to do so."

"Actually, I will. Though you're right, I need to have as much made as possible beforehand. That will just make it easier."

"Can I ask you something?"

"Sure." He set his glass aside and crossed his ankles and arms as he waited.

"What happens if this vendor booth doesn't help? Then you've spent all this money on supplies to do it, which cuts into the money you could put towards the foreclosure."

"I just have to make sure it's a success."

"But you can't guarantee that it will be."

"No. But neither can I guarantee that it won't. There's no fault in trying. If it's a waste, and ends up costing more than it earns, so be it. But I'd be a fool not to at least try. Besides, it's cheaper than starting a business. If I can pull this off, then I won't need to set up that LLC we were talking about. I could just set up a trust and fund the trust by doing this event each year. It should, at least, make enough to cover a year's worth of property taxes. It may not cover more than that, but if it does, great. I'm looking long term."

"You would come back every year to do the Harvest Festival?"

"If it's worth it, yes."

"I hope it is, then."

He uncrossed his arms and smiled. "Is this you saying you want to see me every year?"

He watched as amusement danced across her face. "Not in the slightest."

"I thought so." He playfully nudged her. "You're getting used to me. Admit it."

"I'd rather not."

He laughed as he straightened and began walking towards the door. "I should head out. I've got an early morning of fishing ahead of me." He brushed a hand over a sleeping Puddin' on his way by the couch. "If you aren't busy tomorrow, you should stop by."

"Ramsey—"

"I know, I know." He winked. "But your family will be there, so really you would be coming to see them."

"Are you always going to be this..." she waved her hand in the air to try and think of an apt description.

"Charming? Genius? Fun?"

"Invasive," she finished, and he frowned.

"Invasive?" He felt the insult hit his gut and tighten, spreading tension up into his shoulders. Apparently his dissatisfaction showed on his face because Autumn took a cautious step back. "You're the one who asked me in for cake," he pointed out.

"I didn't mean it to be rude," she said. "It's just, since you've shown up in my life it's like you're everywhere."

"I'm sorry to be such a nuisance." He opened the door with a hard yank and stepped out, insulted and more than humiliated that he'd thought they were slowly becoming friends. That she'd grown comfortable with his presence. When, in reality, she was tolerating him until the blessed day that he left.

"Ramsey!" she called after him as he pounded down the stairwell towards his truck.

She didn't want him around. Fine. That was fine. There'd be no sense in prolonging her torture. He'd head back to the cabin. He had other problems, bigger problems, that required his attention. A pretty lawyer who didn't want him around didn't need to be one of them. Without glancing back, he hopped in his truck and headed home.

~

The sun had been up for quite a few hours. The air was crisp with the scent of leaves and a light breeze blew through her open car window as she sat at the end of Ramsey's drive, trying to muster the courage to keep driving forward. She'd hurt his feelings last night. Unintentionally. Okay, maybe she was a bit forward. *And harsh*, her conscience reminded her. But Ramsey Jenkins had imposed himself right in the middle of her structured and comfortable life. Since the first day she had pulled up this same drive, he'd continually popped up. At her work. At her home. And now he was fishing with her dad and brother? What was she supposed to do with that? She barely knew the man. A knock tapped against her doorframe and she jumped in her seat, hand over her racing heart when she looked up into the questioning blue eyes of Ramsey. "What are you doing scaring me like that?!" she barked.

"Didn't mean to sneak up on you."

"For such a big guy you're extremely light on your feet." She ran a flustered hand through her hair. "And what are you doing here?"

"Shouldn't I be asking you that?" His face held puzzled amusement.

She moaned in annoyance and shoved her door open, climbing out of the car to face him. She saw his truck parked behind her, her dad and brother in the passenger seats. "What are they doing?"

"We had to make a bait run," he explained. "We were headed back, and since you're blocking my drive, I came to check on you."

"I'm fine." She crossed her arms and hugged herself.

"Clearly." Ramsey began walking back towards his truck. "You mind just pulling up towards the cabin to move your car? We're trying to get by."

Mouth ajar at his apathetic departure, she narrowed her eyes at his back before climbing back into her vehicle. "Fine," she fumed. He wanted to play it cool, she'd play it cool.

When she pulled up in front of the shabby cabin, her dad and brother, Calvin, hopped out of Ramsey's truck eager to get back to fishing. Calvin lingered at Ramsey's side, watching the man's every move. Ramsey handed him a rod. "Guard it with your life, kid."

Calvin nodded. "You bet! Thanks!" Pleased to be using one of Ramsey's personal rods, Calvin held it up for her to see. "This is the coolest pole I've ever used, Autty."

She forced an excited smile for him as he darted off to show their dad. "Thanks for being nice to him."

"It's not hard. He's a nice kid." Ramsey lifted a cooler from the truck, opening the lid to check the aerator and that the minnows were still swimming. "You here to bring me more forms?"

"Forms?" she asked.

"For me to sign." Ramsey shut the lid of the cooler and began carrying it towards the bank of the pond in between her dad and brother. She followed.

"No. Why would I need more signatures?"

"Just figured that's why you were here." He walked back towards the truck and lifted the second cooler with ease, his biceps taut.

"Maybe I just wanted to come by."

"Really?" His brow lifted. "Now who's being invasive." He walked the cooler towards the pond and lifted a rod to prep for himself.

"You asked me to come," she pointed out.

"Funny how that works, isn't it?" Ramsey never even looked up as he reached into the cooler and withdrew a small minnow in his hand and worked it onto his hook.

"Okay, I see what you're doing." Autumn sighed. "I'm sorry about what I said last night."

"Are you?" He looked up from his crouched position by the cooler, his annoyance and hurt evident.

"I just... I'm not used to people being so..."

"Nice?" he asked.

"Well, no, just—"

"Friendly?"

Frustrated, she fisted her hands on her hips and stepped into his line of sight and blocked his view of the water. He stood and she felt her confidence waver as her eyes evened with the middle of his chest. "Maybe, okay. I just... don't want you to be upset with me."

"Why?"

"What do you mean why? I just don't."

"Why does it matter if I am?" Ramsey asked, stepping around her and closer to the water to cast his line out. She watched as he expertly flicked his wrist and the small dip into the water could be heard. His eyes surveyed the ripples and she stepped in front of him again, her shoes slightly sinking in the dampness of the water's edge.

"Ramsey," Her voice quieted. "I'm sorry if I hurt your feelings last night."

His eyes briefly darted towards her and then back at the water.

"I've enjoyed getting to know you."

He didn't say a word.

She took another step and felt the water seep up over her shoe. "Agh!" She looked down and saw a line of brown next to her foot. She screamed bloody murder and high stepped away from the pond, slipping as her shoe sank in the mud. She tugged, begging for Ramsey's help as he looked at her baffled. He dropped his rod and reached towards her, her hand taking hold of his arm in a death grip. He tugged and her foot slipped from her shoe and she lunged towards him, half crawling up his side, half hiding behind him as she pointed towards the water. "Sn-nnake!"

Ramsey started forward and Autumn held him back by gripping her fists into the back of his plaid shirt. He reached behind him and freed her hands. "Careful, Ramsey!" Her voice was shrill and face white as he walked to the pond's edge to retrieve her shoe. When he reached down, he lifted a thin curved branch snagged amongst the grass and rocks.

"This your snake?" he asked with a restrained smile.

"W-what?" Autumn smoothed her hands over her light sweater. "I thought... I thought it was." She held a hand to her heart and took a relaxing deep breath.

Ramsey tossed the stick back into the water and bent to fetch her abandoned shoe. He poured water out of it and walked it towards her. "No snake, but way to be alert."

She pushed a hand against his chest as he burst into hearty laughter. Her dad and brother grinned as they watched an embarrassed Autumn try to regain her composure.

"It could have been," was all she could manage as she sat on top of the cooler by Ramsey's side, removing her wet sock. Hearing his deep chuckle, she looked up at him. He stood watching the water, but his amusement at her expense still had him casting glimpses her direction. "Eat it up," she said. "I'm not embarrassed. It could have been an actual snake, and I'm terrified of snakes."

"No kidding? I could hardly tell. Though if you'd crawled any higher, I'd have had to carry you on my shoulders."

She tossed a handful of dirt against his pant leg but felt the corners of her mouth lift. "Good thing you're tall."

He flicked his wrist and cast his rod into a new spot when excitement across the pond had

her brother Calvin frantically reeling in what looked to be a promising catch. Her father cheered him on and when the fish broke the surface, Ramsey cheered as well, her shy brother basking in the positive attention. She watched as he held up his catch for all to see.

"Nice one!" Ramsey held a hand to his mouth and yelled, and they watched as Bobby helped tie the fish on the line.

"This is good for him," Autumn said. "He's a pretty quiet kid, and doesn't always have an easy go of it at school."

"Meaning?"

"He's a shy kid and high school sucks."

"He gets bullied?" Ramsey asked, a protective tone entering his voice that made her appreciate him even more.

"Yes. Not all the time, and from what I gather, it's gotten better. But he's a junior in high school and I know last year was rough. I remember what that's like, and it's hard."

"*You* were bullied?" Now Ramsey looked full-fledged mad, one fist white knuckling his rod, the other gripped into a tight ball.

"When you're smart, quiet, and a bit socially awkward, you tend to be an easy target."

"Kids can be mean."

"You have no idea," she sighed. "Well, I should head out. I just came to apologize and to thank you for including the two of them. They seem to be enjoying themselves." She motioned towards her dad and brother. "Thanks for saving me from the snake."

"The stick," he corrected, accepting the friendly punch to his shoulder. "And Autumn, apology accepted. I'm glad you were at least open about me making you uncomfortable. It wasn't my intention, and I'm sorry if I scared you or made you nervous."

"You didn't. Haven't. I just... I'm not used to someone wanting to be my friend, especially a complete stranger. I'm a bit out of practice at making friends."

"I think you're doing just fine," Ramsey assured her. His serious eyes lingered on hers. "Take care, Autumn."

Wishing to stay longer, but not wanting to seem overly eager, she walked her way around the curve of the pond to say farewell to her dad and to congratulate her brother on his catch before she left. Back in her car, she flashed one more glance towards the pond and spotted Ramsey staring her direction as well. Her cheeks flushed at him catching her, but instead of ducking her head in embarrassment, she lifted her hand in a final

wave; one he returned with that charming, cracked tooth smile.

## « CHAPTER SEVEN »

*Two weeks flew by* and preparations for the Smoky Mountains Harvest Festival kept Ramsey more than busy. He'd purchased a used food truck, and spent an entire weekend fixing and repairing the inside to his specifications. He, with the help of Calvin, gave the outside a fresh coat of paint, and now it was ready for business. He snapped a picture with his phone and texted it to his friends at Friday Harbor. Within seconds of sending, his phone rang.

"Hey big brother," he greeted, Reagan's familiar huff as he sat filling the line.

"Looks good. Meals on wheels. Never thought that'd be your thing."

"Gotta do what I can."

"Speaking of that, Mom is beside herself with Aunt Ceecee."

"I can imagine so." Ramsey shook his head in complete disappointment. "I'm just thankful I don't have to handle the estate business."

"How's the fundraising going? When's the maiden voyage of your new restaurant on wheels?" Ramsey asked.

"Tomorrow morning, bright and early."

"And what's for sale?"

"A little bit of this. A little of that."

"Gee, don't make my stomach grumble." Sarcastically, Reagan sighed. "You talk to Jake recently?"

"The other day. Seems like things are fine. How's your investigation going?"

"Beating my head against a brick wall. Frustrating. We caught a couple teens trying to break into some house boats, but they were just some riff raff from the mainland. Not the thieves I've been looking for."

"Hm." Ramsey rubbed his chin, making a mental note to trim his beard before the following day.

"Mom said you've made a big decision the last couple days about the cabin," Reagan prodded.

"Yeah, I guess so. We'll see if it works out. I'm going to risk it."

"What does your pretty little attorney say?"

"My what?"

Reagan laughed through the line. "Jake said you had a nice-looking attorney helping you out."

"She's not helping me out. She represents the bank in the foreclosure."

"Oh. Jake made it sound like—"

"No telling what Jake made it sound like." Ramsey shook his head and grinned. "Autumn's great though. Her dad is helping me at the festival tomorrow."

"Her dad? Already meeting the family."

"It's not like that, it was just by chance, and—" Ramsey rubbed the back of his neck, not liking Reagan's assumption. "You know what, I've got to go. I've got some last-minute prep to do in the food truck. Plus, I'm making what feels like a thousand gallons of sweet tea as well."

"Well, best of luck, little brother. Keep me updated on how things go."

"You bet. See ya." Ramsey hung up and lugged yet another water cooler into the back of his truck. He'd borrowed several coolers from various people in town, thanks to Bobby doing the asking, and he planned to make as much tea as possible so as not to have to worry about it throughout the day. His hope, however, was that he'd sell so much that he'd need to make more, but it would help to have some already prepped, much like Autumn recommended. And speaking of Autumn, he hadn't seen her in several days, though he'd been swamped in preparation and she was handling her usual workload. He made the effort to pop in on her every few days or so, and so far, she hadn't seemed annoyed by him. In fact, she'd relaxed more and more with each visit. But there was still a line of familiarity she didn't cross, which was understandable considering her position. He hoped after the auction that maybe she'd feel completely free to be his friend. He sensed that might take some convincing, but he wasn't afraid of hard work.

He checked the trailer light connections as a truck pulled into his driveway. Bobby stepped out carrying two more coolers. "Got a couple more."

"You're a magician." Ramsey smiled as Autumn's dad placed them into the bed of Ramsey's truck.

"You setting up tonight?"

"Yes sir. I was about to head that way."

"Want some help?"

"I won't turn it down." Ramsey nodded towards the passenger side of his truck and Bobby walked around and made himself comfortable in the seat as he waited for Ramsey to make last adjustments to the trailer and food truck. When he climbed in and cranked the engine, he slowly made his way down the drive. "I can't thank you enough, Bobby, for all your help with this."

"It's not a problem. I've had fun and I know Calvin's enjoyed helping you. He's come out of his shell the last couple weeks, thanks to you."

Unsure of how to respond, Ramsey navigated his way down the mountain and into Gatlinburg. The festival would spread across the Parkway, Reagan Street, and surrounding side streets. Pavilions were already raised in some areas; barbeque pits, flat bed trailers for musicians sat empty and ready for the early morning. There was a buzz in the air and a warmth that spoke of community and fun, much like Friday Harbor during the touristy months. He pulled up to the barricaded entrance and withdrew his vendor pass. The officer nodded and waved him onward. "I think that'll be us up there." Bobby pointed towards a corner space that, much to Ramsey's delight, was located near a music stand and several large vendor booths.

"This is usually a hot spot," Bobby continued. "Glad we were able to get this location."

"You wouldn't have had anything to do with that, would you?" Ramsey asked him.

Bobby shrugged his shoulders. "Keith and I go way back."

"Keith, as in the organizer of the festival?"

"Yes. He was more than happy to give us the spot."

Ramsey stared at the man.

"What?" Bobby asked.

"I'm indebted to you, Bobby. I just don't know what to say to all that you've done to help me."

"Thanks is enough. Trust me, my daughter and son are like two different people since meeting you."

"I don't know about that." Ramsey backed the trailer into the designated spot and parked.

"I do," Bobby continued. "You've given them confidence, Ramsey. I don't know how, but you have. It's hard on a parent to watch your kids suffer. And though they've had good lives, friends were hard to come by. I'm glad they've found that in you."

"Not sure if Autumn would call me a friend," Ramsey joked.

Bobby chuckled. "Autty's a tough nut to crack, and part of that is my fault. We put so much pressure on her growing up that she never learned how to

just relax and roll with the flow. She lives a very structured life."

"Oh, I've noticed."

Bobby smirked.

"I'm afraid I've disrupted it quite a bit."

"And I'm glad." Bobby opened the door. "Now, let's get this baby set up."

~

"Your dad could barely sleep a wink last night." Wendy laughed as she waved towards someone she recognized in the crowd, her arm linked with Autumn's. "He was so excited. Said Ramsey was a bit nervous last night."

"Was he? I haven't talked to him in a few days," Autumn noted. "What time did Dad come up here this morning?"

"I think they met about six."

"Why so early?"

"Something about making tea," her mom said, which had Autumn grinning.

"That early he should have thought about serving coffee."

"Oh, they are." Her mother beamed proudly. "Ramsey told your dad he wanted to reach as

many people as possible, so he's covering every meal he can. I think their breakfast items are sausage biscuits. Want one?"

"Not right now," Autumn replied, not wanting to venture over to Ramsey's just yet. In truth, she'd somewhat been avoiding him the last week. It wasn't that she didn't want to see him, quite the opposite. And that's what worried her. She wanted to see him all the time and that just couldn't develop any further. Those feelings. Those thoughts and longings for companionship. He lived in Washington, after all, and would be leaving in a couple of months to go back. Her life was in Tennessee, so the thought of something more with him was out of the question. Not that he'd asked for more. In fact, he'd never even shown he was interested in more, which she had to admit, she'd hoped for. He'd politely kept his distance other than being a friend. And even then, she tried to keep him at arm's length so as not to compromise her position at the firm.

"I think this was the first morning in years I didn't have to drag Calvin out of bed. He was just as eager as your dad."

"That's good." Autumn ran a hand over a floral blouse at one of the booths and paused to flip the tag over and gauge the price.

"That's pretty," her mom complimented. "Would look great with your capris."

Sighing, Autumn continued browsing. "Can't really justify anything other than clothes I can wear to work."

"You could if you spent less time there," her mom hummed as she shifted several tops aside on another rack.

"It's work. I can't exactly brush it off, Mom."

"I just meant you don't have to be at the office so late. Leave at five just like everyone else."

"I don't mind working late hours."

"I know you don't, but there's more to life than work."

"I know that."

"Do you?" Her mom quirked a brow and watched as her daughter ran her fingers over the floral top once again. "Get it, Autumn. It would look beautiful on you. And sometimes it's okay to buy something frivolous for ourselves. Besides, if things go well today, we will have a celebratory dinner at Maw's. You could wear it tonight."

"I shouldn't be at the celebration when I represent the other client, Mom."

"Oh, stop it. You know as well as I do that the bank only cares about getting paid."

"Still." Autumn shrugged as they continued walking. She loved the festival. Enjoyed it every year, and even looked forward to it. Gatlinburg's charm was beautiful on any given day, but during harvest festival the town lit up. She passed Ripley's Believe It or Not and watched as several families exited with bright smiles, looking for the next fun activity.

"Ms. Autumn." Sheriff Hendricks stood with a cup of coffee in a Styrofoam cup dressed in his uniform as he chatted with several other men she recognized from the city council.

"Hi, Sheriff."

"Mrs. Simpson," he greeted Wendy.

"Sheriff. Lovely day, isn't it?"

"Quite good so far." He turned his attention to Autumn. "Saw your dad and brother helping Mr. Jenkins at his food truck." He held up his cup of coffee. "Best brew I've had in a long time."

"I'm glad."

"Mr. Jenkins is a good man." He directed his comment more towards her mom, but his eyes remained on her.

"I've meant to ask you how you know him," Autumn mentioned. "You two seem to be good acquaintances."

Sheriff Hendricks chuckled. "Never met him until a few weeks ago, but he's Donald's grandson. My daddy was a pal of his grandpa's. That cabin was a fishing hotspot for the two of them. Ramsey and I just swap old stories and tales we've heard over the years. It's nice to find a young person that will do that. Besides, never seen a man work so hard to save his family property. Seems like you and I post foreclosures on a lot of those old cabins. Don't recall anyone stepping up the way he has."

"He would be one of the few," Autumn admitted.

"Well, I don't mind supporting him. Especially if he can make this coffee by the gallon," he laughed. "This is my third cup."

"Oh my." Autumn grinned. "Pace yourself, Sheriff. I hear he has amazing sweet tea for later."

The sheriff's eyes lit up. "Now that sounds good too. You ladies have a good day." He toasted towards them and turned back to his friends.

"Seems like we aren't the only ones Ramsey has impressed," her mom whispered.

"He's a charming guy," Autumn explained. "Friendly. It's not a big surprise that people like him."

"What about you?" Wendy asked.

"Hm?" Autumn looked up at her mom's inquisitive stare and shrugged. "I consider him a good acquaintance."

"That's all?"

"Why wouldn't it be?" Autumn asked, picking up a pair of silver hooped earrings. Her mom shook her head in distaste and Autumn put them back.

"Just seems like he's the first person you've ever really made time for the last several years."

"I haven't *made* time for him. He forces me to make time. There's a difference," Autumn replied on a small laugh that her mother shared.

"He is an imposing figure." Her mom pointed as they rounded the curve of the street and Ramsey's bright blue food truck sat on the corner, a long line awaiting the goodies from within. Ramsey's upper half could be seen in the back, probably cooking, as her dad and Calvin reached through the small window and handed drinks and food to customers. Calvin's smile was radiant as he worked, and she had to admit it was good to see. Ramsey turned around, and though he didn't look her direction, she felt her pulse quicken. She wondered how all three of them fit in the tiny truck and found herself giggling at the thought.

"What's so funny?" her mom asked.

"Just thinking how tight it must be in that little buggy."

Her mom grinned. "They seem to be managing it just fine. How about some coffee?"

"That is a long line, Mom. I'd rather just walk around the booths."

"Oh, I think we could bypass that line. Come on." Her mom grabbed her hand and steered her towards the side door of the truck that was left ajar to welcome the breeze and help circulate the air inside. "Excuse me," Wendy called. "Can my lovely daughter and I get two coffees?"

Ramsey, without looking up answered. "Sorry ma'am, the line is out fr—" He trailed off when he spotted them, and his concentrated scowl turned into a wide and welcoming smile. "Two?" He held up his fingers and her mom nodded. "I think I can handle that. Kid!" he barked, and Calvin turned around eager to please.

"Yes sir?"

Ramsey pointed towards the door.

"Hey Mom." Calvin beamed.

"Two coffees, please."

"Coming right up." Calvin bustled towards the cylinder at the back.

"How's the festival?" Ramsey asked, as he expertly prepared four sausage biscuits, wrapped them, and placed them on the counter for her dad to hand out. He glanced at Autumn.

"Good. We just got here, so other than bumping into the sheriff, we haven't done much yet."

Wendy accepted the coffee and handed Calvin crisp bills.

"Now, Ms. Wendy, yours is on the house." Ramsey nodded for Calvin to hand her money back.

Wendy held up her hand. "No sir. I'm a paying customer today." She smiled and handed Autumn her own cup. "We'll get out of your hair, Ramsey. Come on, Autumn." She pointed to a booth across from his. "They've got some lovely woodwork over there. Let's go check it out."

"Good luck." Autumn watched as he continued working, never breaking stride as he whipped up breakfast sandwich after breakfast sandwich.

"Thanks. You too." He nodded at her overly eager mom who was already walking away.

Autumn lingered a moment longer, their eyes lingering on one another. She couldn't seem to move her feet. Now that she was finally able to see him, she didn't want to walk away. He handed the next order to Calvin and then walked towards her, stepping down the two small steps that led

into the truck. He wore a half apron around his waist, the sleeves of what seemed to be his favorite plaid shirt were rolled up at the elbows. He leaned down and kissed her cheek.

Autumn hopped back in surprise, her hand flying up to rest where his lips had just been. "What was that for?" Breathless, she looked up at him.

"For stopping by." Ramsey reached out and squeezed her hand. "Thanks." He turned and walked back to his post, quickly making up time for his brief absence. Autumn, stunned and slightly off-kilter, found her feet and slowly made her way towards her mom across the street. She turned several times to look Ramsey's direction, but he was busy. But her heart and her cheek still felt that light brush of his lips.

# « CHAPTER EIGHT »

*"It's all breaded* and ready to go. All you do is plop the basket in the grease, hit this button here and wait for the timer to go off. Then you pour it into the awaiting trays. Got it?" Ramsey looked to an excited Calvin and the teen nodded. "Alright, go for it." He backed away and began helping Bobby at the counter.

"Go. Take a break. We've got this," Bobby told him, the lunch rush slowly winding down.

"What about you?"

"I've been to the festival before. You haven't. Walk around, stretch your legs a bit. If we need you, I'll call."

"Alright, I appreciate it."

"I know you do. Now get." Bobby smiled as he handed change to an awaiting hand.

Ramsey stepped out of the truck, hanging his apron on the doorknob and inhaled a deep breath of fresh air. It felt great stepping out of the confined quarters. He straightened his back and stretched before walking across the street to start perusing the various pavilions. His first thought was to call Autumn and meet up with her, but he wanted to take a few minutes for himself and enjoy Gatlinburg. Growing up, they'd rarely ventured into town except for supplies. He'd never even known about the harvest festival and could have come years ago if he had. There was too much to Gatlinburg to try and soak it all in in one day; so many shops he wanted to visit. So, he decided his brief break would be to just check out the festival booths, and then he'd venture into town to be a tourist another day.

Sheriff Hendricks offered a wave as he passed by and Ramsey nodded in greeting, his hands in his pockets. He walked up to a small booth where an old man whittled away at a lump of wood, the head of a coyote taking shape as he carved. Various animals and figurines graced the table in front of him. Looking them over, Ramsey moved on to the next booth.

"Ramsey." Wendy's voice had him looking up to see Autumn's mom and a gaggle of other women. She beamed. "I was just talking about you with all

my friends." She tugged him over. "This is the young man I was telling you about."

The women openly looked him up and down, which he was used to, in regards to his size, but the gleam in their eyes was new. He wasn't quite sure how he felt about being on display.

"This is Rita," Wendy introduced. "She's the sheriff's wife," she explained. "And that's Tabitha, Denise, and Margaret."

"It's nice to meet you all," Ramsey said, dreading the fact he was to stay and talk longer based on Wendy linking her arm through his.

"He has just been such a jewel to our family the last few weeks," Wendy continued.

Feeling a bit embarrassed at her praise, Ramsey shifted on his feet.

"Mom, what are you doing?" Autumn's clipped tone cut through the conversation as she walked towards them, several bags in her hands. She cast a pitying look at Ramsey's flushed face.

"Ah, there she is. I won't hold you two up." She released Ramsey and nudged him towards Autumn, who burned with fury at her mom's indiscreet wink in her direction.

"What are you doing here?" Autumn asked, her first instinct to lash out at Ramsey.

He held up his hands. "I was just walking by. She nabbed me," he grumbled as Autumn tugged him in a different direction than the whispering ladies.

"I meant, what are you doing out of your food truck?"

"Taking a short break to walk the festival grounds. I needed some air and your dad was willing to cover for me."

"Oh." She stopped her hot pursuit of an exit as soon as she felt they were far enough from prying eyes and ears. She swiped a hand to tuck her hair behind her ear. "How's it going so far?"

"Good, I think. I have no idea how much money we've made, but based on inventory levels I'd say we're doing pretty good."

"Good to hear."

"How about you? How's your day been? I see you've found a few things."

"Oh, yeah, some." She held up her bags and cringed. "This one is heavy though. I may go put it in my car." She pointed to the creases on her arms the bag had made.

"Here, let me lug it for a while." He slid the bag off her arm.

"Thanks."

"Walk with me?" He saw the fretfulness that weaved its way onto her face. "I don't know anyone else really. Would be nice to have some company."

"Okay, I guess for a little while."

He bit back a smile of victory as they ambled through various booths. "I like it here."

"Hm?" She looked up from the decorative wreaths displayed on a table.

"Gatlinburg. I've never really taken the time to tour the place. And so far, the people have been great too. It's a nice place. And the tourists make it feel like home a bit. I'm used to tourists."

"What's it like at Friday Harbor?" Autumn asked. "I mean, the city itself."

"Not as big. And it's mostly boardwalks and small streets. Smells like the ocean. That's one of the things I miss first. But I also like the smell of the trees up at the cabin."

"Maybe you'll be more social next year then, now that you know some people here."

He peered down at her. "As long as I can bug you while I'm here."

She grinned. "Maybe. I might be busy."

"I'm sure you will be." He tugged on her hair. "Pencil me in now so I can get on your schedule."

She patted his arm. "Dinner at Maw's it is then."

He laughed and grabbed the hand that was on his arm and linked it with his own. He brought it to his lips and kissed the back. "It's a date." He pulled her in front of him, forcing their walk to an end. "I should head back to the truck. I want to extend the luxury of a break to your dad and brother as well."

Disappointment crossed her face and he tilted her chin up to look at him. "The festival ends at eight. I'm hoping to be packed up and out of here by nine and then will head to Maw's for a late meal. Will you come?" He brushed his thumb over her delicate chin before she shyly stepped back.

"I'm not sure if I should."

"Oh, right, the foreclosure thing."

"Right."

"How about this? If I raised enough money, you should come. If I didn't, then don't, because then that means the foreclosure is happening and you still represent the opposition."

"Ramsey—"

"Please." He soaked in her deep brown eyes as he saw the war within all over her face. He felt that

same pull, that same tug, that same attraction but hesitancy towards her, but he knew, of all people, he had to let Autumn make the next move and the decision on her own. Was he interested? Yes. He'd missed her the last few days. Tidy, control freak that she was, he missed her. She was beautiful and had no idea, which made her even more so. And when she sassed him, all he wanted was to kiss her.

"We'll see. That's the best I can do."

"I'll take it." He nodded over his shoulder. "I need to get back." He handed her bag to her. "See you later." He waited for her to turn and meander her way back into the crowd before heading back across the street to his truck. When he walked up, Calvin sat smugly on the steps.

"You sitting down on the job, kid?" Ramsey asked, kicking the boy's shoe so he'd stand and let him pass.

"Taking a break."

"You've earned it." Ramsey poked his head into the truck and spotted Bobby sitting on top of one of the coolers taking his own siesta while there were no customers. "Go, walk around." He smiled. "I'll man the fort."

"I'm fine." Bobby waved a tired hand. "I don't think I have it in me to walk around."

"Doing alright?" Ramsey's eyes narrowed in concern.

"Oh, I'm fit as a fiddle. Just tired legs. I want to sit, not walk."

"Same," Calvin echoed on the steps.

"So, how's Autumn?" Calvin asked, his tone leading, as he looked up at Ramsey.

Bobby chuckled at his son's comment and Ramsey ruffled the kid's hair. "She seems fine."

"You sure? Wasn't sure if you guys were going to kiss or hit one another over there." Calvin pointed to his viewpoint of the exact spot Ramsey and Autumn had stood.

"Spying, huh?" Ramsey asked, unashamed.

"I'm a younger brother, it's my job."

"And one he takes very seriously, good or bad." Bobby laughed.

Ramsey looked to Autumn's brother. "And what if I wanted to kiss her?" Ramsey asked. "What would you think about that?"

Calvin turned to face his dad in surprise and Bobby grinned. "I'd say that's just fine." Bobby nodded towards Calvin. "What about you, Cal?"

"It'd be cool." He nodded. "Yeah, I think it'd be cool if you and Autumn... you know."

Ramsey extended his hand towards Bobby and shook it and then to Calvin. "Good to know. Now I will just have to convince Autumn of that as well."

Bobby shook his head. "Good luck, son. Good luck."

~

The noise was deafening. Even as she stepped out of the car and shut the door, she could hear the cheer bursting from inside Maw's shack. Whether or not that was all for Ramsey, she wasn't sure, but the sound confirmed he'd raised enough money to save his family's cabin. Relieved he'd done it, and proud of him too, she stepped inside. She saw them—her mom, dad, Calvin, Sheriff Hendricks and his wife, and Ramsey all crowded amongst two adjoining tables, eating and drinking merrily. Her brother looked like a completely different kid. Her parents looked relaxed and less polished than she'd ever seen them. When she was growing up, they were strict on appearances. It was as if she didn't recognize the people in front of her. Of course, maybe it was just Maw's that brought this side out of them. Her dad spotted her and waved, and she watched as he tapped Ramsey on the shoulder and pointed towards her. Ramsey's face lit up at the sight of her and her heart dropped to her knees. He was happy to see her. He walked over, all eyes on the two of them as he approached her. He grabbed her hands. "I'm glad you made it."

"I take it by the size of this celebration you made your goal."

"I have no idea," Ramsey replied.

"What?" Autumn withdrew her hands and gave them the nervous task of holding her purse strap on her shoulder. "You don't know?"

"No. I haven't counted the money yet. We were a bit fried ourselves after today, so we celebrated a fun day regardless of the amount we brought in."

"Ramsey," Frustrated, Autumn shook her head. "I can't be here then."

"Autumn—"

"No. The deal was that if you met your goal I would come. I can't be here if you don't know."

"Then we'll go count it right now."

"No. You guys are having a good time."

"But not with you. Stay." Those soft blue eyes pleaded.

She shook her head. "I shouldn't be here. Call me Monday when you know for certain. The auction is Friday."

"I know. At least come say hi to everyone." He turned to wave in the direction of the table and chuckled. "They're having a great time. I couldn't have done it without their hel—" he trailed off as

he turned around and Autumn was gone. Angry that she'd slipped out without hesitation, he felt that familiar annoyance with her blind dedication to her work. He knew she was right in her actions. Being here and celebrating would blur the lines of professionalism for her, but at what point would she hang the hat and call it a day? Determined not to let it sour his mood too much, Ramsey headed back to the boisterous crowd at the table. He caught the understanding gaze of Bobby's, but forced a smile.

When Maw made the rounds with a metal pail and spoon, clanking around the restaurant that it was closing time, the herded customers made their way out into the parking lot.

Sheriff Hendricks pumped Ramsey's hand. "Job well done today, Ramsey. I hope it pays off. Literally."

"Me too. Thanks for the support."

"Of course. Call me if you need anything."

"I'm so proud of you." Wendy gave him a tight squeeze that involved rocking him back and forth on his heels as she hugged.

"Thank you, Mrs. Simpson."

"It's Wendy, remember?" She patted his arm before stepping away and her husband stepped forward.

"It was a whirlwind, but a lot of fun." Bobby shook his hand and planted a friendly pat in the middle of his back.

"You and Calvin were my saving grace," Ramsey admitted.

"We were glad to help. Most fun I've had in a long time. And my boy needed it. Thank you."

"No problem."

"Let me know what the total comes to tomorrow. You've got my number." He pointed as if serious and Ramsey nodded.

"I sure will."

"Me too," Calvin told him. "You have my number too."

Ramsey and Bobby chuckled at the boy's enthusiasm at being considered a friend.

"Definitely will, kid."

"Careful going home," Wendy called over her shoulder as they walked away.

Ramsey inhaled the scent of the mountains and sighed. It had been an incredible day. He walked towards his truck and opened the door. A gift bag rested in his front seat. He withdrew the card.

*Saw this and thought of you. – Autumn*

He reached into the bag and withdrew a wooden sign in the shape of a fish that held hooks along the bottom to hold keys or caps. On it, it read: Ramsey's Cabin. She'd had it hand-painted for him. Sliding into the truck, he headed back to his grandfather's cabin, only the fish sign was right, it no longer felt like his grandfather's cabin. It felt like his own. And perhaps after his conversation with his mom and uncle, it was time to stop referring to it as Grandpa's cabin. It was his. It was Ramsey Jenkins' cabin now. And he was determined to keep it that way.

When he parked, he hopped out, grabbing the money bag from beneath the seat. It was time to face the music. It was time to see if he'd earned enough money to save the property.

He withdrew a beer from the refrigerator and sat on the worn couch, sinking slightly in the middle due to the old springs. He reached into the bag and began counting. Stacks of one hundred, then stacks of one thousand. Slowly, the amount continued to build, and he finally had his answer.

## « CHAPTER NINE »

*He hadn't raised enough.* She didn't hear the news from Ramsey himself, but from her dad. He'd called as soon as she was in her office begging her to ask the bank for a longer extension on Ramsey's behalf. Her hands were tied. If Ramsey asked for more time, she'd try, but the bank had made their decision. The cabin and surrounding property would go up on the auction block on Friday morning at 8 AM. He still had the entire week to raise whatever money he needed. Hopefully it wasn't much, and she'd be lying if she said she wasn't curious of the amount he had, but her job was to represent the bank, not Ramsey. By choosing the vendor's booth instead of starting a new business, he did not need her legal services. Therefore, their conversations had to remain brief. And she didn't like it. She didn't like that she

couldn't spend more time with him. She wanted to. She wanted to feel his hands on her face again. Those big hands, tender and gentle, that brushed her hair behind her ear and cupped her chin. But she couldn't. She eyed the clock on the wall and decided that since she could not get her mind off of Ramsey, it was best to head to an early lunch and regroup. She'd come back after some food and feel more herself and be able to tackle the rest of her workload. She grabbed her purse, leaving her leather briefcase by her desk, and headed outside to her car. She started to lift the handle when she spotted Ramsey's truck down the street. He was reaching over the side of the bed and removed a pile of fishing rods. *What was he doing?* She hurried up the sidewalk as he collected the last of what he was needing.

"Ramsey." She saw his shoulders tighten before turning around. His face was serious and hard.

"Autumn."

"What are you doing?" she asked.

He tilted his head. "What does it matter?"

She realized her approach seemed abrupt and backpedaled. "I mean, I saw you here and thought I'd come to see what you were doing with all your fishing poles."

"Selling them."

"Selling?" Her eyes widened. "But why?"

"For money." He moved his fingers as if fingering cash. "I'm sure you've heard by now that I didn't raise enough money to cover the back taxes and fees."

"I did. My dad told me."

"Hm. Well, I've got to find some way to get it, so I'm selling my rods. They're top of the line, so I should get quite a bit. Not enough, but more money to go towards my total."

"How much do you need?"

"About fifteen hundred."

"That's not bad at all." Her voice brightened. "You're so close."

"Yet so far." He nodded towards the sports store. "I need to take care of this. Good to see you." He walked away, his shoulders somewhat slumped, leaving her standing on the sidewalk. She hated that he hadn't met his goal, and she knew it had to kill him to sell his poles. She waited a moment, but when he didn't step back out, she headed back to her car and called her mom.

"Meet me for lunch?"

"Sure! Where at?"

"Gatlinburg. I don't really feel up for driving to Pigeon Forge," Autumn told her. "Maybe the burger place on the corner of the highway?"

"Be there in twenty." Her mom hung up and Autumn made her way to the restaurant. She ordered a chocolate shake to buy her time until she saw her mom's black SUV pull into the parking lot. Wendy Simpson, in all her glamor, walked inside and smiled in greeting as she slid in the opposite booth facing Autumn. "Chocolate shake, hm? That sounds good. I may get one too."

The waitress arrived and took their food order as well as Wendy's request for a shake and disappeared. "This is a nice surprise. We haven't done lunch in ages." Her mom reached across the table and squeezed one of the hands gripping the shake in front of Autumn. Her smile faded. "What's wrong?"

"Nothing," Autumn replied.

"Something is. A chocolate shake on a Monday, that's not like you. In fact, eating out during your lunch break is unlike you, and you have a sour expression. Tell me," she ordered in that concerned tone that only mothers can use.

"I saw Ramsey."

"And?" her mother asked. "How's he doing?"

"Good, I guess. He was selling his fishing poles at the sporting goods store to continue to raise money."

"Good for him." Wendy nodded in approval. "He's doing everything he can."

"His rods though?" Autumn ran her hands through her hair. "This is why they say to keep a distance from your clients."

"But he's not your client," her mom pointed out.

"Yes, but once you become emotionally invested it makes the job harder."

"And are you emotionally invested in Ramsey?" her mother asked, patiently waiting for her daughter to reply.

"Yes. No. Maybe." Autumn growled and pulled at her hair before sliding her hands back around her glass. "I just hated seeing him having to go to such lengths to finish raising the money."

Wendy shrugged. "It's something he can do. Ramsey will not give up without giving it his all."

"I know. And I respect that about him. I've just never had to deal with this side of things."

"You mean actually see the people your job affects," Wendy clarified.

"Well, yes. I usually type the name on the foreclosure, post it, and move on."

"And now you see there's more to it than that. That there are actual people and families behind those names."

"Yes."

"Good people."

"Yes." Autumn sighed and looked at her mother. Her eyes clouded as she felt the burn of tears. "I don't want him to lose that place, Mom. I truly don't."

Wendy extended her hand across the table and Autumn gripped it. "I know, honey, and he knows that too. Your hands are tied, and Ramsey understands that."

"Really? Because he just looked at me like I was the scum of the earth when I saw him just now."

"He's stressed," her mom defended. "And right now he needs to focus on what he needs to do to save the cabin."

"I just wish he could see that I'm not rooting against him. That I honestly want him to save it. I think he sees me as a foe. That I don't care."

"He doesn't think that." Wendy shook her head in dismissal. "He knows you better than that."

"Does he?" Autumn asked. "Because I haven't exactly been super open in that regard either."

Wendy leaned back in her seat. "Autumn, if you have feelings for Ramsey, you need to tell him. Hiding behind your position and your job will only hurt you and him in the long run."

"Feelings?" Autumn asked. "Who said anything about feelings?"

Laughing, Wendy pointed and moved her finger in a circle at Autumn. "Your face gives you away. And this glower mood. Your heart hurts, sweetie, because you care for him. And you want the best for him. It doesn't take a rocket scientist, or a lawyer," She narrowed her gaze. "to see that you have feelings for him."

"But I can't act on them."

"Not right now, no. But once the auction's taken place or if Ramsey pays the back taxes, then you can."

"I don't know." Autumn dipped her straw up and down in the chocolate shake and watched as her mom thanked the waitress for her own. "He lives in Washington. It's not like anything could happen between us because he lives there."

"So?" Wendy's brow furrowed. "Why should that matter?"

"Because he will be leaving in a couple of months, or a month, I have no idea. And that's not near long enough to establish any sort of relationship. And long distance never works out. Never." Her adamancy made her mom smile. "And I live in Gatlinburg. He lives on an island and manages a bar, for crying out loud. A bar."

"And a fishing company," her mom added. "He's a businessman, Autumn. He may appear a bit rough on the exterior, but Ramsey is a hardworking, kind, and genuine man. Those traits are hard to come by."

"But I'm not even looking for those traits. I was fine."

"That's usually when love hits us. When you least expect it."

"Who said anything about love?" Autumn's brown eyes panicked and looked up at her mom. "I was just saying that a friendship with Ramsey wouldn't work because he will be leaving."

"A friendship?" Wendy asked. "I'm not stupid, Autumn. You have feelings for that man, and he does for you. The two of you... honestly." Wendy leaned back as the waitress slid her meal in front of her. "Sometimes you use your brain a little too much, Autumn. You need to listen to your heart on this one."

"Well my head and heart have to be pushed aside until the auction."

Wendy, disappointed, shook her head. "I hope, for your sake, that Ramsey is able to save his property. Because if he can't, then he won't have a reason to come to Gatlinburg again. Ever. Do you really want that to happen?"

Autumn pondered that for a moment. "It doesn't matter what I want right now. My job is to focus on the foreclosure and make sure the bank receives the money it's owed, whether by Ramsey or the auction."

"Then you're a fool." Wendy waved her hand to the waitress. "May I slip this in a to-go container, please?" She motioned to her meal and smiled in thanks. The waitress walked quickly over and arranged Wendy's food into the box and accepted her cash payment. "Think outside of your carefully crafted bubble, Autumn. As your mother, I want to see you happy."

"I love my job."

"But at the end of the day, a job is just a job. Have a good day, sweetie." Her mom kissed the top of her head and left, Autumn watching as her billowy skirt blew in the wind before sliding into her car. Miserable, Autumn ate in silence. Alone. Just like she was used to. Only now, she didn't like it.

~

"I've wired the last of it," Matthew reported. "How close are you?"

"About six hundred from the amount to clear the back taxes and fees." Ramsey appreciated his friend's last contribution of the donations that had been circling Friday Harbor over the last few weeks. "Reagan was wiring another couple hundred as well. So that should put me about three hundred from the amount. I can do that. I'll just dip into my savings a bit. Though I'm beginning to contemplate a different method."

"Haven't you already dipped into your savings?" Matt asked.

"Yes, but I can't let a couple hundred dollars keep me from saving the place... or buying it. The festival brought in the bulk of it and will maintain the property taxes from here on out. I don't mind doing the festival each year to cover the taxes."

"Sounds like that was a huge hit."

"It was. And fun too. Made me miss the harbor though. The buzz of busy season."

"Yeah, it's starting to slow down now. Olivia's getting anxious with the store. I told her it was nothing new and not to take her lack of foot traffic personally."

"It will pick back up."

"That's what I keep telling her. Have you thought about what you're going to do if you can't round up the last several hundred dollars? Will you just come back here?"

"Well, if I lose the place I'm currently staying, I will have to."

"Then let's hope you can bring home a win. Keep us posted."

"Thanks." Ramsey hung up and dialed his brother, but Reagan didn't answer. Busy, he supposed.

The auction was in two days. Two days for him to gather what money he could to cover the cost. Determined, he stormed out of the cabin and headed towards town.

While at the bank, he consolidated what money he had gathered and was pleased to see that Matthew and Reagan's final money wires had processed. His total sum sat before his eyes. *Could he do this?* Now, he just needed to go visit Autumn. Instead of driving, Ramsey walked the couple of blocks to her office. Becky sat at the front desk and welcomed him with a smile.

"Autumn Simpson." Ramsey watched as Becky pressed two buttons on her phone and dialed Autumn's office.

"You can head on back. It's the—"

"I know where it is." His gruff reply had Becky nervously peer down the hallway after him as he stood outside Autumn's door and knocked.

The muffled, "Come in," could barely be heard, but he opened the door, her back turned as she finished typing a sentence in what appeared to be an email. "Please just have a seat, I'll be with you in a moment."

Ramsey sat.

Autumn finally turned and gasped at the sight of him. "Ramsey, what are you doing here?"

"Who did you think it was?"

"I have an appointment at two. I thought you were them."

He glanced at the clock. He had fifteen minutes of her time. "I won't be long then."

"What brings you by?"

"I'm not going to save the cabin."

"What? How? I thought you were close."

"Not close enough for what I want to do."

Sighing, she enveloped her hands on her desk. "I'm sorry, Ramsey. Truly, I am."

"The only way would be if I could get a little more of an extension."

"I doubt that's possible."

"Can you try?"

"I have tried," Autumn admitted.

"Well, try harder," Ramsey barked and then dropped his forehead into his hand and rubbed away a tension headache. "I'm sorry. I don't mean that. I know you've done what you can. I just hate coming this close, you know?"

"I understand."

"So what do I do now?"

"Well, the property goes to auction on Friday. You will need to have all your belongings out of there before then."

He nodded.

"Do you know where you're going to store stuff?"

"No, but I'll figure it out today."

"I really am sorry, Ramsey."

He forced a grim smile. "I know. Thanks for the sign, by the way."

Her sympathetic smile told him she'd hoped for things to be different as well. "Once the auction's over I'll have to head back to Friday Harbor." Ramsey locked his eyes on hers.

"How soon?" Autumn asked.

"Probably by Monday. I've used what little money I can out of my savings to put toward the property. I don't want to tap into it too much for a hotel or anything. And I'll want to return the money to everyone who helped pitch in. But I should be going. I've got years' worth of stuff to go through and get rid of."

"If you need help—" Autumn trailed off.

"You can't help me, Autumn. I know."

"I know. I was going to offer and then realized that I still can't." She huffed. "This is so unfair."

Curious, he narrowed his gaze at her. "What is?"

"This whole situation." She stood, rounding her desk and standing next to him. "You deserve that cabin, Ramsey. You love it. You've worked hard to save it, and here I am... twiddling my thumbs because legally my hands are tied. I can't help, no matter how badly I want to. I just have to sit idly by and watch you painfully accept the fate of the property falling into some stranger's hands, and—" Silence. Blessed silence as he pressed his lips to hers. To his surprise, she didn't pull away, but instead, her hands wound around his neck. He ducked his head and lifted her off her feet as he held her close, their lips melding together in perfect synchronicity. He brushed a hand through her thick hair, the silky waves falling between his

fingers as he set her feet back to the floor, his hands moving to cup her face as he pulled back. Her eyes were still closed, and he gently kissed each one, her soft murmur of his name weakening his knees.

"I should go," he murmured, his voice gruff with emotion and raw with want.

"Ramsey," She opened her eyes, but he'd already started down the hallway. He heard her dart to her office door, but he didn't turn around. If he turned, he'd never leave. And he needed to leave. Needed to take care of the cabin's belongings. His grandfather's legacy. If he couldn't save it from the auction, he had to figure out another way to keep it. However, if he didn't find a way by the time the auction came around, the property had to be ready to sell.

Ramsey couldn't look back and see Autumn's beautiful face with flushed cheeks and tousled hair. He couldn't look back or his heart would betray him. He shouldn't have kissed her. Shouldn't have given in to those wants, those needs, that seemed to spring up whenever she was near him. But he had to. He had to kiss her at least once before he had to leave and head back to the harbor, or he'd kick himself for eternity. Only now that he had, he couldn't imagine leaving her behind.

## « CHAPTER TEN »

*"First up on the* auction block," the announcer's voice called out over the microphone and Autumn sat patiently waiting to hear when Ramsey's cabin came up for sale. She'd execute the proper paperwork with whomever won the bid, but she didn't have to be happy about it. She looked around, and knew, for the tenth time, that Ramsey wasn't at the auction. She'd perused the handful of people over and over again, searching for his face, but he hadn't come. It was too hard, she supposed, for him to see his family's legacy sold to a complete stranger. She couldn't blame him, though she would admit she was disappointed not to see him. She wasn't even sure if he was in Gatlinburg anymore. Now that the property was to be sold at auction, all paperwork could be handled by his mother who was now the

executor of the Donald Rover estate. Ramsey was no longer needed as a representative. She fished in her briefcase for the foreclosure papers and the Deed of Sale that was prepped and awaiting a new owner's name and signature. She hated this. For the first time in her career, she hated her job. Yes, the job itself was what she enjoyed, but this particular part of the job was awful. Tearing away a piece of property from a man who tried so hard to keep it was excruciating. She felt like the wicked witch from the west.

"Sold." The gavel sounded and she looked up to see the exchange happening for a property south of the city. Glancing at her watch, she was impressed with how quickly the auction was moving. Hopefully she'd be done by noon and could possibly drive out to the cabin and see if Ramsey was still there. They could have one last lunch at Maw's. Who was she kidding? She wanted to see Ramsey. Hug him. Kiss him. And beg him to stay. "Real classy move, Autumn," she whispered under her breath.

"Excuse me?" The attorney next to her leaned closer. "Did you say something?"

Autumn adamantly shook her head. "Sorry, just looking over paperwork."

"I hear you." The woman held up a stack. "I have three properties to auction today."

"Three?"

"Yes. Seems like they just stack up every now and then."

"Are you up next?"

"No. I think I'm last."

"You could go before me," Autumn offered. "I'm in no rush, and honestly... I'm hoping mine won't even go through."

"Last minute fundraising, huh?" the woman asked. "Those are always hard. They rarely make it in time. If the person isn't here by the time your turn comes up, I'll go."

"Thanks. I appreciate it."

"No problem. It's nice to give them the best possible chance when you feel like your hands are tied."

"Exactly." Pleased to have found someone with a similar viewpoint, Autumn extended her hand. "Autumn Simpson."

"Shae Griffin. Nice to meet you."

"You too. Have you been—" Autumn's chair tipped backwards off the platform and she squealed, but a comforting arm held the chair from falling and she ascended above the ground.

"Autumn, we need to talk." Ramsey's face was right by hers.

"What are you doing here?" Autumn searched his eyes and felt her lips widen into a bright smile.

Ramsey pressed his lips to hers. "Let the property go to auction."

"What?" Trying to clear her head from his passionate and too brief kiss, she sat baffled. He tipped her chair back onto the platform, Shae looking on in amusement as Autumn turned to face Ramsey. Though she sat on a platform, he was mere inches shorter than where she sat.

"You heard me."

"But why?"

"Because I'm going to buy it." He grinned.

"But—"

"Just... let it go, please."

"Ramsey, if it goes up for auction the bids can be driven higher than the current back taxes and foreclosure fees."

"I get that, but I'm not worried."

"Did you win the lottery?" Autumn asked, baffled at his excitement.

"No," he chuckled. "But I want the cabin in my name. I don't want it falling back into the estate. I'm going to bid on it."

"Ramsey—" He pressed a finger to her lips. "Just do it. Please?"

"Okay..." She watched him rush towards the crowd that awaited the next round of bids and saw her dad standing next to him. She gave a small wave.

"So that's the reason you wanted more time, hm?" Shae asked. "I don't blame you." She grinned with womanly understanding and Autumn blushed.

"It's complicated."

"I bet it is, girl, but if a man kissed me like that, I'd be moving mountains to do what he said." They giggled like schoolgirls as they waited their turns and for the first time in weeks, Autumn felt relaxed. When the cabin came up for auction, Ramsey and her father stepped forward.

~

The auctioneer read off the property details, acreage, current status of the property and the opening bid. Ramsey quickly raised his hand. He'd done it. He'd raised enough money and a little extra to buy the property outright. He'd spoken to his mother and uncle over the last week about allowing the estate to lose the property so he could cut through the red tape and buy it outright. They agreed, hoping the stain of the foreclosure would somehow humble Aunt Ceecee. He wasn't so sure about that, but he was grateful for their willingness to let him purchase it. He hoped that

the extra few thousand dollars he'd rounded up would give him the cushion needed if the price was driven up.

Another man raised his hand and raised the bid. Ramsey turned a concerned eye to Autumn's dad. He held his palms down towards the ground reminding Ramsey to stay calm. He nodded and Ramsey raised his hand again at the next bid option. Back and forth they went for several minutes, Ramsey's budget growing smaller and smaller. "I can't go any further than the next bid," he whispered to Bobby.

"Just wait," Bobby replied. "He's waffling." He pointed to the opposition and saw him shift his feet in uncertainty.

The man raised his hand and Ramsey closed his eyes in restraint to hold his temper and panic. The auctioneer looked to him in response and Ramsey raised his hand, the man quickly raising his again to challenge. "I'm out," Ramsey whispered in shock.

"No you're not. Raise your hand," Bobby ordered.

"I can't. I've reached the amount I have. I don't have anything else."

"Yes, you do. Now raise your hand or you're going to lose it." Bobby nudged Ramsey's elbow until he hesitantly raised his hand.

The other man mumbled to his associate and they waved away the opportunity to bid, forfeiting the property to Ramsey. The auctioneer slammed the gavel against the podium. "Sold." He pointed to Ramsey and pointed towards Autumn who was set up at a small pedestal table to the side with the proper paperwork. She beamed at him.

Bobby nudged him towards his daughter and Autumn held out her hand. "Your bid was in the total amount of—" Before she could utter the amount, Ramsey cut her off.

"I don't have it," he told her.

Her eyes narrowed. "Then why did you bid?" Frustrated, she huffed an exasperated breath.

"He does have it." Bobby fished out his wallet and removed the remaining amount and placed it on Autumn's pedestal.

"Bobby, no." Ramsey shook his head.

"Yes. If it makes you feel any better, you can pay me back. But it's really not much, and I'm not going to let that amount keep you from owning your family property. Now, give her the rest, Ramsey."

Baffled, Ramsey dug the envelope out of his back pocket and set it on the pedestal. Autumn looked to her dad in wonder as he nodded for her to continue. "Well, Mr. Jenkins," she continued in a professional manner. "I need your signature here."

She pointed and Ramsey signed. "And here." He signed again. She stacked the papers and nodded towards the courthouse. "How about we go file these?"

Bobby nudged him onward. "I'll wait for you here."

Ramsey followed Autumn into the courthouse and watched as she filed the Deed of Sale and handed him two copies. "Congratulations, Mr. Jenkins. The property is yours."

Ramsey held the deed in his hands and stared at it in awe. "It's mine."

"All yours." Autumn smiled as she led him back outside and they saw her dad waiting on the courthouse steps talking into his phone, no doubt to her mom.

"Autumn, I... can't thank you enough."

"For what?"

"I heard your conversation with that other attorney. You were going to try and buy me more time to get here."

She ducked her head and he lifted her chin. "Thank you."

"I wasn't even sure you were going to come. I was worried... that'd you'd already left town."

"Without saying goodbye?" He shook his head. "Not my style."

"I'm glad."

"So what happens now?"

"Well, you own the property, so you can do whatever you want. My client receives the payment for the sale and all are happy." She held up her hands that that was all there was to it.

"No, I mean, with us." Ramsey laced his fingers with hers and lifted her hand to his lips. "Now that you don't have to hide behind those legal lines anymore, could I possibly take you out now?"

"Well, I—"

"Hey you two." Her dad walked up the steps. "Is it done?"

"All done." Ramsey shook Bobby's hand and brought him into a fierce hug. "I'll pay you back as soon as possible."

"I know you will. Until then, I just require a good fishing spot."

"That pond is at your disposal as long as I live." Ramsey laughed.

"Deal." Bobby grinned. "Now, are we off to celebrate?"

"Yes," Ramsey affirmed.

"Oh, I can't." Autumn held up her hands to ward off their annoyed glares. "Just yet," she amended. "I need to drop these copies off at the bank and the office and then I will be free to go to lunch."

Ramsey tugged her towards him and into his side. "Get after it then." He kissed her soundly on the mouth and nudged her away. Bobby chuckled at his stupefied daughter and gave a fatherly pat to Ramsey's shoulder as they headed towards his truck.

~

Autumn walked into Maw's at a quarter to one, not bad considering she'd had to make two stops before heading into the mountains. Her mom and dad sat with Ramsey at a table, their heads bent in deep discussion. Her mom spotted her first and waved her over. She slipped her purse from her shoulder and slid into the seat next to Ramsey. He reached under the table and squeezed her knee in welcome before turning to smile at her. She gripped his hand in hers. "Glad you made it."

"Glad you told me where to go." She narrowed her eyes at him.

Laughing, he nodded. "I figured you could guess." His eyes sparkled as he leaned towards her, but he froze and pulled back in shock.

"Ramsey?" she asked.

He jumped to his feet and yelled in greeting as a tall lanky man enveloped him in a tight hug and accepted the bone crushing hug from Ramsey. A petite blonde reached up and allowed Ramsey to lift her off her feet and spin her around before setting her to rights. "What are you doing here?!"

"We had to come and celebrate." The man slid his arm around the woman's waist and pointed to the table. "Can we join you?"

Ramsey turned. "These are my friends from the harbor," he explained. "Matthew and Olivia Summers. They helped raise money on the islands to save the cabin." He pointed to Bobby and Wendy and then when he reached Autumn, he tugged her to stand next to him. "And this is Autumn."

Olivia stepped forward and hugged her tightly. "So nice to meet you. Thank you for helping Ramsey handle all of this." Pulling back, Olivia slipped back to Matthew's side.

"I don't know how much I helped other than to aggravate," Autumn admitted and Ramsey proudly nodded in agreement, receiving a light punch in the arm from Autumn as she waved to the seats near her parents.

Matthew and Olivia made themselves comfortable and Wendy immediately began chatting with Olivia about their flights.

"I can't believe you guys came." Ramsey shook his head in astonishment. Autumn listened as Matthew explained their reasoning.

"Man, we couldn't bear to think of you losing the place, so we flew out not sure what to expect when we got here. But when we arrived, we bumped into the sheriff up at your place, and he said you'd won the bid on the property and were probably at Maw's celebrating."

"The sheriff?" Autumn asked. "What was he doing at your cabin?" she looked to Ramsey.

"Ah, Sheriff Hendricks is now the proud owner of a rusty old pickup truck."

"You sold your truck?" Eyes wide, Autumn gaped.

"I had to. That's why your dad drove me to the auction. I am officially out of wheels. For now."

"But what do you plan to do? To get around?"

"Good thing we came," Matthew laughed. "We have a rental. Should last you a few days while we're here."

"I haven't thought that far ahead." Ramsey tugged on her hair. "All that mattered was getting the cabin."

"But—"

"I'll worry about it later, Autumn." He held his hand palm up under the table and she slid her hand into his. "Right now, I want to celebrate with my friends."

Nodding in agreement, she turned her attention to the couple across from them. "Is this your first time in Tennessee?"

The couple looked at one another and laughed at what must have been an inside joke.

"Matthew has hardly ever left the islands," Olivia stated. "Tends to happen with most everyone who ventures up there."

"But you've traveled?" Wendy asked.

"I was living in Florida until a few months ago."

"What made you decide to move so far?" Autumn asked, watching as Olivia turned loving eyes on Matthew.

"Him."

"So you moved to get married, how wonderful." Wendy smiled.

Ramsey laughed and shook his head. "Nope. That was just a bonus, right Matt?"

Olivia playfully tossed a fry at Ramsey. "What he means to say is that I moved up there temporarily to run my grandparents' boutique. They wanted to

travel, and I was sort of looking for a change. I hadn't been to Friday Harbor since I was a kid, so I went. Little did I know that my long-lost sweetheart was still there." She grinned at Matt. "And he was still *hopelessly* in love with me."

Matthew laughed and nodded unashamedly. "That I was. And am."

"We reconnected and picked up where we left off. We married a few months ago. So I guess I've been up there for what? Four months?"

"Something like that." Matt agreed.

"Wow. Four months and married so quickly." Autumn shook her head in wonder. "Congrats. Though I must say that sounds like a whirlwind to me."

"It has been, but in the best way," Olivia explained. "And this guy," She pointed to Ramsey. "was one of the reasons I chose to stay in the harbor as well. He among others. Everyone there is so welcoming and loving."

Ramsey winked across the table at Olivia and the woman grinned. "Now, Autumn, tell us about you. Ramsey has told us that you're an attorney."

"And stubborn, uptight, and irritatingly beautiful," Matthew quoted, eyeing his friend with a glint in his eye.

Autumn's mom hooted in laughter, which made all laugh except an embarrassed Autumn. "How do I follow up such glowing remarks?"

Matt laughed. "Seems to me they work in your favor." He nodded to their joined hands and Autumn looked at Ramsey.

"It's been surprising, really."

Ramsey tucked her hair behind her ear and rested his forehead against hers before turning back to the group. "Let's just say I'm looking forward to the next couple of months here in Gatlinburg," Ramsey admitted.

"And what will you be doing now?" Autumn asked curiously. "You sold all your fishing rods, you don't have a vehicle, and you live in the mountains."

"Guess I'll have to find other ways to keep myself occupied." He winked at her and she blushed.

"Besides," Bobby butted in, "I've got plenty of rods for the two of us. And I have an extra set of wheels you're more than welcome to use while you're in Tennessee."

"Bobby, man, I appreciate that. You've already done so much though." Ramsey shook his head. "I'm already in your debt."

"Nonsense, it's what friends do." He waved towards Matthew and Olivia. "They fly across the country to come support you. They loan you a

vehicle when you need it." He pointed to himself. "Simple."

"Then I count myself lucky to have such friends." Ramsey shook the man's hand.

"And family," Matt added. "Reagan gave me strict orders to call later and give him all the details."

Ramsey laughed. "He would. He's probably lonely without me up there." He turned to Autumn to explain. "My brother and I are roommates."

"And Jake." Olivia rolled her eyes. "Surprisingly, he's doing a good job for you Ramsey."

"I didn't doubt he would."

"I did," Olivia laughed. "I've been proudly proven wrong with him."

Ramsey leaned back in his chair, Autumn putting a bracing hand on his leg. "I'm not going to fall," he whispered.

"You make me nervous when you do that."

Grinning, he plopped back on all four legs of the chair and leaned towards her. "Will you let me take you out tomorrow night?"

Blushing at the silence around the table, Autumn began shrinking back into the shy woman that lived and breathed her work.

"If it makes you feel any better, I already have your dad's blessing. And your brother's, if you want to toss that in there. I'm pretty sure I have your mom's." He looked to Wendy and she emphatically nodded. "So maybe?" he asked.

"Okay."

Ramsey raised his arms in victory. "She said okay!" He cheered and high fived Matt across the table as everyone celebrated in his second victory of the day.

## « CHAPTER ELEVEN »

"*You don't have to* look fancy." Olivia pulled out the floral top Autumn's mom had convinced her to purchase at the festival. "This one." Olivia handed it to her. "Definitely this one. It's feminine, flirty, and the colors go really well with your hair color and skin tone."

"Thanks."

"No problem." Olivia smiled as she waited for Autumn to change. "You nervous?

"Beyond nervous," Autumn admitted, liking the fact she had another woman besides her mother to talk to about Ramsey. Olivia and Matthew had decided to stay for several days and would head back to Friday Harbor at the end of the following

week, and Autumn had to admit she would be sad to see them go. She and Olivia had bonded quickly, which was a rare occurrence for Autumn. Though she'd only known the chipper blonde for less than twenty-four hours, Autumn could tell Olivia would be a good friend.

"He cares for you," Olivia sighed. "Ramsey's a sweet man, Autumn. I'm glad you see that."

"I will admit he was a bit... imposing at first."

Olivia laughed. "It's the rugged pirate image, isn't it?"

Autumn grinned. "At first, it was. He was so—" she held her hands out wide and then tall. "It was intimidating. But the more I've gotten to know him, the more I see he's just a sweetheart underneath."

"That he is," Olivia agreed. "A big, Herculean sweetheart."

"You know, that was one of my first thoughts of him as well," she laughed. "I feel completely out of my element. I don't go on dates. I've hardly made time for any sort of social life until Ramsey showed up. Puddin' and me just... well we just hang out the two of us, as pathetic as that sounds."

"It's not pathetic," Olivia assured her. "You were comfortable. There's nothing wrong with being content with your life the way it is."

"It is if there really wasn't much life there. I work all the time, I come home, I sit with Puddin' and watch television and repeat. Somehow, Ramsey saw personality in the midst of that, or he was blinded by Cupid's arrow."

"I think both of you got to know and see the person beneath the surface," Olivia explained. "And that's where you two clicked."

"But it can't go anywhere," Autumn added. "He leaves in a couple of months and goes back to Friday Harbor. And then what? I wait to see him until next year? Even now, I'm not sure if I want that."

"Then see each other throughout the year. You can come up to Friday Harbor, stay with me," she grinned. "And then Ramsey can fly down here when he's free. Long distance can work. It just takes work."

"But again, say things do progress, what then? One of us will end up having to make the decision of moving. And I know he loves the harbor. I love Gatlinburg."

"You know," Olivia stood off the side of the bed and rested her hands on Autumn's shoulders. "Why don't you just start with the now. Worry about the future in the future. Right now, let's just take it one step at a time. The first step being your date. Don't over complicate it. Don't overthink it. Don't overanalyze it. Just enjoy it. Okay?"

Autumn took a relaxing breath and nodded. "You're right. I'm thinking too far ahead. Live in the now."

"Exactly." Olivia squeezed her shoulders and then released. "Matt should be here any minute to pick me up. I think I will wait outside to give you a few minutes alone before Ramsey arrives. Have fun." She waved as she exited, shutting the door behind her and leaving Autumn alone with her anxious thoughts.

~

Ramsey grunted as Olivia bumped into his chest on her way down the stairs. "Oh, sorry Rams." She grinned and patted his shoulder. "I'd give her just a couple minutes."

"Is she wanting to back out?"

"Not at all. She's just nervous." Olivia eyed the flowers in his hands. "Those are pretty."

"Thanks. I don't know what her favorite flower is. Yet. But I thought these were bright and cheerful."

"They are. And she'll love them," Olivia encouraged. A horn honked below them. "That's Matt. We're going to go tour around Gatlinburg this evening. Did you know they have a distillery?"

"Yes. And be careful with that," Ramsey chuckled.

"We will. Have fun." Olivia hopped the rest of the way down the stairs and opened the car door with a squeal of welcome to Matthew, her lips moving quickly, as if reporting all she knew about the upcoming date. His friend offered an encouraging wave before pulling out of the parking lot. Ramsey finished climbing the stairs and held his fist up to the door. Two deep breaths later, he knocked.

Autumn opened the door, the light breeze teasing her hair as she soaked in the sight of him. He did the same. She looked... *happy*, he thought, and gorgeous as she smiled in welcome. He handed her the flowers and her face lit up even more. "Thanks." She rushed to the kitchen and quickly found a vase and put them in water.

Puddin' sat across the threshold and stared at Ramsey. "I'll have her back before you know it, little guy." As if understanding, Puddin' walked towards him and rubbed against his pant legs. Autumn scooped up the cat and sat him on the chair, tugging the door closed behind her. She moved quickly, as if in a rush to leave, and Ramsey watched her turn the key and slide the keychain into her purse. She turned, took a deep breath, and smiled up at him.

"Ready."

"You sure?" He grinned.

"Well," She held up a finger and lifted up onto her tiptoes, then reached up and cupped his face,

tugging it down the rest of the way. Her lips were soft and eager, and Ramsey melted. When she released him, she sighed. "Now I'm ready. I know that's typically what happens at the end of the date, but I needed to just," She shook her hands nervously. "work out some of the jitters."

"You're nervous?" he asked, linking his hand with hers as they walked down the stairs.

"A little," she admitted, trying to hide her embarrassment.

Ramsey tugged her towards him and stopped, tilting her chin up so he could look into her eyes. "Me too. Now, let's push the nerves aside. We're friends. We have fun together. We care for one another. It shouldn't be too difficult to go on a date."

"You're right. People do it all the time."

He chuckled. "That they do."

"So, what did you have in mind?"

"I'm taking a play out of Matthew's book."

"Oh really? And what would that be?"

"A picnic," Ramsey told her. "Prepared by yours truly." He pointed at himself. "It will not only be delicious, but it will be in a beautiful and pristine location."

"It's at your cabin, isn't it?" she asked.

He laughed. "Now how did you know that?"

Autumn bit back a smile. "Pristine, as in you do not have any furniture to sit on because you sold it all." She pointed out.

"That's why it's a picnic," Ramsey added. "Part of the charm."

Laughing, Autumn rested her head against the headrest of her father's truck he'd loaned Ramsey and looked at him. "A picnic sounds great, Ramsey."

"I was hoping you'd say that. Besides, the cabin isn't completely empty."

"Really?"

"I have my clothes and a blanket."

She sputtered. "Well, I guess we'll have somewhere to sit then."

"Exactly."

~

Ramsey chattered the entire way to the cabin. He was right, he was nervous, and she enjoyed seeing his jitters as well as experiencing her own. No man had ever gone to such trouble to impress her or to woo her. Heck, she couldn't even remember the last time she'd gone on a date. *Law*

*school? Maybe?* She shook away that thought and studied the handsome man beside her. And Ramsey was handsome. His hair had grown since his arrival, and he wore it short and trimmed, along with his beard. Gone was the scary pirate, and in his place was a good-looking guy with the bluest eyes she'd ever seen. She loved those eyes. The way they looked at her with complete focus, as though she were the only woman in the world. He parked the truck and opened her door.

Escorting her up the porch steps to the cabin, he threw open the door to a candlelit picnic in the center of the room. He was right, he had nothing but what was there, but that was part of the thrill. It was a fresh start and new beginning for Ramsey and the cabin, and she had the privilege to be a part of it. He took the light coat she wore and hung it on one of the hooks on the fish sign she'd bought for him. He pointed at it.

"See, not completely empty."

She nodded, impressed, and he laughed. "Come on." He pulled her towards the blanket and pointed to a cushion on the floor.

"Is that your shirt?" she asked.

"It is. Well, it's several shirts bundled together. I didn't want you to have to sit on the hard floor."

Touched, she reached for his hand and squeezed. "This is beautiful, Ramsey."

He rubbed the back of his neck. "I wouldn't go that far, but I promise one day it will be."

They sat on the blanket and he uncovered several dishes. She squealed in pleasure at the sight of Maw's French fries. "The only thing I didn't make," he clarified. "But I figured you'd forgive me."

"I do." Autumn snuck one while he uncovered more and more options. "I don't even know where to begin." Her brown eyes bounced from one plate to the next.

"How about with me?" Ramsey asked, reaching for her hand. "Here's to a new beginning, Autumn. Wherever life takes us, whatever happens, I look forward to it with you." He kissed her, sweetly, and then sat back.

"Ramsey—" Her tone serious, she eyed him with regret. "As much as I know I'm going to love this and my time with you, we have to be realistic. You leave in just a couple months. You live in Washington. I live here. We're setting ourselves up for failure."

"I think you underestimate how much I care for you. And that's okay," he said. "For now."

"I just don't see myself leaving Gatlinburg." Autumn inhaled a shaky breath at the thought of saying goodbye to him, at the thought of going back to her lonesome lifestyle. But she knew long

distance would only end in heartache. She was doing them a favor by drawing the line early.

He ducked his chin in thought as he looked over the spread of food before them. "Listen, Autumn." His eyes pierced into hers. "I'm not a lovesick kid who wants a fall fling. I'm a grown man. I'm happy with my life in Friday Harbor. It's a great one. I've built a life there. But if what I'm feeling for you grows, then I will gladly leave the harbor and come to Gatlinburg. Because I'm old enough to know that what I feel for you now *will* only grow stronger and I'm man enough to do something about it. If I need to move here to be closer to you, I will. I'm not above doing that. I don't mind doing that. You're worth doing that for. I just want you to be open to giving this a shot. Because if you're not, then you're right, it doesn't need to go any further." He rubbed his thumb over her knuckles. "But *if* you are willing to give me a chance, Autumn, I promise I will do my best at making you happy. I promise you that."

He could see the emotions swirling in her eyes as she pressed a hand to his heart. It drummed, steady and solid. "How does a girl say no to an offer like that?"

"Ideally she doesn't." Ramsey winked and had her snickering.

"Then I guess I won't. I can't say I won't be difficult."

"I wouldn't know how to handle you if you weren't," he admitted and accepted the punch to his shoulder in good spirit.

"But I do care for you, Ramsey. You stormed into my life unexpected and unwelcome at times, but now… I don't want you to leave it."

"Then we're agreed." Ramsey kissed her palm. "We'll see where this goes the next couple of months, and we'll make a decision then on how to move forward. No stressing about it right now."

"I agree."

He kissed her again to seal the deal, and she gripped the front of his shirt to hold him there to soak in his promises and his sweetness for just a moment longer. "Now, let's eat." She lifted a fry and happily popped it into her mouth.

## « CHAPTER TWELVE »

*It was a brisk forty* degrees, but the breeze off the water shot through her bones like pure ice. So, she buried her face within her scarf and weaved her way across the boardwalk down an alleyway that she knew would cut through to Ramsey's bar. Or should. When she reached the ornately carved wooden door depicting an elaborate scene from Moby Dick, she pulled with a small grunt of effort. The place was crowded, warm, and welcoming and all eyes fell upon her. She had been unsure why she'd made such a spur of the moment decision to come to Friday Harbor, but upon seeing Ramsey's comfort zone, she knew why. This was *his* place. And it screamed Ramsey. Her heart thudded at the thought of seeing him again. She unwound her scarf and an eye-catching man walked towards her

with a radiant smile. "Let me help you." He helped her out of her jacket and hung it on a stand by the door with various others. He flashed a dazzling smile. "Welcome to Ramsey's. I'm Jake. Here for a drink or a meal?"

"I'm here to see Ramsey, actually. Is he here?" she asked.

Jake's brow furrowed as he studied her. "Southern accent, beautiful, tiny... are you Autumn?"

She straightened as if being called tiny was an insult and she wanted to lengthen to her full height. "I am."

"Is he expecting you?" Jake asked.

She flushed. "Um, no. I was going to surprise him."

Jake swept her into a friendly hug and spun her around before setting her on her feet. Everyone stared, and Autumn tried to catch her breath, but a loud voice boomed across the room. "Watch yourself, Jake."

Autumn turned and Ramsey stood wiping his hands on an overly used hand towel, his smile and eyes fixed on her. "About time you got here, I was beginning to think you you'd forgotten about me. Everyone around here thought you were a figment of my imagination."

Autumn walked briskly towards him and jumped to wrap her arms around his neck,

planting a hard kiss to his lips. He swung her around much like Jake had, only when he stopped, Autumn brushed kisses on his cheeks and nose and then his lips again. "How's that for your imagination?" She rested her forehead against his and soaked him in, amazed that she'd finally reached him, and amazed that she actually had the courage to surprise him. She'd have to thank her mom for that idea, and for the final push to get her out the door instead of chickening out. She'd never felt the way Ramsey made her feel. Special. Beautiful. Loved. And being in his arms again melted away any uncertainties and fears she'd been harboring the entire trip.

Ramsey grinned and set her to her feet. "Everyone, this is Autumn, my beautiful Tennessee woman you've been hearing so much about."

Autumn stood long enough and then began to fidget under the scrutiny. Ramsey nodded to Jake and tossed him the towel. "You've got the rest of the night. I've got a lady to show around."

Jake caught the towel and laughed. "Nice to meet you, Autumn."

"Likewise," she called over her shoulder as Ramsey pulled her towards the door.

"Ramsey, slow down." Breathless, she stuffed her arms back into her jacket that he held for her and he wrapped her scarf around her neck. He walked outside without a coat and began leading her

away. "Where are we going?" she chuckled as she tried to match his steps and failed. "Ramsey." She finally stopped and placed her hands on her hips.

He turned. "Well, come on. You don't want to freeze, do you?"

"Where are we going?"

"Have you been to Olivia and Matt's?"

"No. They met me at the ferry and took my bags and told me how to find you. Which, to be honest, was a bit more difficult than I thought it'd be."

Ramsey grabbed her hands and smiled. "I'm just happy you're really here. I can't believe it, to be honest. But first things first, you have to meet my brother. He will be sorely disappointed you met the bar first instead of him."

"I'm sure he will understand."

A flashlight shined down the alleyway and landed on Ramsey's back. "This man bothering you, ma'am?"

Ramsey groaned and turned around. "She's fine."

"Oh, well will you look at that, it's my little brother." Reagan's voice sounded amused. "And what would your pretty little Autumn think of you being caught with another lady in the alleyway?" Ramsey's shoulder's stiffened, and Autumn nudged herself around him.

"She'd say it's okay as long as it was her." She gave a friendly wave and the flashlight highlighted her for a brief moment.

"Well, you are pretty, he didn't get that wrong." He grinned, his smile missing one of his front teeth and she remembered the story Ramsey had told her when she'd first met him. Reagan wasn't as tall as Ramsey, but he was similar in build and he had the same mischievous grin that forced people to have no choice but to smile back. "Hello, Reagan," she said, walking towards him. She shook his hand as she felt Ramsey step up behind her.

"So you're the one who's stolen my little brother's heart, hm?"

Autumn blushed as she looked up at Ramsey. "That'd be me."

"Well, you are the first to do so, so I give you points for that. Why are you two walking out in the cold?"

"We were coming to find you," Autumn explained. "Apparently, I had to meet you first."

"But you didn't." Reagan shook his head in mock disappointment. "I see how it is. Big brother's always the last to know."

"By accident," Autumn continued. "I went searching for Ramsey at his bar."

"Are you telling me you met Jake first?" Reagan looked genuinely wounded and Autumn wasn't quite sure what to say or how to answer.

Ramsey laughed. "Again, it was by accident, and Autumn let him know real quick whose girl she was." Ramsey kissed her cheek and winked.

"Good. Don't want him getting any ideas." Reagan nodded over his shoulder. "My patrol car is just up the street. I'll give you a ride."

"To Matt's, right?" He looked at Autumn and she nodded.

"I'm going to stay in their guestroom."

"Good call," Reagan agreed. "You'll like it out at Olivia's house. She and Matt just put the finishing touches on it."

"Sounds great. Though I'm a bit sorry I arrived so late. Having seen you for only a few minutes and not able to see you until tomorrow is not what I had in mind." She felt her heart go haywire as he brushed his finger over her smooth cheek.

"I'll see you first thing in the morning," Ramsey promised. "Bright and early. I'm still in shock you're actually here. What made you decide to come? How long have you been planning this?"

"Just the last couple days," Autumn admitted. "Thankfully, I had ridiculous amounts of vacation

time saved up and…" A blush crept into her cheeks. "I really missed you."

"That's what I like to hear." He winked at her.

Reagan rolled his eyes as he ushered them into the back seat of his police cruiser. "If you two are going to be all mushy the entire drive out there, you're going to have to find your own transportation."

Ramsey reached forward and shoved against Reagan's seat. "Don't listen to him, Autumn. He's just a crotchety old man."

"Old man? I'm two years older than you," Reagan defended. "Besides, I'm not crotchety. It's cold out and I have to do patrols because of those annoying brats who keep burglarizing businesses."

"I've heard about that," Autumn said.

"One step ahead of me and it's getting old," Reagan went on and Ramsey mimicked a mouth with his hand as Reagan talked.

Leaning closer Ramsey whispered. "He could talk your head off for hours."

"How long a drive is it to Matt and Olivia's?" Autumn asked quietly.

"About twenty minutes. Hang in there." He squeezed her knee as she sidled up next to him. A twenty-minute car ride with Ramsey was just

what she needed after long flights and ferry rides to come see him. And she wasn't quite sure how it was possible, but she found her heart and love had only grown in the one month absence of not seeing each other. She rested her chin on his shoulder and looked up at him. "What?" he asked, narrowing his eyes as if to read her thoughts.

"I'm just... glad to see you. And can't fully believe I'm actually here."

He gently kissed her lips. "Believe it."

Autumn nuzzled closer, resting her head on the broad shoulder she knew could carry the weight of the world if needed. She studied their hands that rested on her knee. His large, hardened by years of tough work, hers dainty and soft, and yet, they fit. Quite perfectly. When the car rolled to a stop and a beautiful home was before them, Olivia rushed down the steps in excitement as she hugged Ramsey tight.

He tapped her nose. "Sneaky, sneaky, Olivia."

The woman's eyes danced as she embraced Autumn. "It's not every day I get to pull one over on you, Ramsey." She looked over their shoulders. "Hi Reagan. Want to come in for a coffee before heading back out?"

"Wish I could, but I've got a thermos. Thanks though. You just see about those two crazy love birds."

"Gladly."

"Breakfast. Tomorrow." He pointed at Ramsey and Autumn and they both nodded. Then his face softened. "Glad you're here, Autumn. And glad my brother's found someone special." As if the heart to heart was too much, he then cleared his throat. "And I'm off." He ducked back into his car and drove away.

"Come in, come in!" Olivia led them up the sidewalk into her new home and Matthew was walking down the stairs, barefoot, and freshly showered.

"Oh, you guys are here." He smiled.

"And how long have you known about this?" Ramsey asked.

"Well, my wife did not think I could be trusted with such a secret." Matt looked woundedly at his wife before smirking in understanding. "Which was probably a good call on her part. So, I learned about it when we were headed to pick Autumn up at the boardwalk."

Autumn looked at Olivia in surprise. "You didn't tell him until then?!"

Olivia laughed. "Nope. And believe me, it was necessary. These two tell each other everything." She motioned between her husband and Ramsey.

"So," Matt asked. "What did everyone at the bar think?"

Ramsey's chest puffed slightly as he proudly looked at Autumn. "That the most beautiful woman in the world walked in and swept me off my feet."

Autumn laughed as she slid into his side and wrapped her arms around his waist.

"Everyone's been giving Ramsey a hard time about you, Autumn," Matt explained. "Thought he was all talk about this fantastic woman in Tennessee."

"Well, I hope we stunned them speechless then." She squeezed Ramsey's side.

"I imagine you did." Olivia rubbed her hands together as if nothing pleased her more than mischief. "Come on, I'll show you your room while the men fix us a drink. We have a fire going in the sitting room so we can all catch up. And when you and Ramsey get tired of us, just shoo us off to bed and you two stay up as late as you want. Ramsey is welcome as late as it takes for you two to catch up tonight."

Autumn's voice quieted. "I feel like I'm in a dream. I could stare at him all night long and still need to be pinched because I can't believe I'm really here."

Olivia reached over and pinched her arm, Autumn flinching. "Not a dream." Wriggling her eyebrows, Olivia turned back to leading the way.

~

Ramsey stomped the mud off his boots as he pressed his finger to the doorbell and heard it ring through the house. Matthew answered and looked at his watch. "Didn't you just leave?"

"Three hours ago," Ramsey reported, his tired eyes showing the effects of his late night spending time with Autumn. "But I'm here to sweep Autumn away for an early breakfast with a cranky Reagan."

"Was he patrolling all night again?" Matt asked.

"Yep. I told him we could raincheck on breakfast, but he insists."

"He's happy for you and wants to get to know Autumn more. Can't blame him. She did rock the unshakeable Ramsey Jenkins off his axis."

"That is true."

"Well, come on in. The women are in the kitchen." Matt waved him inside and led the way to the bright and airy room where floor to ceiling windows brought the early morning sunrise sweeping into the room.

"Morning," Ramsey greeted, and Autumn looked up from her mug with a tired, but sweet smile.

"Well, if it's not the man of the hour. We were just talking about you." Olivia trailed off as Ramsey's gaze grew serious as he walked towards Autumn. Autumn nervously set her mug on the counter as if unsure if she'd upset him. Instead of anger, Ramsey scooped her up into a fierce hug and kissed her hard on the lips. Leaving her good and tousled, his hands running through her hair one more time before releasing her, he took a step back and sighed.

"Had to make sure last night wasn't a dream."

Autumn held her fingers to her tingling lips as Olivia and Matt laughed.

"You ready for breakfast?" Ramsey asked.

Autumn, struck mute by his welcome, only nodded, her heart still recovering from his kiss. She suddenly felt like a stranger in her own body. Who was she? Where had the old Autumn Simpson gone? Who was this woman who flew across the country to see a man? Her heart warmed as she stood and walked out of the house with Ramsey at her side. She couldn't even remember that old version of herself. Ramsey had changed her life so much in the few short months she'd known him. And only for the better. He made her feel special and valued, just the way she was. And now she couldn't imagine her life without him. She supposed that's what love did to people. Shake them up, open their eyes, and make them happier than they were before. She wasn't a fool, though,

and she knew they would share hard times together or rough patches; she'd seen that with her parents growing up. But the love they had for one another kept them together. She wanted that. And she wanted that with Ramsey. He tugged her up the sidewalk.

"We'll head to the street corner up ahead. Reagan said he'd pick us up there." He slowed his pace so her short stride could keep up and even that gesture melted her heart a little more.

"I love you."

Ramsey abruptly stopped and turned to look at her, his face serious.

"I love you, Ramsey," Autumn repeated and then, due to his prolonged silence, began to feel the familiar prickles of shyness creep up her neck. "I just... wanted you to know."

Ramsey looked around, the quiet sidewalk only linking Matthew's house with his parents' down the road and the upcoming street where they'd meet Reagan. It wasn't the most romantic spot or delivery, she knew, but the way he searched for the quickest exit had her panicking that she'd scared him. It was too soon. She shouldn't have said anything. Why did she have to ruin a good thing? *Typical*, Autumn thought.

He pulled her towards a cluster of boulders up ahead and nudged her to sit.

"I'm sorry," she began. "I didn't mean to ruin our morning, I understand if you don't feel the same way yet. I just—"

Ramsey held a finger to her lips and knelt in front of her, his eyes glassy as he cupped her face. "You did not ruin my morning, Autumn. You've made my day. My life." He smiled. Finally, she thought, and felt the tumble of nerves in the pit of her stomach slowly slip away. "I love you too. So much." He kissed her and pulled her into a tight hug.

Her shoulders relaxed as she looked up and smiled at his gleeful expression. "I—"

He silenced her with a brief kiss. "Marry me."

Her heart flipped. "What?"

"Marry me," he repeated. "Please?" He tenderly brushed her hair back as the sound of tires pulled up next to them. Reagan rolled down the window to yell but thought better of it as he watched the scene unfold before him. He stepped out of his patrol and onto the sidewalk.

"But we live—"

"We'll figure it out, remember?" Ramsey asked.

"But your family is here." She felt her voice quake as her heart wished to accept his offer.

"And yours is in Tennessee. We'll figure it out," Ramsey repeated a bit more adamantly. "Marry me, Autumn. Please marry me. I love you."

Hearing those words once more soothed her worries. He did love her. They would figure it out. Together. And that's exactly how she wanted to be with Ramsey. Together. "Yes."

He leaned back his head and released a hearty hoot of celebration as he lifted her to her feet and danced her up the sidewalk towards Reagan. He all but shoved her into his brother's arms, Reagan's quick reflexes keeping her from falling. "Hug your future sister-in-law, Reagan! Autumn's agreed to marry me!"

Reagan obliged, his strong embrace welcoming and still a little awkward as he tried to come to terms with the happily dancing Ramsey in front of him. Autumn lightly kissed Reagan's cheek before stepping away and giving a giddy laugh as Ramsey lifted her into the air and swung her around.

"I guess there is more to celebrate this morning," Reagan grinned. "Shall we rally the troops to join us?" he asked.

"No." Autumn held her hand to Ramsey's chest as he hugged her close. "Just us for now."

"Just us. I like the sounds of that." Ramsey kissed her and accepted the congratulatory pat on his

back from his brother as the three of them headed back towards the harbor for a celebratory breakfast she would never forget.

# « EPILOGUE »

*"Calm down, Rams."* Matt slapped his friend's back and grinned as Ramsey continued to pace the small quarters they'd been confined to most of the morning.

"I'm sweating," Ramsey said. "Is that normal?" He ripped off his tuxedo jacket and tossed it towards his brother.

"Yes," Matt assured him. "Completely normal."

Ramsey tugged at the bow tie around his neck. "I feel ridiculous."

"But you look the part of the gentleman," Jake teased.

"How much time?" Ramsey asked.

"Ten minutes, give or take. The wedding planner should come get us when they're ready for us."

"I still don't understand why we can't walk the bridesmaids down the aisle?" Jake asked. "Isn't that what a groomsman does?"

Matt laughed. "Not always. We'll be down front. Besides, you'll escort one of them out."

"Hope it's the tall one. What was her name again? Shae? The other attorney." Jake wiggled his brows and had Ramsey stifling a growl as he continued his march back and forth.

The door cracked open and the elderly woman in charge of today's ceremony took a cautious step back as Ramsey hovered over her, ready to pounce over her and out the door. "It's time." She waved them to follow her and Ramsey rushed out, Reagan grabbing his brother's jacket and helping him into it as he walked.

Jake and Matt walked out first, standing to the side as Ramsey and Reagan, his best man, walked out together to stand nearest the middle where the pastor stood with a warm smile. Ramsey tried to calm his chaotic heart. All eyes were on him. Half the people he didn't know, but Autumn's mother shot him a thumbs up from the first row, and then motioned a hand up and down for him to take a calming breath as if she knew he was about to pass out. Calvin sat beside her. The kid beamed proudly as if he'd been waiting for this

day as much as Ramsey had. Spending the few months in Gatlinburg had given Ramsey time to fish and hang out with the teen, and he was a great kid. And he and Autumn were close despite their age difference. He was glad Calvin had approved of him for his sister as well.

The music shifted and the doors to the back of the church opened. Olivia, in a pale blue dress made her way down the center aisle. She beamed at Matt before giving Ramsey a wink on her way to the other side. Shae followed behind her. Then Autumn's two younger sisters, joint maids of honor, began walking down the aisle. He'd hardly known them, but they smiled excitedly for him and Autumn as they found their place near the front.

Then he saw Bobby step into the doorway and extend his arm, and there she was. Ramsey's knees threatened to collapse as Autumn began slowly making her way towards him. Her dress, delicately laced sleeves and sweetheart bodice framed her perfectly, a long train trailing behind her. Bobby stood, winking at Ramsey as the pastor asked him to hand Autumn over. Bobby extended his hand, but Ramsey swooped him into a tight embrace that lifted the man off the ground and had everyone laughing. Bobby patted him on the back as he smiled and backed away to sit by Wendy.

Autumn's eyes, the warm brown of melted chocolate, were the first thing he noticed. They sparkled with nerves, happiness, and tears, but

they were radiant. Ramsey gripped her hands in his as the pastor began to speak. He'd never seen a more beautiful woman, and she was about to be his wife. The thought had him gently brushing soothing circles across her knuckles as he felt the tremors in her own hands. They'd be happy together. He knew that for certain, because he'd never give up in trying to make her happy.

She'd chosen to leave Gatlinburg and live with him in Friday Harbor. That in itself was a huge step for her and for them. Though owning his grandfather's little cabin by the pond meant they'd spend a few months every year in the Smoky Mountains of Tennessee. And Ramsey couldn't imagine a better life than that. Together. Together, they'd make their own memories at the cabin.

"Ramsey?" Autumn whispered, her eyes concerned.

He blinked and then looked to the expectant faces around him and then to the pastor. The man smiled knowingly and repeated his question. "And do you, Ramsey Jenkins, take Autumn to be your lawfully wedded wife?"

"Yes," he interrupted quickly, the pastor chuckling as he finished the remaining traditional line of questions. Sickness, health, rich, or poor. Ramsey nodded through every one. "Yes," he said again. "I do." The pastor held up his hands and prayed over them and then he granted Ramsey the blessing to

kiss his bride. And Ramsey didn't have to be told twice.

A LOVE FOR ALL SEASONS

# Winter's Call

# The Complete Siblings O'Rifcan Series Available in Paperback, Ebook, and Audiobook

## Claron

https://www.amazon.com/dp/B07FYR44KX

## Riley

https://www.amazon.com/dp/B07G2RBD8D

## Layla

https://www.amazon.com/dp/B07HJRL67M

## Chloe

https://www.amazon.com/dp/B07KB3HG6B

## Murphy

https://www.amazon.com/dp/B07N4FCY8V

## All titles in The Lighthearted Collection Available in Paperback, Ebook, and Audiobook

## Chicago's Best

https://www.amazon.com/dp/B06XH7Y3MF

## Montgomery House

https://www.amazon.com/dp/B073T1SVCN

## Beautiful Fury

https://www.amazon.com/dp/B07B527N57

**Check out the Epic Fantasy Adventure
Available in Paperback, Ebook, and
Audiobook**

# UTHENFADING LANDS

## The Unfading Lands
https://www.amazon.com/dp/B00VKWKPES

## Darkness Divided, Part Two in The Unfading Lands Series
https://www.amazon.com/dp/B015QFTAXG

## Redemption Rising, Part Three in The Unfading Lands Series
https://www.amazon.com/dp/B01G5NYSEO

**Subscribe to Katharine's Newsletter for news on upcoming releases and events!**
https://www.katharinehamilton.com/subscribe.html

**Find out more about Katharine and her works at:**
www.katharinehamilton.com

**Social Media is a great way to connect with Katharine. Check her out on the following:**

Facebook: Katharine E. Hamilton
https://www.facebook.com/Katharine-E-Hamilton-282475125097433/

Twitter: @AuthorKatharine
Instagram: @AuthorKatharine

Contact Katharine:
khamiltonauthor@gmail.com

# ABOUT THE AUTHOR

Katharine E. Hamilton began writing in 2008 and published her first children's book, The Adventurous Life of Laura Bell in 2009. She would go on to write and illustrate two more children's books, Susie At Your Service and Sissy and Kat between 2010-2013.

Though writing for children was fun, Katharine moved into Adult Fiction in 2015 with her release of The Unfading Lands, a clean, epic fantasy that landed in Amazon's Hot 100 New Releases on its fourth day of publication, reached #72 in the Top 100 in Epic Fantasy, and hit the Top 10,000 Best Sellers on all of Amazon in its first week. It has been listed as a Top 100 Indie Read for 2015 and a nominee for a Best Indie Book Award for 2016. The series did not stop there. Darkness Divided: Part Two of The Unfading Land Series, released in October of 2015 and claimed a spot in the Top 100 of its genre. Redemption Rising: Part Three of The Unfading Lands Series released in April 2016 and claimed a nomination for the Summer Indie Book Awards.

Though comfortable in the fantasy genre, Katharine decided to venture towards romance in 2017 and released the first novel in a collection of sweet, clean and wholesome romances: The Lighthearted Collection. Chicago's Best reached best seller status in its first week of publication and rested comfortably in the Top 100 for Amazon for three steady weeks, claimed a Reader's Choice Award, a TopShelf Indie Book Award, and ended up a finalist in the American Book Festival's

Best Book Awards for 2017. <u>Montgomery House</u>, the second in the collection, released in August of 2017 and rested comfortably alongside its predecessor, claiming a Reader's Choice Award, and becoming Katharine's best-selling novel up to that point. Both were released in audiobook format in late 2017 and early 2018. <u>Beautiful Fury</u> is the third novel released in the collection and has claimed a Reader's Choice Award and a gold medal in the Authorsdb Best Cover competition. It has also been released in audiobook format with narrator Chelsea Carpenter lending her talents to bring it to life. Katharine and Chelsea have partnered on an ongoing project for creating audiobook marketing methods for fellow authors and narrators, all of which will eventually be published as a resource tool for others.

In August of 2018, Katharine brought to life a new clean contemporary romance series of a loving family based in Ireland. The Siblings O'Rifcan Series kicked off in August with <u>Claron</u>. <u>Claron</u> climbed to the Top 1000 of the entire Amazon store and has reached the Top 100 of the Clean and Wholesome genre a total of 11 times. He is Katharine's bestselling book thus far and lends to the success of the following books in the series: <u>Riley</u>, <u>Layla</u>, <u>Chloe</u>, and <u>Murphy,</u> each book earning their place in the Top 100 of their genre and Hot 100 New Releases. <u>Claron</u> was featured in Amazon's Prime Reading program March – June 2019. The series is currently being produced in audiobook format with the voice talents of Alex Black.

A Love For All Seasons, a Sweet Contemporary Romance Series launched in July of 2019 with

Summer's Catch, followed by Autumn's Fall in October. Winter's Call and Spring's Hope scheduled for 2020 release dates. The series follows a wonderful group of friends from Friday Harbor, Washington, and has been Katharine's newest and latest project.

Katharine has contributed to charitable Indie Anthologies as well as helped other aspiring writers journey their way through the publication process. She manages an online training course that walks fellow self-publishing and independently publishing writers through the publishing process as well as how to market their books.

She is a member of Women Fiction Writers of America, Texas Authors, IASD, and the American Christian Fiction Writers. She loves everything to do with writing and loves that she is able to continue sharing heartwarming stories to a wide array of readers.

Katharine graduated from Texas A&M University with a bachelor's degree in History. She lives on a ranch in south Texas with her husband, Brad, and three year old son, Everett.

By Katharine E. Hamilton

A LOVE FOR ALL SEASONS

## 2 / DEAN

D<small>EAN WATCHED THE DUDE GO AND SIGHED</small>, <small>TURNING INSTEAD TO HELP</small> the next group of guests. Not that there was usually much to help with, and he'd done it so many times he didn't have to think about it. The words came out of his mouth, and his hands made the gestures of pulling the harness down on autopilot. Which left his mind free to worry over how he'd talked to the guy who wanted to go on the ride but also apparently didn't at the same time.

How had Dean not caught his name? He'd been in the queue. He'd had his staff ID on a lanyard around his neck. His name had been right there, and Dean hadn't thought to look. He'd been too busy focusing on his face, which, well... that was probably a good thing. The guy had needed encouragement and eye contact was important.

*And he was gorgeous.*

The ride came back in, and he pulled the lever to release the safety harnesses. But that wasn't the point at all. The point was that Dean had offered to help him and he'd walked away like the devil was on his tail, and Dean hadn't even introduced himself. He hadn't got his name, and he didn't know who he was aside from that he worked at the park and in the security team.

It didn't really matter if he didn't know him - except he really did want to help him with the ride. Helping people out was the best thing about his job.

And the guy hadn't asked *his* name, which was par for the course. Dean was pretty much invisible. He was the guy who ran the ride, the guy who helped people on and checked that their security harnesses were in place. He waved to the people heading off on the rides, and they usually ignored him. Well, some of them waved back, but mostly they were busy talking to each other or excited for the ride.

But none of that really mattered to Dean. The thing that mattered was that he was part of their experience. People loved Spaceship Mayhem, and part of the reason they loved it was that it was a smooth experience. He was one of the reasons for the smoothness of that experience. They might not pay attention to him personally, but they didn't need to. He made things easy.

It wasn't the noblest profession, sure. But it was noble enough.

Jessica came to relieve him at the front of the line about an hour later. She was the same age as Dean – twenty-three – and similarly perky about the roller coaster. She had red hair and an Irish accent.

"Gimme the clicker and the satchel," Jessica said. She nudged him with her elbow. "Good shift?"

"Yeah, pretty good. The usual. Well, except for this one guy." Dean chuckled and shook his head. "He chickened out pretty hard, and he's tried a couple of times this week, too. He works at the park, in security."

"Oh yeah?" Jessica grinned, took the satchel off him and slung it over her shoulder. "And you noticed him, huh? Is he cute?"

*Was he cute? Cute wasn't exactly the word. More like dangerously handsome.*

"Kinda. He had a sort of chiselled thing going on. Hard jaw and these dreamy eyes."

"Sounds more than kinda cute. You get his name?" Jessica went to help the next lot of guests onto the ride, and Dean waited. Once she was done, he shook his head.

"No, I'm a dumbass. Didn't even read his ID."

"Not a problem, we can check out the staff directory," Jessica said. She flipped her hair over her shoulder and flashed him a toothy smile. "You should get to know him. When was the last time you went on a date?"

"I don't even know." His mouth had gone dry,

Jessica snorted. "You're pathetic," she said. "Go on break and check the staff directory. Track down the handsome stranger."

"Roger, will do." He gave her the handover high five and left her to look after the ride, but he took his time. He never left the ride in a hurry. He always looked around at the decorations and listened to the soundtrack. The lights and things were all so interesting. There was a concealed staff exit behind the big purple alien cut out but they didn't have to use it.

He had a bit of time outside in the sunshine, then he slipped behind the Intergalactic Diner and went up the back stairs to the staff room.

The staff room in Hidden Galaxy was kind of like a clubhouse. Dean enjoyed hanging out in there – there was always someone else around to chat to, the sofas were comfortable and there was free tea, coffee and cocoa. Usually, someone brought in cookies or donuts or leftovers from the Intergalactic Diner as well.

The room was on the second floor above the diner. It was large, with scattered sofas and armchairs around the room and windows looking out over the park. You could watch the guests walking towards the roller coaster, or coming out of it, or heading into the shops. It was usually only the ride staff who used the room, but sometimes the people who played the Hidden Galaxy characters stopped by to hang out.

Dean made himself a cocoa and said hi to the people already in the room, then headed to a desk in the corner where they had a shared computer. It had internet access and all the staff information, like the shift schedules, and they all had private sign-ins so they could check their timesheets were correct. It also had access to the staff directory, complete with ID photos.

Dean sat down and signed into the computer. He checked his timesheet so that it wasn't super obvious that he was only signing in to stalk someone. Then he casually opened the staff directory. He selected the security team and scrolled through the profiles.

Dean pumped his fist in the air. There he was. Cody Buchanan. He worked in the Enchanted Forest and his position read Character Guard. That meant he would usually be working as a bodyguard to one of the groups of characters over there.

Cool.

The Enchanted Forest was filled with princes and princesses and forest creatures. Dean smiled, imagining Cody at work.

*This big, tough guy with massive shoulders running away from my roller coaster and then going back to protect a princess? I love that kind of contradiction. People are so interesting. I want to meet him. I want to be his friend.*

Dean resolved to take a wander over to the far side of the park. To see if Cody wanted coaching to ride the coaster, of course. And definitely not just to perv at the good-looking guy in his natural, magical forest habitat.

## 3 / CODY

FRIDAY AFTERNOONS WERE ALWAYS BUSY IN THE PARK, AND AS SOON as Cody got back to the muster area of the building the princes and princesses got changed in, Lennon grabbed him.

"There you are, I was this close to paging you over the park intercom." Lennon was part First Nations and had long brown hair, pulled back in a low ponytail. They were non-binary and kind of ran things for the princes and princesses and their entourage – even though their formal job title was just 'Character Handler.' Cody was sure they were due a promotion, and a big one, soon.

"Uh, I have my earpiece in, and you didn't say anything." Cody tapped the thing to make sure it was working and was rewarded with an annoying test beep.

"No, probably because I'm so used to finding you lurking somewhere nearby," Lennon said.

"Excuse me? I don't *lurk*." Cody fought off a grin and put a hand on his chest as if he were offended.

"Yes, you do. You sit by the window so you can see who's coming and going. You hang out outside if someone's having a private conversation so you can eavesdrop."

Cody finally let the grin hit his face. He didn't know Lennon noticed stuff like that. It was sort of comforting to know someone paid attention to him.

"That's just doing my job. If one of the character actors is outside the airlock they need supervision, just in case."

"Right. So that's why you were watching Nate and Dash make out against the back wall the other day?" Lennon raised an eyebrow. "You lurk like the lurkiest lurker in lurksville."

"It's all in a day's work," Cody said airily. "Anyway, I'm here now. Is it time to head out?"

"Yes, of course it is, it's afternoon meet and greet time," Lennon said. They checked something on their clipboard and then set it down. "Cody, bring up the rear, like normal."

"Roger that." Cody moved in behind the fussing group of character actors.

Nate looked up from adjusting the hem of his shiny blue brocade vest and gave Cody a big, warm smile. Cody returned it happily. Nate was exceptionally good looking and a perfect match for Prince Valor, the character he played. He was half Jamaican with curly dark hair and a wide, friendly smile. Dash, who played Prince Justice, was your classic all-American – a blond, blue-eyed hunk. He had straight, even teeth and a serious manner. Cody sidled up to Nate, feeling particularly lurksome.

"Hey Nate, ready for another exhausting encounter with the public?"

"Always," Nate said. "You ready to fight off the fans driven to hysteria by Dash's signature dreamboat handsomeness?"

Dash coughed and shoved Nate gently in the shoulder. Cody couldn't help but laugh. The two of them together really cracked him up. "Always," Cody mimicked. "They've been *particularly* hysterical this week."

"Very funny, you two." Dash rolled his eyes. He was blushing a little. Cody was pleased Nate and Dash were together – and not only because it had mellowed Dash out considerably, and he had needed the mellowing.

Cody had briefly considered asking Nate out himself, but it was so clear that Nate only had eyes for Dash that Cody had decided it wasn't worth trying to get in between them.

Greer pushed between the couple to take Dash's arm. "I'll need to take this one for a bit," she said, smiling at Nate.

Greer wore the curled auburn wig and tiara of Princess Honesty, along with the sparkling and voluminous purple ball gown. In the movies and the stories, Princess Honesty and Prince Justice were madly in love. That meant out in the park, Dash and Greer had to act that way, too.

Nate leaned in to give her a kiss on the cheek before turning to take the arm of Ariana, who played Princess Patience. Her wig was a long blonde one, and she leaned in against Nate a little.

"I'm so tired! I don't care that it's late summer, it's still too hot and this wig is going to cause me heat stroke," Ari said, fluttering her eyelashes dramatically.

"Ugh, don't even *joke* about that," Nate said, he nudged her with his elbow. "I nearly died when I went out as Treasure the Unicorn."

"Yeah, as if we haven't already heard that story a million times," Greer teased.

"And we're walking!" Lennon called out from the door. The group took off and Cody, walking behind, could instantly see the transformation. As they walked out the doors of the airlock, Dash, Greer, Nate and Ari's backs straightened, their walks turned into a glide and they became the quintessential fairytale princes and princesses they were dressed as.

It was like witnessing a little of that Fairyland magic Lennon was always on about.

As a security guard, Cody didn't have to worry about his gait or his smile or his appearance. As long as he was wearing his blue polo shirt with 'Security' written on the back coupled with black pants, and had his earpiece in, he was good to go. He slipped on his sunglasses as they went out into the park. Ari may have been joking about heat stroke, but it the sun was relentless with no cloud cover.

Cody followed the entourage to the Reflecting Lake, falling easily into the heightened awareness he needed for the job. He scanned the crowds, on the look-out for anyone rushing towards the characters. The walk was uneventful and he settled into his usual spot to the left of the group, keeping an eye on the people already lining up to meet the characters.

The encounter went normally enough. Well, until he saw someone in a pink and silver T-shirt. Someone with a boy-next-door look about him and sandy brown hair. And a nice tan, he could see, now that they were out in natural light. He swallowed and ran a hand through his hair.

*What the fuck is Spaceship Mayhem guy doing here, in the Enchanted Forest? He couldn't really have been waiting to meet Princess Honesty, could he?*

Cody licked his lips and left his post, though he still kept an eye on the crowd as walked over to meet him.

"Hey."

Dean smiled wide when Cody approached him, his whole face lighting up. His eyes practically sparkled, and his hair looked blonder in the sunshine.

"Hi! I found you!" Dean said. His voice was pitched higher and sort of strained - was he nervous?

"You did," Cody nodded. "Um, why?"

"Oh like, I didn't stalk you or anything." Dean's eyes widened. He rubbed the back of his neck. "Well, I mean, I sort of looked you up on the staff directory and saw which part of the park you worked in. And then I came here to find you, so I guess it was sort of stalky. My bad. Anyway. Um, hi. I'm Dean."

Cody tilted his head at him. "Okay? Um, why are you here?"

"Well, I thought it was a pity you didn't get to ride Spaceship Mayhem, and I wanted to check on you, see if you wanted me to, like, help you through it?"

Cody narrowed his eyes and looked around to see if anyone was listening. He didn't want Lennon, Neve or any of the character actors to overhear. A big, tough security guard who used the chicken door? He'd never hear the end of it. He tugged Dean to the side of the path, slightly behind one of the trees.

14

Lennon raised an eyebrow at them and spoke to him through the earpiece.

"Everything okay, Cody?"

"Yep, just need a second," he said. "I'll still keep an eye on the line."

Lennon nodded to him and turned back to watch the princess encounter.

"Uh, it's fine, I don't need help," he mumbled, trying to think of the best way to get Dean to leave as quickly as possible.

"Sure, yeah. That's why you kept on coming back and trying," Dean said. He noticed Cody's scowl and widened his eyes in panic. "Look, I don't want to sound weird or anything, I just noticed you."

"Except you are sounding pretty weird," Cody said. But despite himself, he was amused – Dean was flustered and Cody barely had to do anything. And he liked having that effect on people, especially someone as cute as Dean.

"R-right. But I wanted to see if it was something you wanted to work through. I mean, I know the ride better than anyone. Who else would be a better Space Mayhem buddy?"

"That's surprisingly sweet but you don't have to." Cody chuckled a little, the earnestness in Dean's face was disarming. He shifted his weight to one side and then the other and cleared his throat. "I don't even know you."

"Yeah... I actually thought that could be a benefit." Dean ran a hand through his sandy hair and then gestured widely with both hands. "I mean, you don't have to be embarrassed in front of me. Like, it doesn't matter if you barf in front of me or whatever, because we don't have a history."

"I'm not going to barf," Cody said, a little too quickly. He wasn't, was he? How intense was this roller coaster? "It's not barfing I'm having trouble with." He cleared his throat and looked around. The queue was moving in an orderly fashion, no one was crowding Ari, Greer, Dash or Nate. Everything looked under control, but he felt the sudden urge to get back to his job.

"Whatever it is, I want to help. Let me help. Please?" Dean

gave Cody a huge, encouraging smile and reached to take one of his hands. Cody's eyebrows shot up.

*He's holding my hand, because he wants to help me. This guy doesn't just wear his heart on his sleeve, he's got in printed on his T-shirt. It's intense, but sort of appealing.*

Cody took a deep breath and let it out, tapping the fingers of his free hand against the side of his thigh. Dean's encouraging face was so cute, and he looked so hopeful. Saying no to him would be like kicking a puppy. And try as he might, Cody just couldn't make himself turn him down. "Fine, okay. I'll let you help."

"Great!" Dean bounced a little on the balls of his feet. "Come by after your shift, okay?"

"Okay, alright, calm down." Cody said. He cleared his throat and looked away. "Now I gotta get back to doing the thing I'm paid for before that person over there banishes me from the Enchanted Forest." Cody hooked a thumb in Lennon's direction.

Lennon folded their arms and tilted their head towards the queue.

"Sure, me too." Dean squeezed Cody's hand, then he pulled back quickly, his eyes widening. "Sorry, I'm a touchy guy. Is it okay? I didn't mean to touch you without asking."

"It's fine." Cody chuckled a little. This guy was kind of adorable. Like how Cody felt watching one of the character actors play Treasure the Unicorn. "Just don't sneak up on me from behind or my training might kick in."

"*Suuure*, your training," Dean chuckled. "Like, full ninja training or plain old gamma ray exposure?"

"Neither. I was a Sergeant in the United States Air Force." Cody felt his back straighten as he said it. Old habits, and all. He cleared his throat as Dean's eyes widened even further.

"No way," Dean breathed.

"And mixed martial arts. A little tai chi. Now get back to your ride." Cody nodded in the direction of Space Mayhem.

"Got it. See you soon, sergeant!" Dean took off, almost running. He seemed so excited.

"Just Cody is fine," he called after him.

But as he walked back to his spot by Reflecting Lake, he noticed his heart started racing. He wiped his palms on his pants and folded his arms across his thumping chest.

*What did I just agree to?*

DEAN'S AFTERNOON TOOK *FOREVER*. ALL HE COULD THINK ABOUT WAS meeting up with Cody again.

*New friends are the best, especially when they're all cute and dangerous.*

Wait – dangerous wasn't the right word.

*Muscular.*

Yeah, muscular. That worked.

He threw himself into his job to get through the hours, and when it was knock off time and one of the evening crew took the satchel off him, he bounded straight down into the park to wait for Cody.

*I didn't plan this well, I just said come by. That meant to the ride, but now I'm done with the ride and I just need to wait around... Lurk. I'm not good at lurking.*

He was biting his lip and dithering at the entrance to the ride when he saw Cody approaching. He sighed as his body flooded with relief – he had half expected that Cody wouldn't show up at all, but there he was. Cute and muscular. Dean bounced a little, happy to see him. He waved an arm and Cody nodded and raised his hand before letting it drop again.

"You totally came!" Dean said.

"Yes, I did totally come," Cody tilted his head to the side slightly. "You're surprised?"

"Yes. No. Well... A little bit," Dean said. He chuckled to hide his own awkwardness but that just made it worse. "So, um, you want to try and ride Mayhem right now?"

Cody looked past him at the ride, a serious expression on his face, then he looked at Dean with a particularly piercing gaze.

*Are his eyes hazel or just brown?* Dean wondered faintly.

"No. Let's just get a drink or something," he said.

"Sure, I love drinks!" Dean said. He cringed internally.

*Get it together Dean! I love drinks? Seriously. Who says that?*

Cody smiled, albeit with a flicker of concern maybe. Dean had already taken his hand before he remembered Cody wasn't as much of a touchy guy as he was, so he dropped it again and flashed Cody an awkward wince of a smile. "This way, we can go to the Intergalactic Diner."

"Lead on," Cody said, so Dean did.

Once they were settled in a booth in the diner with drinks and a bowl of Martian Nuggets to share, Dean felt extra pressure to carry the conversation. After all, *he'd* suggested the whole meet-up and friendship thing, so he had to make it happen, right?

He cleared his throat. "So, Cody," he began. "How long have you been working at Fairyland?"

Cody picked up a Martian Nugget and examined it. "About six years, I guess," he said. "You?"

"Six months," Dean said. He dipped a nugget in barbeque sauce and nibbled it. "They hired me when they started the process of opening Spaceship Mayhem."

Cody took a bite of nugget and chewed thoughtfully. Dean leaned forward. For some illogical reason he really felt like the fate of their friendship rested on whether Cody liked the nugget or not. He smiled and swallowed it, reached for another. Dean leaned back in his chair, relieved all over again.

"They're good, aren't they? Made with soy."

"I thought they were chicken?" Cody's eyebrows drew together and he scrunched his nose as he broke one open, examining the insides like he was a scientist with a new specimen.

"They're made to taste like chicken, but they're entirely plant matter. Part of the whole futuristic sustainable food thing Hidden Galaxy is trying to promote."

"Huh, you don't say." Cody popped both pieces of nugget into his mouth and chewed.

"Didn't expect they'd taste that good if they were soy. Good texture, too."

Dean's stomach dropped at the brief lull in the conversation and he scrambled to find another topic. Sure, small talk was important for breaking the ice - but they had to establish common ground to get to know each other properly.

"So. Err... what's your favorite Fairyland movie?"

"Um, I guess I don't really watch them – besides, like, what I had to watch when I was hired."

Dean's mouth dropped open. "What? How can you work here and not care about the movies?"

Cody shrugged. "I like the atmosphere," he said. "Besides, it's better than working security at a nightclub and dealing with violent drunks."

Dean imagined Cody fighting multiple drunks in a nightclub. He pictured him defeating all comers with ease, punching, kicking and flicking his head up as if to say 'anyone else feeling lucky?' or something like that. It was badass.

"What?" Cody quirked an eyebrow at him

"Huh?" Dean's face was deadpan.

"You were grinning all..." Cody gestured at Dean. "Goofy."

"I-I was?" Dean flushed and shook his head. "N-nothing. Um, well, yeah. So my favorite Fairyland movie is *Typhoon Season*, you know, with the explorers and the pirates?"

Cody nodded. "Sure."

"And Jessica's favorite one is *Fairy Gentle's Bad Day*," he went on. "Which is also great. And obviously all the ones with the princesses, I mean, they're total classics, right?"

Cody raised his eyebrows and nodded again. Dean was boring him.

*Why am I talking about Fairyland movies when he said he didn't watch them? Come on, Dean, you can do better than this.*

He cleared his throat, pushed his hair back from his forehead and regrouped.

"So. What kinds of movies *do* you like?"

"I used to like Westerns," Cody said. "I guess I don't watch a lot of movies now, though."

"Okay, so what do you like to do after work?"

Cody considered for a moment, tapping a Martian Nugget against his lips.

"I like to drive around, I guess," he said finally. "Go to the gym. Sometimes I'll read a book or something. But I'm not like, an avid reader or whatever."

Dean sat up straighter and smiled. "What kinds of books?"

"Science fiction, I guess. Like, far futures where there's aliens and humanity's all over the universe, that kind of thing."

Dean sat up straighter, catching on. "No wonder you want to ride Spaceship Mayhem, then! It's total science fiction."

Cody chuckled and shrugged one shoulder. "Well, yeah, maybe that's part of it."

Dean slapped his palms on the table, and Cody started. Dean picked up his hands and looked at them, horrified. Then he pulled them back into his lap, feeling sheepish.

"Sorry! I didn't mean to…" he trailed off. "I just thought about how great it'll be when you finally *do* ride the coaster. Jessica and I will be there to cheer you on, and we could ride it, like, a million times."

Dean felt his face crack into a huge grin. And after a brief flicker of trepidation, Cody joined him, too.

"Okay, so how about tomorrow morning? What time do you start?" Dean asked.

"Not tomorrow," Cody said "The day after?"

"Looking forward to it."

## 5 / CODY

CODY ARRANGED TO MEET DEAN AT THE ENTRANCE TO THE PARK. HE didn't usually get in early, but he made a point to today. Despite the frank weirdness of someone like Dean paying interest in him, he was enjoying the time they spent together.

*Maybe it's not so weird that we get on.*

Dean put him at ease. It felt a little like being back at school – making a new friend. Sure, he'd made friends while he served, but that was due to proximity – same with how he was friends with Nate, Dash and Lennon. They were forced together so you had to get on or things would be difficult.

Dean just wanted to be friends with him and help him, because it seemed like Dean was just a fucking good person. It was adorable, really. It made Cody feel wanted, and not in a sexy way, just in a worth-getting-to-know way, which was unfamiliar. Thinking about Dean was pleasant too. It was like the guy genuinely believed everyone around him was a good person.

*If only he were gay,* Cody thought. *And a few years older.*

He heard footsteps and turned. A couple of actors who worked over in Pirate Bay were approaching. Cody watched them together, they looked comfortable but not in a sexy, dating way. They didn't touch each other enough for it to be a relationship. But they were smiling and joking with each other.

*Why is everyone at Fairyland is so damn attractive?*

Which was, of course, a benefit to working here as opposed to working security at some random bar. Cody loved to people watch, and the opportunities at Fairyland were almost endless.

He broke into a smile as he caught sight of Dean walking towards him. He'd come from the direction of the public transport stops, and he was dressed in his Mayhem uniform with a denim jacket over the top.

He looked like he'd walked out of the recruitment pamphlet for the Fairyland intern programme: *Join the all American, clean-cut youths and work the Fairyland magic!* It would be adorable if it wasn't so predictable.

"Mornin', Cody!" Dean said, waving as he approached.

"I thought we would walk and talk today," Cody replied, before Dean could ask him about the roller coaster. "That's all."

"Great!" Dean added a bounce to his step. "You going to walk me to my roller coaster, or am I walking you to your handsome princes?"

Cody side eyed Dean. "*My* handsome princes?"

"Isn't that what you do all day? Protect the princes?" Dean was loving this – Cody could feel the amusement radiating off him. Cody grunted.

He couldn't count how often he'd been involved in dragging Nate and Dash out of their changing room since they started dating. Protecting? Mostly he was protecting them from being fired for being terminally late from sucking each other's faces.

"I... I guess I thought we could walk around the park a little and then I could drop you off at your coaster."

"Perfect," Dean slid his arm into Cody's and then pulled it back again. "Sorry, I know you're not a touching guy. I am, but I *will* remember, I promise."

"It's all right, I don't mind," Cody mumbled, but he mumbled it just as they went through security and Dean was wishing the gate guards good morning, so he didn't hear him. Maybe Cody had timed it that way on purpose.

Security had two desks at the same station, so Dean went to one and Cody the other.

"How was your night, Shirley?" He asked.

Shirley chuckled and handed Dean back his bag – they had to do bag checks on everyone, including all staff. Cody sighed. He didn't miss the early days when he'd been on gate duty.

"Oh, it was fine, Dean, thanks for asking. Morrie made dinner last night."

"He *did*? Aww, that's awesome! Was it edible?"

Shirley laughed. "I didn't have to make it myself, so it was delicious!"

Cody watched Dean. He didn't take nearly as long to go through security, he just said good morning and good day and was done. Dean was apparently friends with everyone.

After a few minutes, he caught up to Cody, somehow even happier than he'd been beforehand.

"Who's Morrie?" Cody asked.

"Shirley's son. He's fifteen, but he's really growing up well," Dean said.

"And... *How* long did you say you've worked here?"

"Only six months." Dean chirped.

Cody whistled. "How many of the people on staff do you know stuff like that about?"

Dean shrugged and his smile faltered a little. "I don't know. It's just being friendly, there's nothing wrong with that."

"No, I'm not saying there is," Cody said. How could he tell Dean he admired him without it sounding weird? "It's just unusual is all, I don't know many people who..." he trailed off. What was he trying to say, exactly? He pulled his beanie off and pocketed it, taking the walkway towards Pirate Bay, expecting Dean to keep up.

"I don't know a lot of people who go out of their way to get to know everyone around them. And then, it seems like you check in on people – actually make an effort, you know?"

"Well, sure," Dean said. "It's the people in this place that make it magic, right?"

Cody gave him a sidelong glance. A lingering one, because

Dean was looking forward and hadn't noticed he was watching him. His face was totally open, trusting and contented.

*Did they construct this guy in a Fairyland cyborg factory? And why is he so damned... endearing?*

*On anyone else this would be annoying, so why does this feel so comfortable?*

SCHEDULING TIME AROUND HIS OWN SHIFTS AND CODY'S SHIFTS wasn't as hard as it could have been. Cody finished at much the same time every day, and although Dean's shifts were a little more unpredictable, he could usually find time before or after to meet up with Cody. He looked forward to seeing Cody every time.

This time, they met up at the Forest Kitchen. Dean ordered the Halloween special – a huge iced pumpkin cookie, a milkshake and a collectible straw with a ghost on it. Cody ordered coffee.

"You really keep all that stuff?" Cody asked, pointing at the straw.

"Oh yeah." Dean admired the straw. The Halloween designs were adorable. "I have a whole cabinet for limited edition Fairyland stuff. It could be worth a lot of money someday."

"If it's had your spit all over it, I don't think it will be," Cody smirked at his own joke and Dean smiled back, unphased.

Cody liked to make jokes, and he'd been carefully directing Dean away from riding on Spaceship Mayhem, which is fine, but Dean did want to see if they could make progress.

"How about we try you on a gentle ride first?" Dean suggested, looking down at the table.

Cody looked at Dean skeptically. "If you're about to suggest we go to the Enchanted Forest and ride the spinning lily pads, I can tell you right now the answer is no."

"Why not?" Dean asked. He picked up his drink and took a sip. "The lily pads are fun."

"Because I'm not a fucking five-year-old. Also, I have no problem with the spinning lily pads."

Dean's laughed. "No problem? So, you're saying you've ridden them before?"

Cody nodded. "In my first week I rode every ride in the park. That was before your one opened, though."

Dean took a sip of his drink. "Wow. I can't imagine you getting on the spinning lily pads." His eyes widened. "Oh my god – did you ride the Kiddy Coaster as well?"

"Okay, aside from that one. I couldn't fit in it," Cody said. Dean choked on his drink and set it back down, wiping his mouth. "I mean, it's kiddy sized."

Dean looked him up and down. He was tall. From the size of him he could probably barely fit in one of the lily pad cars – he must've had to fold himself in half.

"Okay, so no problem with the swinging pirate ship?" Dean asked. It seemed like a bit of a step up from the spinning lily pads and the kiddy coaster.

"The pirate ship was fun, I got into a whooping contest with some high school kids," Cody said, smiling. Dean smiled. That was a cute image as well. Big, tough ex–Air Force Cody and the kids all whooping it up.

"How about the other big coaster in the park – the Kraken. Have you ridden that one?" All of a sudden, Dean felt nervous. He didn't get nervous at all riding any of the rides, he absolutely loved them, but looking at them from a 'this is scary' perspective made his heart speed up a little. Like he was nervous on Cody's behalf.

"Kraken's okay," Cody shrugged. "I mean, it's fine, I guess. I find it a little intense when it goes all dark and the kraken appears around the corner. You know, when it does that jump out thing? But I can ride it."

"So it's really Spaceship Mayhem that's the problem?"

Cody nodded. "The control panel's a bit too real, reminds me of... well. Of stuff I'd rather not remember."

"You were in the Air Force, yeah? So maybe we should talk about that a little. It seems to be getting in your way." Dean picked up his milkshake and took a sip. It tasted so good. All the park food tasted amazing.

Dean saw Cody's shoulders tense. "I didn't agree to this so you could shrink my head," he said, frowning. "And I have a piece of paper that says my PTSD isn't bad enough that I need a disability benefit, so. Whatever's happening in here-" he tapped his forehead. "Isn't serious according to the brilliant health insurance system."

Dean whistled a little and shook his head. "Yeah, but the medical system is pretty messed up, especially when it comes to veterans. My mom couldn't get any support when she got back from Iraq and she had nightmares almost every night."

Dean's stomach squirmed. It wasn't the most pleasant time in his life to think about.

Cody frowned and tilted his head a little. "Your mom served?"

"Yeah, she was in the marines," Dean said. "I probably should've told you that earlier, huh? She served in Iraq and she got an honorable discharge after her last tour."

"You didn't want to follow in her footsteps?" Cody looked genuinely surprised by the idea that Dean would be here and not serving. Dean shuddered and shook his head.

"Oh, no. After I saw what it did to Mom, I didn't want to. I had thought about it as a teenager, but..." He took a deep breath, steadying himself. "Nah. She supports us no matter what we do."

Cody nodded and swallowed. "Probably for the best, you seem kinda chirpy and optimistic."

"I *am* optimistic." Dean took a bite of his special Halloween cookie and relaxed some. Something about Cody and the cookie filled him with warm feelings. "Like I know we'll be able to get you on Spaceship Mayhem."

"Maybe," Cody pulled a face which could have been

amusement or could have been a grimace. Dean didn't know him well enough yet to tell. "By the way, how old are you?"

"What is this, twenty questions?" Dean laughed. "Twenty-three. And how about you?" Dean asked. He gave Cody a smile to show he knew he was being cheeky.

Cody surveyed him with a raised eyebrow. "Well, you look like a teenager, so I guess that's a good thing. I'm thirty-seven," Cody said. "I know, I know, I'm an old man. Staring down the barrel of forty. You don't have to make the jokes, I hear enough of them from Prince Justice over in the Enchanted Forest."

"I wasn't going to," Dean said. He liked that Cody was sensitive about his age, it showed a crack in the bad ass tough exterior which Dean hadn't expected. "You look good, you don't look old at all."

"I do, but thanks." Cody sighed. Dean thought he saw Cody soften a little.

*Maybe I should've spoken about my mother earlier, it seems like it's done some good.* Dean's sat up straighter in his chair. *I'm about to be brilliant, I think...*

"Hey, you want to come around and meet my mom sometime?"

Cody spluttered on his coffee. "Now, now. Let's take this one step at a time," He said. "How about we start by riding the Kraken. I'll see if it freaks me out, and you can let me know which bits are like Spaceship Mayhem."

"Deal," Dean nodded once. He offered Cody his cookie, somewhat embarrassed by the size of the bite he'd taken out of it. As he did, his stomach rumbled, and he felt his cheeks start to burn. "Cookie?"

Cody chuckled. It was the best sound Dean had heard all day. "Tempting, but no."

## 7 / CODY

A WEEK LATER, CODY WAS IN THE AIRLOCK WAITING FOR THE FIRST prince and princess meet and greet and texting Dean. It turned out Dean was the kind of person who messaged a lot. And it wasn't annoying stuff like 'what you up to?' or 'why aren't you replying?' It was stuff like 'here's a neat rock I found'. Stuff from his shifts like 'while I was running the ride these two young guys got on and I swear they were on a date and they were like quintessential jock and emo and it was ADORABLE'

Often it was selfies of him enjoying his coffee or milkshake or whatever Fairyland beverage he was loving in that moment.

It wasn't the kind of thing Cody thought would make him smile, but to his own surprise, he did. Each picture Dean sent was cute or endearing. They sometimes made Cody snort air out of his nose a little too loud, and he'd send back stuff like 'wtf' or emojis of faces looking confused or raising their eyebrows.

"Who're you messaging?" Nate asked from behind his shoulder.

Cody's stomach lurched and he gripped his phone tight so that his instinct to turn and punch didn't kick in.

*Nate is my friend.* He breathed in.

*Nate isn't trying to kill me.*

"Just Dean." Cody showed Nate the latest picture Dean had sent him, which was Dean in the Hidden Galaxy staff room, drinking a hot cocoa and crossing his eyes. His hair had a fascinating swoop thing happening in front.

Nate peered at the picture and grinned. "Who's Dean? He's very... happy looking."

"He works over in Hidden Galaxy," Cody said. "He runs the Spaceship Mayhem roller coaster."

Nate put his hand on his hip and cocked his head.

"Okay, so, you're into him?" Nate asked. He nudged Cody in the arm and grinned even wider somehow. He was in his Prince Valor costume. He looked just like he'd stepped out of a picture in a Princess Patience story.

Cody shook his head.

*No way Dean would be interested in a messed up old dude like me.*

"You're ridiculous, he's a friend," Cody said. "A very enthusiastic friend who likes to share the things he's excited about, which seem to be mostly food-related. He's ridiculous – a little bit like you." Cody ran his fingers through his hair. "What is it about me that attracts ridiculous people, do you think?"

"You're really smiling, though," Nate looked almost hopeful, in an abandoned puppy kind of way.

"I don't *not* smile." Cody felt a little defensive. "I smile all the time."

"Yeah – but usually at other people's discomfort."

"Still counts," Cody muttered.

He wasn't sure why he felt defensive, except that Nate was probing something which he didn't want probed. Some nascent emotional attachment, or feelings which he didn't want to be having about someone who'd never like him that way. Someone with a girlfriend.

"Sure, okay. But this is all genuine and stuff," Nate continued. Cody looked down at the pictures of Dean and minimized the app, buying himself some time to respond. Maybe hiding him from Nate as well. He felt uncertain all of a sudden. He looked back at Nate again.

"I mean, he's a friend. He's offered to help me with something.

I tried to ride Spaceship Mayhem but I kind of freaked out about it."

"Freaked out, how?" Nate frowned. It looked so wrong with his current costume – Prince Valor would never risk angry forehead wrinkles. "I didn't know. I'll ride it with you, if you like."

"No, it's fine, Dean's helping. It's just all a bit…" Cody sighed and waved a hand. He wasn't comfortable admitting to weakness like this – especially not with someone he worked so closely with. It made him feel exposed.

He swallowed the lump in his throat. Still, this was Nate, and Nate would never do anything to intentionally hurt anyone. So why was he still so afraid? "I guess it reminds me too much of Afghanistan. The control panels, the cockpit and everything."

Cody's stomach churned as Nate's eyes went really wide and he nodded, reaching out to gently touch Cody's arm.

*Why is everyone touching me lately? This is why I don't tell people this shit. They get all 'oh no' and touch me and look at me like they pity me.*

*I hate it.*

"I'm sorry, Cody, I had no idea."

"It's fine." Cody shook his head. "Like I said, I'm working through it, and Dean's helping." he paused again, considering. As much as he hated talking about it, he valued Nate's opinion on things like this. "You don't think this is a stupid idea, do you?"

"What? No, I think it's a great idea. If you get to unravel some stuff from your past and you get to ride a badass roller coaster in the process, that all sounds good to me. Besides, Dean is really good looking. Show me again – I think he had a really good nose."

Nate reached for Cody's phone and Cody swiftly shoved it in his pocket.

He cleared his throat. "I think we're about to go out. You just focus on Dash and keeping him happy."

Nate nodded and gave Cody an encouraging smile. "Yeah, okay. That's almost another full-time job," he joked.

"And we're all looking forward to the Royal Wedding," Cody said, nudging Nate back a little harder than he meant to. "Are you going to be serving lobster rolls? Raw vegan rice rolls? What can we expect on the buffet?"

"Shut up." Nate blushed and bit down a smile. "Let me know if there's anything I can do to help, okay?"

Cody checked his security lanyard was outside his shirt. "Yeah, I will," Cody said. And the smile Nate gave him made him feel like opening up was the right thing to do. He could trust Nate, and that was a good feeling, even although he still felt a little jittery. "Do you really think this is a good idea?"

"Yes, it fucking is," Nate raised an eyebrow. "Also, he's cute."

Cody scowled, despite his heart doing a little excited skip. "That is not the point."

DEAN COMMUTED TO AND FROM THE PARK ON THE BUS. ON THE WAY home, he liked to catch the same bus as the people who'd just left the park. He loved to see them all tired out, the kids sacked out in their parents' laps, the people with bags of merchandise, going through their photos and sharing them on social media.

He liked to stand up and give grateful, tired-out parents his seat.

Sure, his feet hurt from his shift, but being able to do one more nice thing for someone topped off his day. If he could get a smile out of someone exhausted and starting on a long journey home, then he'd have a bounce in his step on his walk from the bus stop to his apartment.

He lived in an apartment his mother had bought in a suburb near the university. He'd have to share it with his younger siblings when they decided to move out of home, but for now it was his to enjoy. A modest two-bedroom, one-bathroom apartment with a huge living area and a kitchen from the eighties. Not exactly up-to-date, but it was comfortable and it felt like home.

He had his cabinet, second-hand from the thrift shop, which was two-thirds full of limited-edition Fairyland merchandise. The top shelf had the best stuff: the Christmas costumed plushies of Treasure the Unicorn, Sparkles the Dragon and the other forest characters. They were all so cute in their little fluffy Santa hats!

The next shelf down had his seasonal mugs and figurines of the princes and princesses.

The third had sipper cups, special straws and tiny mugs that you could get at the eateries in the park. It was a small collection, but Dean liked to see everything out on display. It was like having a little bit of Fairyland at home with him.

He added his newest straw to the collection - that made him think of eating at the Enchanted Forest, and that made his stomach rumble. He gave his display another look and went to the kitchen to make himself an omelet. Looking in the fridge he found some leftover chicken and mushrooms that he cut up to add to the pan.

*I wonder if Cody cooks for himself,* he thought. *Could be he's the kind that orders in all the time. Then again, if he's served he'd have some kind of routine around eating regularly and stuff that's at least halfway decent, right?*

*Maybe I should ask him over for dinner sometime.*

Dean switched on the radio and had a bit of a dance in the kitchen as he cooked. When the omelet was done he sat in front of the TV with a drink. Once he'd eaten the last bite he called his mother.

"Anne speaking." She picked up after three rings.

"Hey, Ma," he said. He resettled himself on the couch, slouching down and draping a leg over the arm of it.

"Deanie, baby, how are you?" He could hear the smile in her voice. He smiled, too.

"I'm really good, Ma. How's things with you?"

"Oh, the same old thing, you know how it is."

"Mm-hmm, how're the kids?" Dean stifled a yawn and sat up a bit more, shoving a robot cushion behind his head. He and the rest of the family all referred to his younger siblings as 'the kids'. He was five years older than the next younger sibling, Meryl, and she was two-and-a-half years older than their brother Jacob. Seven years younger than Jacob still were the twins – Abby and Alex.

"Meryl's having girlfriend troubles, but honestly, I think she's better off without this one. She's so full of drama."

Dean frowned. "Yeah, I think so, too. She's been texting me all sorts of weird stuff. I kept telling her to look after herself first."

"Mm-hmm, and the others are pretty busy with school work. How's your job going?"

"It's great," Dean said. "I think I've made a new friend, this guy, Cody. He works security and he was having issues with riding the roller coaster. He has PTSD, I think."

"Oh yeah?" Anne's voice changed, became more interested, and he heard the clank of something being set down. She'd stopped multi-tasking.

Dean got up from the couch and carried his dishes into the kitchen.

"Yeah, he served in Afghanistan, in the Air Force," he continued. "He said the coaster cart reminds him too much of the control panel on his plane."

"Hmm. I could see that," Anne said. "It is weirdly realistic compared to some of the other rides in that park." Her tone had shifted, got a little more faraway. Dean's chest ached to hear it.

Dean had taken the whole family to the park a few times – and of course they had all ridden Spaceship Mayhem a few times. His father, Louis, seemed to love it especially. He continued to explain to his mom how he'd met up with Cody.

"He's like, kind of awkward, I don't think he hangs out with friends that often. But he seems sweet. He hasn't once told me to stop messaging him with selfies or anything."

"Uh-huh." Anne's tone had lightened again, there was a noise like she was back to multi-tasking. Dean ran the faucet over his plate to rinse it. "And what's he look like?" Her knowing tone of voice gave her away.

"It's not like that, Ma. He's a friend," Dean said. He bit his lip. "I'm helping him through something is all. Maybe we hang out a bit as well, but it's not like I'm gonna *kiss* him."

"All right, all right," Anne laughed. "I'm glad you made a new friend. You should bring him around some time."

Dean bounced happily and did a little spin on the kitchen tiles. "Yeah, I thought so, too!" Dean said. "Good. I'll see when he's free and let you know. Love you, Ma."

"Love you too, Dean."

Once he'd hung up, Dean couldn't keep up with all the thoughts bombarding his brain.

*I could introduce Cody to my mom, and he could meet Meryl and Jacob and Alex and Abby, too. Maybe he'd even get on with my dad!*

He took a selfie of himself with his post-phone call cocoa – complete with duck shaped marshmallows – sent it to Cody and waited expectantly for his reply as he folded his laundry.

## 9 / CODY

"So, you think you're ready?" Dean asked. "It's pretty soon..."

"I think so," Cody said. His voice had cracked slightly so he cleared his throat to cover it. His heart was speeding up - it knew what he was about to try.

They were in the staff lounge in Hidden Galaxy, which Cody was starting to recognize purely from the backgrounds of the endless selfies and food shots Dean sent him.

They'd spent an hour watching illicit videos guests had filmed while riding Spaceship Mayhem online. It was the kind of thing Cody was pretty sure Dean was meant to stop, but with cameras getting so small, Dean had said there were always ways to hide them – though he did confiscate a few Treasure the Unicorn nanny cams most weeks.

The videos were fine. Cody could watch them, at least. There was a particularly high-quality one that he'd watched several times over. He knew when the turns happened, when the ride went out of the building and when it plunged back into darkness. Some of it was hard to make out because the video was dark and you could just hear screaming, but Dean had talked him through those bits of the ride.

So why were his palms still so sweaty?

Cody rubbed his hand over his eyes and nodded. "Yeah, it's fine. I can do this."

"Cool, if you're sure. And we can always leave – just say the word." Dean stood up and Cody followed him out of the staff room. The sunlight seemed extra bright and Cody squinted as he fumbled to put his sunglasses on.

When he opened his eyes again, he saw Dean wave at someone as they walked towards Spaceship Mayhem.

He blinked. He suddenly felt an odd sensation... like the building was getting taller and the ground under his feet was sinking down. His feet felt steady on the paved walkway, but when he looked at the ground, it seemed to be sloping away.

Cody swallowed and shook his head a little. This was silly. Nothing was actually happening. Nothing like *that*, anyway.

"You okay, buddy?" Dean stood beside him. Cody looked at him and the world kind of righted itself. He was a good, steady point to focus on. Something to keep him grounded.

"Yeah," Cody mumbled. He sort of wanted to say something. Something about Dean being a steady point of focus, maybe, but when he imagined saying it to him it sounded ridiculous. Like a line out of some corny romantic comedy. So he straightened his back and stayed quiet, looking up at the entrance decorations as they walked into the Spaceship Mayhem building.

"I'll go first," Dean said. He led the way up to the express path, waving his staff ID at a cute red-haired girl.

"Oh, I know who you are, Dean," she said in a clear Irish accent.

"Okay, but do you know my friend, Cody?" Dean turned to wave Cody forward. He gave the redhead a tight smile.

"Hey."

"Why, no, I don't know Mr Tall, Buff, And Mysterious." Her smile was warm and enthusiastic. Cody didn't know how these ride staff could do it all day – all that smiling would hurt his cheeks within a half hour.

"This is Cody," Dean said. "Cody, meet Jessica."

"Mm-hmm, well. Welcome, Cody." Jessica reached out and

squeezed Cody's arm before turning to Dean. "Oh my god, you would not believe the family who came through just before. They were all wearing the same Sparkles the Dragon T-shirt and matching purple baseball caps. They were *so cute!*"

Dean beamed and nodded, as if this was the best news he'd ever received. "Yes! That is so good! The whole family?" Cody looked between them, wondering what he was missing.

"Yep – Mom, Dad, two kids and the baby."

"You let a baby ride Spaceship Mayhem?" Cody asked.

"No, silly! They did a rider switch," Jessica said. "One parent rode first and the other held the baby then they switched over so they both got to enjoy the ride."

Dean turned to Cody. "I'm not allowed to hold the babies," he said, sadly.

"That would be weird, is why," Cody said. He took a slight step back, disarmed by Cody's adorableness. "They don't know you, why would they let you hold their babies?"

"Because I'd take *such good* care of them!" Dean's eyes were as wide as saucers. For a second Cody almost thought he might cry from the unfairness of it all.

Jessica rolled her eyes and shook her head, but she scrunched her nose and smiled affectionately at Dean.

*These two are so well matched. She's like girl Dean, I can see why they're so crazy about each other.*

"Well, maybe you should open a daycare center for the park," she said.

"Oh God – that'd be the best thing," Dean's voice practically quivered. "But, one, that would never happen; and two, we're gonna go ride. I'm glad you two got to meet. Come on, Cody."

Cody's breath caught as he started walking up the express path. He'd kind of forgotten what they were here to do. But now he was looking at the dayglow paint and his heart was racing all over again when the damned robot jumped out at him.

He focused on watching Dean's back. His shoulders relaxed and he could breathe easier. It was like he was just following his friend on a walk. Yeah. Just a plain, ordinary walk – through the nightmarish Hellscape that was the bleeping, blooping all-too-realistic spaceship ride.

Cody clenched his fists so hard his nails dug into the fleshy part of his palms.

*I can do this.*

*I can do this.*

Dean turned the corner to the platform where the ride cars came to a stop. As Cody turned around the same corner, Dean was already talking to the guy running the ride. His breath caught in his throat. How did this happen so fast? It was like they'd teleported right from talking to Jessica to here.

*I need more time.*

"Come on," Dean called encouragingly. He reached his hand out to Cody. Cody looked at his hand, then he looked at the guy running the ride. He looked at the open ride cart, the safety harnesses up, the music and sound effects playing. His ribcage felt like it was constricting, pressing all his internal organs into glue.

*I can't do this.*

He turned away from Dean's outstretched hand and walked out the chicken door.

Every step he took away from the ride platform felt like freedom. It became easier to breathe and hear and think and his chest stopped contracting.

Cody walked out into the sunlight. In the distance he could hear an Irish accented voice calling out to him, but that wasn't his problem.

He slipped his sunglasses back on and marched toward the Enchanted Forest.

He didn't have to come back. He didn't have to tell anyone about this – not ever.

*No one had to know.*

Lennon summoned Cody into their office shortly after he got back to the airlock.

"Big changes," Lennon said. Cody's stomach was still tied up in knots. Lennon handed Cody a heavy A4 envelope.

"Are you firing me?" Cody's hand shook slightly as he felt the heft of the papers inside the envelope.

"No, I'm not firing you," Lennon frowned. "Don't be an ass. There're changes to our protocols coming. Rumor is that the fabled Max Jones is coming for a visit."

"Max Jones…" Cody said. His shoulders relaxed. He really needed to get a grip – for a moment there he really did think Lennon was about to cancel his contract. "That name rings a bell."

"And so it should, because he's the son of legendary Dracine Jones." Lennon made air quotes with their fingers around the word '*legendary*'. "The founder and owner of the park, if you need reminding. Which means that he's going to inherit the whole business someday soon."

Cody raised his eyebrows. "Sure. Yes, that's exactly what I was about to say."

Lennon sighed and turned in their chair, typing a couple of things onto their laptop and then sighing again, more heavily. "The management team are freaking out. They want everything extra double good around here and that means all of us have to step up our game. More security at the front gates, more orderly lines in the meet and greets, more moving people on from sitting around in the park randomly and of course, more merchandise. They're adding more carts for merchandise and snacks."

*New merchandise, Dean will be stoked.* But then he swallowed down thoughts of Dean. He'd probably never see him again.

Cody nodded at Lennon. "Okay, makes sense, I guess. What do you need me to do?"

"Well, it might be extra shifts, some weekend work. I'd like you to head up a squad if you're into it. We'll be recruiting, of course, the agency's on that, but they'll still need park training."

"Extra shifts?" Cody frowned, imagining giving up his spare time. He wouldn't have time to do a few things, not that he exactly had hobbies. It'd cut into the nights he went to the club, or the hours on the couch playing that damn app game Dash'd got him hooked on. "Overtime?"

"Yes," Lennon said, they tapped the envelope in his hand. "The details are all in the packet – but it'd be double-time plus some extra leave days for weekends worked. I've also secured you a pay rise for taking on training. If you agree to do it, that is."

Cody looked Lennon in the eyes and they returned it. Their expression said they already knew he'd agree.

He thought it through and all the tension he'd been holding in his shoulders, neck and jaw eased. He could breathe easier.

*This could be just the opportunity I need. If I'm busy with totally legitimate work then I won't have time to meet up with Dean and we can forget about the whole Spaceship Mayhem thing.*

He'd have no choice but to cancel their meetings and focus on training the newbies, to get them up to scratch. And he was sure he wouldn't lose touch with Dean entirely. Guy couldn't stop sending photos.

As he thought about it, his phone buzzed in his pocket. Just the prickle of vibration against his thigh made his heart leap in his chest.

"Yeah, okay. Count me in. I'll sign this stuff now." he said. He spotted a pen on Lennon's desk and leaned forward to grab it.

"Read it first, please," Lennon said. They snatched the pen out of his reach and arched an eyebrow. "I'll sleep easier if I know you're not just going around signing anything anyone gives you."

Cody flashed Lennon a smile. "Okay, I'll take 'em home, read 'em and bring 'em back in tomorrow." Cody stood up, folding the envelope in half and shoving it in his back pocket. "It's nice to know you're worried about me, though."

"I'm not worried exactly." Lennon waved a hand dismissively. They huffed a little and opened their desk planner, looking for their next appointment no doubt. "I'm just not sure that you *ever* think things through before you do them."

"I think things through plenty, don't you worry." Cody gave them a friendly salute and turned to go. Okay, maybe he didn't *always* think things through enough. But Lennon didn't have to know that. Besides, they were already focused on whatever was on their screen.

Cody pulled his phone out as he left the office to find a picture of Dean looking contrite with a sad cartoon bunny filter over his face. It was sweet, and it made Cody smile.

*Aw, damn it. I'd miss Dean's selfies if I skip out on him entirely.* It was a relief to have a totally legitimate reason to drop the Space Mayhem stuff but still stay friends with Dean.

He messaged him back.

Let's meet up after this shift.

Dean replied within seconds.

Awesome! HMU when you're done! <3

"Hey, Nate," Cody said, approaching the group of princes and princesses getting ready to go out into the park. He didn't look up from his phone.

"He's still getting ready," Dash said. Cody looked up and gave Dash a dry smile, a polite one. He was never as excited or happy to be talking to Dash, even though he'd known him longer. Dash always had some sort of barrier up. Well, and there was that time

Dash had almost punched him. Sure, all Cody had been doing was trying to help Nate out with a bottle of water when he was close to passing out, but Dash had wanted to be the one to help him. And he'd shown no fear of Cody in that moment.

"Dash, do you know what HMU means?" He showed his phone to Dash.

"Hit me up," Dash said, without looking at the phone screen.

Cody huffed out a breath. Dash had a tendency to be difficult – especially with things like this. "I *was* hitting you up, I was just asking you what HMU means."

"It means hit me up," if Dash's voice could have rolled its eyes, it would. Cody looked at the text again and his cheeks started to burn.

"Okay, right. Got it. Makes sense." He nodded.

"New boyfriend?" Dash asked. He looked at Cody's phone and then raised his eyebrows at Cody.

"No, he's just a friend. From over Hidden Galaxy way."

They both looked at Cody's phone for a moment. Dash lowered a single eyebrow. Cody had just kind of worked out how to reply to HMU when Dean sent through a photo of him and Jessica doing peace signs and grinning.

"I think he's dating her," Cody said, relieved to have a way to divert the conversation.

"Too bad, he's cute," Dash said. "If you like the boy-next-door type."

"Who's cute?" Nate appeared at Cody's other elbow, a little out of breath. "Oh yeah – Cody's new boy. He's really cute."

"*You* like the boy-next-door type," Cody indicated to Dash while nodding towards Nate. Dash looked affronted.

"Uhh, no. I like the gallantly handsome prince type."

"Kind of you, but I'm totally the boy next door." Nate grinned. "I'm just masquerading as a prince."

"You'll always be a true prince to me," Dash said, his eyes widening a little.

Cody snorted. "You two are ridiculous, and I'd like to get out of the middle of this conversation now." He joked but his insides were squirming. He moved back to where Lennon was briefing Neve and some tall, buff dude in a security T-shirt who Cody hadn't met before.

Lennon turned to Cody. "Neve'll be in charge for this one – and we got you one of the new recruits I mentioned as a backup."

"That was quick," Cody frowned.

"Meet Francisco," Neve said. "Francisco, this is Cody, he'll be your boss for the next couple of weeks, all going to plan."

"Pleased to meetcha," Cody said, sizing him up. Francisco was unshaven, had startlingly bright brown eyes, wavy black hair and olive-toned skin.

They shook hands and Francisco's grip was firm but not crushing. Cody squeezed extra hard – just to show him he was the boss. It reminded him of his commanding officers in the military. Whatever, he did it without thinking. Francisco squeezed back briefly and then let him have it.

"The pleasure's all mine."

Argh, he had that South American accent that made Cody go all gooey.

"Sure. Just stick by me for the first bit. We'll need to make sure people aren't trying to get at the characters." He gestured at Nate, Dash and the others. "I don't expect any trouble. You got your earpiece?"

Francisco nodded. Cody had to look up to meet his eyes. He was so tall! It was comforting talking to someone who wasn't miles shorter than him for once. "Yes, sir. Neve tuned it in for me."

"You don't have to call me sir, for the record. Let's get out there, then."

*Just gotta get through this, show the newbie the ropes and then I can catch up with Dean.*

## 11 /DEAN

DEAN WAITED IN THE INTERGALACTIC DINER, BUT IT WAS HARD TO stay still. He kept shifting in his seat, and if he tried to stay still his leg jiggled so hard it rattled the table. He got up twice to see if he could see Cody out the door.

Cody had bailed hard at the ride, and he was sure he'd be feeling embarrassed about it. Dean blamed himself – he'd tried to move too fast and pushed Cody to go on the ride before he was ready. He'd bustled along right up to the ride without checking in on how Cody was feeling, and they hadn't unpacked any of the issues Cody had with his experiences in the Air Force.

He sighed into his Nebula shake. It was a weirdly brilliant purple color and tasted like delicious grapes. Yet, he was fiddling with the straw rather than drinking it. He watched the door, his heart leaping every time it slid open with a kitschy 'woosh' sound from some seventies science fiction show. The door had opened probably twenty times since he had sat down, and none of those times had been for Cody.

When he finally did walk through, Dean leapt out of his chair and waved him over, waves of relief flooding his body.

Cody looked serious, his jaw set and his eyes blazing in a dangerously handsome way. Dean jiggled in place until Cody was nearly at the table then threw his arms around him.

Cody went stiff in his arms, and Dean realized with a start that they hadn't actually hugged before. He'd just gone and done it like they were old friends. He pulled back with a full-teeth awkward grin.

"Sorry, didn't think. I was just so happy to see you!" Dean's cheeks were flushing red, he could feel the heat in them. "S-sorry."

"It's okay," Cody said. He was smiling the way he did sometimes when Dean was particularly silly. A kind of wry, reluctant smile where half his mouth would pull up and the other stayed neutral. Then he pulled Dean back in gruffly for another hug. "Hugs are okay."

"Good." Dean relaxed. He squeezed him, closing his eyes and relaxing into the hug. And if, maybe, he turned his head slightly to smell his neck, then that was just reflex. And besides, there was nothing theoretically weird about smelling someone's neck, right? The neck was just where everyone smelled the best to Dean. And it made him happy to smell that quintessential *themness* of them.

He cleared his throat and pulled back before he sniffed in behind Cody's ear. That would definitely be weird, and Cody would probably notice.

They sat down. "Did you want something to drink or eat?" Dean said. "I just got the shake but you're welcome to share it with me, or?"

"I'm okay," Cody said. "I can't stay too long. I just wanted to…" he trailed off. His eyes dropped from Dean's to look at the shake. He frowned. "Uhh, are you sure that's food? It's a horrible color."

"Oh, I know, but it tastes really good! Like grapes, like the tastiest grapes you've ever eaten."

"A grape milkshake?" Cody frowned deeper and stuck out his tongue. "Sounds disgusting."

Dean pushed the shake towards him. "Try it."

"Yeah… no," Cody laughed. "Look, I just wanted to thank you for your help and stuff, but I'm gonna have to call this off. My job's just got a helluva lot busier and I'm not going to have time. Besides, I think we can both agree it's not working."

Dean's heart sank and he shook his head. "You don't mean that, we only just started."

"No, my job really *is* gonna be busier. Have you heard the rumors Max Jones is coming to check the park out?" Cody's tone was light.

It felt like he was trying to distract Dean instead of basically saying he didn't want to be his friend anymore. Because that's what 'call this off' meant, right? That they wouldn't hang out anymore?

"No, I hadn't heard that." Dean's voice sounded far away, like he'd left his body.

"I guess he'll be taking over the park and the business," Cody said. One of his hands went to fuss with the clip on his staff ID, fiddling with it. "So the management team are going the extra mile, tightening up security. I'm going to be heading up a team."

"That's a great opportunity," Dean almost wasn't thinking about what he was saying. It was good news – it was practically a promotion – so why did he feel so deflated?

*I'm really gonna miss hanging out with him.*

"Mm-hmm." Cody frowned. "Are you okay, Dean?"

*Oh, have I been spacing out? I thought I was still being supportive.*

"Yeah, I just... I mean, you could still come see me, uhh, I mean, you could still come and we could work stuff through in your lunch break or after shifts, right?"

Cody shook his head. "Sorry, bud. I'm going to be too busy," he said. "Lennon mentioned weekend work and overtime and I guess... I just don't know when my shifts will end. I don't want to mess you around, or anything. So, I think it's best we just call it off."

Dean's stomach twisted. He remembered when he was in high school and he'd make a cool new friend. Then he'd just be too *Dean* at them and they'd start hanging out with other people. Not answering his messages. Too busy to catch up. He'd done it again. He'd gone too hard and pushed Cody and now he wanted space.

But Dean had grown up some, he could pull back a little. He could be the kind of friend Cody would like. He just had to try and do it in a smart way.

"But we can still be friends, right? Jessica really wanted to get to know you better, and I, like, wanted to introduce you to my family and stuff." Dean thought about how excited he'd been to tell his ma about Cody, they'd get on so well.

"Sure," Cody said. He cleared his throat. "I just won't have too much time. I don't want to set something up with you and have to cancel it at the last moment."

"Oh, okay. That makes sense I guess." Dean picked up his shake and took a sip. His emotions were all over the place. He felt sad and angry and bereft and basically like the rug had been pulled out from under him. Wait. Angry? Why was he angry? He frowned as he kicked at the table leg.

He was angry that he wouldn't see his friend. Angry that he wouldn't get to spend time with Cody. Angry that Cody was going to be so busy, sure, but there was something more. Was he angry that Cody was using extra work as an excuse? Was that it?

"This isn't just an excuse, is it?" Dean's heart thumped. He wasn't usually confrontational like this. In fact, he usually just smiled and let things happen and then resented everything about it later on.

"An excuse?" Cody's eyebrows raised and he sat back in his chair. He shook his head slightly and his hair fell over his forehead a little. He rubbed his nose with one hand and sniffed. "No, this stuff is really happening."

Dean frowned and folded his arms. "Yeah, sure. But maybe you just don't want to try going on the coaster anymore. Maybe you're just... just taking the easy way out."

Cody looked away to the side. "I-it's not like that," he said, clearing his throat. "I should get going."

He stood up.

Dean stood up too. "Wait, I didn't mean to–"

Cody cut him off. "Don't worry about it. This has been fun."

"I, yeah. Yeah, of course," Dean said, deflated. He sat back down as Cody left.

His heart pulled in his chest. Had he just lost his new friend? It really felt like it. And he hated that feeling. He texted Jessica a sad face emoji as melancholy started to rise.

He finished off his shake alone, hardly tasting it.

*Beeping. What was beeping? Cody scrambled to find the switch that would make the beeping stop.*

*The controls were all flashing lights at him. That couldn't be good. He checked the fuel gauge – low, but not dangerously so. He checked his altitude meter – it seemed fine.*

*Wait… No. No, it wasn't.*

*The needle swung wildly around and then swooped downwards.*

*It was plunging – the plane was plunging. He was going down. His stomach fell and tightened all at once. He gasped for air.*

*Where was his mask? He felt around for it. Why wasn't he already wearing it?*

*The beeping got worse, sounding more like alarms or sirens. It was shrill. Demanding. Demanding he do something immediately to stop disaster.*

*But he couldn't draw breath. He tried to radio an SOS, but he couldn't speak beyond a gasp.*

*He saw flashes of white lights and realized his eyesight was spotty. A bad sign – he was running out of time.*

*There was an explosion nearby, close enough to deafen and hot enough to scorch his skin.*

*There was nothing he could do.*

*He was out of time.*

• • •

Cody woke up grabbing at his own throat, trying to find an oxygen mask that wasn't there.

He was tangled in his sheets, sweating hard. The old Air Force training academy T-shirt he wore as a pajama top was riding up to his chest, constricting him.

He pulled the shirt off and tossed it across the room before he worked at freeing his legs. Well, his leg and his stump.

His heart was still racing as if he'd really been in the crash again. As if he was in danger, instead of just fucking sleeping.

He pulled the sheet aside and stretched his entire leg out, then the stump. His hand moved to rub at the tender end of it, where it had been amputated just below the knee. It wasn't sore at all, but he always felt extra aware of it after a dream like that.

He looked over at the digital clock on the wall. Five AM. There was no way he was going to try and sleep after that – he knew from experience he'd just fall straight back into the same dream. That was, assuming he could even get back to sleep at all.

He reached for his preferred prosthetic leg and fastened it around his knee and thigh, then got up to use the bathroom.

His apartment was easy to navigate, even in the pre-dawn darkness, in part because it was so small. He'd never seen the point of a big house, or lots of possessions. Maybe it was a habit from the military or maybe he was just minimalist by nature.

He lived in a bedsit apartment, one big room for living, bedroom and kitchen, and a bathroom to the side. The bathroom wasn't too small, though – he needed room to move around with or without wearing the prosthetic leg.

Once he'd pissed and brushed his teeth and glared at himself in the mirror for being weak, he folded his bed back into the wall and got dressed.

Saturday.

He didn't have work, so he pulled on a black T-shirt and his motorcycle leathers. If he could do anything that would blow away the dream, it'd be riding. Down the Pacific Coast Highway and stop at one of the beaches. See the sun come up over the wild, restless sea.

An hour later he was sipping a protein shake overlooking the beach near Venice. Venice Beach was a bizarre and fascinating place – it reeked of broken dreams and lost hope, but it was shiny and full of tour buses during the day time. All those people who'd turned to selling tourist junk advertising Los Angeles or Hollywood. Venice felt like where Hollywood idols came to die in a drug-infused stupor. He should probably move there, he thought, rather than spending his time in a literal fantasy world.

Or maybe he should've kept on riding up to Santa Monica. At least there he could watch all the gym heads working out on the beach, watching to see who was watching them. Which was always amusing.

What was he doing here?

What was he doing with his life?

Since coming back from serving he'd been surviving. The job was good, and he felt like he had friends at the park, but it wasn't like he spent any time with them outside of work. Fairyland was a joy to be in, but as soon as he drove away the magic faded and he was left with himself.

Maybe he should do what Dean did and take bits of it home. A souvenir straw and a plushie Treasure to brighten up his place.

And through it all this lingering stress. This trauma that he couldn't let go. It wasn't even as if he'd had it that bad in his tours. Sure, he'd lost half a leg but at least he was still alive.

He had a lot to be grateful for, considering how different things could have turned out.

He dug his hands into the sand beneath him. Well, that could be a reason he felt shitty all the time, couldn't it? What was it called, again? Survivor's guilt. The guilt of having lost friends and still being here himself.

He was broken out of his reverie to watch as two young people jogged along the beach - a guy and a girl. They were in their nice designer workout gear, but they didn't have headphones or earbuds in that he could make out.

Jogging together? Not listening to music?

Cody made a bet with himself that they were a new couple. He watched them jog slowly past the palm trees, turning their heads towards them.

Then the guy tripped on the sand somehow and stopped running, bracing his hands on his knees. The girl stopped too, throwing back her head in obvious laughter, her hand clutched over her stomach.

*Oh yes, definitely early stages of dating,* Cody thought.

He watched as the girl ruffled the guy's hair and he pulled her in for a kiss. She kissed him back a while and then pushed him away, taking off down the sand with extra speed - making him chase her. Cody smiled and watched them until they were out of sight behind the skate park. The beach was always good for people watching.

He looked around for someone else to watch but it was still too early for it to be busy. His thoughts turned to Dean, and the horrible conversation they'd had the day before.

Dean had looked so sad.

*I lost friends in the war. I more or less lost my family. Maybe I shouldn't push away my new friend, either.*

*Maybe... maybe there was something with the rollercoaster that I needed to do.*

*Maybe I've been a fucking dumbass.*

"Fuck." He turned and tossed the empty smoothie cup into the nearest garbage container. He pulled out his phone and looked at it. Dean hadn't texted him since he'd walked out of the diner the day before, and that felt shitty.

It was early still. Six-thirty, but he opened up his messenger app and texted Dean.

Hey, I fucked up. I still want to do this thing. Want to get breakfast or something?

His phone beeped after thirty seconds – Dean had replied already. Why was he even up?

Sure thing. Gimme twenty minutes and I'll meet you... where?

Cody smiled and messaged back the address of a nice-enough diner out Fairfax way. Why did they always meet up with food and drink? He shrugged. Dean was always eating. It made sense.

After a moment Dean replied.

It'll take me a while to get out there, gotta take the bus and it's a few connections

What's your address? I can come get you

Dean replied with three thumbs up emojis and his address.

Cody sighed, feeling a familiar churning in his stomach.

Now he just had to work out how to explain how he was feeling to Dean.

## 13 / DEAN

DEAN DIDN'T USUALLY GET UP EARLY ON THE WEEKEND. BUT HE WAS a light sleeper and his phone's notification beep had woken him. He never put it on silent, he didn't want to miss anything.

Hearing from Cody was worth waking up for, and he agreed immediately to meeting up with him.

Feeling excited, he bounced out of bed, used the bathroom and tried to do something with his hair. He had some hair wax which, when the stylist had used it on him at the salon had made his hair perfectly wavy and cool.

Dean sighed – he could never replicate it himself though. He tried, but it always just ended up doing the same thing it always did, making a vague cowlick to the left. He frowned at his appearance in the mirror and washed his face, then went to pull on some clothes. He texted Jessica a picture of his favorite Hawaiian shirt.

Is this okay?

Jessica didn't reply, which he wasn't surprised by, as it was before eight on a Saturday morning, but just sending the picture off made him rethink his decision. He didn't want to wear a Hawaiian shirt when he first met Cody outside of work. Instead, he chose a purple and black striped polo shirt with a Spaceship Mayhem logo on the left breast. It had been a limited-release shirt for the launching of the ride. Dean had been so excited when he'd picked it up on his first day on the job.

Gnawing at his lower lip, he rethought again. Maybe it was a bit on the nose though? He took a picture of himself wearing it and sent it through to Jessica.

Or how about this one? It might be too much Spaceshippy, don't you think?

No reply.

He tugged on pants and shoes and headed outside to wait for Cody.

It was as chilly as Los Angeles got, which was to say, it wasn't hot yet. Just pleasantly warm. The sky was clear, and Dean felt at peace with the world. His phone vibrated. Finally, Jess had replied.

*Wtf are you doing up this early in the morning? And why are you wearing your fancy shirt, have you got a date?*

He quickly typed back:

Dean: Nah, just meeting Cody for breakfast

Jess: Yeah that totally doesn't sound like a date

Dean: Don't be an ass, he's not even gay

I don't think

Do you think he's gay?

Jess sent a shrug emoji.

Dean laughed at the idea. Cody didn't strike him as gay at all! Jess must've been asleep and still dreaming to think that a handsome, tough, funny and generally sexy guy like Cody would take any interest in Dean. It was ridiculous, anyone could see that!

Dean heard the roar of a motorbike getting closer, which generally wasn't a cause for attention, but he felt his stomach flip as it got closer. When it pulled up right outside his house – practically at his feet as he stood on the front step, waiting – he felt his mouth drop open.

The dude on the gnarly bike, which frankly, looked like something out of an anime from the eighties, pulled his helmet off. Of course it was Cody. Cody had come to pick him up *on a motorbike*.

Dean hurried over, his heart in his throat. "You have a motorbike?" he said, instead of hello. Right, yeah – he should probably say hello. "Um, I mean, hi."

"Morning. My bad. Should I have warned you about the bike?" Cody asked. He reached behind him and produced a second helmet – apparently out of nowhere.

"I mean, yeah," Dean said, immediately kicking himself after the words had escaped his lips. Urgh, that just made him sound like a square or a dweeb or some other kind of weirdly outdated slang, didn't it? He cleared his throat. "No, no. It's cool, I can ride a motorbike."

"You ride?" Cody tossed him the helmet, it was gunmetal grey. Cody's was black with a painting of a white bird on it. Maybe a crane? Like a Japanese crane? Dean had so many questions.

"Me? No, I mean, I ride the bus. I've never been on a bike before. I mean, I've been on like, a pedal bike. I've cycled on the Santa Monica beach trail same as everyone, but–"

Cody laughed. "You're nervous. I should've warned you, I'm sorry."

"It's fine," Dean bit his lip and tried to work out which way round the helmet went. If he paid enough attention to the helmet, maybe he wouldn't start babbling again.

*Why am I so nervous all of a sudden? It's just Cody. And a motorbike. And Cody looking gorgeously rugged and sexy on a motorbike.*

Maybe it was that crap Jess had said about Cody being potentially gay. Yeah, that damned shrug emoji was throwing him off. He shook his head to shed her dreamstate weirdness and shoved the helmet onto his head. Cody reached over to help him with the straps.

Dean was very aware of Cody's knuckles brushing his throat as he fixed the straps. Almost like Dean was a cat Cody was chucking under the chin.

*Where is my mind today?*

"Okay, so you've never ridden before. All you need to know is to hold onto me tight. Or the bars, there's bars you can hold onto if you don't want to hold onto me."

"I can hold onto you," Dean said. He wasn't sure why he felt such a need to prove himself to Cody. Maybe the bike was intimidating him a little.

It wasn't like he could exactly see Cody in a tidy little city car. The bike made so much sense, really, but he also hadn't mentally prepared himself to risk his life on the road before eight in the morning.

"Cool," Cody said. He turned away and pulled his own helmet back on, climbed back onto the bike and started revving it.

Dean climbed onto the cushiony back part of the seat, which was more difficult than he'd thought, as the bike was wider than he'd expected. He wrapped his arms around Cody's hard torso – he could practically feel his abs, even under the motorcycle leathers. All of a sudden Dean felt overwhelmingly underdressed in his silly Space Mayhem polo shirt.

"Lean when I lean," Cody said, shouting over the roar of the engine.

"What does that mean?" Dean shouted back, unable to hide the nervous tremor in his voice.

"And squeeze with your thighs," Cody added.

*That's not an answer at all.*

Dean adjusted his grip so his arms were around Cody's waist and his fingers were interlacing on his abdomen. His chest was pressed tight to Cody's leather clad back.

Then the bike roared even louder and they started moving. Cody leaned forward and Dean leaned forward, too, because he wasn't going to hold onto him any looser – not when the asphalt was blurring under them like that.

When Cody took the first corner Dean realized what he had meant about leaning into it, and actually there wasn't too much Dean had to do because he was squeezing the bike so hard with his thighs out of pure self-preservation, and he was wrapped so tightly around Cody that he leaned with him anyway. Leaning down towards the road took Dean's breath away, and he was sure his life was about to flash before his eyes.

It was terrifying.

But after a few blocks, it was also sort of brilliant. He even managed an enthusiastic whoop at one point – although he didn't dare remove his hands from Cody's waist.

It was… fun. Like a far more intense ride than Spaceship Mayhem, because this was actually real. And holding onto Cody like this, well, that was nice, too. He trusted Cody, he knew Cody would protect him. Cody was his friend. And hey, when he felt the hardness of his muscles and the strength in his back as he made turns, well. That was really, really nice. It made Dean feel all squiggly inside, in the best possible way.

They were at the diner before he knew it. The whole ride was a kind of adrenaline-fueled fear blur. Cody cut the engine and waited, and Dean realized he had to get off the bike first.

He eased his arms back from around Cody and swung his jellified leg around. It was kind of like getting off a horse. Like, a tiny, ridiculously fast horse.

His legs were a bit wobbly, but he covered it up by making a big show of removing his helmet and shaking out his hair.

Cody was beside him in a flash.

"You okay?"

"Yeah! I'm super fantastically awesome!" Dean beamed at Cody. "That was fun! And also scary! How come you can do that, but you can't ride a rollercoaster? Rollercoasters are so much safer."

Cody tilted his head a little and licked his lips. He looked over Dean's shoulder, considering. Dean resisted the urge to glance over his shoulder to see what his gaze had fixated on.

"I'm in control of my bike. I know how to handle it. I guess with a coaster, I'm giving up that control to… to the ride. I dunno. I guess it doesn't make a whole lot of sense."

Dean shrugged. "Nah, that makes sense."

"Come on, let's get some breakfast. My shout." Cody slapped

Dean heartily on the back and Dean stumbled forward a little and tried to cover it with a skip. Because a skip was so much more dignified? An inward groan at his own awkwardness echoed around his head.

*Get it together Dean.*

## 14 / CODY

SOMETHING HAD HAPPENED. IT WAS THE BIKE RIDE MAYBE, OR THE adorable way Dean had pretended not to be totally terrified. Or maybe it was the warmth of Dean's body against his back, the feel of his arms around him, holding on fiercely.

*It'd felt so good.*

Cody hadn't been held like that by anyone for a long time. He didn't give people rides on his motorbike. And he hadn't been with anyone since he'd served. And even then... that hadn't gone well at all.

But he didn't want to think about John.

Actually, he didn't want to think too much about what he was feeling for Dean, either. Instead, he had patted him on the back and headed into the diner. They sat at a window booth and Cody focused intently on the menu.

"Can I take your order?" The waitress appeared beside their booth, notepad in hand and gave them both a bright smile.

"Yes, please! Thanks so much, Carol," Dean said. Cody looked up, wondering if Dean knew her. He was beaming at her, his eyes practically sparkling, and she sparkled right back. "I'll have the short stack, Canadian maple syrup and an order of blueberries, please."

"Sure thing, Sugar, and to drink?"

"Oh, a drink – have you got pink lemonade?"

"Sure do."

"Pink lemonade would be perfect, thanks, Carol."

Carol turned to Cody and her smile flickered just a bit. He tried to smile the way Dean head but it felt kind of strange and... well, maybe he'd imagined it, but it seemed like there was a little fear in her eyes. He cleared his throat and gave up on the smile.

"Coffee. Bacon and eggs, with sausage, hash browns, biscuits and gravy, please," he said.

"Mm-hmm, and how d'you like your eggs?"

"Over easy," Cody said. "Thanks."

Carol nodded, repeated back their order and then she and Dean flirted some more. Cody watched, a pang of regret or something shooting through him.

When Carol left, Dean tilted his head. "What? You're looking at me all weird."

"How... how do you do that?"

"Do what?"

"Charm everyone you meet," Cody said. He gestured towards the counter where Carolwas filling their order and shook his head. "You just... You just smile and everyone loves you. How do you do it?"

Dean's cheeks turned pink and his eyes widened. He didn't answer right away but stuttered – and goddamnit it – that was all adorable as well.

"Not *everyone* loves me."

"You could've fooled me." Cody wondered if maybe he'd played his hand too much and freaked Dean out by implying that he loved Dean – because he'd count as everyone too, right? And spontaneous bike ride feeling aside, he was fairly sure he didn't love Dean. And besides – Dean was with Jessica, presumably.

Dean's phone beeped and he picked it up from where he'd laid it beside his knife. He smiled as he read whatever message had come through, his attention entirely focused on what he was doing, before his thumbs moved in a blur. After a moment, he set his phone back down.

"Sorry, that was really rude," he said to Cody. "What were you saying?"

"Nothing." Cody felt a wave of relief that Dean hadn't thought he was professing love, and busied himself with his cutlery so Dean couldn't read anything in his eyes. "Who was the text from?"

"Just Jessica," Dean's eyes lit up again. "I told her you had a motorbike and she freaked out. She said that it was too dangerous. But I told her I'm still alive."

Cody chuckled, glad that Dean had someone who would worry about him like that. "Well you can tell her not to worry, I'm a very experienced driver," he said. "And I've never had an accident, either."

"Okay." Dean brightly picked up his phone again to text Jessica, looking up to smile and thank Carol as their drinks arrived.

Cody watched him. Trying not to think about his sudden warm feelings for Dean was really hard when he was right there, being all cute and focused. A bit of his hair had fallen forward onto his forehead and Cody's hand twitched to fix it for him. Madness.

*Get it together, Cody. You're not sixteen and this isn't a school dance.*

Cody laced his fingers together on the table and breathed out slowly. There was no need to lose his head. So, he had a crush on his friend – probably it was just his body getting excited about touching someone other than in a 'removing people from the park' kind of way. It wasn't like he had a lot of close contact with people, so it would make sense for his body to overreact in this way,

Just ignore it, he told himself. Ignore it and think of him as a friend, which is after all, what he is.

"So, what brought about the change of heart?" Dean asked, after putting down his phone again.

Cody spluttered and choked on his own saliva. Had Dean realized what was going on with him? Had he been staring at Dean and giving away all his weird sudden feelings? He picked up his coffee and took a sip to give himself some time to recover. "Hmm?"

"Are you okay?"

"Yeah, just, uhh, inhaled wrong," Cody said. "What did you ask?"

"About Spaceship Mayhem," Dean raised an eyebrow. "What happened overnight that changed your mind?"

"Oh, just nightmares," Cody said. "Made me rethink some stuff."

Dean's forehead crinkled as he frowned. Damn, he was cute – even when he wasn't meaning to be. No... it was just because he looked sad. Sad for Cody. Which made Cody feel kind of strange. Because it was the first time he'd mentioned the nightmares to someone who actually, genuinely seemed to care.

"Oh no, I'm so sorry," Dean replied, reaching out across the table for Cody's hand.

"Not your fault," Cody said. "It happens every now and then. I just..." he hesitated, trying to work out how much to share, and how much to hold back. He didn't want to reveal everything and see Dean's even sadder face or freak him out too bad. "I just realized I still have some issues to work through, and maybe the coaster is a part of that. It definitely taps into some memories and I–I should confront those, or work through them somehow."

"Maybe you should also consider going to see a therapist?" Dean looked a little afraid. He bit his lip, waiting to see if Cody would snap at him, presumably.

"I had one for a while. She suggested meditation and crystals and, yeah. It didn't really work out," Cody said. Thinking about how confused he'd been, when this woman had suggested crystals would help with his PTSD, he shook his head again. "She didn't get how I was feeling about losing part of my leg and getting a prosthetic either."

"Oh. I mean, there are other therapists, though. I'm sure you could find one who would suit you," Dean's voice rose at the end of the sentence as if it were a question.

"Maybe." Cody shrugged. He was saved from the rest of that

particular conversation by the food arriving. His shoulders relaxed and he licked his lips, it all smelled incredible.

Carol and Dean did their little 'Sugar' back and forth thing again as she asked him if there was anything else he needed. Cody noticed her nudge a little bowl of applesauce next to Dean's pancakes, which he was pretty sure didn't come standard.

Cody's plate didn't have any extra things, but the food here was always amazing so it didn't matter, and he definitely wasn't jealous.

"Have you been here before?" Cody asked, grateful to be able to change the subject.

Dean shook his head. "No, I'm hardly ever out this way. I usually hang out, like, Westwood by home, or go down to Santa Monica." Dean started to spread the pancakes with the applesauce and then topped it off with the maple syrup. Then, he sprinkled the berries over the top before he finally started to eat.

"No wonder she called you Sugar," Cody said. "How much do you ingest in a day?" Cody started in on his eggs. They were perfectly cooked, proper free-range eggs with orangey yolks, delicious.

"No idea," Dean shrugged. "But it tastes great."

Cody let the egg yolk run over his tongue before swallowing.

"So, you didn't go to college?" Cody asked. He felt bad for not asking earlier. Dean did seem to work full time but maybe he had time for a study break here and there.

"Naw, although my mom would like it if I did," Dean replied. He looked down at his pancakes and frowned a little before he started eating again and perked back up.

*Touched on something tender there,* Cody thought.

*Best to go gently around that in future.*

HE'D ONLY RIDDEN ON CODY'S MOTORBIKE TWICE. AND EVEN THEN, it had only been for about ten minutes, maybe fifteen, each time. But Dean was addicted. The rest of Saturday, Dean felt buzzed about it.

He started on his laundry and while he waited for the clothes to wash, he thought about the rumble of the engine between his legs, of leaning against Cody's back and the smell of the leather.

He tried to distract himself by thinking about other things, but that was a sharp spiral down a 'what am I doing with my life?' hill, and that was no fun. So, he kept on thinking about the motorbike instead.

*The excitement of the ride, the pleasant feeling of the bike vibrating between my legs. Pressing myself against Cody and feeling his abs under my fingers...*

Once he was done with his laundry, Jessica came over to hang out. She always came to his place because her own was a tiny hellhole in the South of Los Angeles. They settled on the couch to watch some movies together. They both liked old style science fiction stuff, and this time Jessica had dug up the old *The War of the Worlds* movie.

"What was it like? Riding the hog?" Jessica asked. She sprinkled a generous amount of extra salt over the microwave popcorn and scoffed a handful.

Dean laughed and tossed some popcorn at her. "I don't think it was a *hog*, it was all cool, shiny and fancy. Maybe Japanese," Dean threw a couple pieces of popcorn in his mouth, too, and munched away happily.

"Cool. So what was it like?

"Amazing! Like, it was scary at first. Actually, it was scary the whole time – but it was so much fun as well."

"Uh-huh, and how's Cody? You two tight again?"

Dean picked up his phone and grinned, bouncing in the couch cushions. There was a picture from Cody. It showed the entrance to a gym.

"Hold up, he's messaging me, pause the film?"

She nodded and hit the button, and went into the kitchen for sodas. "Tell him you can't stop thinking about his machine between your legs."

"You're gross," he said. And tapped out a message to Cody.

Dean: You're supposed to show me pictures of you working out

Dean: It's like you haven't Instagrammed at all

Cody: Because I haven't.

Cody: Why would you want to see me all sweaty and gross?

Dean didn't know how to respond. "*Because it's hot*" sounded too forward. He bit his lip and replied with the safer option.

Dean: because that's what fitspo people do

Cody: now you're just making up words.

Jessica leaned over his shoulder to read what Cody was saying and smirked. "Oh yeah, you're tight again."

"Yeah, I guess we are." Dean leaned against her a little. "Hey, um. I know this is, like, out of the blue… but do you think I'm wasting my potential?"

"Err, what?" Jessica pulled back so that she could look him in the eyes and he fell against the back of the couch. "What's Cody been saying to you? If he's making you feel crappy, then I'll pound his face in."

"I don't think you could do that," Dean said. "You're too short to reach his face. Besides, he's literally a security guard, he tosses people out of the park for a living."

"Still, if he hurts you." She narrowed her eyes and flexed her arms. She spent a moment examining her bicep – or lack of one – when she flexed. "Okay, okay. Whatever, I'll still take him down. I'm Irish, we have a history of being scrappy. Plus, like, leprechaun luck."

Dean smiled at the thought of Jessica challenging Cody to protect his honor. "He didn't say anything," he said. "Stand down, don't attack anyone, please! Keep your leprechauns to yourself!"

Jessica smirked and punched him in the arm.

"Ow!" Dean did his best to look injured. "No, I mean, I was just kind of thinking. Mom bought this place so me and my siblings could use it while we study. Only I never studied, I went into the Fairyland internship and then just never left."

"So? You love it there," Jessica said. "What's college got that Fairyland doesn't?"

"I do love it there," Dean said. He raised a hand to his mouth to chew on a nail, but they were already chewed down. "But I guess... I guess I got some perspective. Cody's been through so much. He served in the Air Force – he has nightmares about it, he's had experiences. And what have I done? I've run a rollercoaster. And before that I was a greeter at the gates, briefly. Like, it's not going to change the world, is it?"

Jessica slouched back against the couch as he spoke, leaning her shoulder against his and sighing. "I know what you mean," she said. "But we do some good stuff, too. Look at all those people whose day is brighter – every single day – just because you're around to make them smile."

"Yeah, I guess that's true," Dean said, meaning it. He loved to make things easier for people. "But I think maybe I could be doing more. I'm good with people, maybe I should be... I dunno. A teacher?"

Jessica tilted her head to one side. "Yeah, I could see you with a class of kindergartners. They'd love you so much."

"Yeah, I think so. And impressing young minds feels like it would be worthwhile. But I dunno, maybe something like helping Cody out, too. Like a social worker?"

It's an idea that had crossed Dean's mind before but he'd shuttered it away as too ambitious - beyond someone like him. Too much to try for.

Jessica turned a little to look at him. "Holy shit, you'd be an amazing social worker."

"...You think?" Dean gnawed on his lower lip and pressed back against the couch, somewhat intimidated by the intensity of her expression.

"Hell yeah! people love you because you put them at ease. You'd make a real difference. I mean, it's hard work, though," she trailed off, frowning. "They say it really wears you down."

"I guess it would, but I'd also be helping people so it should also build me up, right?" Dean said. The idea was making his breath come faster. If Jess believed he could do it, maybe he could? "Like, *literally* helping people."

"Sure, you'd be great at it. You can handle the studying and stuff, and being a little older than the other freshmen might be an advantage." She leaned forward.

Dean frowned and rubbed his eyes. He didn't like the thought of sticking out in class as older. "Wait... now it's like you're trying to talk me out of it. Why?"

"I'm not!" Jessica shook her head and leaned in to look Dean right in the eyes. It was intense, and kinda scary. Dean felt like his whole world was spinning faster than he could keep up. His pulse quickened and he took a deep breath to stave off the anxiety. "I'm just not sugar coating it. I want you to succeed, but it won't be all popcorn and fairy tales if you go to college. It'll be late nights and lots of reading and tests and assignments and going to classes when you're hungover and didn't sleep enough." She shrugged.

"I *like* popcorn and fairy tales," Dean said. He chewed on his lower lip again. The stuff Jessica had said kind of freaked him out – he'd hated tests and reading and assignments in high school. He was a visual learner, and he did well in group situations when he had a chance to talk things through. Just sitting on his own and reading and making notes was so boring. "I dunno, I guess I'll think it over."

"Urgh, I totally freaked you out, didn't I?" Jessica sat back and picked up a packet of jellybeans, handing it to him. "I didn't mean to actually make it sound scary."

"Well, you did." Dean sniffed. "Scary and hard." He took the jellybeans and tore open the packet, helping himself to a handful of them.

"I was hoping if I mentioned how challenging it would be, you'd get all heroic and be like 'I can do it! I'll do all of it and come out successful and be the best social worker in the world!'"

"Oh." Dean licked his lips. "Sorry."

Jessica leaned against his shoulder and chuckled, but it was a bit of a sad chuckle, Dean thought. "You don't have to apologize to me. Sorry I freaked you out. I do think you can totally do this."

"Don't worry about it, I'm fine." Though if he was being honest, Dean kinda felt like the air had just been let out of his balloon.

"You should totally do some research on PTSD online," Jessica said after a moment. "If you're gonna help Cody without like, scarring him worse or something."

"Wooow, you are *so* not comforting today, Jess." Dean scrunched his nose up and stuck his tongue out at her.

"Sorry! I just know you don't always, like, think everything through. And we are talking about a war veteran's psyche."

"Right, makes sense." Dean sighed. "And it's nice to know that you care about Cody's psyche."

Dean leaned against Jessica's shoulder and he gave her a tight smile. He would think college over, and maybe he'd research some stuff online, but he still felt fear penetrating his gut. The idea of leaving Fairyland was way too much – he loved it there, why would he ever leave?

And to leave just to lose himself in books and study and fall out of touch with all his friends? It sounded hard, and lonely and horrible.

He screwed his mouth to the side. Best just to leave things as they were. He could help people at the park, by running the roller coaster. Things didn't have to change just for him to do something meaningful. He had Cody, after all.

Because freak outs and bails aside, Cody still wanted to be his friend.

And a friendship with Cody was something he really didn't want to miss out on.

AFTER CODY'S SHIFT ON WEDNESDAY, DEAN ASKED TO MEET HIM.

They stood outside, looking up from the back of Spaceship Mayhem. Out here there was a good view of where the ride shot out of the building and zoomed up into the sky. Every few minutes the cars full of coaster-goers would rocket out of the building, do a loop, and everyone would scream their heads off.

"I'm not sure this is helping," Cody swallowed the lump in his throat. He couldn't help wincing a little every time the screams started again. There was no warning for when they'd next tear out of there and scream. His heart was racing.

"I read about this thing online called exposure therapy," Dean said. He was standing beside Cody and looking up at the loop as well. "Like, if you're scared of spiders then you sit there and people bring you small spiders, and like, you sort of get used to them, and then they can bring you bigger spiders. And then you get used to those and then you're like, holding tarantulas and it's all fine."

"Please don't bring me any tarantulas," Cody said, quickly. He couldn't in good faith put it past Dean to have taken this whole 'exposure therapy' thing literally.

"I won't! I wasn't going to do that, I was just going to show you this. If this works, I can take you to the other outside loop. We can access it from the maintenance scaffolding."

Cody looked at Dean skeptically. "Maintenance scaffolding sounds unsafe."

"Nah, it's fine, weren't you ever involved in school productions as theatre crew? It's just like running around in the flies."

"The flies?"

"You know, the rafters and crossbeams above the stage and the audience? Where lights and pulleys and things are all secured."

"Err... no," Cody said slowly. "I wasn't in the productions in high school."

He hadn't expected Dean to be running around the rafters above the audience in high school, it was kind of impressive. Fearless. He nodded and said "Hmm."

He looked back up at the loop as another set of screamers tore through the air. Cody winced.

*Why is this so different to the screams on the swinging pirate ship? Oh yeah, because those are screams of excitement and happiness. These are screams of 'I'm about to die'.*

"I bet you were too cool," Dean said. "You were like, in the football team or lacrosse or something." He laughed a little, but it sounded self-conscious. Cody glanced at him and then shook his head.

"I was a bit of a loner in high school–" He'd been going to continue but Dean cut in.

"Oh man, did you have a motorbike in high school? I bet you had so many girlfriends and skipped class to go smoking and stuff."

Cody laughed and shook his head. Where did Dean get this stuff? Dean's ideas about him were so far removed from reality they may as well have been a fairy tale. He decided to play along – who was he to destroy Dean's dreams? "Yes, exactly. I was the bad boy from a teen romance movie. I had the beat-up leather jacket and the long hair and everything."

"I knew it!"

Dean really didn't seem to have understood that he was just teasing him, he just grinned. Cody cleared his throat to set him straight. "I was on the track team, because I could run alone. That, and taekwondo."

"Oh, that's super cool." Dean chuckled. "But the teen romance movie thing would have been epic. You'd look so badass with long hair."

"Well, I did have the long hair." Cody admitted, taking a breath in through his nose as another coaster car of people screamed overhead. "Dean? I dunno if this is working."

"Only one way to know for sure. Let's see if you can get on the ride now that you've experienced this bit." Dean took Cody's hand and tugged him back towards the entrance to the building. Cody didn't resist exactly, but he wasn't used to holding hands and he didn't grip back or anything. Should he grip back? Was that what he was supposed to do?

Cody's stomach fell a little as Dean let go and led the way inside before he could figure out what to do.

The staff access tunnels weren't themed, they were weathered wooden boards with bits of primer on them here and there. The tunnels were kept pretty clean, though. Cody swallowed. Wait, why was he noticing what the tunnels looked like? Was it so he wouldn't think about how right Dean's hand had felt in his, or was because he didn't think about what he was about to attempt?

But not thinking about what was coming next didn't mean it wasn't going to happen, and as they got to the top of the line through a side access panel, there were the bleep-bloop noises and the line of people waiting and the cars and the coaster cars with their all-too-realistic control panels.

"Dean," Cody said. He heard himself like he was miles away, he could hear the urgency in his own voice.

"Come on, it's exposure." Dean reached back for Cody's hand again and led him to the front of the line. Jessica was running the ride that day. She waved them both forward.

"Go ahead, good luck. You got this, Codester!" She trilled.

"How much have you told her about me?" Cody frowned. His heart was racing and he snatched his hand back from Dean's again.

"Talk later, ride now," Dean said. He climbed into the front of the first car on the coaster and patted the seat beside him. "Come on in, the water's fine."

Cody swallowed and climbed in, kicking the plastic molded centerpiece between the seats with his prosthetic foot and half falling into the seat. He landed with a painful bump.

"That's the way, here." Dean reached up to pull the safety harness down over his head.

Cody's hand shot up to brace against the base of the safety harness. "Wait."

"It's okay, I'm right here with you," Dean said. He tugged on the harness again. "Don't overthink it, just go with it."

He pulled on the harness and Cody's stomach exploded with fear. He wrenched the harness back up with both hands.

His heart was beating so fast, and his breathing was so quick he thought he might black out.

"I-I can't do it," he hissed. Dean frowned, looking at him like he didn't understand. Which was ridiculous, surely Dean should've expected this. The whole basis of their friendship was that Cody couldn't ride his stupid, terrifying ride.

Cody went to get up and stumbled a little. His legs shook, his prosthetic felt large and cumbersome. The damned thing tripped him up and he swore.

"Cody, it's okay." Dean stood up. He felt his hand on his elbow, helping boost him back out of the ride. "It's not gonna hurt you, it's okay." But Cody couldn't help but notice the tinge of disappointment in Dean's voice – and he hated the thought of letting Dean down.

"It's not about that," Cody said. He could see all the people in the line staring at him. Couples and families and school kids, all these people looking at him like he was a freak. All these people who could ride the roller coaster without freaking out like a damned coward.

*They could see I couldn't do it, how I'm getting out again and stumbling because... For fuck's sake! My leg doesn't bother me for months at a time, but now it does?*

*All these people can see how damaged I am. And guess what comes after that?*

*Pity. Pity, the useless fucking emotion that makes me feel like a stupid child. Like someone who can't do simple things. People will shake their heads and say things about how brave I am. But if there's pity in their eyes... I can't stand it.*

Cody took a breath, found his feet and strode out of the place, right past the chicken door and down the long way, past all the people waiting in line. He glared at each and every one of them. Some averted their gazes and some took steps away from him... but not the people up the top.

Because the people up the top had seen him fail like some crybaby weakling. Cody's stomach somersaulted.

*Dean saw me fail. Again.*

*He saw me meltdown.*

He couldn't stand that. He had to get out – right out of the park and away from everyone in it.

Dean was mentally kicking himself. No, make that *thrashing* himself.

*How could I be so epically stupid? A little Googling and suddenly I'm an expert on therapy? And now Cody will absolutely definitely never talk to me again!*

And Dean wouldn't blame him if he never did.

He'd be sad, and he's miss him and he'd wish forever that things had been different, but he'd been a gigantic doofus and he'd hurt his friend and now he was left texting and messaging and calling and getting no response.

It'd been three hours since the incident and Dean hadn't eaten or gone home or even breathed, it felt like. He was just clenching his jaw and wandering the park, hoping that he'd turn a corner and see Cody sitting and sipping on a slushie, or in the staff areas of the park chain smoking or drinking from a hip flask.

He had no idea where to find Cody. He'd gone all around the park, and then headed into the Enchanted Forest area and looked around for the people he worked with. He'd found the staff access area where the princes and princesses got ready but the people there said they hadn't seen him since the end of his shift.

"Have you tried calling him?" The pretty guy who played Prince Valor asked.

"Yeah, I've tried calling him," Dean said, gnawing on his thumbnail. "It rings for a bit and goes to voicemail." He looked at the guy in desperation. "I'm so sorry, I've totally blanked on your name."

"It's Nate," he said. "Look, don't worry about him, Cody's a tough guy, he's probably just riding it off on his bike or something."

"His bike, yeah." Dean shook his head. "I dunno, he seemed really upset."

The guy who played Prince Justice – Dash – Dean could remember that one for some reason. Maybe because it was a weird name. Dash appeared over Nate's shoulder. "Who's upset?"

"Cody," Dean replied. "Do you have any idea where he might've gone?"

Dash frowned and shook his head. "I wouldn't worry, though, Cody's got it together, he'll be okay."

Dean felt tears starting to well in his eyes. "You guys don't know him at all!" He said. Well, *blurted*. He bit his lip. Dash and Nate both took steps back and he flushed. "S-sorry. It's just that he has a lot of stuff going on and he's trying to work through it and I totally pushed him too far and he ran away! He could be anywhere, I'm worried something could have happened!"

*And it'd be my fault if it did*, he added.

Nate cleared his throat and reached out, trying to calm Dean down with a hand on his shoulder. "Right, okay. I see what you're saying. Um, what can we do to help?"

Dash looked like he was trying to decide between getting angry or saying sorry. Dean focused on Nate. "I don't even know. Do you know where he hangs out after work?"

Nate shook his head and Dash did too. "But I drove Nate to work today so I have my car, we could drive around and try and find him, maybe?"

Dean sighed. "Look, just... Just let me know if you hear from him, all right? I'll give you my number."

He pulled out his phone and it vibrated in his hand. Cody's face flashed up on the screen – his awkward smile and the 'don't take my photo' expression was so freaking cute that it made Dean's heart ache, thinking he could be hurt or doing something stupid somewhere.

"He's calling me back." Dean answered it. "Cody, where are you?"

"C'n you come'n get me?" Cody's voice was slurred and messy. "I don't think I can ride. Can't ride the ride, can't ride my bike, I just…"

"No, it's fine, I'll come get you," Dean said, quickly. "Tell me where you are."

"Bar," Cody said. "Forgot the name."

"Turn on the location on your phone," Dean said. "I can track you with GPS. Just stay put, and maybe have some water." He paced a little, back and forth. Nate and Dash were watching him, looking spooked.

"Thhink I c'n work it out," Cody said. Dean could hear Cody take the phone away from his ear. "Damn buttins! Why don't phones have buttins anymore? Just… just do what I tell you."

"I'll come get you real soon, Cody. Stay put."

"Thhanks, Dean." Cody said. Then he hung up the call and Dean chewed his lip so hard it started to hurt.

"You can take Dash's car," Nate said. He turned to Dash. "Where're your keys, babe?"

"Aah, no, he can't take my car," Dash frowned. "How will we get home?"

Nate huffed out a breath. "Then we'll drive you to get him," he said.

"No, it's fine," Dean said. "I can borrow my friend's car, thanks, though."

Nate scowled and punched Dash in the arm. "Not everything is about you, you know."

Dash glowered and looked at his feet.

"Um, thanks, you two." Dean turned and raced away from them. He dialed Jessica. She answered within a single ring – he'd been keeping her updated on the search for Cody.

"What's up?"

"I know where he is, I need your car," Dean replied.

"Sure darlin', I'll get a lift back with Sal," Jessica said. "We're in the Galactic diner, swing past and you can take my keys."

Dean breathed out a sigh of relief. "Thanks, Jess, you're the actual best. See you soon."

He had been running towards the park gates, but now he veered towards Hidden Galaxy, dodging past slow groups of tourists and people stopping to take photos of the lights on the castle in twilight.

He was well out of breath when he crashed through the doors into the diner, but he didn't need to give any explanations. Jessica held up her keys as soon as she saw him. He kissed her on top of the head, gasped out a 'thank you', and then ran for the staff car park.

As he got to Jessica's car and clicked the unlock button, his phone buzzed. Cody had worked out the location sharing function and he had a destination.

"Perfect timing," he said to the car, and started it up. Dean didn't drive that often, but when he did it was usually Jessica's car. If they went out and she drank a few too many then he'd drive, or if he borrowed it to do a big food shop or something. He didn't feel too worried about being behind the wheel.

He made his way as carefully as he could while still being a few miles over the speed limit and pulled up outside a seedy-looking bar. There was an array of men standing outside in leather jackets and leather vests. They all looked at him as he got out of the car. Dean dialed Cody's number.

"'Lo?" Cody slurred.

"I'm here, where are you?" Dean said. He tried to keep the panic out of his voice but now that he was here his nervousness had tripled. What was he going to see when he found Cody?

"I'sside, Imma come out," Cody said. Dean sighed and headed inside, after double checking that Jessica's car was locked. He kept the phone plastered to his ear.

Inside the bar it was dark, the only lights were those old-fashioned saloon-style stained glass lampshades, and they were hung over pool tables. The bar was a huge wooden plank with a big crocodile head over the corner of it. The place was full of men who looked drunk, angry and ready to fight. They all seemed to be watching Dean with interest.

Dean straightened his back, and tried to pretend he wasn't wearing a cute shirt for a roller coaster in a fairy tale theme park. He tried to project the kind of badass 'don't mess with me' vibe that Cody seemed to have naturally.

He couldn't see Cody anywhere. He coughed into the phone. "Uhh, Cody? Can you be more specific about where in the bar you are?"

"Booth," Cody said.

Dean stopped next to a pool table and spun around slowly. He hadn't even noticed any booths. But now that he was looking for them, yes. The wall on the far side of the bar was lined with booths that were recessed into the wall. He hurried over towards the wall and then remembered where he was and tried to stifle the natural bounce in his step.

"I'm here. I'm gonna find you." Dean's eyes moved back and forth, desperately searching the gloomy booths for his friend.

"Marco," Cody said in a singsong voice, and then giggled.

*Man, he was really far gone.*

"P-polo," Dean replied.

"Maaaaarco!" Cody sung. Finally – Dean's shoulders relaxed. He'd heard that in real life as well as over the phone. His body flushed with relief as he made a beeline to Cody, who was sitting – well, more like slumping – in the corner of a booth.

"Hey there, buddy," Dean said. He reached for Cody with both hands and tugged him towards him. "Let's get you home."

Cody was heavy, or strong, or big, or something. When Dean tugged, he didn't budge. Cody swung his head up like it was made of lead.

"Hey, it's Dean!" His eyes grew wide. Then he laughed.

"Yes, it's me, you called me, remember? We were literally just talking on the phone, now walk towards me." Dean was really worried about Cody now. He hadn't realized just how much of a state he was in on the phone. Forgetting he'd called him? Raising his head like he was a bear coming out of hibernation? That and the number of empty glasses on the table in the booth all painted a concerning picture.

Once Cody was out of the booth, Dean draped Cody's arm around his shoulders and took some of his weight. He secured an arm around Cody's waist and led him out of the bar. It wasn't easy, as Cody was half asleep, and the other half of him was distracted by everything.

After several attempts to get to the bar and then the pool table – the latter of which involved Dean practically straining something in his shoulder to haul him back on track – they finally got to the car and Dean stuffed Cody into the passenger seat. He fastened Cody's safety belt for him because Cody didn't seem to be capable of anything requiring motor skills right now.

Dean had climbed in on the driver's side before he realized he had no idea where Cody lived.

"Cody, dude, where do you live?"

"Over there," Cody said, waving his arm in a broad sweep. Dean blinked at him for a second. He'd just gestured to pretty much half the city. Even if he could communicate his address, was Cody going to be alright by himself for the night? What would happen when he started to sober up? Dean was sure Cody had mentioned he lived alone before... he didn't think he was willing to leave Cody on his own right now.

"Forget it, you can crash on my spare bed." Dean pulled out and headed for home. Cody went quiet and when Dean looked over, he'd closed his eyes and leaned his head against the car window. His mouth hung open. He looked younger, somehow, less guarded for sure. Dean felt a warm, protective need rise up – the kind he felt when he thought about his little sister in trouble.

*I want to take care of him so badly.*

Well, now was his chance, it seemed.

After a few minutes Cody snorted a little and sat up, yawning. "Wait... where're we going?" His voice wasn't as slurred as before, but it was still different. It was messier somehow, a little deeper pitched, gravelly. It reminded Dean of the weird mornings when the fog rolled in off the sea and the usual haze of smog was augmented by mist.

"I'm taking you back to my place," Dean said. "I didn't think it was a good idea for you to be on your own."

"I'll be fine," Cody said.

"Okay but, I mean, you also couldn't tell me your address."

"I thought I did." Cody sounded surprised. He moved around, hands roving over the dashboard and into the cup holder. "Where's your drink?"

"My drink?" Dean raised an eyebrow and glanced at Cody before refocusing back on the road. "I wasn't drinking with you."

"No, not like that. You always have a park cup with something sweet in it. Melon soda, grape shake... bubble fizz tea, I dunno. So where are you hiding the sugary stuff?"

"I don't have one right now, and this is Jessica's car so you'll wanna stay out of the glove compartment."

Cody sat back with a sigh. "Oh, yeah. Jessica."

Dean didn't know what that meant, so he just let the silence stretch out and concentrated on driving for a couple of minutes. Then, in an overwhelming surge of guilt, he remembered that he was largely responsible for Cody's current state. He should say something about that, shouldn't he? He should apologize.

He swallowed.

"Hey, Cody?" He said, when they were stopped at some traffic lights. He looked over to see that Cody was already watching him, his eyes shiny in the reflected streetlights.

"Yeah, Dean?"

"I'm sorry for trying to push you. Earlier, on the ride. I was a dick about it."

Cody frowned so hard it scrunched up his entire face. "No man, you weren't. You were really good. You're trying so hard and it's so... it's so..." Cody trailed off, his eyebrows pulling together as he worked to finish the sentence. "No one's ever done that for me," he finished.

"Wait, you mean no one has ever tried to force you to confront your fears with coercion and physical force?" Dean asked blankly. He probably wouldn't be this blunt if he thought Cody would remember any of this in the morning. It was kind of freeing.

"No. No, no, no – I mean… no one's ever cared about me like this," Cody said. He put a hand on Dean's thigh and it landed so heavily and so unexpected, Dean jumped.

Cody's hand on his thigh felt heavy and warm. It was nicer than he'd expected, not that he'd been expecting Cody's hand to land on his thigh or anything. But it was weirdly comforting, even if Cody was only doing it because he was still inebriated.

"It's okay." Dean chewed on his lip. They were nearly home now, and he pulled Jessica's car into his little parking spot that usually sat empty. "You're my friend. Of course I care about you."

He thought about how terrified he'd been for Cody only moments before. How horrible he'd felt knowing that Cody was somewhere out there, in pain, all because he'd pushed him too hard.

The relief that Cody wasn't actively angry at him was palpable, he could practically taste it in his mouth.

"It's… it's really beautiful," Cody said. His voice broke a little and Dean swallowed, suddenly nervous. Was Cody about to cry? Shit, he really was drunk. Dean had definitely done the right thing by bringing him home to his place. Now he just had to get him settled for the night. Preferably with a bottle of water, and whatever aspirin he had in the house. After that? Cody could cry all he wanted. Because Dean would be there to reassure him that he wasn't alone.

"It's beautiful, yeah. Now you think you can get out of the car?"

"Mmm," Cody said. Dean got out and went around to help him, and together with a lot of leaning – and Dean catching Cody twice and bumping into three walls – they got up to Dean's apartment.

"This is the spare room," Dean said. Cody was leaning on him hard and his fingers were digging into his upper arm, not in an entirely unpleasant way. He swung Cody onto the bed and knelt down to undo his boots for him.

Cody cleared his throat huskily. "Something else you could do while you're down there."

Dean froze, his fingers partially in Cody's bootlaces. He held his breath.

*Wait, what did he just say?*

Dean felt his face immediately flush red and he looked up to see Cody leering down at him, his eyes unfocused and his smile wide and saucy.

*Like a rugged, sexy pirate*, Dean thought and then shook his head.

"Ha ha – very funny," he said, weakly. His heart started pounding and his breathing came back but much too fast.

Then he felt Cody's fingers tease at his temple gentler than he could've imagined Cody was capable of being just then, and his fingers were threading through his hair and rubbing his scalp in a very nice way. His fingers almost gripped at him, tugging gently at Dean's hair with each touch. A hot feeling shot through Dean from head to toe and he felt a tightening below his stomach.

"No, wait, you're too... this can't happen." Dean pulled away.

He tugged Cody's boots off and rocked back on his heels and then stood up. Cody was out of his mind on alcohol – he probably thought Dean was someone else. If he'd even forgotten where he lived this evening, then he probably thought Dean was his girlfriend or... well, maybe boyfriend. Maybe there *was* a gay vibe to what had just happened.

Regardless, Cody wasn't in his right mind. And Dean couldn't possibly take advantage of Cody being drunk.

Cody looked up at him confused. "Can't happen?"

"Can't. Happen." Dean said, as firmly as he could manage, which felt not firm at all, because his body was zinging from the ghost of Cody's fingers in his hair and he was pretty sure his voice had cracked a little.

"Okay. Can't happen," Cody sighed and plonked his head back on the pillow.

"Here, I'll get you a bottle of water and some aspirin," Dean squeezed his eyes closed for a second.

Cody nodded mournfully and started taking off his shirt. As he did, Dean left the room as quickly as he could to track down a bottle of aspirin, some mineral water and a spare T-shirt that Dean thought might just fit over all of Cody's muscles.

He brought back the supplies to find Cody with his jeans off, fiddling with the buckles on his thigh that held his prosthetic leg in place. Dean swallowed.

Cody had mentioned having a prosthetic, hadn't he? At some point? But Dean had never seen it.

But beyond that, he hadn't expected to see so much of Cody's skin. His body was a hard, muscled masterpiece. He had a few tattoos over his torso and his legs. Or, leg. One and a half legs, Dean mentally corrected himself. He was absolutely gorgeous, but perhaps not in the conventional sense.

*He'd never get hired as a Fairyland prince, but... He could maybe be one of the pirate characters. Sexy and a little dangerous.*

"You need some help?" Dean asked. He set the water and pills down beside the bed.

"Nah, it's fine," Cody yawned. "Been doing this for years."

"I'm sorry," Dean said. He wasn't even sure what he was apologizing for. For Cody's struggles? For saying no to hooking up with him? For everything that had happened with the exposure therapy stuff?

*All of the above.*

"Don't be sorry, I'm good." Cody looked up to meet Dean's eyes. He seemed almost sober. He gave him a faint smile. "You rescued me."

Dean's heart did a sort of extra hard pump and then fluttered super-fast. He had to get out of there before he did something he couldn't possibly do.

"Okay, so, uh, take some aspirin, drink the water, and get some sleep. The bathroom's through there, and I'll see you in the morning."

"Thanks, man," Cody said. He grabbed Dean by the thighs

and pulled him in for the most awkward hug Dean had ever had, with Cody sitting there, one leg half detached, Dean standing and trying really hard not to respond physically to the warmth of his touch.

"You're welcome," he replied. And then he fled the room.

CODY WOKE UP WITH BRIGHT LIGHT SHINING IN HIS EYES AND A splitting headache. He groaned and turned over, throwing his arm over his face to shield his eyes. The bed was soft – much softer than his bed had ever been before.

*Holy shit, where am I?*

He sat up quickly and immediately regretted it as his head swam. He groped at the side table where he noticed a bottle of aspirin and took some, washing it down with a bottle of water.

Oh, no.

Things were coming back to him now.

The disastrous attempt at Spaceship Mayhem, going to his favorite gay bar to drink and then… *and then?*

His heart sank as he remembered.

*Calling Dean.*

He groaned a little and rubbed a hand over his forehead. He must be at Dean's house. He closed his eyes and tried to remember. He'd called Dean.

He didn't want to think about what it meant that he'd called Dean. A bunch of guys at the bar knew him, and would've helped him out if he'd asked. He could have called Nate. He could've called…

It was depressing how quickly the list of possible people to call ran out.

That's all it meant that he'd called Dean. Dean was his friend for real and he was top of his mind, he was coming up first in his contacts for recent use.

He'd called Dean and Dean had turned up because he's him and of course he did. And then Dean must've brought him home? To his home? He didn't want to think about what that meant either.

Something else stirred, deep and uncomfortable, something he didn't want to remember. Had he…? No, he couldn't have.

Oh, fuck.

Yeah, he had. He'd come onto Dean. In some kind of horrible, sleazy-drunk way. Which was ridiculous because for one, Dean was definitely in a relationship with Jessica and two, Cody was pretty sure he didn't even swing that way and three, it was horrible manners to come onto your friends. Or… something. Cody's head was still muzzy.

But he remembered one thing very clearly. Once he'd remembered that he'd come onto Dean, he recalled Dean's reaction. He'd said it couldn't happen. And there was an emphasis and a gravitas to those words. Cody could see his face, all stern and flustered like he had freaked him out. "Can't. Happen."

Well, yeah – of course it couldn't happen. Cody had just been too drunk to hold back whatever stupid, primitive urge he'd had to touch the pretty boy. He groaned, rubbed his face and took another swig of water. And now Dean would probably be all uncomfortable and weird around him.

He hauled himself to the side of the bed and pulled on his prosthetic leg. Leaning forward produced a horrible pounding in his temple, but he breathed through it. He downed the rest of the water bottle and then went to find the bathroom.

Dean's place was much larger than Cody's, which wasn't difficult - Cody's was tiny - but it was a little surprising. Cody had half imagined Dean in a student room-sharing situation or something. A crappy kitchen and a bookshelf made of planks of wood and breezeblocks. But this place was nice, like a show home.

The bathroom was roomy, with a shower and vanity which had been updated sometime in the last five years. And there was a towel folded on the side of the sink that Cody assumed was left out for him, so he stripped off and took a shower.

I wonder if I can sneak out? He thought. He helped himself to Dean's shampoo and body wash, since he was sure he smelled like a stale barseat. And sweat. He was a sweaty, beery mess. The shower had good, strong water pressure. He even took the time to condition his hair. Maybe he should grow it out again? Dean seemed to think it would look good on him.

Whatever. He sighed – he'd just have to act like normal and pretend that he *hadn't* come onto his best friend, or that he wasn't disappointed that he'd been turned down. Then, hopefully, everything could just go on like normal.

He got out of the shower and dried off, put his underwear back on and realized he'd come out without a T-shirt, so he draped the towel over his shoulders to somewhat cover himself up.

He walked out into the apartment just as Dean opened his bedroom door and emerged yawning, soft with sleep, his hair standing up at all angles.

Damn, he was cute.

*Can't keep thinking of him like that.*

"Morning," Cody said, with as much cheeriness as he could muster.

"How're you doing?" Dean knuckled his eye and yawned again. "I hope you weren't up all night throwing up."

"Uhh, no. I slept. I don't usually puke – strong stomach. I do have a headache, though. Thanks for the water and the aspirin, and uhh, everything." He cleared his throat. "And for coming to pick me up, obviously. That was… that was really good of you."

"Don't mention it." Dean seemed to be having trouble looking at him. He'd meet his eyes for a moment and then his gaze would glide off to the side. "That's what friends do. You'd do the same for me."

"Sure," Cody shrugged. He headed for the spare room. Maybe if he put proper pants on Dean would stop feeling so awkward. "I'll just," he hesitated. "Go get dressed."

"Yeah, yeah. I'll just shower then I can make breakfast, if you're hungry, that is?"

"Coffee's fine, thanks. I guess we'd better go soon if you're gonna drop me off at the bar."

"Why would I be dropping you off at the bar?" Dean frowned. He was halfway inside the bathroom and stripping. It seemed that Dean wasn't used to having other people around, and therefore saw no need for privacy. Or maybe he was just still sleepy and had forgotten.

"Oh – just to pick up my bike," Cody called, closing the spare room door before he saw too much of Dean.

Because if he saw too much of Dean naked there was every chance his resolve would crumble and – straight or not, cute Irish girlfriend or not – Cody would go full seduction-mode on his ass. And that was clearly the worst possible idea.

He rubbed the empty water bottle against his forehead in an effort to cool down, but it didn't achieve much.

"Get it together, Cody," he hissed to himself as he got dressed.

DEAN COULDN'T GET THE IMAGE OF CODY'S ALMOST ENTIRELY NAKED body out of his head. He thought it'd be better once he dropped Cody at the bar to collect his bike. Then, at least, he wouldn't be breathing the same air as Cody. But in reality, once Cody got out of the car it got worse. It was like his mind was intent on replaying everything that had happened the night before – like it had been holding back while he still had company.

He was on a loop of Cody pulling off his own shirt, Cody's hand in his hair, Cody suggesting… what he had suggested… and then flashing to Cody in a towel and underwear this morning. Just round and round and round in his head.

Cody hadn't said anything much about his suggestion this morning. He'd been pretty circumspect all round, and he'd hurried to get his clothes on after the bathroom – which meant that Dean had been right. Cody wasn't interested in Dean at all, he'd just been drunk and a little horny.

*And that's… fine. Cody is my friend after all, and I don't go around sleeping with my friends. That would be weird and* so *not cool. So not what I'm about.*

Dean shook his head. He was overcompensating, even inside his own head. Truth was he didn't even know what his feelings for Cody were. He liked him a lot, and clearly he thought he was hot. But he hadn't even realized Cody was gay, which probably meant Cody wasn't flirting with him, or Dean would've noticed, right?

He drove to the park, the route unfamiliar because he'd never come to Fairyland from a biker bar before. That, and he almost never drove. He pulled into the staff car park and then realized he should've asked Jessica if she needed picking up. He checked his phone but there was no message from her, and no message from Cody.

He took a deep breath, telling himself that no messages didn't necessarily mean anything bad, and went into the park.

Jessica was in her usual place at a table in the staff common room, sipping on a steaming cup of tea and flipping through the newspaper.

"How'd things go last night?" Jessica asked, as soon as he pulled up a chair at the table and pushed her car keys over the table's surface to her.

"Good. Weird. I don't know."

She closed the newspaper, pocketed her keys and leaned her chin on her hand. "Explain further, Deano."

"Um, well, he was pretty out of it. He'd been drinking and he was all…" Dean broke off to gesture with his hands and stick his tongue out. "He was forgetting stuff, he said he'd come outside to meet me but actually he just stayed inside, and I had to physically help him to the car, like, he was gone."

"Uh-huh." Jessica took a sip of her tea. "And?"

"And I figured he was so out of it, he'd better come to my place so if he, I dunno, started projectile vomiting in the night he'd at least have someone to clean it up."

"Eww. Is that really why you took him home?"

"I was worried he'd choke on his own vomit, yes," Dean said.

"And did he?"

Dean shook his head. "Nah. Once I got him to drink some water and take painkillers he went right to sleep. I checked on him a couple of times in the night, but he was fine."

"You checked on him in the night?" Jessica raised her eyebrows. "Dean! Creepy."

"I didn't watch him sleep!" He protested, although he admitted to himself the thought had crossed his mind. "I just got up and listened at the door once or twice. I could hear his snoring, so I knew it was all right. You know I'm a light sleeper, I didn't set an alarm or anything."

"Still kinda creepy," she said, pulling a face. "I guess you're *super* into this guy, then."

Dean flushed before he could even say anything in his own defense. "N-no, it's not like that, he's my friend."

"Yeah, he's your *friend*. And you're his friend that he calls when he's out of his mind and needing help. It sounds like he thinks of you as more than a *friend*." Jessica's eyes pierced into Dean and she didn't say anything more. Dean had to cut off this line of reasoning, fast.

"I think I'm maybe, like, his *only* friend outside the park, I mean, the guys he works with care about him, but I don't think they hang out." He cleared his throat. "And besides, he's not into me like that."

Jessica tilted her head, and between that and the eyebrows raised she resembled an inquisitive bird. All bright and tropical with her auburn feathers. "Something else happen?"

"Well, when I was helping him with his boots—"

Jessica cut in. "You helped him with his boots?"

"Yes, Jessica! He was really drunk!" Dean huffed out a breath. What was with the twenty questions all of a sudden?

Someone else came into the staff room. Dean waved at them and then leaned forward to hiss to Jessica in a low voice. "He said while I was down there, taking off his boots… I could… *you know*. And he touched my hair. But I think it was all a mistake."

He sat back and rubbed his hand over his cheeks, feeling how hot the skin was there.

"He is *so* into you!" Jessica crowed. She clapped her hands together.

"Yeah, but I don't think he is." Dean said. He swallowed hard. Cody was older, and super cool. Dean was nothing like the kind of person he'd be into.

"And why not?" Jessica raised her eyebrows and shoved him gently in the shoulder. "Everything you just said absolutely contradicts your position, so you'd better have a really good reason."

"Because! Because he's gorgeous – you've seen him, right? He could make out with any person in the world if he wanted to make out with them, any person at all. Guy or girl or any gender at all... and knowing *that*," Dean took a shuddery breath in to prevent his voice from cracking. "Why would he be into me?" He looked around. He'd got louder.

Jessica sighed and rolled her eyes so hard it looked like it probably hurt. "You're ridiculous. You're a catch, Dean."

"I am not," Dean protested. "I'm a gangly, pimpled mess with weird hair!"

"You do not have pimples, and your hair is great." Jessica shook her head. "You are deluded, is what you are. You're cute as fuck. Okay, so maybe you need a little Queer Eye transformation, but let's face it – who doesn't?"

"I still don't think he was flirting with me, okay."

"Oh my god, Dean! How can you be so dense when it comes to matters of the heart? You have to follow up. You're into him, right?"

Dean swallowed. "Well, I don't know. I'm confused. And more importantly I don't think that what happened means he's into me, I think it just means he was drunk, and I was there."

Jessica softened and rubbed her thumb on his arm, comforting him. "Nah, he's into you. He called *you*, Dean. He wanted *you* there. And then that happened... I dunno, but even drunk I don't come onto people I'm not into."

Dean raised an eyebrow. "You came onto that surfer girl with the ugly tattoos once." Dean grinned, hoping maybe he could turn the conversation around on her. Jessica, naturally, saw right through him.

"She was still cute, and this is not about me. I think there's something there. And additionally, I think you're being intentionally slow on the uptake so you don't have to deal with it."

Dean frowned and chewed on the inside of his cheek. He thought for a moment. Could she be right?

"You really think so?"

"Yes, I really do." Jessica nodded and gave his hand a little squeeze.

"So, then… why do you think *I'm* into him?" Dean hated how his voice gave away all his vulnerability and uncertainty.

"I don't know, Dean, maybe it's the way your face lights up when he texts you back, and the way you get so excited if he sends you a selfie, and the way you can't fucking stop talking about him all the time?" She shrugged, spreading her arms wide. "Little clues, you know?"

Dean swallowed. "I really do all that, huh?"

"Yes, you do." Jessica sighed. "Okay, so now I'm thinking you're actually just slow on the uptake and not doing it on purpose."

She got up and went to the vending machine, stuck in a few dollars and brought him back a can of green melon soda imported from Japan. "Drink this, get your head together, and think it through. You haven't dated anyone in twenty-seven years, and this could be a really great thing for you."

"I'm only twenty-three," Dean said. "And I'm not slow." He took the soda and cracked it open. But secretly, he thought she was probably right. "Thanks, Jessica. What do I do from here?"

"Keep on seeing him and see what happens. Be nice, try and flirt some and maybe one of you will get a clue, something might happen. You never know. Miracles do happen."

"Yeah, but it's almost Halloween. Not Christmas," Dean said, trying to make a joke.

Jessica shrugged. "Halloween miracles are a lesser known but still valid," she got up and reached over to ruffle his hair.

Dean drained his soda and then folded his arms and buried his face in them.

The feeling of her hand in his hair did nothing for him – at least not in *that* way – and it highlighted how awesome Cody's hand had felt there… and…

*Oh damn.*

*I have it bad, don't I?*

Dean brought his head up for a moment only to bring it thudding back down on his arms again.

*How could I be so clueless?*

CODY'S HEAD WAS STILL POUNDING BUT THE COFFEE HE GOT OUT OF the machine took the edge off. Then Lennon called him in for a meeting.

"You look like hell." They fixed him with a concerned look. "Are you well?"

"Yes, thanks," Cody said. "Had a big night. I'm fine though – I'll be fine today."

"Good, okay, because as you know Halloween is in a week, and we've got the special Halloween parade. We always get really big crowds for that. How's Francisco doing?"

"Good." Cody rolled out the stiffness in his shoulders. Actually, he'd been so distracted with the whole riding Spaceship Mayhem thing that'd he'd forgotten all about giving Lennon regular updates on Francisco. "He's doing well, picking stuff up quickly. He's slotted right in with the crew. I'd be happy to head out with just him to the meet and greet this morning if you want to trial that?"

Lennon shook their head. "I'll leave that decision to you. I want you to step up and take responsibility for the security detail for the Halloween Parade. Show Francisco how it's done."

"Yeah, of course." Cody straightened up in his seat – organizing the security detail over Halloween? That was a big deal. "Any word on when the big heir guy is coming into the park?"

"Nothing just yet," Lennon said. They frowned and opened their calendar app, tapping through it. "It's still rumors really, but someone said before Christmas. We don't really know, but we have to be prepared all the same."

"Makes sense," Cody said.

"Ahh, looks like Francisco's just come in," Lennon said, looking past Cody and out their office window. "Go ahead and get him briefed before the meet and greet."

Lennon seemed distracted, and kind of dry. They hadn't teased him about his big night, and had barely made eye contact.

"Are you doing all right?" Cody asked, before he got up. He frowned. He didn't usually make small talk like this – maybe he was more hungover than he felt. Or maybe it was Dean's influence.

*But Lennon's my friend, right? We've been working together for years. If they're stressed out I want to know if I can help.*

Lennon looked as surprised as Cody felt, their back straightened and their eyebrows shot up. For a moment, Cody felt a pang of guilt shoot through his chest. Was he a really a bad friend, because he didn't ask this kind of stuff?

"Um, yes. I'm fine. Overworked, but what else is new?" Lennon tugged on their signature pony tail, tightening it. "This thing could be gigantic. I'll be in trouble if our bit of the park doesn't pull things off seamlessly."

"You got this." Cody nodded. He meant it, too. "You're the best in the park. And you got me and Dash and the others backing you up."

Lennon broke into a huge smile. "Thanks, Cody," they said. "Now go do your job – that'll help me immediately"

Cody got up grinned back, feeling the stress melt away from his temples. "I know you're not as mean as you make out."

"Hey – you keep that to yourself!" Lennon pointed a letter opener at him. "I don't want anyone to hear I've gone soft."

"You have my word as a boy scout." Cody chuckled as he turned to leave the office.

"You were never a boy scout!" Lennon shouted after him. Cody winked broadly and heard a tinkle of laughter as he closed the door behind him.

Francisco was at the coffee machine, steaming milk, or possibly summoning banshees given the noise the machine was making. As Cody leaned against the table and waited for him to be done, he thought more about his interaction with Lennon. Maybe he *should* reach out to people more. Be a little more... Deanish. Francisco finished torturing the milk and gave Cody a smile.

Cody cleared his throat. "Good morning," he said. "You know, I can show you how to properly steam the milk without it making all that noise, if you like."

"Oh, I don't mind the noise." Francisco chuckled, his cheeks turning red.

"It'd be for the benefit of the rest of us, not you," Cody gave Francisco a playful nudge. "I'd quite like to keep my hearing. Anyway, the Halloween parade's coming up and Lennon wants us to head security. Think you're up to the challenge?"

Francisco nodded. "What does it involve?"

Cody sat down at the table and waited until Francisco was settled opposite him before he launched into the details. "Well, in addition to the regular parades, there's a couple of special Halloween ones on the thirtieth and thirty-first. It draws some really huge crowds and the princes and princesses ride on horses for it for some reason, so there's animal-wrangling to factor in as well." He sighed and ticked off the points he'd made on his fingers. He'd missed something – oh, yes. "And people who visit the park are allowed to dress up. Without masks, of course, so you have to deal with people getting excited about being in costume, and make sure no one's slipped on a mask."

Francisco frowned some. "Do people try to put masks on?"

Cody shrugged. "Sure. They all get checked and approved at

the ticket gate, bag checks and everything, obviously, but if they bring in a mask they might slip it on after that."

Francisco shook his head. "Weird. All right, what else?"

"Well, it'll be a lot of crowd control and constant vigilance," Cody said. "And we'll be in charge of the whole security detail in the Enchanted Forest."

"Sounds good."

Cody looked at him for a moment and smiled. Asking Lennon about themself had worked well. Maybe he could try it again now. He ran his hand through his hair. "So, how're you liking it?" Cody asked. "The job, I mean."

Francisco grinned. "I like it very much. Every day is a little different, and no one has shot at me yet, so…that's a bonus."

Cody raised his eyebrows. "Sure. What did you used to do?"

"I was in the security detail for the Secretary of Defense," Francisco said. "It was very different to here. Much more intense."

"I can imagine." Cody had once seen the Secretary of Defense at a military training base. It was from a distance, but the sea of security personnel that surrounded her had been staggering. He wondered if Francisco had been one of them.

"Thank you for all your help, through the orientation process," Francisco said. His eyes crinkled up when he smiled, making him even more handsome than he was usually.

*Handsome but too similar,* he thought. *I couldn't be with someone who was constantly reminding me of my past. Dean's the absolute opposite of military… but he understands me.*

"It's no trouble," Cody said. "Compared to the Secretary of Defense gig this place must seem like a cinch."

"It has its own challenges," Francisco raised an eyebrow as he looked over Cody's shoulder. "Like this one," Francisco added quietly. Cody turned just as Dash and Nate walked in, arguing over something. As they came in Cody caught the tail end of their argument about coffee.

"They're not so bad once you get to know them," Cody said, turning back.

"*They're* not. *Dash* is…" Francisco paused, his eyes wide as he searched for a word. "A challenge." Dash and Nate disappeared into the changing room. But they could both hear their voices, continuing the tiff.

Before Cody could come up with something to say in Dash's defense, Greer and Ariana came in. Greer made a point of coming over to the table and saying good morning to both of them.

"How're my favorite big, strong, handsome men?" Greer fluttered her eyelashes.

"Morning, Greer. Don't let Dash hear you say that." Cody winked. Greer leaned in and kissed him on the cheek all princess-like.

"But it's true," she said, and pouted her lips prettily. If she was making a point of acting all precious and cute, she must be after something.

"Okay, okay. What do you want?" Cody sighed.

"It's nothing much. I just wondered if you could maybe tell Lennon that having horses in the parade is too much of a security hassle." Cody glanced at Francisco, who was smiling broadly at Greer. He frowned. Did Francisco flirt with everyone?

"Sure, it's annoying, but we've had the horses a couple of years running now, it's not that big a deal," Cody replied. "Why?"

Greer made a frustrated groaning noise and slumped her shoulders. "Because I already asked, and because I *hate* managing that freaking dress on a freaking horse. But they said no, point blank." Greer folded her arms – she was back to the normal Greer that Cody knew. Francisco chortled a little.

Cody shrugged. "I don't think it'll change their mind if I say anything, but I'll try. For you."

"Aww, thanks, Cody! You're a doll. And you make sure he does it, 'Cisco," she wiggled her finger at the both of them and sashayed into the princesses changing room.

"Well she's a spitfire," Francisco said, approvingly. Cody nodded his agreement.

"Sure, she is. Don't ask her out until you've been here at least a month, though, we gotta get you through the trial period – and me through the Halloween parade."

Francisco chuckled and winked at him. Cody was sure he was flirting with him now. "Yes, boss. And does that go for *anyone* who works here, who I, err, might be interested in?"

He raised an eyebrow and his eyes twinkled at Cody. Okay so that was definitely flirting.

Cody dug his fingernails in harder. "Yes, anyone." He took a deep, steadying breath. "Come on, let's go do some prep for the parade."

A week ago he wouldn't have minded – he may have even welcomed Francisco's advances. But now, even when he was sure that Francisco was flirting with him, all he could think about was being alert to the weight of his phone in his pocket so he could feel if it vibrated. So he could catch the second Dean messaged him with another selfie – if he ever did again, after last night.

And it was totally fine that Cody was hanging out for a selfie from a straight guy with a steady girlfriend because… because… ?

*I'm totally fucked, aren't I?*

DEAN TOOK A DIFFERENT BUS AT THE END OF THE DAY. CODY HAD texted to say he'd been given the security gig for the whole entire Halloween parade so he wouldn't have much time in the next couple of days to catch up.

He felt irrationally angry at the Halloween parade for taking Cody away from him.

*But I love the Halloween parade, I can't stay mad at that. So, I'm actually annoyed… that I don't get to see Cody for a few days. Sad face emoji.*

He must be tired if he was thinking emojis to himself. He rested his forehead on the bus window and shuddered with it when the bus stopped, letting more people on.

Dean had admitted to himself he liked Cody, which was one step. But it opened up this big can of worms - how could he talk to Cody about it? Could he try and put the moves on him? What kind of moves did Dean even have? He didn't. He was a move-free-zone.

And yeah, Cody had sort of made a move on Dean the night before but that was almost certainly the alcohol talking, so he didn't want to count on Cody being interested in Dean in particular.

So, Dean texted his mom and told her he'd come around for dinner.

The bus to his parent's house was a long, winding route. He stood up for a pregnant woman and his feet started to hurt. His head went swimmy from the exhaust fumes and it was such a relief to get off the bus and open the gate to his parents' house he almost cried.

The twins, Abby and Alex, were playing some kind of mobile phone game together at the base of the tree in the front yard. When they heard the squeak of the gate opening and closing, they leapt up from the ground and raced towards him.

"Dean! Dean! Hug me first!"

"Did you bring me anything?"

Dean laughed weakly and crouched on one knee, catching one in each of his arms. He hugged them close. "I missed you two!" he said. "And yes, I brought you treats. Just let me get inside and I'll dig them out of my bag."

Abby had been reaching over his shoulder and trying to get into his bag already – she was always the more outgoing twin. She pulled back as soon as he'd spoken. "Is it robot candy? I love that stuff!"

"You'll just have to wait until we're inside," Dean laughed. He let go and as he stood up the twins laughed and ran inside.

"Dean's here!" Abby called out to the house.

"Okay?" Jacob's voice echoed from somewhere in the house.

As soon as Dean got inside, he put his bag down on the sideboard to retrieve the Halloween cookies he'd got at the Enchanted Forest. The chef there had really gone all out this year. There were cookies in the shape of creepy haunted trees, and Treasure the Unicorn and Sparkles the Dragon with Halloween masks on. They were beautifully detailed, and they tasted incredible, too – Dean had low key gotten hooked on them the day they'd been released, so he'd bought a stack of them for dessert.

"One for you, and one for you," Dean said, handing them to the kids.

"Thanks, Dean!" They chimed in unison.

"You're welcome, And there's more for after dinner. Now, where's Mom?"

"In the backyard," Alex said. He was already tearing into his dragon cookie. "She's doing barbeque and it's taking aaages." He drew out the word 'ages' and rolled his eyes to demonstrate just how bored he was with the process – which would have been cute, if he didn't have a mouthful of cookie.

"Thanks." Dean kissed the twins on the tops of their heads, which they only endured because of the cookies, and then went out the back.

Their backyard wasn't huge, but it had a big deck his father, Louis, had put up when Dean was about the twin's age. It was wide and wooden, and the barbecue sat in the corner. There was a picnic table big enough for the whole family to sit around and deckchairs enough for them all plus a few in case they had guests. Anne was at the barbecue cooking some sausages, vegetable skewers and pork chops.

"There you are." Anne's face lit up when she saw him. She was wearing a big pair of sunglasses, but she still shielded her eyes as he came over to give her a hug.

"Yup, here I am," Dean said. They embraced and he smiled. There was nothing like a mom hug, he felt some of the weight on his shoulders lift just from the warmth of her arms around him and her familiar mom-scent.

"How're you doing, baby?" She pulled back, looked him up and down and rubbed his arms before going back to cooking. She picked up the long-arm tongs and started turning the steaks on the grill.

"I'm okay," he shrugged. Although after everything that had happened in the last couple of days, 'okay' was kind of an overstatement.

"There's gotta be more to it than that, tell me what's going on!" The corner of his mouth twitched with a smile. He could always count on his mother as a sounding board, she could sense any sort of bad mood or trouble on him. He looked around and frowned.

"Where's Dad?" Dean couldn't see a sign of his father. His younger sister Meryl sauntered out of the house. She had a big floppy black hat on, huge round black sunglasses, a black tank top and black leggings.

"Hey, Dean," she mumbled. She took a seat on a deckchair and put her earphones in, disappearing into her phone.

"He's got an extra shift, so he won't be here until after ten. And hey, you. Don't dodge my question."

"I wasn't." At least, not exactly. Dean sighed and leaned against the back fence so he could stand close-ish to his mother, and the delicious smells of cooking meat, while he answered. "Things are kind of… going well? But also kinda confusing. Wow. Meryl's deep in the Goth thing, huh?"

Anne raised an eyebrow. "She says it reflects the darkness in her soul." She turned to point the tongs at him. "Okay, so explain what's going well and what's confusing." Anne reached down to the cooler, pulled out a can of beer, and tossed it to him.

He caught it and cracked it open. "You know the guy I told you about, Cody?"

"The Air Force vet?" Anne nodded. "I recall."

"Some stuff kind of happened last night and I'm pretty confused about if…" he broke off, trying to gather his thoughts. "Well, I don't know if I want us to just be friends or if I want us to be something more."

Anne smiled some. "You don't have to decide right away, you know."

Dean took a long swig of beer. His shoulders relaxed some. Anne had always been cool about Dean being queer. He'd dated both girls and boys in high school, but lately he'd hit a bit of a dry spell. Whoever he brought home, his mother had treated them just the same – as a valued guest. His father had taken a little longer to adjust, but after a while he'd reassured Dean that he loved him and he just wanted him to be happy.

"Right, I know."

"But you should bring him round, either way. I want to meet this guy," Anne said. She was busy stacking the meats onto a serving dish. "Now go inside and get the salad out of the fridge. Meryl!" she raised her voice to get Meryl's attention. Meryl pulled the earbuds out of her ears.

"Yeah, Mom?"

"Go inside with your brother and bring out some cutlery and plates. We'll eat outside. Oh, and Dean – call the twins in to wash their hands."

Within a half hour they were all settled at the picnic table.

Jacob had torn himself away from his video game and had heaped his plate with as many meat products as he could. "How's the magical space world?" he asked Dean.

"It's wonderful," Dean said, grinning. "You wanna come by and ride Mayhem again soon?"

"Maybe," Jacob shrugged.

"We want to!" Abby said. "Invite us!" The twins were picky eaters, so they just had sausages and potato salad and bread rolls.

"As soon as you're tall enough, I'll give you the best VIP Mayhem experience ever," Dean promised, giving them a wink. "So, what's new with you, Meryl?" Dean asked.

"I'm thinking of going into fashion design," Meryl said. She had a little of everything on her plate, which she was cutting up into tiny pieces.

"Oh yeah?" Dean smiled at her. "You'd be great at that."

Meryl nodded, as if that was obvious and she didn't need his validation. Which she probably didn't, to be fair, it was just that Dean liked to give it anyway. "I know." She shrugged. Then she put down her knife and fork and looked at him critically for a moment. "Are you gonna work at Fairyland your whole life?"

Dean flushed and licked his lips. That stung a little. He knew she wasn't trying to be mean it was just that out of all his siblings, Meryl was probably the most ambitious. "I don't know. I had kind of wondered about going back to study, maybe."

Anne's face lit up. "You were? Oh, Dean, that'd be wonderful, what are you going to study?"

He felt a little like he was on the edge of a cliff. His mother was so excited about the idea of him studying, and he didn't want to disappoint her, but he hadn't exactly settled on anything either.

"I mean, I don't know if I'm gonna do anything at all, but I was thinking of maybe social work or something like that. Helping people, you know?"

"My son, the social worker," Anne beamed.

And her smile ignited a warmth right through Dean's chest.

It'd been a couple of days since he'd seen Dean, what with the Halloween parade planning and everything. But he didn't want to make Dean think he was running away again, so he kept texting him, and even sent him some random pictures and selfies.

Dean had lapped it up. Every picture Cody sent garnered replies with multiple exclamation points, emojis and excited reply selfies. Cody hadn't realized reply selfies were a thing, but here was Dean sending them. It was, frankly, adorable.

He made a time to meet up with Dean after work on Thursday, for two reasons. One: Dean had stopped trying to get him to ride Spaceship Mayhem. The drunk incident seemed to have put a stop to that, which was a relief. And two: because Cody missed him. He didn't like admitting that he missed someone because it made him feel all self-conscious and vulnerable. But he couldn't deny that his heart hurt a little when he thought about Dean. He mentally added a third reason to the list: he missed the way Dean made him laugh.

They met up at the Enchanted Forest Kitchen because Dean was obsessed with the Halloween cookies they made there. Cody recognized them because Nate brought them in sometimes – he was best friends with one of the chefs and got to take the extras some mornings when they carpooled in together.

Charlie, Nate's friend, was behind the counter when Cody

went in, and they gave each other friendly nods. Cody sat in a corner booth. He didn't have to wait long before Dean arrived, flushed and happy, as usual. He leaned over the corner of the table to give Cody a one-armed hug before he sat down opposite him.

"Cody! How are you?"

"Apparently not as good as you," Cody said. "What's going on?"

"I'm thinking about making some life changes," Dean said. He took a deep breath, like he was nervous. "I've got some stuff for a college. I'm thinking of studying."

"Isn't it, like, totally the wrong time of year?" Cody asked. He had an instant wave of nervousness at the idea of Dean going to study. "Didn't you just miss the intake for new classes?"

Dean blinked at him and opened his mouth. His chin twitched a little. "Umm. Yes? But I was thinking of starting with Summer school."

Cody frowned. "Why do you want to study, anyway? What's wrong with things as they are?" Cody said. He could feel a flicker of muscle tensing in his jaw. This was really pissing him off, for some reason.

"Well, I–I mean, I was just starting thinking that maybe there's more to life than roller coasters." Dean lowered his gaze to their carefully distressed wooden table.

Cody snorted derisively. Then he wondered why he had snorted. Dean winced. Cody held his breath.

*Oh shit, I'm being a dick and Dean's so excited about this. I can't be a dick to him or he'll never talk to me again.*

"Sorry," he said. "Yeah, of course." He rubbed his face. "It's a good idea."

"I think I'm just gonna get us some cookies and cocoa," Dean's shoulders slumped as he walked to the counter to order. Cody's stomach was churning with nervousness. The anxiety he usually felt thinking about riding Spaceship Mayhem bubbled inside him. But why was this such a problem for him?

Then it hit him. If Dean went to study, he wouldn't be at the park every day anymore. In fact, he might not be in the park at all. He'd be out of Cody's life, and he'd probably forget about Cody. There'd be no reason for them to stay in touch if he wasn't working the roller coaster anymore, and Cody would lose Dean from his life.

And everything would suck.

He swallowed and bit his lip.

This wasn't about him, though, was it? It was about Dean. And the fact that Dean wanted to do more with his life was fair enough, too. What kind of life was it if all you ever did was load people into a roller coaster day in and day out? He wanted Dean to have the best life he could, and maybe that would include studying and finding a better job.

But, he was slowly starting to realize, he also wanted Dean.

Which wasn't going to happen because Dean was with Jessica, anyway, and similarly to how they happened to stop talking about Cody riding the coaster, they also happened to not talk about how Cody had awkwardly tried to come onto Dean that one night.

They weren't talking about a lot things. But they should talk about *this*, right?

*I just have to suck it up. This is about what's best for Dean and I shouldn't get a say. I should encourage him. Even if I never see him again…*

Dean brought over a tray with two large hot cocoas and a stack of Halloween cookies on it. He put it in the middle of the table.

"How're you doing?" Dean asked.

Cody shook his head a little. "I don't matter. I mean, I do, but what I want doesn't matter. I mean," He shook his head again, harder this time, and tried to get out what he actually meant. "How I *am* doesn't matter right now. We were talking about you going to study – we should keep talking about that."

"We don't have to if you don't want to." Dean sounded extra cautious, like he was afraid of talking too loud in case Cody spooked.

Damn it, he really *had* hurt him. And Cody did feel spooked. Like he was losing his grip.

"No, I want to know. What would you be studying?"

"I was thinking anthropology, or psychology or maybe social issues stuff," Dean said, shyly, looking at his cocoa. "You know, like, helping out people in need."

"You mean... people like me?" Cody didn't know how to feel about that. On the one hand it felt a lot like pity. Like Dean saw him as a charity case who needed fixing. On the other hand, it was kind of nice to feel like he'd inspired something – pity or not. And Dean *did* have a gift for putting people at ease. He genuinely cared and wanted other people to be happy, and if going back to study was going to make him happy, it was a good thing, and Cody should do his best to support him, right?

"Yeah. I mean, no, I mean–" Dean looked flustered. "I don't mean like 'you're a sad sack who needs rescuing' or anything. I just mean, I felt like I was helping you out and it felt good. I want to do that more."

Cody picked up a cookie in the shape of Treasure the Unicorn and bit the horn off. "You have helped me out." He paused. He swallowed a wave of annoyance at being called out so accurately. "And I am a sad sack, and you did rescue me at the bar, so."

He took a deep breath and bit into the cookie again. If he'd kept talking he was going to say something really inappropriate. Something about how Cody was so grateful he'd do anything to thank him or like, that he wanted to make love to him down by the ocean or some sick shit like that.

Dean smiled at him, all goofy and pleased and adorably Deanish. "You think?"

"I think you rescued me? Yes." Cody sipped his cocoa – anything to stop the stupid, inappropriate feelings which were threatening to spew out of him.

*I don't even like cocoa that much.*

"That's cool. Thanks for saying that, man."

Cody nodded, time to change the subject before he couldn't

damn up his feelings any longer. "So. What're you up to this weekend?"

"Oh, uhh, I was gonna go see my folks. Dad wasn't around last time I went over, so we're catching up again. I said I'd take over some stuff and we could have a kind of Halloween feast thing."

"That sounds fun," Cody said. Not because he really thought so but because Dean looked so excited about it.

"Oh my god, you should come!" Dean said. His eyes widened, and he reached for his phone. Cody regretted saying it sounded fun.

"I couldn't," he said. "It'd be such an imposition."

Cody had never turned down an invite to a family dinner before – mainly because he'd never had an invite to a family dinner. But that's what people on TV said to get out of these kinds of situations, wasn't it?

"No, not at all. We always have too much food, and my mom wants to meet you. She was a marine, so I've told her all about you."

Cody swallowed hard. "No – that's like, more reasons not to go," Cody said. "Besides, I, um, have something on."

"Uh-huh, you have something on?" Dean folded his arms over his chest and raised an eyebrow. "What have you got on?"

"I have to…" Cody paused, trying to think of something that sounded plausible. "I have to help Nate with his… car. Yes. Nate has car problems."

"Ha! Well, that's weird because Nate doesn't have a car, Dash does," Dean said, triumphantly.

*Shit.*

"Will Jessica be coming to this family Halloween thing, too?" Cody said, he could see Dean wasn't about to let this go, and he could feel himself giving in. He was going to have to go to Dean's house and meet his family and have a meal together. If he wanted to stay friends with Dean when he left Fairyland to study, there was no getting away from it.

Dean looked surprised. "I guess I could ask her? I kinda

thought it could just be you and me, but if you'd rather she was there too, that's cool."

Cody tapped his fingers on the table. Yes. Jessica would be a safety net – a safety net to stop him from getting too carried away with his crush. He couldn't just go around falling head over heels for a guy with a girlfriend. That wasn't cool. And so, Jessica should be there. To remind him.

"Yeah, invite her, it'd be cool."

"Ohh-kay, so does this mean you're coming?" Dean opened the messaging app on his phone and started tapping it.

"Yeah. I'll come with." Cody tried his best nonchalant shrug to hide his nervousness, but he suspected it came across like a shoulder spasm. He smiled at Dean as mildly as he could manage.

*Oh god, what did I just agree to? A whole night with Dean and his family? I bet they're all exactly like him. I hope this isn't a huge mistake.*

"WHY DO YOU WANT *ME* THERE?" JESSICA ASKED. THE TWO OF THEM were doing the pre-opening clean of the coaster cars. It was a quick process because they'd both done it so many times – wipe down the outside of the car with a microfiber cloth and then spray and wipe the inside, focusing on the seats. Once one car of six seats was done, they hit the button to move things along and did the next car.

"Cody wants you there," Dean said, he shrugged. "He's nuts on you, I guess."

Jessica made a fart noise with her mouth. "The fuck he is. It's you he's into."

"I don't know about that," Dean said. He ducked his head down like he was trying to get to the middle section of one of the cars so Jessica wouldn't see him blush. He felt a wadded-up cloth hit him in the shoulder.

"He came onto you, doofus."

"When he was drunk! That's an extenuating circumstance." Dean protested. He straightened up and tossed the cloth back at Jessica. She caught it with one hand. "He was off his head. He probably thought I was someone else."

"Yeah, because he seems to have so many people around him all the time," Jessica rolled her eyes.

"Rude!" Dean pointed a finger at her.

"I'm just telling it like it is. He's obviously chilled out a lot since he got to know you, and he's into you, and he sent you a freaking selfie from his bed this morning. What more do you need? A sign from outer-space? Bingo the alien to turn up with a sign saying 'Cody likes you'?"

"Yeah, okay. But he only sent that photo because I sent him a wake-up selfie first," Dean mumbled.

*I was so excited to receive that picture. Maybe I shouldn't have shown it to Jess... she's obviously reading too much into it.*

*There's no way he'd be into me anyway. I'm too young and silly and he's all tough and cool and older. It's just not happening.*

"Dude's hot for you. End of. Now can we get back to work?"

"It's so not the *end of* anything," Dean mumbled, then raised his voice to address the next part to her. "So. Will you come to dinner or what?"

"Fine, I'll come. But you never know. Maybe I'll leave early, or I'll get sick at the last minute and have to cancel," Jessica teased. He fixed her with a stern look. "Jokes! I'm joking."

"You'd better be," Dean scowled.

"Relax, Romeo. I'll be there, I'll be charming, I'll distract the kids, and you can have a lovely dinner with your folks and your soon-to-be husband."

Dean blushed again and cleared his throat. "Stop it. There's nothing going on. He's not into me like that, okay. He hasn't done anything to indicate he is, not since that one drunken come on."

"Except for the sexy bed pic, you mean? Seriously, Dean. Do I have to whack both your heads together? Because I'll do it. And I'll probably enjoy it, too."

"You send me good morning selfies all the time!" Dean shook his head. "I don't know why you keep coming back to that."

Jessica was being totally ridiculous. Just because he had a gorgeous 'sleepy Cody who may or may not have been wearing anything under the blanket' picture didn't mean it meant that Cody liked him for sure. It wasn't like, a thirst trap picture or anything.

Dean wondered if Cody even knew what thirst traps were. Probably not. Which, again, only further proved his point.

"Mine are different," Jessica said. "I know there's nothing between us but friendship. And you know it, and we've actually *discussed* that like normal adult human beings who are capable of having normal adult conversations about feelings, so there's no subtext."

Dean sighed. It was true. They had discussed it. When they first became close a couple of years back, someone had joked they were dating, and it'd put the idea in both of their heads. They'd tried one kiss one time, but they both agreed it was all wrong.

*There's no passion there*, Jessica had said. *It was like kissing a wall.*

Although feeling a little insulted, Dean had agreed wholeheartedly.

So they'd just been best friends instead. And actually clearing the air like that had been wonderful. So, maybe that's what Dean needed to do with Cody. Just lay it all out in the open and make sure they both agreed about what their relationship was.

Dean scrubbed extra hard at a grey spot on the seat of the last car on the coaster, narrowing his eyes until it finally came clean.

But they'd do family dinner first – because talking like that might spook Cody and he might back out. And Dean really wanted Cody to meet his family. Just the idea of showing off Cody to his family made him smile.

*Imagine if it goes really well, and Cody starts coming to family dinners regularly. I'm sure that'd be good for him. And it'd be nice to have him around more outside work too.*

*I'd really like to see Cody more, I'm into him, and I want him, but there's no way he'd go for someone like me. I'm not good enough for him. I'm a jerk who tried to force him onto a roller coaster.*

*There's just no way the word boyfriend would ever stick to Cody. But I still have to talk things through. Put everyone out on the table and clear the air and all that good, adult stuff which is utterly terrifying.*

*No problem, right?*

## 24 / CODY

CODY FELT SOMEWHAT NERVOUS ABOUT THE WHOLE DINNER THING. He spent Saturday low-level worrying about how it would go. He'd woken at about eight-thirty and picked up his phone to see a good morning text from Dean which ended with 'see you tonight, can't wait!' and a text from Dash.

The Dash text was unusual, so he opened it, frowning. Dash had invited him to work out with him. Cody couldn't think of a good reason to turn him down – and he didn't have anything to do today but worry – so he texted back a yes. Dash replied with the address of the gym.

Cody wasn't used to spending so long worrying about something. It wasn't like not being able to ride the roller coaster, which was a much more incident-based terror rather than a creeping dread. A workout would be a nice distraction from the inside of his head, and he knew Dash, unlike Nate, wouldn't make him talk about his feelings or anything, which was a relief.

He and Dash could work out in peace, he'd have company to distract himself from his nervousness and they'd probably not talk at all. Sounded great. In theory.

He met Dash outside the gym and got signed in as a guest. They started with weights. Cody got the bench press sorted the way he liked and lay down. Dash stood over him, spotting for him. Once Cody had the bar in his hands and had started to take the weight, Dash cleared his throat.

"So, what do you need to do to be happy?" Dash asked.

Cody froze, the bar just slightly up from the rest. "Sorry, what?" His breath hissed out of his lungs.

Dash didn't meet his eyes, just focused on the bar in case he had to take it. "Look. Nate's worried about you, after the other night when your little friend came by looking for you, and you were all out-of-it the next day. I don't want to talk about feelings or whatever–"

"Okay, good." Cody scowled as he put the bar back down. This was *so* not happening right now.

"But in my experience, if you're in love with someone you have to do something about it."

While Dash had been talking, Cody had picked the weights up again and just about dropped them on himself when he said the word 'love'. Dash had to grab them and bring them back to the rack.

"What the hell, Dash!?"

"If you're in love with that boy – whatever – the ride jockey–"

"Dean," Cody ground out between gritted teeth. "He's just my friend." He shot Dash a glare and lifted the bar again.

"Look, if you want to mess around and pretend nothing's happening, I don't give a shit."

"Surprised you give a shit anyway," Cody grumbled in between reps.

"Nate's worried," Dash said. "And that means I have to hear about it. If you sort your shit out, he'll be happy, and then *I'll* be happy."

"Okay, genius. Well, what about if it doesn't matter because he has a girlfriend," Cody said.

"He does?" Dash snorted. "I'm sure you can convince him not to."

"Dash!"

Dash shrugged. "If Nate had a girlfriend I would have." Dash paused, apparently thinking through the scenario. "I mean, I still would've kissed him up against the wall, so he knew how I felt."

"You didn't know how you felt!" Cody exclaimed. "We could all tell you were confused."

"This isn't about me, anyway," Dash raised an eyebrow. Cody cleared his throat since it was clearly Dash that brought up his own case, but whatever. He could just focus on lifting and not on the drivel coming out of Dash's mouth.

The silence stretched out as he pressed the weights. He realized he'd better say something or Dash would start in again.

"I don't know," Cody said. "I think Dean's amazing, and I'm terrified of losing him from my life and I don't know what to do. And I'm going to dinner with his family tonight! I had to tell him to invite his girlfriend, or it was just going to be him and me and his parents." Cody sighed. "He's so clueless sometimes."

Dash frowned again. Saying all that while bench pressing had winded Cody. He replaced the bar and sat up.

"Wait. He *hadn't* invited his girlfriend to dinner?"

"No."

"Are you absolutely sure that relationship is what you think it is?" Dash asked, slowly. Cody stood up and took a deep drink from his water bottle as Dash adjusted the weights got onto the bench.

"I mean, yes? He's always talking about her, and they hang out all the time and he sends me cute selfies with her."

"Hmm." Dash didn't sound convinced.

Cody moved into spotting position and frowned to himself. *Have I misread the situation? Was it possible?*

He shook his head. "Well, either way I guess I'll find out tonight."

"Before that happens, just ask yourself one thing, Cody," Dash said. He took the weight bar and started his reps.

"What?"

"Ask yourself what you really want. And I don't even mean with Dean, necessarily. I mean, in life. Do you want to work at

Fairyland forever? Do you want to travel to the Bahamas? Do you want to get married and have kids?"

Cody thought about it. Really thought.

*What do I want? When was the last time I really considered that, instead of just living day to day? Beyond knowing what I want for dinner.*

He thought of beaches and roller coasters and the possibility of a wedding with a fancy suit and someone beside him in an equally fancy suit. But imagining that felt like he may as well have been imagining himself in outer space. There was something… something closer to home.

"I don't want to be afraid," he said.

Dash didn't say anything for a moment. Cody didn't really expect him to have an answer for that, anyway. He just paid attention to the bar in case Dash needed help.

"Everyone's afraid though," Dash said eventually between reps. "You can't miraculously become a man without fear. But you can do shit regardless. They say that true bravery is being afraid and not letting it stop you."

"Who says that?"

"It's a famous quote – I don't know. Someone important."

"Hmm." Cody let the idea of it wash over him.

Whoever said that quote probably hadn't been living with post-traumatic stress disorder, it likely wasn't about people with crippling anxiety or sweat-drenched nightmares or anything like that. But even still, maybe there was something in it.

*Why am I afraid of, for instance, telling Dean I'm into him?*

*The worst that could happen would be, what? Dean freaking out and us not being friends anymore? But I can't really see Dean reacting like that. He's easy going.*

It'd probably just be awkward and when Dean said he had a girlfriend and they'd just keep on being friends.

"Do you feel better now?" Dash asked. He was straining a little so Cody helped him replace the bar on the rest.

"Yeah, you know what? I think I do."

"Good. Then let's do cardio in silence," Dash said.

Which, of course, left Cody alone with his new thoughts, and the same old confusion.

As much as he wanted to ride on the motorbike again, Dean insisted that he pick Cody up in Jessica's car and bring him to his folk's place. If they were all in the car together, Cody couldn't bail. He couldn't suddenly invent a Nate emergency, or forget about the evening or anything.

Jessica drove, and Dean navigated to the address Cody had given him. It was a bit of a crappy apartment building. Dean looked up at it doubtfully, but this was the place. He texted Cody.

Dean: We're here. Come on down.

Cody: Heading down

A couple of minutes later Cody emerged and slipped on his sunglasses, giving Dean and Jessica a tight smile.

He was wearing a black short-sleeved button-down shirt with a print of white daisies scattered across it. The top few buttons were undone revealing a black T-shirt underneath.

He had a dark pair of jeans on with no rips or fades. He was freshly shaven – and it even looked like he'd combed his hair. He had obviously dressed up fancy for the occasion, and he had a big bouquet of flowers in one hand and a canvas tote slung over his other arm.

*He looks incredible. Like he's had the cast of Queer Eye do a makeover on him.*

*Dreamy.*

Jessica wolf whistled. "Look at you!" She called out through her wound-down window.

Cody laughed and climbed into the back seat. "Hey, you two."

"Looking amazing!" Jessica said. She grinned and shoved Dean's arm. "Tell him how good he looks."

"You look really good." Dean turned to smile at Cody, feeling a warmth in his cheeks all over again. He even thought he caught a whiff of something that smelled fantastic.

"Thanks. You do, too." Cody looked Dean up and down and grinned.

"Who are those flowers for?" Dean asked.

"Your mother," Cody said. "My mom taught me to always bring a hostess gift, or a host gift, or… something."

"What is your mother like?" Dean asked.

Jessica started driving them out to Dean's parents place.

"She's very down-to-earth. Traditional," Cody said. Dean sat back in his seat a little, facing forward so Cody could talk or not talk and not have to look him in the eyes. "She's never quite gotten over me serving, I guess. When I came back like I did, she didn't really know what to do."

"Do you see much of her?"

"No," Cody said. "I didn't even go up for Thanksgiving or Christmas last year. I guess I feel like we're all happier if I'm not there."

"I'm sure that's not true." Dean frowned. He didn't know how much *was* true, but now he was even more pleased than before that Cody had agreed to come to dinner tonight. Cody needed some family time. Whatever he said about his own family being happier without him, no one could be *entirely* happy with no family connections, right?

"How about you, Jessica? Are your family nearby?"

"No, they're all in Ireland still." Jessica grinned. "I go visit once a year and my mam comes here once a year and we skype like, all the time. I just adopted Dean's family as my local family."

"Of course," Cody said.

"You're welcome to adopt them, too," Dean said, quickly. "They're definitely going to want to adopt you, so."

"They are?" Cody sounded skeptical.

"For sure," Dean nodded. Jessica nodded as well.

"You're all cute and wounded – they'll adore you," Jessica affirmed.

"But not, like, wounded in a way that means people pity you," Dean said, quickly, shooting Jessica a pointed glance. "Anyway, I have four younger siblings. I can't remember if I've told you before."

"I don't think I know much about the specifics, beyond, you know, constant texts," Cody said.

"Right. So Meryl's the next oldest – she's the Goth – and super cranky so you'll probably get on well with her," Dean said. "Then it's Jacob. He's kind of, you know, when teenagers just kind of stop talking because they're so cool or whatever? Yeah. He's sort of there."

"Mostly he just plays a lot of video games," Jessica said.

"Okay," Cody said. "Then there's the youngest two – the twins?"

Dean smiled, warmth spreading through his chest because Cody remembered something about his family.

"You remember!" Dean said. He bounced in his seat and turned to look at Cody. "Yeah, the twins are Alex and Abby. They're gonna jump all over you."

"Any pets?"

"No, dad's allergic," Dean said. "Just kids – he doesn't seem to be allergic to those."

"Great," Cody said again.

"It *is* great," Dean agreed. He absolutely adored his family, and he was psyched that they were going to meet Cody. He just knew they'd all get on like a house on fire.

Jessica pulled the car in to park in the driveway.

"Here we are, then." Jessica sighed. "Gird your loins, Cody,"

Dean saw her catch Cody's eye in the rearview mirror and wink just before the three of them piled out of the car.

"Loins are well girded," Cody said, dryly.

*This was going to be so freaking excellent.*

DEAN'S PARENTS LIVED IN A TIDY HOUSE WITH A BACKYARD, A LITTLE driveway and a second floor. The house was painted a pale yellow and the window frames were white. It was like something out of a picture book about happy families. Or an advertisement in a suburban real estate catalogue.

Jessica had warned Cody to gird his loins and he took that advice quite seriously, although he wasn't sure he'd be able to actually prepare for meeting the people who created Dean.

He took some deep breaths, clutched the stems of the bouquet tightly and checked that the gifts he had in the tote bag were all present and accounted for. They were. Dean walked straight into the house, he had a key, and he apparently didn't think they should knock.

"We're here!" Dean shouted. Jessica gestured for Cody to go next, so he nodded and stepped inside. The house smelled of fresh-baked bread and something smoky and delicious.

"Come in, we're in the kitchen!" A male voice called out.

"That's my dad," Dean said, nodding to Cody. He led the way to the kitchen.

The kitchen was some fifties confection of white and pink, with lots of cupboards and shelves above the countertops.

Dean's parents both stood in there. Cody swallowed hard as his heart pounded.

"This is Cody," Dean said. He tugged Cody forward by the upper arm.

Panicking, Cody thrust the flowers towards the woman, Dean's mother. She raised her eyebrows and smiled.

"Cody, these are my parents, Anne and Louis. Parents, meet Cody, he's my friend I've been telling you about."

"These are lovely, thank you. Welcome to our home."

Louis went to shake Cody's hand and then he kind of tilted his head, smiled, said 'aah' in a kind of knowing way and pulled Cody in for a hug. Cody hadn't expected that. He raised an arm to hug him back, the other stiff at his side, clutching his tote bag.

"Any, ah, *friend* of Dean's is welcome here anytime," Louis said. He squeezed Cody closer for a moment and then let him go.

Cody felt a flood of warmth course through him, prickling his veins. If this was what a normal family was like, he knew he'd been missing out.

"Thanks you," Cody said. Then Cody felt his eyes bug out, and he coughed, his throat thick. "Thanks. I mean, thank you. It's good to meet you."

Anne appeared beside Louis and wrapped her arms around Cody as well. He had to fight an overwhelming instinct to press himself tight against her and start crying. "You look hungry, Cody, I hope you like salmon. Louis has been smoking it all afternoon."

"Oh yes, salmon's great," Cody said. He tried not to be too awkward about the hug but trying not to be awkward just kind of ended up making it more awkward. It was a relief when Anne let go of him – he was afraid he was about to lose it.

"Thank you for the flowers, they're beautiful."

"Isn't he sweet?" Dean embraced his father and then his mother. Then Jessica was next on the hug queue. Cody moved back and set his tote down on a clear spot on the countertop.

"Yes, dear," Anne kissed Dean's cheek and then hugged Jessica. "Good to see you, love."

"How's the garden coming?" Jessica asked.

"Well, I've given up on everything that isn't a cactus," Anne sighed. "Come on out back and I'll show you."

"How're you going, Dad?" Dean asked. He went to give his father another hug.

Cody tried to remember the last time his own father had hugged him, but he couldn't. The combination of 'gay' and 'military' had been more than he was willing to accept, apparently. Maybe he'd hugged Cody when he was a kid, but since then? He couldn't think of a single hugging incident. He swallowed, but whatever was happening with the lump in his throat, he couldn't easily push it away.

"I'm great, son, but I have more dinner to prep. You get Cody a drink and make sure he's met everyone. We'll catch up a little later."

Dean turned to Cody with a comfortable smile. "What're you drinking?"

"Err, just something non-alcoholic, please," Cody said. He shoved his hands in his pockets and tried to look normal. How did people look when they were visiting and being normal?

"Did Meryl make lemonade, Dad?"

"She sure did, should be a couple pitchers in the fridge." Louis had turned back to where he was chopping vegetables. "What did Cody bring in that bag?"

Dean had already opened the fridge and he pulled out a big curved glass pitcher of lemonade. "I dunno. Cody, what's in the bag?"

"Oh, just some chocolates," Cody said. He pulled out the box. "You said the kids liked sweets, so I got a big box at the Enchanted Forest gift shop. I thought I'd… y'know." He looked at Dean's father and trailed off. Louis had such a kind face.

"Hype them up on sugar?" Dean asked, grinning.

"Bribe them?" Louis suggested, laughing.

"Yeah, bribe them," Cody said. He chuckled a little. "I'm not really used to kids."

"I thought you worked at Fairyland?" Louis raised his eyebrows.

"Yeah, in security," Cody said. "Most of the time I'm dealing with violent or rude grown- up people. The character guys are the ones interacting with the kids. Or people like Dean, running the rides." He rubbed the hair at the back of his head and shifted around a little. He still felt weird and tingly, but he was relaxing. He didn't feel like he had to watch what he said, too much.

"You don't have to bribe them, they're gonna love you," Dean said, beaming. His smile made Cody feel a little more confident. Louis's easy conversation made Cody feel – what? Comfortable? Or maybe just less nervous, like his baseline anxiety levels were dropping.

Dean handed him a tall glass of lemonade, clinking with ice.

"Thanks." Cody's pulse jumped a little when he brushed Dean's hand as he passed him the glass.

"C'mon, let's go find the kids so you can bribe them. Bring the chocolates," Dean said. "Abby! Alex!" He called out.

"I think they're out the back," Louis said.

Cody and Dean went out the back door to the yard where a picnic table stood, stacks of plates and cutlery piled on top ready for the feast.

Two children of about eight years old were climbing a tree, but they dropped down out of the branches when they saw Dean. "Dean! Did you bring us anything?" The girl asked, rushing up to them and looking up eagerly at her big brother. Cody took a step back, uncertain. What was an appropriate thing to say to an eight-year-old?

Dean knelt to hug her. "I brought you a Cody," he said, laughing. "And Jessica. I thought you liked Jessica, too."

"I do, but she's busy with Mom." Abby scrunched up her little button nose. She looked up at Cody. "Hello. I'm Abby. And this is Alex."

Alex hugged Dean and then looked shyly up at Cody.

The resemblance was clear - Alex and Abby both had the same sandy Dean hair, and their eyes were the same. It was like Cody was looking back through time at how Dean must've been as a kid.

"I heard you like sweet things," Cody said. He offered her the box of chocolates. "Do you like these?"

Abby looked the box over carefully and read the label before taking it off him with both hands. Her eyes grew so wide he thought they might pop out of her skull. "Wow! I haven't had this kind before, they look awesome!"

"Maybe you should say thank you?" Dean raised his eyebrows at his little sister.

Abby beamed up at Cody. "Thank you, Cody," she said sweetly.

"You're very welcome," Cody said. His chest flooded with warmth. He smiled at her and Alex, and Alex looked Cody up and down solemnly.

"Thank you, Cody. I like your flower shirt," Alex said. His voice wasn't as loud as his sister's. He seemed a little shyer all round.

"Thank you, Alex." Cody took a sip of lemonade and looked at Dean, still uncertain about what to say. Dean nodded at the kids, who raced off to where Anne and Jessica were contemplating a cactus as tall as Dean.

"All right, so far so good." Dean reached over to pat Cody's upper arm. "You want to sit down?"

"Um, sure," Cody said. Then he leaned a little closer to whisper. "Wait – what would you usually do?"

"I guess I'd sit down." Dean shrugged. "Or help, but it looked like Dad had all that under control."

A tall Gothy girl version of Dean appeared in the doorway and sauntered out into the backyard. She had a huge floppy brimmed black hat on over a short black lace dress and ankle boots. She raised a hand at Dean and Cody.

"Hi."

"Meryl, this is Cody," Dean said. "Cody, meet Meryl. She's the oldest after me."

Cody offered her his hand to shake and she looked at it with raised eyebrows before taking it in her fingers and shaking it once. "Charmed, I'm sure," she murmured.

Cody got the feeling that maybe she was acting up, trying to impress him. He nodded in response. He could be cool about it. He knew how to handle flirting. "Pleasure's all mine."

Dean smiled approvingly. "I knew you two would get on!"

Meryl and Cody exchanged a 'can you believe him?' look and then Cody grinned at Dean – probably ruining everything he'd just built with Meryl.

"I got chocolates for the little kids. If you like chocolates, they're over there," Cody said, nodding. Meryl glanced over and then sighed like she didn't really care.

"Maybe later. So," she flicked at the rim of her hat nonchalantly. "Dean said you have a motorbike?"

Cody grinned. Thank goodness, he finally had some familiar ground. He could talk about his bike all night, that was easy. He and Meryl chatted away about bikes as Dean listened, his eyes sparky – his smile never fading once.

Jacob came out shortly before dinner was ready, nodded hello to Cody and sat at the table, playing a mobile game. Cody took a sip of his newly replenished lemonade and sighed contentedly.

*I just have to stay on easy topics like this,* he thought. *And who knows? Hopefully the night will go smoothly and I won't make a fool of myself.*

DEAN'S HEART WAS WARM AND FULL OF HAPPINESS. SEEING CODY sitting next to his mother at dinner and hearing the two of them talking about their units and their favorite experiences was a dream come true. Dean tried not to just creepily watch them the whole time, but it was hard. He was so excited to see them getting on.

Meryl nudged Dean while their father was telling a story over dessert. "Hey," she whispered. Dean leaned towards her.

"Yeah?"

"How single is he?"

"Meryl, no! You're jailbait. You can't even *think* about that," Dean said. His heart instantly started speeding. No way his little sister was going to flirt with Cody. *No way.*

"Eww, okay. I just think he's a snack, that's all." Meryl pouted.

"He is gorgeous, you're right," Dean hissed back. "But stop thinking about him like that, please."

Meryl gave a long-suffering sigh and rolled her eyes. Jessica, who was sitting on Dean's other side, was watching him.

"What?" Dean asked, leaning towards her now. She leaned in and pressed her mouth almost to his ear. Her breath tickled him a little and he bit his bottom lip to stifle a giggle.

"How into him *are* you? Be honest, now."

"Shut up," Dean whispered, throwing in a glare for good measure. "Behave, you."

Jessica sat back with a smile, shaking her head. Dean looked over to see Cody watching him with a strange expression. It was a sort of desolate look, which evaporated as soon as he saw Dean was looking at him. Dean's stomach dropped a little. Cody turned to say something to Anne and they shared a laugh. Whatever he'd just glimpsed in Cody's face was raw, visceral, and it made him want to do anything he could to make Cody happy again.

When dessert was finished, Dean stood up to collect the plates and stack them. Anne stood to help, but Dean waved her down. "I got this."

Cody stood and started taking the large platters with the leftover chocolate-covered strawberries and brownies. Abby snatched a piece of brownie as he lifted it, and Cody gave her a warm smile and a wink.

"You shouldn't be doing that, you're our guest!" Louis said. But Anne put her hand on his arm.

"If Cody wants to help, he can help," Anne said. "That is, assuming Dean will let him."

"Cody can help." Dean felt a little fluttering in his stomach as he took the plates inside to the kitchen. Then he set them gently down next to the sink and started rinsing them. He intentionally didn't look up when he heard Cody come in behind him – he just focused on the water and the traces of food going down the drain.

"Your family's really great," Cody said. Dean smiled and looked up at him.

"They are, right?" Dean turned and scrubbed the platter of the last few bits of dessert. He picked up a chocolate strawberry and toyed with the stem of it, he felt impulsive, flushed with the success of the night. "They adore you. Maybe a little too much in Meryl's case, but hey."

"I like them a lot, too," Cody said. He moved in closer to the sink, slipping a hand past Dean to place the serving spoons into the water. He was close – so close Dean felt a heated tingle curl up his spine.

"You want a strawberry?" He asked. His heart pounded louder and he smiled up at Cody, feeling wild and shy all at the same time. He never did things like this. But he was so happy and excited.

Cody swallowed, his eyes on the berry and then on Dean's hand holding it. Dean offered it to him, holding it higher, pressing it towards Cody's lips. Cody's lips were obscenely luscious this close-up.

"I-I can't," Cody stuttered. He took a step back. "I don't want to–" he broke off, looking at Dean helplessly, his eyes wide.

"You can't what? It's just a berry, you were eating them just before."

"No, I mean… I can't. I can't do *this*," Cody turned and picked up the leftover platters, putting them in the fridge. As he headed back outside, Dean was left in the kitchen still holding the strawberry. His eyes prickled and his vision blurred and rippled. A single tear plopped down into the sink.

*What just happened? What did I do wrong?*

Everything got much quieter once the little kids were sent to bed. Jessica and Dean went inside, too – into the kitchen to make tea and coffee. Cody settled in beside Anne. He felt surprisingly relaxed. Almost like he'd had a drink or two, although he'd only had Meryl's lemonade.

*It's easy to be around Anne.*

Her service might have been a few more decades behind her than Cody's was, but she understood. And aside from that he genuinely liked her. She was funny and warm. He could plainly see how much she cared for each of her children.

"Thanks for tonight," Cody said to her, quietly. "Dinner was amazing."

"I'm very glad you came." Anne gave Cody a warm smile that reminded him of Dean. "Dean thinks the world of you, you know."

Cody looked away, down at his feet. "I'm sure I don't know why," he said. He didn't feel at all worthy of Dean's admiration or Anne's gentle care.

"You're a good man," Anne said. "I can see it, and so can Dean."

Up until that moment, Cody had successfully pushed the image of Dean offering him a chocolate-covered strawberry out of his head. But, in a flash as clear as the sun on the Reflecting Lake, there it was. Dean all innocent and cute. Offering to hand feed him what had to be the most romantic food in the universe.

No matter what Dash had suggested at the gym, he couldn't tell Dean how he felt. Not after an incident like that. He still had the girlfriend after all and he probably had no idea he was even giving off sexy vibes to Cody.

"Mo-om!" The call came from upstairs and sounded like it was Abby. Anne shook her head and pushed herself up out of the deckchair.

"Please excuse me," Anne said. "I have to take care of some brats."

"Of course," Cody said. He was relieved he didn't have to respond to her 'good man' statement. He smiled at her and she disappeared into the house.

He looked around the darkened yard. Dean had reappeared with drinks and was talking to his father. Jacob and Meryl were squabbling, but Meryl had kept half an eye on Cody the whole night. She caught Cody's eye, smiled and stood up.

"–Oof," Jessica sat down in the chair Anne had just vacated. Meryl frowned and sat back down next to Jacob.

"Hey, Jessica," Cody was certain Jessica had just saved him from an uncomfortable moment. Meryl was sweet, but she was also quite full-on. Jessica handed him a bottle of beer, which he took gratefully. He hadn't been drinking – mainly because it hadn't seemed like a good idea after the whole bar incident – but, one cold one would hit the spot perfectly. "So. How's the evening going?" She clinked her beer bottle against his and they both drank.

"Good," Cody said. "They're all really lovely people."

"They really are," Jessica agreed. She looked around a little. "I meant what I said in the car, they're like my family away from home. If I miss my ma, I come 'round here and get a fix." She chuckled a little.

Cody smiled too. It was a nice thought, to have a family like this. One that was just *there* when you needed them. "So, uhh, how long have you and Dean been together?"

Cody's watched as Jessica's eyes slowly widened and suddenly he had a sinking feeling. She took a big swig of beer and then grinned widely. "So *that's* the problem!" She'd exclaimed it, loudly, and Cody looked around nervously to see if the others had heard.

"W-what's the problem?"

"You think Dean and I are *together*?" She laughed and shook her head. "No way! He's my friend, that's all. And he's bi, just in case you need more information."

Cody downed half his beer. "Bi as in…?"

"Bisexual, you ass. You want me to draw you a diagram?"

Cody's stomach dropped away. He felt like it was one of those moments in a movie where the director uses a dolly zoom, zooming in hard on the character's face as the world shoots away behind them.

His mouth still felt parched. "What did you just say?"

Jessica leaned in and grinned at him. "Dean is single, and bi, and he thinks you're incredible. If you've been holding back this whole time because you thought he and I were a thing? Well, we're not a thing. Now fucking go and boink him already so he stops torturing me about how much he likes you, all right?"

Cody swallowed. He couldn't process this. "But… but you two, you're always together. And you were kissing his neck during dinner."

"I was?" Jessica giggled. "Well that's news to me. Ohhh, I know what you saw, I was whispering to him. About how good-looking you are actually, you gigantic doofus."

Cody drained his beer bottle dry and in the time it took to do that, his brain had caught up with what she was telling him.

*Dean is single. And queer. And into me.*

*There's no reason I can't go full seduction mode.*

Well, except that they were literally surrounded by Dean's family right now.

"You're serious?" He said, finally. "You're not like, setting me up for a three-way or something?"

Jessica snorted. "Uhh, no. Kissing Dean doesn't do it for me.

We tried it once and it was about as stimulating as kissing a dish towel. He's into you, boyo, though I can guess it'd be hard to tell because he's nice to everyone." She leaned back and shook out her hair.

Cody nodded. What was it about today that everyone could see he needed help? He was glad of it, because heaven knows how long he would've thought Jessica and Dean were together without someone spelling it out to him like that. No wonder Dean hadn't invited Jessica to the dinner to start with.

And he'd insisted she come along, like a weirdo. He held his forehead against the cool glass of the beer bottle.

"Great. Okay, good information to have. Thank you," Cody said. He made to get up, but Jessica put a hand on his arm.

"Hey, just before you do something rash," she started. He sat back down and looked at Jessica quizzically.

"I mean, you're the one who just told me to boink him, I think. And now you're saying don't be rash?" He grinned at her. He couldn't help it. He felt an outrageous amount of excitement bubbling inside him. It was all he could do to stop himself from giggling like a little kid meeting Princess Honesty for the first time.

"Yes, but also, don't break his heart, okay?"

"I wasn't planning on it." A little of his excitement died down as he realized how serious this was. Dean had a lot of people who cared for him, he wore his heart on his sleeve, and Cody was no Prince Valor.

"Right, but like… don't just think of him as a short-term fling or whatever," Jessica leaned in, one hand on his arm, gently squeezing his bicep. "He's a gold star magical pixie dream boy, and you've got to treat him like one. Like sunbeams shoot out of his fingertips. You got that?"

"I…" Cody tilted his head. "A pixie dream boy?"

"A *magical* pixie dream boy," Jessica corrected. She nodded solemnly. "So, you'd better be in as in love with him as I think you are. Or I revoke my order for boinking."

"Please stop saying boinking," Cody wished his beer bottle

would refill itself, his throat was scratchy and he was far too sober for this particular conversation. "But I hear you. And I am into him, and I don't want to hurt him." He made eye contact, so she'd see how much he meant these next words. "The idea of Dean hurting is abhorrent to me. I want him to be happy, and if I can make that happen then I will do everything I can to do it."

"Good," Jessica sat back with a smug smile. "Now for the love of Heaven, please go and tell him that?"

Cody nodded and got up off the chair. He was halfway to where Dean sat with his father before he lost nerve. He made it to sit down beside Dean but he and his father were deep in conversation about college and what Dean may or may not try out.

*I can't interrupt him while he's talking with his father about his future. That's way too important. And totally has nothing to do with the fact that my heart is beating out of my chest right now.*

Soon, it was time to leave, and Cody hadn't managed to get Dean alone. He kept catching Jessica giving him stern 'go on' looks, but he didn't want to be rude and pull Dean away from his family. And he also didn't 100% know what to say.

Should he just blurt it out? That he wanted to be Dean's boyfriend? It felt so weird even to be thinking about that at Dean's parent's place.

When he finally left, everyone hugged Cody. Even Jacob, who Cody had said very few words to all night, gave him a one-armed, back-patting hug.

Louis embraced him warmly. "Come back any time. I mean it. You're always welcome here, with or without Dean," he said.

"Thanks, Louis," And the tingle in Cody's chest let him know that Louis really *did* mean it.

Anne enclosed Cody in a bear hug, her strong arms pulling him close. "You're a good man," she whispered to him. "And you're going to be alright. Just give it time."

Cody returned the hug with equal ferocity, feeling tears well up, which rarely happened to him. He swallowed them down and breathed out heavily.

"Thank you, Anne."

Anne and Louis waved from the door as they piled into Jessica's car and she started driving them off. The car was silent for a moment before Dean half turned to Cody in the back seat.

"You have a good night?"

"Yeah," Cody said. "I really did. Your family's lovely."

Jessica met Cody's eyes in the rearview mirror. She widened her eyes and raised her eyebrows. He shook his head slightly at her. Now wasn't the time to say something to Dean about his feelings. And Jessica's insistence wasn't making it any easier.

"They are, right?" Dean sat back. A contented silence permeated the car for a couple of minutes. Then Jessica sighed loudly. "Are you okay?" Dean asked her.

"Yeah, just tired," she cleared her throat and flicked her eyes back to Cody again.

"I'm not tired at all," Cody said. "I was thinking we could have another drink or something. At my place, maybe?"

"Sure," Dean said.

"I think I'll leave you two to it," Jessica smiled. "I can drop you both at Cody's and you can have a nice night together."

"Oh, I don't want to put you out," Dean turned again, biting down on his bottom lip.

"It's fine," Cody said. "You're welcome to come up."

Jessica dropped them off and Cody realized with a flash of terror as she drove off that Dean was about to see his place. His place was so tiny compared to Dean's. And compared to his parent's place it was both tiny *and* pathetic.

"Actually, maybe we should go to your place." Cody shoved his hands in his pockets.

Dean looked at the building and then at Cody. He wrapped his arms around himself, as a cool breeze hit them. "I'd like to see your place," he said. "But if you'd rather I just went home that's cool, too."

Cody's heart thumped. Now that Jessica was gone, things were starting to feel awkward. "No, I don't want you to go home."

"L-listen, I'm sorry about the kitchen," Dean blurted.

"The kitchen?"

"I was. I…" Dean broke off, embarrassed, and then raised his chin to look Cody in the eyes. "I thought I was getting a vibe, and I went for it, but I guess I was wrong. And I'm sorry."

"You weren't wrong," Cody's heart sped up and he took a breath. This was almost as bad as trying to ride the damned roller coaster. "I was wrong about… about a couple of things, and I didn't know I was wrong, then. In the kitchen."

Dean frowned. "I don't understand."

"Let's just go inside," Cody sighed. "I'm sorry about my house. I'm just gonna say that now. Up front."

He led the way into the building and Dean followed, his arms still wrapped around himself for warmth. In the elevator, Cody swiped his keycard and punched the floor number and then turned to Dean.

"Dean, I thought – I thought you and Jessica were together," he said.

Dean's eyes widened. "What? We're not, though, we're just friends."

"Well, I know that now," Cody said. He moved closer to him, his heart pounding in his ears. Dean's arms tightened around himself on instinct, as if he were afraid of Cody getting too close. But his eyes were wide, his pupils blown. His lips parted.

In… anticipation?

He was leaning back against the wall and Cody had the urge to plant his hand beside his head, lean in and kiss him hard. But before he could the elevator dinged, and the doors opened for them.

Cody huffed and turned, every inch of his body on edge as he led the way down the hall to his apartment. He could hear Dean's footsteps behind him, hurrying to keep up.

He unlocked the door and went in, switched on the light, and turned back to Dean. "I'm sorry. It's not much," he said.

Dean walked in and looked around. "It's fine, I mean, it's nice," he said, his voice a little cracked and husky.

"It's small," Cody shrugged. He was pleased that was it clean at least – he didn't have enough stuff to make a mess, but he had left a couple of dress shirts over a chair, discards from when he'd been choosing which one to wear tonight.

"It *is* small." Dean looked at the shirts on the chair and then at Cody. "Where do you sleep?"

"The bed folds into the wall," he said, nodding at it.

"Right." Dean swallowed and nodded. "Right."

Cody felt all his mojo deflate some. How could he seduce Dean now? He was obviously confused and feeling pity and who knows what else about him now that he'd seen his apartment.

"What was that you were saying in the lift? About Jessica?" Dean said, turning back to Cody. He stuck his hands in his pockets like he was trying too hard to be nonchalant.

Cody looked at him and his heart skipped.

*Maybe I could try something.*

But before he could work out the next move, Dean was slouching a little closer into him.

"And if you had known, what would be different?" He smiled shyly – an unusual smile on Dean.

"I guess I would've…" Cody licked his lips and moved closer. "I would've eaten that strawberry."

"Y-you would have?" Dean blinked up at Cody, his lips staying slightly parted.

*Damn, his eyelashes are beautiful. Look at that face…*

"Would you have done anything else?"

Cody swallowed the lump in his throat. "Yeah, I would have asked if it was okay to kiss you way, way sooner than now."

Dean's eyes were shiny. He bit his lower lip and Cody wanted nothing more to bite it for him. He swallowed.

"I'd really like to kiss you, if that's okay, Dean." Cody breathed. He felt tingles shooting all over his body. He moved in closer and inhaled, smelling the barbecue, the tea and the sugar of Dean.

"Y-yeah. Yes, I mean." Dean leaned in and closed his eyes.

Cody closed the distance between them and, finally, kissed him softly.

Dean's lips were warm and soft, and he tasted like sugar cookies. Cody's blood thundered in his ears, and he pressed harder, slipping a hand around Dean's waist and pulling him closer.

Dean moaned softly, opening his mouth and inviting him in with his tongue.

It was delicious. Cody's whole body relaxed as Dean's arms wrapped around his neck and they kissed and kissed until Cody had no choice but to pull back for air.

Dean chuckled and Cody did, too, lifting his hand to touch the angle of Dean's jaw. His skin was so soft – like he'd never grown a beard. Maybe he couldn't. It didn't matter. Beard or no, Dean was the most beautiful person he knew.

"Was… was that all you were going to ask?" Dean's voice was breathy. Cody's stomach twisted, whirling with excitement.

"Maybe not." Cody cleared his throat. "Do you – would you like to stay the night?"

Dean paused. "You go to fast for me, Cody," he breathed.

"I mean, no pressure," Cody said. He pulled back a little to look Dean in the eye and check he was okay.

Dean nodded. "Um, assuming two of us can fit on your bed."

"It's horrible, isn't it? You can just say you hate it," Cody laughed a little, feeling giddy instead of embarrassed. "Do you want to go to your place?"

"I… no. No, I'm happy here, if you're here, and you want to kiss again."

"Kiss, yes." Cody mentally classified his program for the night from R18 to just PG. "Kissing would be great."

With that, he leaned in and kissed him again, this time aiming for the downy fuzz in the corner of his mouth and daring to reach up and touch his hair. It was softer than he'd imagined. Dean had softness all about him – his hair and his jaw and his face – but his body was all hard angles and tension.

Cody pulled back and turned to look at the kitchen bench. He had to – before he lost his head.

"Would you like something to drink? I have beer or whiskey?"

"Just water is fine," Dean said. He touched Cody's waist and Cody looked back to see him smiling. "I'm sorry, it's just… We only just like, said things and kissed. I don't want to, like, get drunk and fuck because I'm scared you'd be gone in the morning and I'd never see you again."

"I don't mind taking this slow," Cody said, and he meant it. More than anything he wanted for Dean to be happy. And if Dean was happy kissing him and sleeping in the bed beside him? Then Cody was over the moon. "Dean, you're… amazing. I just want you to be happy."

"I'm happy, are *you* happy?" A single crease formed between Dean's eyebrows.

Cody went to the kitchen and poured a glass of water for Dean. He handed it to him with a smile. "Honestly? I'm just ecstatic you kissed me back."

DEAN DIDN'T THINK THERE WAS ANY EARTHLY WAY HE COULD possibly sleep, since his heart was racing and all he wanted to do was press himself against Cody and kiss him for hours.

Cody's body was so warm. He was so warm and so well-muscled. They changed into pajamas, or what Cody used for pajamas since he didn't seem to have any proper ones. Cody had given Dean a pair of soft, clean gym shorts and an Air Force Training Academy T-shirt. It was loose on Dean's chest and he licked his lips as he imagined the muscles that usually filled it out.

Dean changed while Cody used the bathroom, and then Cody changed while Dean did. Cody had brought the bed down out of the wall and was taking his prosthetic leg off when Dean quietly emerged, and Dean watched him for a moment. Cody wore a similar T-shirt to Dean's, and a pair of boxer briefs with longer-than-normal legs. Still, it showed off a lot of his thighs. Dean focused on the prosthetic instead.

"Can I help?" Dean asked.

"No, it's fine," Cody said. "I'm used to it." He looked up at Dean. "You don't have to watch, if it makes you uncomfortable."

"It doesn't," Dean moved closer and sat down beside Cody. "I think it's a really neat leg."

"A really neat leg?" Cody raised an eyebrow and looked over at him. He laughed and set it aside. "Really?"

Dean gave him a toothy grin. "Sorry, I guess I'm nervous."

*Nervous is an understatement. God, he's going to think I'm a total idiot, and he'd be right. I'm not handling this well. I'm making it more awkward.*

"You don't have to be. You can ask anything you want. I give you permission, just this once," Cody said.

"No, I don't... I don't need to know, unless you have something you particularly want to share."

Cody shook his head and scooted back up the bed, patting the mattress beside him. "Not really. Although I should probably warn you that sometimes I have nightmares and thrash around."

"I think I can cope with that," Dean moved up to settle in beside Cody on the bed. "Is there something I can do that would help, if that happens?"

Cody didn't reply right away. Dean sneaked a sidelong glance at him and saw he was considering.

"I don't know, I guess... I usually wake myself up from them so don't freak out. I don't want to lash out at you instinctively so like, don't grab onto my arm or anything." Cody's voice was soft and uncertain and Dean realized with a warm glow that this was the most vulnerable he'd ever seen him.

Dean nodded. "That makes sense. Do you think if I rubbed your back that might help?"

Cody shrugged a shoulder. "No one's ever done that for me, I don't know. Maybe?"

Dean inhaled, feeling suddenly like he might cry if he wasn't careful.

*Time for a change of subject. This is getting awkward and emotional.*

"The bed's quite comfortable, isn't it?"

"Your guest bed was nicer," Cody said. Dean reached out and took Cody's hand, squeezing it.

"I can't believe you thought me and Jessica were together," he sighed, thinking of how different things could have been. How much easier they could have been, if he'd just told Cody how he felt outright.

Cody cleared his throat. "Have you ever actually paid

attention to any of the pictures you send me?" He asked. He squeezed Dean's hand back. His palms were rough, his skin harder than Dean's. But that was probably to be expected.

"Um, I guess not," Dean said. He wasn't sure what to do to get rid of this awkwardness between them. A flash of fear sped through his tummy. Had he ruined things by saying he didn't want to go further tonight? Or was it just that neither of them knew what to do next?

He looked over at Cody, who was staring at the ceiling, his body tense.

Dean exhaled, hesitated, not at all sure if this would help or not, but he wanted to try. He shifted closer to Cody, scooched down the bed a little and cuddled in, resting his head on his shoulder. Cody moved his arm around his back.

"I-is this okay?" Dean asked.

"Yeah, this is good," Cody sighed gently, almost dreamy. He reached up with his other hand and turned off the light.

Being this close to Cody, smelling his sweat, and whatever he used in his hair, and the clean laundry scent of his shirt… all of it together had a calming effect on Dean. He was excited as Hell to be there with Cody. To be feeling how warm his body felt, pressed against his own. To have kissed him. To hope that there'd be more kisses – that is, if Dean hadn't entirely freaked him out or frustrated him – but overall? He just felt safe.

*Wait – was 'safe' something I didn't usually feel? I didn't think that I was walking around feeling unsafe. But with Cody's arm around me, and his body right there, his chest under my cheek, I feel like nothing could ever hurt me.*

And even with his brain still jumping around excitedly, he fell asleep within minutes.

Dean slept deeply and probably wouldn't have woken up for hours, except for a phone beeping. His alarm? No, his alarm didn't sound like that. And it certainly didn't sound like annoyed grumbling.

Cody stirred beside him, extracting an arm from under Dean's neck where he'd been using it as a pillow. Dean made a sad whimpering noise, without even meaning to. He swallowed it down, mortified. He hadn't even known that he could make noises like that – especially in the company of a big, sexy man he wanted to do more than sleep next to some time.

He felt Cody run his hand through his hair gently, then Cody sat up and the beeping stopped.

"Ahh, fuck," Cody's voice was rough with sleep. It made Dean shiver slightly.

Dean rolled over and forced his eyes open. "What is it?"

Cody turned his head and gave him the warmest, most affectionate looking smile Dean had ever seen on his face, which did things to Dean's stomach, making him feel all warm and treasured.

"It's Lennon. I have to go," Cody hung his head. "I'm really sorry, I can drop you home?"

"Isn't it Sunday?" Dean asked. He was going to say more but a huge yawn consumed him.

"It is Sunday. But there's been some complication with the shift workers for the Halloween parade, they need me to go and sort it out. Everyone needs confirmed schedules before work on Monday, so…"

"Oh," Dean nodded. "Okay, yeah." He tried to smile but he was still mourning the loss of morning cuddles, Cody stroking his hair and the possibility of making breakfast pancakes. Or even the chance to talk through what had happened and what was going to happen next – he couldn't exactly ask Cody if they were boyfriends while he was clinging to him on the back of the motorbike.

Cody bent forward, fastening his prosthetic leg. "Sorry," He said. Like he had heard Dean's thoughts and shared his sadness.

"It's fine," Dean yawned again.

*Man, I must've been deep asleep.*

"I guess you could always just come to the park with me?"

Cody sat back up and looked at Dean, twisting at the waist to face him. Dean bit his lip.

It'd be really nice to spend some more time with Cody – of course it would – but he couldn't help but feel he'd be in the way. Plus, if he just lay down again, he'd be right back to sleep and that would be really, *really* nice. Sleep was good.

"No, it's okay. The park is always packed on the weekend, anyway," Dean said. "You can just drop me home."

Cody ruffled his hair again, like Dean was a friendly puppy or something. Dean didn't hate the feeling, though. It felt really nice. Then Cody went to the bathroom.

"This is not how I saw this morning going," Cody called out from the bathroom.

"Neither, but that's okay," Dean replied. He shuffled off the bed and changed out of the pajamas Cody had loaned him and into his clothes from last night. He was just pulling his shirt back on when Cody walked in.

"What did *you* imagine this morning would be like?" Cody asked, grinning. He was ogling Dean's chest. Dean took a little longer than necessary to get his shirt in place.

"Pancakes," Dean said. "And snuggles. And kisses."

"Snuggles?" Cody laughed a little. He moved in close to where Dean was standing, put his arm around his waist and kissed him. Dean threw his arms around his neck again, instantly, like they knew that's where they were supposed to be.

Cody's phone beeped again.

Dean breathed out and let go of him.

"Sorry," Cody said. "Raincheck?"

"Yeah, sounds good." Dean went to use the bathroom and brush his teeth while Cody got changed. But, wait... it'd be weird to use Cody's toothbrush though, right? He checked in the cupboard and carefully didn't read the labels on the medicine bottles. No spare toothbrush. He squirted a little toothpaste on his finger, rubbed it over his teeth and rinsed.

He emerged to see Cody in his work security polo and black

pants, pulling on his leather jacket. Dean's knees went all weak. Cody was like a bad boy fantasy come to life.

*And he wants to kiss me!*

Dean grinned like an idiot. He didn't need anything else this morning. As long as he had a raincheck for more kissing later, he was happy.

The bike ride was just as thrilling as last time, possibly even more so because now Dean felt like he had permission to hold on extra tight and slip his fingers under Cody's leather jacket. He pressed the pads of his fingers against Cody's abs through the soft fabric of his polo shirt. He pressed his cheek against the shoulder of the leather jacket.

And he felt like the luckiest man on the planet.

Dean's fingers under his jacket were distracting to say the least. Cody was flushed hot, and feeling a tug between his legs, which the bike just amplified with its vibrations. It was all he could manage to not pull to the side of the road and push Dean against a wall, kissing him so hard their mouths bruised.

He just tried to ignore it instead, but Dean's fingers kept moving.

*Damn. Probably doesn't even realize he's doing it.*

When he pulled up at Dean's apartment, he didn't get off the bike – he didn't trust that his pants weren't bulging and it didn't seem gentlemanly, somehow. Dean hovered a little, saying goodbye. After he'd driven off, Cody realized he probably was hoping Cody would take off his helmet for a goodbye kiss. Ahh well. It was too late by the time he realized.

Cody walked into the airlock just as Prince Magnificence and Princess Constance were heading out with their handlers. He stepped out of the way, since Constance's dress was a gigantic confection of yellow silk with swirly white flowers woven into the fabric. The skirt was a little bigger than the one on Princess Honesty's dress, which he knew was a point of contention between the women playing the roles.

That wasn't his problem, though. He just had to get out of the way of the skirts and then inside the Airlock.

"Morning, Cody!" Lennon called as Cody walked in.

"Hey, you came in, too?" He grabbed a breakfast coke from the vending machine and went to join Lennon at the table, where they'd laid out stacks of papers. They were looking stressed.

Francisco appeared moments later with a tray of coffees from the Enchanted Forest Kitchen. "I figured we could all use a pick-me-up this early on a Sunday," he said, setting the coffees down.

Lennon took one and sat back, sighing. "I'm really sorry about calling you both in today," they said. "We have some pretty solid advice that Max Jones is going to be at the park this week, maybe even as early as tomorrow, so everyone's panicking."

Francisco cleared his throat. "Someone remind me why we care so much what this guy sees?" He cracked open his coffee lid to add some sugar to it.

"Because he's going to own it – the entire place," Cody said. He drained his coke in a few short gulps and picked up a coffee. He could use all the caffeine he could get his hands on.

"Well, no matter what we do, he's going to want to make changes. To put his stamp on the park," Lennon said. "That's a given. But what we *don't* know is where he'll make those changes. If our section of the park runs beautifully, then it won't be the obvious choice."

"Changes can be good, though, right?" Cody said, frowning. "What if he wants to pump a whole lot of money into the area and we all get more to do?"

"Right. And what if he decides that the Enchanted Forest is outdated and needs to be leveled to make room for a new virtual reality roller coaster?" Lennon fired back. "I'm not sure I'd want to take that chance."

"A virtual reality roller coaster *does* sounds really fun," Francisco said. He looked up from stirring sugar into his coffee and raised his eyebrows – then slumped in his chair when Lennon gave him a death glare. "Sorry. I follow now, thanks."

"So. I have everyone's availability for the week," Lennon said. "We'll need more staff on than what we'd normally have and it's a puzzle to get them all to work out. Cody, Francisco, I need you to match up the people who work best together. And tell me who shouldn't be anywhere near each other, too. That way we can sort the ultimate teams for the week. It shouldn't take too long."

They got down to work.

Three hours later, they had a schedule that worked for the next month and Cody had a pounding headache.

"Okay, that's it for today. Thanks, you two. Let's get out of here," Lennon said. They closed their laptop, shuffled their papers into a folder and dumped the lot into a Treasure the Unicorn shoulder bag.

Cody picked up his phone. He had two messages from Dean. One was him kissing the camera with a slogan *'thinking of you'* over the picture, and the other was him in bed, covers pulled up to his shoulders, head on the pillow and a contented smile on his face. He'd written *'nap time'* on that one.

Cody smiled and texted back.

Finally finished.

"Want to get some lunch?" Francisco asked. Cody nodded. His stomach had been rumbling for the last hour, but they'd been so close to cracking the schedule that he hadn't wanted to say anything.

"Forest Kitchen? Intergalactic Diner? Somewhere else?" Francisco asked.

"Forest Kitchen," Cody said. "It's closer and it won't be as busy."

Sure enough, they got a table at the kitchen, close to the counter, and didn't have to wait too long in the queue for food.

As Cody was ordering he heard a familiar voice.

"Our new batch is ready! New designs!"

Nate's friend Charlie came around to the front counter and set down a huge basket of Halloween cookies. These ones featured the Fairyland Castle but in purple and orange, and weird haunted-looking trees.

"Hey, Charlie," Cody said. He picked up a couple of cookies. "These are really, really good."

Charlie blinked at him, then saw the staff ID and 'security' emblazoned over Cody's chest. "You're Cody, right? Nate's told me about you. And I've seen you around."

"Yeah, I watched you tell Dash off once," Cody said with a grin. He may not have talked to Charlie before, but he had mad respect for him for intervening with Dash.

Charlie grinned back. "Didn't he need it, though?"

"Can't argue with that. Charlie, this is Francisco," Cody said. Francisco and Charlie nodded at each other.

"How's your love life going?" Charlie asked. "Need me to tell someone off for you? I can be very persuasive."

"Nah, I'm good," Cody said. "I just started something last night, I think."

Francisco made a surprised noise. "Y-you did?"

"Oops," Charlie said, grinning. "Sounds like someone's disappointed. Awkward." Charlie's eyes shifted from Cody to Francisco. Cody's stomach twisted in a giant knot.

"Anyway. What're you eating? Actually, you know what? Never mind, you two can be my guinea pigs. No charge. Go sit." Charlie shoved a table number at them and bustled off.

"*Are* you disappointed?" Cody asked Francisco as they sat down again.

*Sure, he'd been flirting with me a bit, but I didn't think he was really serious, after all he flirts with everyone.*

Francisco shrugged. "A little, but I was trying to play it cool, so I can't complain if you've found someone else in the meantime."

"It'd be all kinds of wrong for you and me," Cody said, although he did feel flattered that Francisco had been thinking of him like that. "I mean, I'm your boss."

"Only temporarily," Francisco said. "But it doesn't matter, I'll find someone else."

"Yeah you will." Cody said. He picked up his phone, but there was nothing from Dean. He was probably still asleep.

Charlie brought them two trays laden with food. It all smelled incredible and Cody's stomach rumbled in anticipation.

"So, what we have here is the experimental new menu. I'm hoping to roll it out once I get the head chef's approval," Charlie said. "Roast lamb with house-made mint jelly, extra-crispy roast potatoes and seasonal vegetables. There's a dinner roll with smoked butter – and for dessert, either a cinnamon and apple cake or spiced creme caramel. You can fight over who gets what."

"*Dios mia*, this looks incredible!" Francisco said. His eyes were as wide as saucers. "Thank you."

"Don't thank me, just give me honest feedback," Charlie said. "Once you're done, I mean. I'm not gonna hover around while you eat, that'd be weird. Enjoy!"

He and Cody exchanged nods and then Charlie strode back to the kitchen. The confidence of a man who knew he'd just laid some delicious food down and was waiting to be praised.

"So, what's this about your love life. Give me the intel," Francisco gave Cody a conspiratorial smile and started eating.

Cody frowned at his lamb. He didn't want to say too much when he himself wasn't exactly sure what the deal was. "I – I don't think there's any details to give, really," he shrugged.

"Then how about you just tell me what happened?" He cut himself some lamb, popped it in his mouth and groaned with happiness. "It actually tastes better than it smells, if you can believe it."

Cody looked up at Francisco. He wasn't exactly the type to gossip, well, not about his own life anyway. But Francisco was clearly offering an olive branch, trying to smooth over the awkwardness and be friends. Cody could appreciate that. He just had to open up a little.

*I just have to say some words, right? I should do that.*

He took another mouthful of lamb that practically melted in his mouth and swallowed. "Mm-hmm, that is delicious."

Francisco was watching him. He raised his eyebrows.

"Well, his name's Dean."

"Ahh. The boy you've been texting?"

"Yes, the boy I've been – how did you know about that?" Cody ate some more lamb. It was really, *really* good. Tender and a little smoky. He moaned softly.

"You've been texting him a lot, and I'm not blind," Francisco said. "Go on."

"Well, I thought he was dating this girl, but I found out last night that they're just friends. I went to dinner at his parent's house. Met the whole family."

"Intense," Francisco said. "I usually put the whole 'meet the family' step off as long as I can."

"I thought we were just friends. I mean, we *are* friends. Then I found out that him and this girl aren't together and we kissed." Cody wolfed a crispy potato. "And he stayed over at my house."

"There it is!" Francisco grinned and gave a little whoop. Cody hushed him, his cheeks burning, and looked around to see if anyone was looking at them. As far as he could tell the only person watching was Charlie, and he was mostly looking excited about the food.

"Nothing *happened*," Cody said, turning back to Francisco. "He wants to take it slow, so we just slept."

"Still, sleeping and cuddling is nice," Francisco said. "How long has it been?"

Cody thought about the feeling of Dean's warm body beside him in his bed. The way he'd slept peacefully, no nightmares or even vaguely stressful dreams. He hadn't woken at weird times in the early morning. And he'd still had his arm around Dean when his phone had gone off.

"Far too long."

"Ahh, look at you," Francisco said. He shook his head, smiling. "You totally have it bad for this boy."

Cody ducked his face, embarrassed, but unable to stop the goofy grin slowly spreading across his face.

*Francisco is right. I do have it bad.*

Charlie, who despite his assurances otherwise had been hovering close by, finally hustled over. "I'm sorry, I can't stand it," He said, worrying his bottom lip. "How's the food?"

"It's… amazing." Cody speared a potato on his fork and took a bite. "Absolutely mind-blowing. I'd like seconds, please."

"The best I've tasted in the park," Francisco agreed. He even kissed his fingers to emphasize the point.

Charlie breathed out and his whole body relaxed. "Oh, that's such a relief! Yeah, that's what I thought. Okay. Keep in touch about the desserts." He practically danced back into the kitchen.

"Well, I'm happy for you," Francisco said. "And just know I'm still around, if things don't work out with the cute texting boy." He gave Cody a subtle wink.

Cody hesitated before swiping his last bit of lamb through Charlie's mint jelly. He wasn't sure he wanted that pressure.

DEAN WOKE UP FROM HIS NAP FEELING LIKE HE WAS WAKING UP TO A new world. A world of opportunities he hadn't realized existed.

He was full of possibilities.

He sat up and looked around his bedroom, wondering what to do with this feeling. Jumping out of bed, he started with tidying. He put all his dirty clothes into the hamper, all the dirty cups into the kitchen sink and vacuumed the floors. He even cleared the top of one of his low shelves so that if Cody were to stay over, he'd have a place to put his leg.

That done, he went to check his phone, but he hadn't charged it overnight at Cody's. Then he'd fallen asleep with it on the bed beside him and hadn't plugged it in, so it was quite dead. He finally started charging it and went to take a shower.

Halfway to the shower, Dean stopped. He had too much energy to waste time washing himself or just wait around for Cody to be done with work. And he didn't want to sit around the house at all, either. He wanted to get out into the world.

So, he pulled on his workout clothes, dug out his old iPod and headphones and did something he rarely did, ever. He went for a run.

To start with, Dean felt amazing. He was out in the sunshine, in the fresh air, using his body and stretching his legs. His iPod had a whole lot of songs on it that he loved and he hadn't listened to in over a year. Listening to them was like reconnecting with an old friend.

All the while the feeling of possibilities was still thrumming in his head and making sparks in his heart.

*Maybe I could write a book? Maybe I could design a new roller coaster! Maybe I could start a behind-the-scenes at Fairyland blog and get a million followers! Oh, right. I'd have to check what my contract said for that last one.*

Maybe he really *could* quit his job and go to school and learn all sorts of things. Not just Anthropology, but English literature and marine biology and astronomy, everything cool and interesting. Maybe even film studies!

He could make a whole lot of new friends and take notes in fresh new notebooks and wear scarves and whatever else cool students did.

After about twenty minutes of running he was struggling to draw breath, and his legs ached. He slowed to a walk. Which seemed to hurt his legs worse, somehow.

He walked a couple of blocks and then looked around, confused. He'd been so caught up in his thoughts that he hadn't been paying attention to where he was going.

He turned around and headed back the way he'd come, but he was sure he'd been turning corners, crossing roads at random, high on the feeling of freedom and possibilities. And outside of the route he took to the bus stop, or the local bodega or the takeout places he liked, he didn't know his neighborhood. He was lost.

Dean's stomach sank as he went to pull out his phone only to realize that he'd left it charging on his bedside table.

He licked his parched lips, stopping at an intersection and looking around for some kind of landmark that he recognized.

Nothing.

Running a hand through his hair, he took stock of what he had. He had his house key, an iPod… had he brought any money? He checked his pockets. No. But then again, why would he have needed money on a run?

"Fuck," Dean chose a direction at random and walked that way.

He was starting to realize why everyone in LA went to the gym instead of running outside. It was very, very hot. The sun beat down on him and the concrete pavement reflected the heat back from below. He could feel the heat radiating through his running shoes, they started to feel like they might melt.

Finally, he saw a 7-Eleven and went inside.

"Excuse me," he said, to the woman behind the counter. Her name tag said 'Laverne'. "Laverne, I'm so sorry. This is going to sound really stupid and unbelievable, but I'm lost."

"Ooh-kay," Laverne said. She narrowed her eyes like she was thinking *what has this got to do with me?*

"I was just wondering, I mean, I left my phone behind. And I don't have any money, would it be possible to use your phone?" Dean asked. He felt a little better in the air conditioning, but he was still a complete idiot for getting himself into this mess.

"Err, no," Laverne shook her head.

Dean licked his lips. "Please, I'm really sorry, I can come back in like, an hour with money and buy some stuff if that would help. I just need to call someone to come pick me up, and then I'll be out of your way. It won't take any time at all." He tried his best, most winning Fairyland host smile on her.

She shook her head again. "I'm sorry but it's store policy, honey." She looked behind him and he glanced back to see someone waiting with a bottle of Powerade.

*Oh man, a Powerade would be so good right now.*

Dean stepped aside and waited. Once the person had left, he moved back in front of Laverne.

"I understand that it's store policy, truly," he started. "But please, I really need your help. And it would make my day just, a whole lot better. I mean, it already started pretty well, but I'm a bit of an idiot."

Laverne nodded then, and Dean couldn't blame her for how unconvinced she looked. "Mm-hmm."

*Maybe I should just go all in and explain the whole ridiculous situation.*

"You see, the thing is," Dean cleared his throat. "I'm in love with this guy, and I thought he was too cool for me, 'cause he's like, older and really awesome. But actually, it turns out he's into me too, so that's kind of amazing. And last night we worked that out, and we kissed, and I slept over at his house–"

Laverne's eyes bugged out a little and he shook his head. "No, not like that!"

*Whoops, maybe a bit too far.*

He ran his hand through his hair and winced as it came out sweaty.

"Nothing raunchy, we just, like, slept. He's a veteran, and he has this prosthetic leg and I guess he's trying to be a gentleman but also, I mean, I didn't want to put out on our first date. And it wasn't even a date, really, he was just meeting my folks. You see, my mom's a vet, too, so I wanted them to meet and they got on really well, and I think Cody – that's the name of the guy – I think it made him feel less alone." He paused to take a breath. Laverne was leaning forward on one elbow, listening. He thought maybe he finally had her interested.

"Go on, honey," she said.

"Right. So he met all my family and we had this great barbecue and then it turned out he'd talked to my best friend, who he'd thought I was with, but I'm not, because, well... It just never felt like that with her."

"Sure," a voice said behind Dean. He turned. There was a guy in his mid-twenties, holding a loaf of bread and a quart of milk. "Sometimes it's just not like that, right?" Apparently, he was invested in his story, now, too.

"Right, exactly. And so we kissed and I slept over, and – like I said – I didn't want anything X-rated to happen, and he was really cool about it. But first thing this morning he got a call to go into work."

Laverne made an annoyed noise. "What timing," she said, shaking her head.

"I know, right? So he dropped me home and went to work on his bike. He has this amazing motorbike, and I went to sleep at home but I didn't charge my phone. So I woke up and I got this idea to go for a run – and it's stupid because I never run – but I was so out of my head about Cody and how good I feel all over that I didn't pay attention to where I was… and now?"

He shifted, stretching out his left leg before it started to cramp. "Now I'm in pain and I – I stink, and I don't know how to get home, and I don't have my phone. So, it would really be amazing if you could let me use your phone, maybe?"

"You can use *my* phone," the guy with the milk said. He dug his mobile out of his pocket.

"It's okay, I can bend the rules this time. For love," Laverne said, smiling. "I feel like you're in a romantic comedy and I should be one of those people who helps you get a happy ending."

She produced a wireless phone from below the counter and offered it to Dean.

"Thank you so much," Dean's whole body felt jellified, exhaustion finally catching up with him. As he took the phone and his knees wobbled, either from relief or from the unexpected running, he wasn't sure. He moved to one side and the bread-and-milk guy nodded at him, set his stuff down and then went to the fridge for a sports drink which he purchased then handed it Dean.

Dean mouthed 'thank you' and looked at the phone. He'd memorized Jessica's number, and he could absolutely call Jessica, but he didn't want to bother her. No, he wanted to call Cody. He wanted Cody to roar up on his motorbike and rescue him.

But he didn't know Cody's number by heart.

Maybe his mother would have Cody's number? They were getting on really well last night. But then, he hadn't noticed Cody getting his phone out at any point, and surely his mother would've mentioned if they'd traded numbers.

Nate would have his number, but Dean didn't know *Nate's* number.

Laverne was watching him, and he was just staring at the

phone. He had to dial someone. Work. He could dial the park. They'd have Cody's number, and since Dean was also a staff member, surely they'd give it out to him, right?

He dialed the number staff had for calling in sick.

It took about five minutes, and Dean had to say that Cody was his boyfriend and it was an emergency, but someone eventually agreed to call Cody and get him to call Dean at the 7-Eleven.

Dean hung up the phone and clutched it to his chest. Laverne and the bread-and-milk guy were watching.

"You gonna be okay?" Bread-and-milk guy asked.

"Yeah, just as soon as..." Dean jumped when the phone rang and he picked it up. "H-hello?"

"So, I heard that my *boyfriend* is having an emergency," Cody drawled. He sounded amused. Dean felt a wave of relief wash over him. He smiled and closed his eyes.

"Yeah. I'm sorry about that, they wouldn't give me your number unless I was like, family or significant other."

"It's all right, what's wrong? Are you hurt?"

"Nope, I'm just an idiot. Can you come pick me up?"

"Where are you?"

Dean gave him the address and hung up, handing the phone back to Laverne. "Thank you so much." He took a drink from the Powerade and turned to bread-and-milk guy. "And thank you for this. Um, I can get you both complimentary tickets to Fairyland, if you like. As a thank you?"

Laverne smiled wide. "Yeah? I love that place, but it's so expensive."

Bread-and-milk guy grinned, too. "Oh, I'd love to take my kids there."

"Great! Um, give me your email addresses and I can set it up."

By the time Dean heard the roar of Cody's bike outside, Laverne, Mario and Dean were all laughing together. Mario had added them both on Facebook, so Dean had made two new friends. The run hadn't been a failure after all!

He hurried outside as Cody pulled up, Mario and Laverne right behind.

"You don't have to watch, folks," Dean said, laughing.

"Are you kidding me? I have to see what superman looks like," Laverne said.

Cody removed his helmet and Mario whistled with appreciation. Cody looked at Dean, bemused.

"Um, hi. What's going on?"

"I got lost," Dean said. He hurried over to Cody and gave him a thank you kiss. Okay... maybe it was for the benefit of the audience, a little, but he was also genuinely happy to see him.

"You're all sweaty," Cody said.

"Take this boy home before he hurts himself," Laverne chastised, looking all motherly.

"Gladly," Cody nodded. "Dean, who are these people?"

"My new friends Laverne and Mario," Dean said. "They've heard all about you."

"Oh, God," Cody shook his head. He handed Dean the spare helmet. "Put this on and let's get out of here. Nice to meet you, Laverne and Mario, but I gotta get this one into a shower."

Dean complied happily, climbing up behind Cody and wrapping his arms around him.

Laverne and Mario waved happily as they left.

CODY WAITED WHILE DEAN HAD A SHOWER. HE STARTED WITH wandering the apartment, looking at the Fairyland merchandise Dean had on display, the few books on the shelf and then checked out the fridge to see what was inside. Alongside some fresh looking vegetables and cold cuts, Cody spotted toaster waffles, chocolate milk and leftover pizza. He helped himself to a slice.

He sat on the couch and switched the TV on. It was on some kind of Japanese cartoon channel. Figured. He watched it for a little while and then channel surfed, smiling when he heard Dean singing in the shower. He didn't have too bad a voice, either.

Dean emerged a few minutes later, his hair damp, dressed in a fresh white T-shirt with a Hidden Galaxy logo on it and torn jeans.

"Hey," Cody said. He switched the TV off and half turned to face Dean. Dean sat on the other end of the couch, folding one leg under him. "Do you have any items of clothing that aren't Fairyland branded?"

Dean shrugged. "I think I have a fancy shirt which isn't. So, here we are again," Dean said. He smiled wide. "Thanks for rescuing me."

"I guess it was my turn," Cody said. He stretched his arm out to gently rub Dean's hand. "Though I'm not entirely sure why you needed rescuing from a convenience store three blocks from your house."

Dean blushed and ducked his head. His drying hair flopped forward over his forehead in a very cute way. "I didn't know where I was; in relation to my house."

Cody shook his head, feeling affection swell his heart. "Man, you're hopeless. How do you even function?"

"Usually Jessica would stop me doing things like leaving the house without my phone, or going for a run in prime L.A. heat," Dean said, sheepishly. "But I didn't want to call her."

"I guess you didn't." Cody moved his hand to Dean's knee. "So. What do you want to do?" He asked, his voice lower, a bit gravelly. Okay, he was activating full seduction mode. He rubbed his thumb against the exposed skin of Dean's lower thigh. Hey, ripped jeans were good for something.

Dean looked up, his cheeks pink. "What do I really want?" He repeated, like he was in a dream. Success! Full seduction mode was working. Cody pulled his good leg up onto the couch and shuffled a little closer to Dean.

"Yeah! Sky's the limit, you can have anything you want," he murmured, coming in closer to Dean in hopes of planting a kiss on his neck.

"To marry you," Dean replied, giving him a shy, one sided smile.

Cody froze. "What?" His voice came out strangled. It had to be a joke – Dean was messing with him. His hand tensed on Dean's knee.

"Oh gosh, I didn't mean to say that." Dean went pale and his hand went to cover his mouth.

"But you did," Cody said. "It was a joke, right?" He forced a laugh. "You're just being whacky. And you only said you were my boyfriend to get my number, right?"

"I did say it." Dean frowned, his eyebrows drawing together when Cody laughed. "Wait. You don't want to marry me?"

"I only just kissed you yesterday." Cody sat back against the couch, ran both hands through his hair. "This is absurd."

"What's so absurd about it?" Dean asked. "I mean, obviously it's a rush and we shouldn't like, rush in and get married, but why is the idea of marrying me absurd? That... that kinda hurts."

"No, I didn't mean it like that," Cody sighed. "I'm freaking out here, you basically just asked me to marry you and we haven't even slept together yet."

"We have to *sleep* together before you'll even *consider* marrying me?" Dean's voice got louder. "Holy crap, I'm glad we're having this conversation."

Cody shook his head. "I'm just trying to be reasonable! Listen to yourself, it's the twenty-first century, who waits to have sex until after they're married?"

"I might!" Dean said. "I don't know, I've never thought about it before." He folded his arms, frowning. His lip was actually beginning to quiver.

Cody's heart raced. He had that 'get out' feeling that he got on Spaceship Mayhem. He couldn't stay here. Dean was sweet, but he wasn't about to jump into a lifelong commitment when they'd kissed less times than Cody had fingers. This was nonsense.

"I think I'd better go," Cody said. He stood up and took a quick breath. "You're not making any sense."

"It's just kind of horrible for you to say you don't want to marry me. And now you're going to go?" Dean said, sounding worried. "I thought we could get dinner."

"You didn't say you wanted dinner, you said you wanted to get married." Cody turned away and headed for the door. "Maybe you just need to drink some water or eat something, I don't know. But I'm gonna leave you to it."

Dean didn't say anything as Cody walked out. The door closing behind him sounded extra loud, and final. Cody paused for a moment in the hallway. He wasn't overreacting, was he? No – it was unreasonable to talk about marriage the day after they'd hooked up. And not even hooked up, just kissed and slept in the same bed.

Sleeping in the same bed had been wonderful though. He hadn't even had any nightmares.

But it was just one night! And they'd barely seen each other all day. It was anyone's guess what was happening in Dean's head right now, but he was clearly moving too fast. Dean was a lot younger than he was, maybe he was just being over optimistic, or not thinking about what it really meant to be married.

Cody couldn't still himself long enough to wait for the elevator, so he took the stairs. It was a little jarring on his prosthetic leg to run down stairs as fast as he did, but it felt real at least.

The conversation he'd just had with Dean felt completely unreal. Like something out of a stalker horror movie. Not that he was afraid of Dean at all, but still. It had been super weird. Perhaps he was wrong. Wrong about this whole thing – the roller coaster, the family dinner... wrong about liking Dean.

He got on his bike and drove home. His mind still a whirl.

## 33 / DEAN

DEAN CRIED A LITTLE. AND THEN HE THOUGHT ABOUT WHAT HAD happened and was absolutely perplexed. Why had he said that? Of course Cody had freaked out and left! *Anyone* would say that it was moving too fast.

But the way Cody had laughed had hurt. He did what he always did when he needed someone. He called Jessica. She picked up after a few rings.

"Hey Deano, how's lover boy? You two do it yet?"

"No," Dean's voice cracked. Then he sobbed a little and Jessica's tone changed.

"What happened? Did he hurt you? I'll beat him up if he hurt you. I told him to be good to you!"

"No, no it's not like that," Dean said. "I kind of… I've had a really, really weird day."

"I'm coming 'round and I'm bringing pizza," Jessica said. "Hang in there, baby boy."

Within twenty minutes Jessica let herself in the door. She set the pizza down on the coffee table and gave Dean a hug.

"Tell me what happened."

He caught her up, not leaving out any details and emphasizing how foolish he'd been. "And now he's never going to text me or see me or kiss me or cuddle me again," Dean wailed. He wiped his eyes on the sleeve of his T-shirt. Jessica passed him a box of tissues.

"Now, then. You don't know that for sure. Yeah, it sounds like you freaked him out a bit, but I reckon if you tell him you feel stupid and you're sorry he'll forgive you." Jessica patted his arm.

"You really think that?" Dean felt so pathetic. He could even *hear* how pathetic he sounded, whimpering to Jessica.

"Yeah, I really do," she said. She handed him a piece of pizza and he munched it, feeling slightly better just from the cheese.

"Okay, I'm going to do it." Dean cast around for his phone, patting his pockets. He was sitting on it. He unlocked it, his heart soaring at the thought that Cody might have messaged him. Maybe he'd come back for dinner?

"No new messages." Dean sighed, sadly.

"Okay, Prince Pity Party, just tell him you're sorry and plead temporary insanity."

Dean crafted a 'Sorry, I was stupid, please forgive me and let's pretend that didn't happen' message. Jessica read over it before he sent it.

"I don't know about the 'pretend it didn't happen' bit," she said. "He's going to remember that it happened."

"Yeah, but I want him to know that I won't be thinking about it," Dean said. "Forget it ever happened is a safety net. Like, we can both go on with our lives like I never said anything about marriage."

Jessica shrugged. "I'd take it out, but I see your point."

Dean left it in and sent the text. He watched his phone but there was no immediate reply.

"I've ruined it. He's never going to reply to me." He shoved his phone under the couch cushion and then immediately pulled it back out.

"Give him some time, he's going to need to process this. Don't catastrophize, okay?"

Dean ate another slice of pizza and pouted. Jessica put on a Fairyland pirate movie and they watched it together. By the third movie, Dean had started sending a text to Cody every half hour. That was, until Jessica took his phone off him.

Then he just bundled himself into a warm Fairyland hoodie and sulked.

On Monday morning Cody woke up with his alarm. He'd largely been ignoring his phone. Dean had texted once and he wasn't sure how to respond so he'd turned his phone off. He needed time to process this on his own.

The whole marriage thing had freaked him out for sure. How could anyone be like 'yes, let's kiss' and then twelve hours later it was 'marry me'? It was like a crazy celebrity story, like getting drunk married in Vegas by a dude dressed as Elvis.

But he was also relatively sure that he didn't want to break things off with Dean altogether. The feeling he got in his stomach when he considered breaking things off was akin to needing to vomit, so he figured that was a no.

Probably they just needed to have a talk. Dean was adorable, and he'd obviously been over excited and... something. Maybe he just spent too much time riding roller coasters and the ups and downs had become normal to him.

What was it Jessica had said?

He's a gold star magical pixie dream boy. And he needed to be treated well. That sounded about right.

And Cody *wanted* to treat him well. He wanted to be the one making Dean smile, making Dean bounce with happiness. He thought of the way Dean's eyes had sparkled the day before as they talked. The warmth of his skin under Cody's hand. The way all Cody's worries seemed to melt away when they kissed.

He thought it through during his shower and brushing his teeth.

When they'd slept together the other night, Cody hadn't had any nightmares. It was too small a statistical sample to conclude from, but Cody would take a gamble that Dean's presence was soothing him psychologically, too.

He thought of Dean's fingers creeping under his leather jacket as he drove him through town on his bike. The press of his chest against Cody's back. His cheek resting against Cody's shoulder.

He didn't want to lose any of that, in fact, as he thought about all those things, he realized he wanted all of that to be his life from now on. And, imagine if they *did* get married? He could go around and see Anne and the family regularly. He could wake up next to a warm sleepy Dean and kiss him all over his face. He could know that he'd never be alone again, even when things got scary.

*There was nothing as important as that.*

He felt a flare of panic and rushed to turn on his phone, half dressed. As it came back to life, it vibrated with message after message, all from Dean.

"Oh, shit," he breathed. The messages became increasingly desperate.

Cody's stomach seized into a knot of anxiousness, imagining how Dean must've been worrying. He texted him back immediately.

Cody: I just needed some time to think. It's okay. Are you okay?

Dean texted back after a minute, which Cody spent scrolling through the messages he'd missed.


Dean: Dunno. Will I ever see you again?
Cody: Yes.
Cody: Today. I'll come see you

Dean: K

The lack of excitement in Dean's reply had Cody even more worried. His stomach filled with dread the same way it did when he approached Spaceship Mayhem.

He felt awful for turning off his phone and not checking on Dean. He had to do something to make it up to him. But what could he do?

It wasn't in Cody to do a grand romantic gesture. He wasn't going to dress up in a tuxedo and show up at Spaceship Mayhem with a wheelbarrow full of red roses. Was that even romantic? He had no idea.

He was so used to avoiding situations with real emotions in them. Used to avoiding his own emotions. He had to quit that.

First thing's first, though. He got ready for work and drove in on his bike. He couldn't just ride Dean into the sunset, he had work, he had to focus on that.

Cody set the problem of how to make it up to Dean to the back of his head, letting it bubble away there. Maybe something would come to him over the day. Or maybe he'd just have to buy out all the Halloween cookies and beg Dean for forgiveness.

## 35 /DEAN

DEAN USUALLY LOVED MONDAYS. THE BUS RIDE TO WORK. HEADING in and flashing his staff ID and walking into the mostly empty park.

But the sick, sad feeling in his stomach wouldn't leave him alone.

He'd screwed things over with Cody for sure. Cody's text was so dry... He'd said they'd see each other, but Dean knew exactly what he was going to say. He was going to tell him that he was too much. That they should cool things off and stop hanging out. That he had gone too far too fast and scared him off. Well, he may not say that exactly, but it was clear that was what had happened.

He sighed as he walked into the staff room. Jessica was waiting for him at a table with an extra-large, caramel-colored latte. She nodded at the chair opposite. He sat down, or more accurately crashed down, his legs sprawling out to either side.

"Here you go, big guy. How're you holding up?"

Dean shrugged and took the drink when she pushed it at him. He hadn't even managed to eat any of Jessica's cold pizza this morning.

"That bad, huh? You never heard from him?"

"I did. This morning." Dean showed Jessica his phone and the pathetic texts from Cody. He sighed, feeling like he would burst into tears at any moment.

"Drink your coffee," she said. "These aren't that bad! He said it's okay and then asked how you were."

"Yeah but he didn't reply to any of the stuff I asked him last night. He didn't mention the whole getting married thing. He didn't say he still loves me."

"Has he…" Jessica paused, speaking very cautiously. "Did he ever say that he loves you?'

Dean curved forward and rested his forehead on the cool surface of the table. "I'm doing it again! I'm spinning everything out of proportion. No one thinks like this," Dean said, aghast. "No, of course he didn't. Because he's not a freak like me who tells someone they want to get married less than a day after their first kiss." He slumped forward further, folded his arms on the table and buried his face in them. "I'm the worst."

Then, he felt a hand in his hair. It was very gentle, petting the back of his head.

It made him think of the gentle scratching way Cody had caressed his hair that night he was drunk. He stifled a tiny sob.

Jessica's hand was somewhat comforting. She made a soothing noise.

"There, there, you're not the worst. You just got really excited and that's sweet, really."

"Cody doesn't think so," Dean mumbled.

"I don't know about that. I don't think he's cut you off, he texted you. He's still interested, I think."

Dean sat up and rubbed his face. He took a sip of the coffee and a deep breath. "Thanks, Jessica, that did help. A little."

"And even if he *does* break things off with you, there's other fish in the sea," she said. Dean pouted.

"But I don't want other fish. I don't want *fish* at all." Dean left off the rest of that thought, which was that he wanted Cody and nothing but Cody. Urgh, why did his brain have to work this way? Obsessing about someone he could probably never have.

The day passed slowly. Dean did his job without feeling any of his usual joy, and although he still smiled and helped people, he knew he wasn't making anyone's day magical. He was just sorting people onto the cars and making sure their safety harnesses were on. He was doing his job on autopilot.

He ate lunch on his own and barely tasted it. He entertained the idea of wandering over to the Enchanted Forest and seeing if he could find Cody, but that seemed like he'd be being too much all over again.

What he needed to do was back off and let Cody sort himself out. Cody needed time to think. He needed to work out if Dean was worth the drama and the random marriage proposals. If being with him was worth the steep inclines and the sudden drops.

*Maybe he needs time to miss me?*

So, for his entire lunch break, Dean didn't text him, or go visit, or anything. He just played a mobile game and went back to work.

Just after four in the afternoon he was about due for his last break when Jessica got in touch on the ride's walkie-talkie. She was up the front, ushering people in like normal.

"Hey, Dean, heads up," she said. The walkie-talkies were just for work stuff – they'd both had very stern warnings from their supervisor never to use it for chatting. Only to keep in touch if there was an emergency, or something went wrong.

"What is it?" He asked. "Someone throw up again?"

"No, just… you've got an incoming," Jessica said.

"Incoming what?" Dean looked towards where the line fed into the ride loading zone. "Drunks? A tour group? Teenagers?"

"Cody," Jessica said. "Brace yourself."

"Oh shi–" Dean bit off the swear word, looking at the people waiting to get into the ride car.

*Whoops.*

"Thanks for letting me know!" He set down the walkie-talkie.

His heart instantly started racing. He felt sweat starting to bead on his forehead. Why was Cody here? What was he going to do? Was he going to break up with Dean right here on the ride? How could he keep going with his shift if that happened? Were they even together enough to break up?

Dean's stomach did a double-corkscrew loop as Cody rounded the corner, wearing his security polo and staff ID. He looked determined. Dean's breath caught in his throat. In fact, Cody sort of looked like that assassin guy that was sent to kill Captain America. It was intense, and it was freaking hot.

Jessica hurried up behind him.

"How about I take over running the ride for a bit?" She asked, falsely cheerful.

"Cody, hi," Dean said, breathlessly. "How're you doing?" He put his hands in his pockets to hide their clamminess.

Cody stopped in front of Dean, looked right into him with his blazing blue eyes and took a deep breath. "I'm going to ride Spaceship Mayhem," he said.

"Oh-kay? Right, sure. Um, go ahead?" Dean gestured to the car waiting. The people in the rest of the line shuffled a little but didn't explicitly protest. It seemed like Cody was intimidating everyone just with his presence.

Cody looked at the car and then looked back at Dean. He huffed a little and ran a hand through his hair. Dean recognized all the nervous signs from the other times Cody had tried to ride the coaster.

*Wait, was he actually going to ride it this time?*

"I need you," Cody said. He inhaled through his nose and then reached for Dean's hand. Dean let him take it. His heart spun with emotional g-forces he couldn't explain. Cody's hand was cold and sort of damp. "Please. Maybe… maybe if you sit next to me, and I know you're there, I can ride it. I'm afraid still, really, *really* afraid, but I also have this feeling like if you're with me, I'll be able to do it."

Dean's heart did a happy flutter.

"You, really? What?"

Cody smiled then, Dean's total confusion seeming to cut through his fear. "Come on, let's ride this fucking thing."

Dean squeezed Cody's hand. "You really want me to go with you?"

"Yes, come on, before I change my mind and run as fast as I can to that damned chicken door," Cody said.

Dean climbed in first. He watched Cody hesitate before stepping in. Then Cody met Dean's eyes and just looked at him as he climbed into the seat.

He sat down and took a deep breath.

"It's okay, it'll all be over in three and a half minutes," Dean said. He reached over to pull Cody's safety harness down. Cody's hand caught his and he squeezed it hard.

"I trust you," Cody said.

"It's really, really fun. I promise."

"Dean. I don't want to lose you," Cody's voice was all scratchy and tight. He turned to face Dean. Dean pulled his own harness down over his head, not letting go of Cody's hand.

"You're not gonna lose me. I'm gonna be right here beside you." The ride rocked a little as more people climbed in and pulled harnesses down.

Cody inhaled sharply and squeezed Dean's hand. Dean squeezed back.

Jessica walked the length of it, checking everything was secure, flashing Dean a slightly worried, slightly hopeful look.

"You got this," she said to Cody. She gave them both a thumbs up.

"Thanks, Jess." Cody glanced at her, and then at the fake control panel he'd been avoiding and Dean heard his breath catch.

"Just keep looking at me," Dean said. Cody met his eyes again and Dean smiled encouragingly.

"I don't want to lose you," Cody said again. "And I mean, in life. Not just in the ride." He swallowed. His hand squeezed Dean's harder.

"You're not losing me, not unless you want to," Dean said.

"I don't want to–"

"Here we go!" Jessica called out. The ride started to move, slow at the start. Cody's hand gripped Dean's so hard Dean could feel his bones grinding together, but he didn't flinch or try to let go. If this would help Cody, then he'd do it. He'd do anything.

"Will you be my boyfriend, please?" Dean asked. Cody breathed out, his grip on Dean relaxing to a manageable level. He smiled, turning to Dean and trying to lean to kiss him, but the safety harnesses kept them from reaching each other.

"Yes. Please. I'd love that. Though I would have preferred to ask *you* that question when I'm not fearing for my life."

Dean grinned and gave Cody's hand an extra squeeze.

The car tilted back as they started the initial climb.

"Oh, what the fuck! Why am I here, why did I think this would be a good idea?" Cody cried out.

"It's okay!" Dean called back.

As the soundtrack volume increased and the people behind them whooped, Cody

started to yell.

Dean's heart soared.

"I love you!" He shouted, confident that Cody wouldn't hear it over his own screams.

## 36 / CODY

He yelled quite a lot, and quite loudly. And that was all right, because everyone else on the ride seemed to be doing the same.

And it felt good to scream, like he was letting go of something. Letting go of anger and confusion and fear.

Well, the fear was still there. But as the ride zipped through the darkness, taking turns Cody couldn't anticipate and dipping and zooming, Cody felt the fear take a back seat to exhilaration. The ride definitely was a lot of fun. The wind rushing past, making his hair blow out. The surprise of being out in the bright sunlight one moment and then plunged back into darkness, his eyes seeing stars from the change in light. But he didn't let go of Dean's hand, not once.

Finally the coaster hit the brakes and Cody was thrown forward, then back.

"You did it!" Dean shouted beside him.

"I did it," Cody breathed. Shouting had left him hoarse and a little out of breath.

And, honestly? It felt like more than one triumph. It felt like he'd overcome an impassable roadblock. Some kind of wall he'd built up inside.

He'd knocked it down today – or maybe he'd just stood aside and let Dean smash through it.

Either way, he felt free.

Like he'd left something he didn't need on the tracks of the coaster. And maybe he'd even be keen to ride it again.

Still, as soon as the safety harnesses lifted, he was glad of the chance to get out.

Cody tried to get up, but he had to wait for Dean to move first. Dean got off the ride and turned to offer Cody his hand, like Cody was a seventeenth century lady rather than an ageing, grumpy, one-legged veteran.

Cody took his hand.

"Well? What'd you think?" Dean asked. He bounced on the balls of his feet, his face sparkling with happiness and expectation.

Cody didn't answer, he just tugged on Dean's hand to pull him close. He kissed him passionately and warmly, his heart full of possibilities.

Jessica whooped and cat called from the other side of the ride platform. A few people in the line joined in with laughter and applause.

"Oh, shoot!" Dean said. "You should get a badge!"

"A what? No, I don't need anything," Cody trailed off.

"Jess, a first-time badge!" he called out over Cody's shoulder. Then he let go of Cody, his attention on Jessica. She dug into the satchel Dean usually wore with the ride operator's important bits and pieces. Then she tossed something over the roller coaster to Dean.

"I'll cover the rest of your shift, you two love birds go have fun!"

On the way out, Dean insisted they buy a copy of the ride photo which Cody had to admit was funny. Cody's mouth was wide open and his eyes wide, like he thought he was about to die. Which, he admitted to himself, he totally did think at the time. Beside him, Dean was smiling wide, and instead of looking forward, his head was turned, watching Cody.

"What else?" Dean asked, looking around the gift shop.

"I don't need anything else," Cody said. "I have my button."

"Put it on," Dean said.

Cody sighed and rolled his eyes. The button was large, a few inches across, and it said 'My first time!' over a brightly colored Spaceship Mayhem logo. "D-do I have to? This is humiliating."

"Absolutely you do, and I'm getting you this, too." Dean held up a soft, plush robot on a keyring.

"You don't have to," Cody said as he pinned the button onto his chest.

"I know I don't, but we should commemorate this momentous event."

Once Cody had finally extracted Dean from the gift store – where he'd picked up three *more* important souvenirs for Cody – they kissed again.

"I'm really sorry," Cody said. Dean blinked at him.

"For what?"

"For bailing yesterday," Cody said. "I should've just... I should've talked to you. I'm sorry I freaked you out. I want to be with you, Dean. I want us to be boyfriends and hang out and ride home together on my bike."

"Ride home?" Dean asked. His eyebrows shot up. "Wait. You mean, does that mean... you want to move in together? Isn't that too fast?"

"Yeah, probably," Cody shrugged. He smiled at Dean and felt indulgent and silly and happier than he could remember being. "But I'm into you, and it feels like the right thing to do. What do you think? A smaller step before marriage?"

Dean laughed and ducked his head, his cheeks filling with color. "Yeah, I'd love that."

Cody wrapped his arms around Dean and they kissed softly.

"Your place, though," Cody said. "Mine's a hole."

"My place," Dean agreed. "I already made a spot for you to put your leg." Dean pressed his face behind Cody's ear and inhaled.

"What're you doing back there?" Cody squirmed. Dean could feel him laughing from the vibration of his chest.

"Sniffing you," Dean said. He sounded a little embarrassed.

"Um, why?"

"Because people smell the best back there," Dean said. "And you smell really, really, *really* good."

"Weirdo." Cody ruffled Dean's hair. "I thought I could cook for you while you study – you know, when you go back to university." It was an offer, more than a suggestion.

"I don't want to leave Fairyland, though," Dean said. Well, more like mumbled. He'd buried his face in Cody's neck now and it took a moment to parse what he'd said.

"So, go part time," Cody said. Dean pulled back to look Cody in the eyes.

"How are you such a genius?" he asked, his eyes wide and his tone one of absolute awe.

"Just gifted." Cody kissed the curve of Dean's jaw and took a deep breath in. He felt lighter than he had in a long time. The adrenaline of the ride was starting to wear off, sure, but he was buoyed up by Dean and the idea of moving in together. Of course, it was too fast, but it also felt right.

And if it wasn't, then they could sort it out.

Something inside him told him they'd be just fine.

- fin

For more Fairyland, check out Book 3 – Recipe for Chaos
Featuring Charlie and heir to the park, Max Jones

---

Did you like this book? Please consider spreading some Fairyland magic by leaving a review online

Indie novels thrive or perish on reviews so even if you just do a star rating and one sentence, it will make a big difference!

## ABOUT THE AUTHOR

Thanks go to my demon, my only, my wife.

Thanks to Zephfi, whose beta reading and insightful comments improve my work.

Big thanks to my Wednesday night writing group, who helped with some names and

Finally, thanks to Fairyland's magical Godmother, Emma. Her enthusiasm and insight raise my prose right up the biggest incline at the start of the ride and send the story whirling through the loops, the drops and the bit where you actually get to catch your breath.

Jaxon Knight loves theme parks, Japanese food and happy ever afters. A non-binary author from New Zealand, Jaxon spends their days writing the stories they'd like to read and stressing over deadlines that they set themselves. Jaxon also publishes under the pen name Jamie Sands

Find me online:
https://www.facebook.com/JaxonKnightAuthor/
https://www.goodreads.com/author/show/19244965.Jaxon_Knight

*UNTITLED*

The recipe is simple:
  Charlie cooks an amazing meal
  Charlie impresses heir to the theme park Max Jones
  Charlie gets a promotion and a dash of control over his kitchen

But the perfect recipe becomes unpalatable with one wrong ingredient and Max Jones is not behaving how Charlie expected…

Max is meant to inherit the entire Fairyland theme park but he just wants to party, have fun and bed as many people as possible. That is, until he meets Charlie and falls for him so hard he can't even finish the delicious meal.

Charlie doesn't have time for clubs or helicopter flights over the city, but Max is accustomed to getting what he wants, and he wants Charlie.

Featuring one part Billionaire, one part sensible chef, six cups of attraction, a generous dose of snark and a freshly prepared Happy Ever After.
  Buy now

*FAIRYLAND BOOK 3: RECIPE FOR CHAOS*

The recipe is simple:
    Charlie cooks an amazing meal
    Charlie impresses heir to the theme park Max Jones
    Charlie gets a promotion and a dash of control over his kitchen

But the perfect recipe becomes unpalatable with one wrong ingredient and Max Jones is not behaving how Charlie expected…

Max is meant to inherit the entire Fairyland theme park but he just wants to party, have fun and bed as many people as possible. That is, until he meets Charlie and falls for him so hard he can't even finish the delicious meal.

Charlie doesn't have time for clubs or helicopter flights over the city, but Max is accustomed to getting what he wants, and he wants Charlie.

Featuring one part Billionaire, one part sensible chef, six cups of attraction, a generous dose of snark and a freshly prepared Happy Ever After.
    Buy now

Haru is a single dad, a widower, doing his best to balance his career and raising his little girl, Minako. Thankfully Fairyland theme park is a haven for both of them. However, when both a prince and a pirate start courting Haru, his balancing act gets a lot harder...

Cillian plays a pirate at Fairyland theme park and he loves playing the rogueish character in and out of work hours. The last thing he wants is to settle down with a guy with a kid, so can't he stop thinking about handsome single dad Haru. And why can't he stop looking at pictures of Prince Magnificence and his stupid symmetrical face? And why does he keep running into both of them?

Grayson feels he's found his home in the role of Prince Magnificence, but he's more likely to run from love than seek it out. Until he meets Haru, that is. Christmas is complicated by Grayson's role being featured in a special Christmas celebration. Not only that, but his feelings for Haru, and his possible rival Cillian keep on growing. Maybe it's time to stop hiding who he really is?

The Good, the Bad and the Dad is a sweet MMM romance featuring a single father, a rogue and a trans prince with a heart of gold. No cheating, just the tentative first steps into polyamory.

Buy now

*FAIRYLAND STORY: NEW YEAR'S EVE*

MAX AND CHARLIE GOT TOGETHER OVER THANKSGIVING - THIS SHORT story finds them a few weeks later, celebrating New Year's Eve together with Blaze and Coco, and doing some bar hopping. But Charlie's trying to find the perfect moment to ask Max something important...

An MM short story, following on from Recipe for Chaos and The Good, the Bad and the Dad.

Buy now

*FAIRYLAND NOVELLA: TAILOR MADE
CHRISTMAS*

https://books2read.com/tailormadechristmas/

Sparks fly and old hurts flare as two men too afraid of their feelings discover some things can't be buried. Teddy loves his job working in the Wardrobe department of a theme park, but his love life needs resuscitation.

The last thing he expected was his high school best friend and crush walking in to be fitted for a prince costume. Art wants to make it big in Hollywood, and getting a job as a handsome prince might not seem like the obvious first step, but if the rumors are true it could be the break he needs. Instead, he comes face to face with Teddy, the one he left behind.

---

Tailor Made Christmas is a sweet second chance romance with queer characters, set in a fairy tale themed amusement park. Guaranteed HEA. Some cursing, no cheating. This is a shorter length novella style book

## FAIRYLAND BOOK 5: THE TROUBLE WITH ORDER

https://books2read.com/troublewithorder/

Opposites attract, right?

Link's past was difficult but he learned to skim through life and have things work out right, Teayang has worked for what he has and sacrificed things along the way.

When Taeyang is cast as Lord Order, the villain opposite Link's fun-loving Fairy Mischief, there's instant chemistry that can't be denied.

Outside of acting at Fairyland, Link's life is falling apart and he has no idea how to handle it alone. But years of putting up walls and projecting a happy image makes it impossible to ask for help as well.

Taeyang may love playing a villain, but in real life, he yearns to reach out to his acting partner, if he'd only accept that help... Can a villain become a friend? Or something even more?

--

The Trouble with Order is a slow burn, opposites attract MM sweet romance featuring team building, silliness, troublesome parents, assumptions, green smoothies and a HEA. It can be read as a standalone but is best read as part of the Fairyland series.

## SANTA'S SACKING
### AN M/ENBY SWEET WITH HEAT CHRISTMAS ROMANCE

https://books2read.com/santasacking/

Darian knew from the moment Nole Ox took over BirdTalk that their ideal job writing code for a social media platform was done.

They packed up their things and went home to Snowfall, Oregon, tail between their legs for a quiet Christmas with their folks.

However, their folks want Darian to stay busy by contributing to the community so Darian finds themself signed up to help with the Christmas pageant. Thrown in at the deep end and with only days until Christmas, their only lifeline is handsome Connor, the handsome barista-turned-handyman.

Can Darian make the sound tech work so the kids have their musical cues?

Is Connor really the perfect hunk he appears to be?

And why can't Darian just sleep in?

Santa's Sacking is a sweet, tropey Christmas story that will fill your heart and tickle your funny bone. This story is Standalone but there *may* be a return to Snowfall for next Christmas...

*ALSO PUBLISHED BY GREY KELPIE STUDIO*

OVERDUES AND OCCULTISM BY JAMIE SANDS

Busy now

A witch in the broom closet probably shouldn't be so interested in a ghost hunter, right?

That Basil is a librarian comes as no surprise to his Mt Eden community. That he's a witch? Yeah. That might raise more than a few eyebrows.

When Sebastian, a paranormal investigator filming a web series starts snooping around Basil's library, he stirs up more than just Basil's heart.

Between Basil's own self-doubt, a ghost who steals books and Sebastian, an enthusiastic extrovert bent on uncovering secrets, Basil's life is about to get a lot more complicated.

Overdues and Occultism is a sweet, no heat contemporary novella about a witch living in Auckland, New Zealand. MM romance, HEA.

Buy Now

Cedric has been kidnapped by pirates.

...they have no idea how much trouble they're in for.

Cedric was living his best life, partying in the colonies, bedding whomever he pleased and trusting that his parents' money and affluence would get him out of any unfortunate scrapes.

Until he was kidnapped by the fearsome pirate Lucifer, who planned to trade him for a hefty ransom. Unfortunately, he's not the only one after Cedric, and the strange secret society who have Cedric in their sights might just be more dangerous than Captain Lucifer.

Now Cedric is trapped on a pirate ship with a dashingly handsome captain, a quartermaster who won't stop staring at him and an overwhelming desire to find some fun, all while saving his hide from an unknown organisation who will stop at nothing to track him down.

ALSO PUBLISHED BY GREY KELPIE
STUDIOS

HIS PIRATICAL HAREM BOOK ONE - CABIN
BOY BY DRAKE LAMARQUE

Buy now

I've never been what I was supposed to be. Wealthy sons of Port
Governors aren't supposed to be ejected from the British Navy
after less than a year, they're not supposed to like pulp romances
or daydream about the handsome heroes of the stories instead of
the heroines.

When my Father issued me an order to marry a woman, I
knew I had no choice but to make my own way in the world, and
I found a berth on the first ship out of Jamaica.

I didn't mean to join a pirate ship, and I certainly didn't intend
to find myself the cabin boy to an incredibly charming Pirate
Captain. Or that I'd also be attracted to the mysterious First Mate,
or that both of them would show me all sorts of unspeakable and
salacious pleasures while on board. How can I choose just one of
them when I want both?

In addition to confusion on board the ship, there's also
enchanting genderfluid merfolk, a cat which seems to understand
a lot more than it should, an unseasonable storm and a sea witch
with a serious grudge... and with all these complications, I am
definitely in over my head.

Come and meet the crew:

Gideon: an innocent with a lot of forbidden desires and a lot of love to give

Tate: a huge, muscular ship's captain with a sweet side

Ezra: a dominant and closed off first mate

Ora: a genderqueer, curious and affectionate merman

## HALLOWEEN COOKIES FROM THE ENCHANTED FOREST KITCHEN

1 1/2 cups sugar
   1 1/2 cups softened butter
   2 large free-range eggs
   2 tablespoons vanilla extract
   4 cups all-purpose flour
   1 teaspoon salt
   1 teaspoon baking soda
   1 teaspoon cream of tartar

Preheat oven to 350 degrees F.

Cream the butter and sugar together in a mixing bowl until fluffy. Beat in the vanilla extract and add the eggs one by one. Sift together the dry ingredients in a separate bowl, then gradually mix into the butter-sugar mixture until just blended.

Flatten dough into a disk, cover in plastic wrap, and chill at least 30 minutes.

On a lightly floured surface, roll dough to 1/4" thickness. Cut with Halloween shaped cookie cutters and transfer to lined baking tray.

Chill cookie shapes for 5 minutes before baking (this stops them spreading) then bake for 10-12 minutes or until the edges are lightly golden.

Cool on sheets for five minutes, then transfer to a wire rack and cool completely before frosting.

Frost with your preferred frosting recipe and flavor then give them to your family as a bribe to behave, to your crush to show them you care or just eat them all yourself.

## THE OMELETTE DEAN WOULD HAVE MADE CODY

2 large or 3 medium free-range eggs
  Leftover roast potatoes
  Some ham or chicken or bacon or whatever meat you have around, or no meat is good too, shred them
  Mushrooms, sliced
  Garlic
  Salt and pepper
  Butter
  Cheese, grated

Heat a frying pan on medium with butter and crushed garlic for about a minute. Add in the sliced mushrooms and shredded whatever meat you're using (or not), cut the leftover potatoes into small pieces and add them to the pan as well.

While those are frying - multi-task and keep stirring them as you do the next part - break the eggs into a bowl and add a small splash of water, season with salt and pepper and whisk until the eggs are a bit frothy.

Turn on the grill and move the oven tray to the top level.

Once the stuff in the pan browns, pour the egg mixture over them and cook until the surface is just barely liquid. Spread the cheese over the top.

Put the pan into the oven on the top shelf and finish the omelette off in the grill. It's done when the cheese goes puffy.

Serve on a plate to your crush and watch them fall even further in love with you.